Praise for
Chasing

MIDNIGHT

"A smooth prose
Big Easy vibe disti
the shivers are worthy of a Lisa Jackson."
—*Publishers Weekly*

"Filled with suspense and mystery and
centered around a compelling plot with a
terrifying villain...this is one riveting read."
—*RT Book Reviews*

"A romantic thriller that continually
keeps you on the edge of your seat."
—*Fresh Fiction*

"*Midnight Caller* is a heart-thumping page turner...
Ms. Tentler's debut plants her solidly into the
romantic suspense genre with a bang."
—*Romance Junkies*

MIDNIGHT FEAR
"...Mesmerizing... Tentler's ability to draw out suspense
while wrapping it in captivating,
visceral fear is amplified in this exceptional thriller...
impossible to put down."
—*Examiner.com*

"The chilling look inside the mind of a
serial killer will haunt readers long after
[it] reaches its stunning conclusion."
—*The Reader's Round Table*

"It isn't too often that I read a good mystery
where I don't see the ending coming...
all of the twists and turns make this story
a roller coaster of a ride [and] well worth the read."
—*Nocturne Reads*

"An amazing story.
The murders and mystery are chilling...."
—*Romance Books Forum*

Also by Leslie Tentler

MIDNIGHT FEAR
MIDNIGHT CALLER

leslie TENTLER

EDGE OF *midnight*

MIRA®

ISBN-13: 978-0-7783-1313-7

EDGE OF MIDNIGHT

For questions and comments about the quality of this book please contact us at Customer_eCare@Harlequin.ca.

www.Harlequin.com

Printed in U.S.A.

For my husband, Robert.
I love you.

Prologue

Atlantic Beach
Outside Jacksonville, Florida

Officer John Penotti took a sip of his rapidly cooling coffee, fighting the drowsiness that always came in the last remaining hours before daybreak. Listening to the command radio's static, he peered through the cruiser's windshield as it traveled along a remote portion of state road A1A. His partner, Tommy Haggard, was behind the wheel, humming a tune that had been playing at the all-night diner they'd recently departed. The rain had ended and beside them, the endless stretch of the Atlantic appeared to be nearly one with the blackened sky, with only the foamy whitecaps of ocean waves breaking through the darkness.

"You taking vacation this summer?" Tommy asked.

"You sound like my wife. I keep telling her we already live at the beach."

Tommy kept his left arm poised coolly on the window's rim as he used his right hand to steer the cruiser. He was younger than John by a decade and still had the energy to do more than sit in front of his television with a cold beer on his days off. "So do something different. Go hiking in the mountains, or take the kids to Disney World."

"They're getting too old for it."

Tommy gave him a look. "Too old? I had my *honeymoon* at Disney, man."

A snide comment formed on John's tongue, but he let it pass as he placed his foam cup in the holder and nodded toward the road ahead of them. "Look up there."

"Great," Tommy muttered, annoyed. He slowed the cruiser and activated the light bar on the roof as they approached.

The silver Acura had taken out a good ten feet of wooden stake fencing that separated the environmentally protected sand dunes from the highway. It had veered off the still-wet road and plowed into one of the mounds, its crumpled front end embedded into white sand. The driver's side door hung open. They'd had a quiet night so far, John thought, with only a minor traffic violation and some teens trying to buy beer at the local Gas 'N Go with a fake ID.

"Probably a DUI," he surmised. "Idiot's probably passed out on the beach."

Tommy cut the engine but kept the cruiser's light bar on, staining the Acura with rhythmic blue streaks. Getting out, John pulled his flashlight from his utility belt and trained its beam into the car's darkened interior.

"Empty," he confirmed as he moved to the open door. The air bag had deployed in the crash and hung from the steering wheel like a deflated balloon. "Tennessee plate. Want to call in the tags?"

Tommy headed back to the cruiser as John leaned into the car for a closer look. Blood droplets, still wet, were visible on the air bag. Frowning, he raised the flashlight higher, illuminating more of the interior. While it was possible the bag's release had broken the driver's nose, there was a lot of blood on the seats—drying brown smears that looked as though rusty fingers had been wiped against the leather.

"The car's stolen." Tommy returned to John's side. "The owner's vacationing here and reported it missing two days ago."

"We've got blood."

Tommy peered inside. "Any open containers?"

"No." Straightening, John walked around to the front end of the car. He put his hand on the hood. It was still warm. Squinting onto the darkened beach, he filled his lungs with briny sea air, then sighed in resignation. "Let's go look for the driver."

As they crossed one of the walkovers—plank bridges that provided access to the beach while protecting the dunes from foot traffic—John unsnapped his holster. He noticed that Tommy—always in search of excitement— had already unsheathed his firearm and held it poised in front of him as if he were part of a SWAT team conducting a raid. Normally, he gave his partner hell about his gung-ho tendencies, but this time he acknowledged that the car's stolen status did increase the possibility of an armed perp.

"Footprints," Tommy noted as John's flashlight swept

the packed sand at the bottom of the wooden steps leading onto the beach. The prints were narrow with only
a shallow indention, indicating that whoever had abandoned the crashed vehicle wasn't too remarkable in size,
and was also barefoot.

They followed the trail for a couple hundred feet
before it veered into another village of sand dunes anchored by thick ocean grasses and vegetation. John
raised the flashlight, sweeping the area. A shadowed
form crouched behind a scraggly cluster of oak trees,
barely visible and as still as a rabbit trying not to end up
as quarry.

"This is the Atlantic Beach Police," John announced
in an authoritative tone, removing his weapon. Tommy
stood beside him, already in shooting stance, his gun's
barrel pointed into the trees. "Come out slowly with your
hands on your head!"

The form remained motionless.

"Come out now!" John stepped carefully closer and
focused the flashlight's beam directly on the figure.

"You think we won't shoot you, asshole?" Tommy
yelled. "There's two of us and only one of—"

John laid a hand on his partner's arm, pushing the
gun's nose down. "Christ. Put that away."

The huddled form was a woman. She squatted on the
ground, her slender arms wrapped around herself in a
protective gesture. A curtain of sleek, dark hair concealed her face, but the flashlight illuminated her skin
and the dried blood on her hands, arms and legs. At first,
John thought she wore a bathing suit, but realized with

a jolt it was only a skimpy pair of panties and a lace bra. She trembled in the beam's filmy swath.

"Ma'am? You all right?" He came a few steps closer, one hand stretched toward her. To Tommy he said, "Go back to the car, get a blanket and call for an ambulance."

Once Tommy had taken off, John sank on his haunches to the woman's level. If she was aware of his presence, she gave no indication.

"Ma'am?" he asked again. His fingers grazed her shoulder, which seemed to break the trance she was in. She cried out and scrambled backward, her chest rising and falling rapidly with her ragged breathing.

"It's gonna be all right. I'm a police officer. We're sending for help."

Her brown eyes were wide with fear or confusion, her pupils dilated, a likely indication of a head injury, or possibly drugs. Her nose was bleeding a little but didn't appear to be broken, and John wondered how badly she was hurt. She had a lot of blood on her, but he couldn't ascertain its source. Her wrists, however, were red and badly abraded.

Wherever she'd come from, she'd been tied up.

"What's your name?"

The woman blinked at him warily.

"M-Mia," she managed to say after a long moment. She sounded uncertain, her voice barely audible above the roar of the ocean waves behind them. Even in her current distress, she appeared pretty and a little exotic, with an oval face and delicate features, and was maybe in her late twenties or early thirties. John noticed the fresh bruise shadowing her jawline.

"Can you tell me what happened to you, Mia?"

A fresh wave of tremors racked her body as she squeezed her eyes closed. "I—I don't know."

"You don't remember?"

She shook her head, biting her lip. Her long, dark hair lifted in the ocean breeze. John noticed a wide section of it was several inches shorter than the rest, as if a handful of it had been carelessly lopped off.

She jumped at the sound of Tommy bounding back across the walkover toward them.

"It's okay," John assured her. "That's my partner, Officer Haggard. I'm Officer Penotti. You're safe now, all right?"

Tommy appeared beside him, out of breath from his speedy trip to the cruiser. "There's a bus on the way."

She recoiled as he moved forward to wrap her in the blanket he'd brought back.

"Sorry…I'll just hand it to you." Tommy held it out. Her left hand shook as she inched forward, tentatively reaching out to take it.

Two of her fingernails were completely missing, the exposed nail beds raw and oozing blood. Had they been ripped out in some kind of struggle? John swallowed hard. What appeared to be the number eight—or maybe the infinity sign—had been carved into the pale skin of her stomach, the wound angry and red. He watched as she managed to drape the scratchy blanket around herself, her petite frame nearly disappearing inside it. She continued to shiver and rock.

"You think she was raped?" Tommy asked a short

time later, voice low. They had stepped several yards from the dunes and allowed the paramedics to take over.

"I don't know. Maybe." *Probably.* A female medic had coaxed the woman onto a gurney, and John could only catch glimpses of her through the gaggle of emergency workers. Overhead, blue-and-red flashing lights from the road reflected into the still-dark sky.

"Hey, Carl," John called to an EMT as he went past, headed back to the ambulance. "What's the deal?"

"We won't know until we get her to the E.R. for a tox screen, but my guess is she's on something. She's pretty out of it. Doesn't even remember driving here."

"What about all the blood on her?"

"Other than her fingers and stomach, there are no other wounds—at least none significant enough to account for all that blood. I gotta get something out of the bus, all right?" Carl trotted away.

Which meant what? That some of the blood belonged to someone else? John removed his uniform cap and ran a hand through his hair.

Nearby Jacksonville was no stranger to violence. Like any large city, it had its share of assaults and homicides, drug deals gone wrong. But for the large part, the surrounding beach communities were quiet, with occasional rowdy teenagers and drunken tourists their most typical problems.

He thought of the two women who had gone missing in Jacksonville over the past two weeks and wondered if there was a connection. Neither had been found, but to his recollection neither of them had been named Mia, either. John had heard the young woman telling the female medic that her last name was *Hale.* It rang some kind of bell, but he couldn't quite put his finger on it.

Regardless, he didn't like what was going on here.

1

FBI special agent Eric Macfarlane faced the cluster of oak trees, his suit coat discarded on the warm, pale sand. His eyes were closed, the strong ocean breeze ruffling his light brown hair, and the sun's heat was like a brand through the back of his blue dress shirt. Seagulls cried in the air overhead.

He tried to imagine what it felt like to crash on an isolated beach road, in a strange car and with lost hours that couldn't be accounted for.

Eric had read the Atlantic Beach Police incident report multiple times—in his office yesterday at the FBI's Violent Crimes Unit in Washington, D.C., then again on the plane bound for Jacksonville International Airport early that morning. Despite the warmth of the Florida climate, even now the similarities contained in the document made a chill crawl beneath his skin.

If it was *him,* if he had finally resurfaced…

The thought caused his emotions to skitter like stones skipped on water.

"Eric."

He turned to see Florida Bureau agent Cameron Vartran walking toward him, looking as out of place in suit pants, tie and a dress shirt on the beach as Eric did himself.

"I thought I might find you here," Cameron said. Dark-haired, grinning, he shook Eric's hand warmly, then gave him a congenial back slap that denoted familiarity between the two men.

"Your investigative skills are that good?" Eric asked.

"That and the field office told me you'd checked in and asked about the crash site."

Eric and Cameron had known one another for years. They had gone through training together at the FBI academy in Quantico, then been partnered as agents for a time before Cameron had transferred back to his native Florida and Eric had joined the VCU.

"How's Lanie?" Eric asked.

"Pregnant."

He raised his eyebrows. "Really? Congratulations."

"She can't wait to see you. It's been way too long." Standing with his dress shoes planted in sand, Cameron wedged his hands on his hips just above his holstered gun. As he looked at Eric, his expression faded into seriousness. "When the match came up in ViCAP, I thought that you'd want to know."

Eric nodded, peering off briefly into the distance. "So how did this end up with the Florida Bureau?"

"Some of the local beach communities have their own police forces, but they're small and not equipped for major crimes. So the report was passed to the Jacksonville Sheriff's Office as a possible tie-in to two other missing females in the metro area over the past couple of weeks. The JSO called us in for assistance. I called you."

"Have either of the two other women shown up?"

Cameron shook his head. "Alive or otherwise. It's suspected Ms. Hale was the intended third victim, but somehow managed to escape her abductor."

"In a stolen vehicle and without any memory of her ordeal."

"Right. Her toxicology results just came back. Combination of Rohypnol and gamma-hydroxy-butyramine—the date rape drug and liquid Ecstasy—which explains the severe memory loss. The attending physician classified her as having complete anterograde amnesia."

Eric thought of the victim's wounds that had been detailed in the report—the second and third fingernails on her left hand excised, a section of her hair cut off, and the numeral that had been carved into her skin. It seemed too precise to be coincidental. He felt a spiraling disquiet. The Collector had been off the VCU's radar for thirty-four months now, fueling internal speculation that he was either dead or incarcerated somewhere on unrelated charges.

Eric had never been able to accept that.

"Damn, it's hot." Squinting against the light, Cameron removed the sunglasses clipped to his shirt pocket and slid them on. "Maybe we can grab a quick bite to eat and catch up before the briefing with the JSO detectives at one. There's a great seafood place down the road from here. Only the locals know about it."

They began walking across the sand, and Eric bent

to retrieve his suit coat, slinging it over his shoulder. As Cameron talked, he gazed back toward the water. Although the beach here wasn't as commercialized, he noticed there were still a few people strolling along the shore. The ocean appeared calm under an azure sky and farther out, the grayish outline of naval ships floated on the horizon.

"So Mia Hale—she's a reporter for the *Jacksonville Courier?*" Eric said as they came down the planked stairs that led back to the road. The information was still surprising.

Cameron nodded. "A *crime* reporter. She'd been covering the missing women—both assumed abductions since the women's families are adamant they aren't the type to just disappear. Ms. Hale's last story ran on Monday morning, and she vanished that same night out of the newspaper's parking garage. The beach police found her hiding here some eight hours later, stripped to her underwear and in pretty bad shape. My guess is that her articles got *someone's* attention."

"What about the vehicle? Any leads from it?"

"The Sheriff's Office processed it. Forensics on the car is expected back this afternoon. Ms. Hale doesn't recall how she got in possession of it or even where she drove it from. The vehicle was reported stolen a couple of days earlier from an outlet shopping mall popular with tourists. The mall's on the other side of the city."

A few dozen feet away, a wide section of fencing that cordoned off the dunes was missing, its wooden stakes scattered like broken matchsticks between clumps of brown sea oats. It was all that was left of the crash scene. Eric studied the area.

"I'm going to want to talk to Ms. Hale."

"She was released from the hospital yesterday. We can schedule some time with her."

The government-issued vehicle the other agent drove was parked behind Eric's rental sedan on the sandy shoulder of the A1A. Cameron provided directions to the nearby restaurant, then removed his sunglasses again. Concern was evident in his eyes. "The truth is, I wasn't sure the VCU would want you involved, Eric, considering."

Rebecca. Her image, her voice, had faded a little in his memory, the realization tightening his jaw. The last time Eric had seen Cameron and Lanie was at the funeral. That had been nearly three years ago.

"I pulled a few strings," he admitted.

"I bet. And you came down here without a partner?"

"Resources are limited. I told them I'd be better off working with my *old* one down here."

"The timing works. My partner tore his ACL. He's out on leave." Cameron appeared to choose his next words carefully. "If this really is the guy…are you going to be able to handle it?"

Eric specialized in serial murderers at the VCU. He was all too aware that unsubs had relocated in the past, had gone into hiding to evade capture. But ultimately, their innate desires drove them to hunt again.

"I want closure," he said simply.

Cameron sighed as he gazed at a passing car on the highway. "I know you do."

* * *

"I don't want you coming into work, Mia," Grayson Miller said over the phone. "That's final."

"I could just attend the editorial meetings—"

"Give yourself a little time to recover, all right? You live on the coast for a reason—go soak up the sun or something." He paused to speak to someone in his office, and Mia imagined Grayson sitting at his desk at the *Jacksonville Courier,* bifocals perched on his nose as he red-penned the hell out of someone's story. When he returned to the conversation, he lowered his voice. "Look, I'm going to come over there after work and check on you."

"You don't have to. I've got Will and Justin downstairs—"

"Indulge me. I need to see for myself that you're all right."

The sincerity in his words made Mia's throat ache.

"When I came into work that morning and saw your car here with the door open and your purse inside it, it scared me. I've been executive editor here for thirteen years and nothing like this has ever happened. One of my reporters, taken right out of the parking garage. You're special to me, Mia. It's a miracle you're alive."

She closed her eyes, swallowed down the emotion that seemed to be at her surface these days. "Grayson…"

"I'm bringing dinner. Pizza from Mario's or Thai from that place around the corner. I expect an email by six letting me know which."

"Thai food," she whispered, and disconnected the phone.

Mia remained on the balcony of her apartment, hating the fact that she was shivering despite the sun's warmth. Placing the phone on the glass-topped patio table, she pulled the sash of her short, kimono-style robe more tightly around herself and stared blindly over the canopy of trees at a lush park in Jacksonville's historic San Marco neighborhood. Grayson was right, she conceded—she wasn't ready to go back to work. But the truth she would never admit to anyone but herself was that she didn't want to be alone. The bustle of the newsroom, a story assignment, even a simple one, could help take her mind off things.

The only problem was, she was part of the story now. Or at least the one everyone was talking about. Mia felt another tremor pass through her.

Try as she might, and she'd tried hard, she couldn't remember anything. Detectives from the Jacksonville Sheriff's Office, as well as an agent from the local FBI field office, had quizzed her, but not even a fragment of those lost hours had returned. Her last memory was of leaving the office late after filing a breaking story. She'd said good-night to Ronnie, one of the evening janitors, and walked out to her car in the balmy evening. Mia had clicked the key fob, deactivating her ancient Volvo's security system, and tossed her purse into the front seat.

Her next memory was of awakening in a crashed car that didn't belong to her, on an unfamiliar stretch of darkened beachside road. Covered with blood, trembling and confused, her inner voice had screamed at her to run.

Hide. Even now, the cold fear of the unknown pooled inside her.

The beach police who'd found her, the emergency workers at the scene and then later, the doctors and nurses in the hospital E.R.—it had all been a blur of people poking at her, taking blood and checking her vitals, asking myriad questions she couldn't answer. Her lungs squeezed at the recollection of the invasive, degrading rape examination and her acute relief when it appeared she hadn't been assaulted in that way. Mia had asked one of the nurses to call Grayson, knowing he typically arrived at the paper well before daylight, and discovered that he had already reported her missing.

Remnants of the dull headache that was like a hangover were still with her—the result of the illegal, black market drugs in her system, she'd been told.

What *had* happened to her? Who had she escaped from and how?

Speculation was that whoever had taken the two women Mia had written about had targeted her, as well. And those women were still unaccounted for. As a reporter, she'd always tried to maintain a level of objectivity. That was all gone now. She felt a kinship with those women, wondered if they were still being held somewhere. Or if they were dead.

The warm breeze lifted her hair. Mia pressed one hand against her stomach, her gaze lingering on the ugly abrasion encircling her wrist. Through the robe's silk material, she could feel the raised edges of the bizarre, scabbed carving on her skin. *No bikinis for me anytime soon,* she thought, trying to inject some humor into an otherwise terrifying situation. The tips of the second and third fingers on her left hand were bandaged and sore.

You're tough, Mia. You've been through bad things before and you'll get through this.

She went back inside her apartment, which was large and airy, with high ceilings and antique heart pine floors. From down the hall she could hear the police scanner she kept in her home office, its low chatter a strange but familiar sound. Walking to the granite-topped island that separated the kitchen from the living area, she eyed the copy of the *Jacksonville Courier*. Mia had taken it from her doorstep hours earlier but so far had been unable to read it. The headline below the banner was innocuously political—a standoff between the county and state over shoreline zoning rights.

Gathering her courage, she unfolded the paper, scanning the front-page news first and then opening it to the second page, which she laid flat against the countertop. Grayson had already warned her that Walt Rudner, a senior reporter nearly twice Mia's age, had taken over the story on the local abductions.

A story that now included her, at least anonymously. As she read Walt's follow-up article to the larger one that had appeared earlier in the week, she felt her stomach flip-flop all over again.

A thirty-one-year-old woman believed to have been a third abductee managed to escape during the early hours of Tuesday morning. Due to her sustained injuries, the victim has so far been unable to provide any information that could be useful to

*the investigation, according to a spokesperson for
the Jacksonville Sheriff's Office...*

The concluding paragraph stated that the FBI's Violent
Crimes Unit out of D.C. had been called in as a special
consult.

A rap at the door made her jump. She moved to the
foyer and peered out through the peephole, her shoulders
sagging in relief when she saw Will Dvorak, who lived
on the first floor and also co-owned the building. It bothered her that a simple knock had kicked her pulse into
overdrive. Despite all of this, Mia vowed she wouldn't
turn into a frightened shell of who she'd once been.

"Get dressed. We're going to be late," Will announced
as he entered the apartment, kissing Mia's cheek. He was
medium height, with russet hair and blue eyes. As usual,
he was immaculately dressed in khakis and a pressed,
short-sleeve shirt, and his designer sunglasses hung from
a cord around his neck.

"Dressed? Where are we going?"

"Justin called from Élan. One of his hairstylists had
a cancellation and you're the lucky girl." Justin Cho was
Will's partner and a successful entrepreneur who operated a number of ventures around the city, including one
of Jacksonville's top day spas. "I told him I'd bring you
down."

Mia shook her head. "That's sweet. But I'm really not
up to it."

Will gave her an understanding smile but ignored her
comment. "Afterward, we'll have lunch at that place you
like on the Riverwalk. The fresh air will do you good."

She must have appeared unconvinced, because he placed his hands on her shoulders and gently turned her around, guiding her toward the hall bathroom. Will was a good friend. In fact, in many ways he was the closest she had to family.

"Will…"

"This is for your own good." He flipped on the light, bringing Mia face-to-face with herself in the beveled mirror above the marble vanity. She flinched at her own pale, haunted reflection.

Her dark hair was a mess. And it wasn't just the fact that it hadn't been brushed with any recent regularity. The wide swath that had been chopped off during those missing hours gave her a lopsided appearance—as if she were a child who had attempted to give herself a haircut.

"It's just not a good look, honey," Will said softly.

Mia frowned, touching the faint bruise on her jaw with her bandaged fingers. Her cocoa-brown eyes were liquid and questioning. She tried again to remember something about what had happened to her, but it was like trying to see through a black mist. She looked at Will in the mirror as he stood behind her. His gaze held concern.

She wouldn't let this wreck her.

Sucking in a tense breath, Mia left the bathroom to get dressed. "All right. Tell Justin we'll be there."

2

The Jacksonville Sheriff's Office was a combined city and county agency that handled law enforcement in both Jacksonville and the greater Duval County. Eric sat in the JSO conference room on East Bay Street with Cameron and the two detectives who had initially been assigned to the missing-person cases. Detective Boyet was heavyset and balding, while his partner, Detective Scofield, was a blonde, athletic-looking woman in her mid-forties.

"There was more than one blood type in the Acura," Eric noted as he scanned the forensics report on the car Mia Hale had crashed.

Boyet nodded, his chair squeaking as he shifted his weight. "The blood type on the steering wheel and air bag are a match to Ms. Hale, as are the fingerprints found inside the vehicle. But the larger smears on the front seat are the same blood type as Cissy Cox, our second missing person. Although DNA testing isn't completed yet, Ms. Cox is O negative. That's a rare blood type—only about five percent of the population. Its presence makes it likely she was also in the car at some point."

"Or, the smears were a transfer from Ms. Hale's hands." Seeing the detective's puzzled expression, Eric explained further. "She could've come into contact with the second abductee's blood at the location where she was held. It's possible she had it on her when she escaped and wiped her hands on the seat before driving away."

Cameron rose from the table, and he leaned his tall, athletic frame against the wall near a plate-glass window overlooking a line of palm trees. "Speaking of, how *did* she drive away? The car was stolen—were the keys inside it?"

"It was hot-wired," Boyet supplied. "Whether she did it herself or the perp did it, Ms. Hale knew at least enough to twist the wires together properly to get the ignition started. I'd say that's an interesting skill for a journalist. Especially one blitzed out on roofies."

"Any other prints inside the car?" Eric asked.

"Just hers."

Detective Scofield spoke. "We've had a few dealings with Ms. Hale as a reporter, including the recent disappearances. She's young, but she's smart. She was pretty shook up when we spoke to her at the hospital, which is to be expected. It will be interesting to see how she handles all this."

Photos of the first two missing women, as well as several Polaroids of Mia Hale that were taken during the E.R. examination, lay on the table. Eric studied the closest one, which focused on her face and revealed a faint bruise on her right jaw. She was pretty, he noticed, with a pale olive complexion, dark hair and doelike brown eyes that in the snapshot were glazed with a combination of drugs, confusion and fear. He felt a hard tug of sympathy. His gaze moved to the two other E.R. photos, which displayed the injuries to her abdomen and hand. The interconnecting loops of the number eight were visible on her flat, tanned stomach.

"What kind of twisted bastard does something like that?" Boyet indicated the third Polaroid. Open, raw wounds existed where two of her fingernails should have been. "The E.R. doc said her nails were probably pulled out using pliers or some other tool."

"Her injuries are consistent with the signature," Eric said.

Scofield gave a shiver of revulsion. "She's probably glad she doesn't have any memory of what happened to her. I know I'd be."

Eric tried not to think of Rebecca, what she'd gone through. "Are there any similarities or connections between the abducted women? The same socioeconomic status, or maybe they had similar jobs, took the same yoga class or shopped at the same grocery store?"

Cameron pushed off from the wall and began pacing the room. "From a victimology perspective, we haven't been able to find anything so far. Cissy Cox works at a retail job at the River City Marketplace. Pauline Berger is a stay-at-home mom with a McMansion in Ponte Vedra Beach and a country club membership. Mia Hale lives in the artsy San Marco community, and as you know, works for the *Courier.* Those are pretty diverse locations and lifestyles."

"Not to mention, the victims are all over the map, physically." Scofield pointed to photos of all three women, tapping each with the tip of her ballpoint pen. "A curvy redhead, a tall, Nordic-looking blonde and a petite brunette who's possibly of mixed Latino or Spanish descent. If you really think this could be a serial killer at work, don't they have a preferred type?"

"Some do," Eric acknowledged. "But if this is a resurgence of a past unsub, as I suspect, his tastes are diverse, intentionally so."

She tilted her head. "I'm not sure I follow."

"He's indicated that he likes taking a variety of women. He refers to them as his 'collection.'"

Scofield blinked. "You've spoken to him?"

"He sent digital recordings to the VCU during the previous investigation, although it was likely his voice was altered." Eric recalled the audios that had been delivered one by one after each woman had gone missing. Even though he didn't look at Cameron, he felt the weight of his gaze. "The recordings were of his victims being tortured and killed."

"The VCU deals with some pretty sick shit." Boyet picked up another of the photos. "What's the story with the carving?"

"He numbered his victims. There were five women abducted and killed in Maryland before he vanished three years ago. If this is the same guy, your two missing women could be numbers six and seven—"

"Making Mia Hale victim number eight," Scofield uttered in realization. "Or that was the plan before she got away."

"Technically, this is still a missing-persons case until a body turns up." Boyet's expression was grim. "But if you're right about the abductor's identity, Agent Macfarlane, it's not good. We're heading into the beach tourist season—Jacksonville doesn't need a serial killer on the loose."

"What were you getting at with the second blood type in the car being a transfer?" Cameron asked as he and Eric traveled through the busy JSO lobby a short time later. Although it was still April, heat hit them in a muggy wave as they pushed through glass doors that led to the building's plaza, then headed west toward the multilevel garage where they had both parked.

"During the Maryland investigation we were able to pick up sounds of two women at once on the recordings." Eric loosened his tie as he walked. "The first woman—the one being intentionally recorded—was in the foreground. But the AV techs also isolated the sound of a second female in the background on each audio, although the voice was muffled, probably due to a gag."

Cameron stopped, halting Eric, as well. "Meaning what, exactly?"

He looked out across the water. Jacksonville was known as The River City, and an expanse of the St. Johns that ran through the heart of the downtown was visible from where they stood. He worked to lay out the theory as impassively as possible. "It's believed the unsub kept two women captive at once. He'd make the newer abductee watch as he killed the woman he'd taken earlier, as a show of power. Then when he brought another woman in, it would be that abductee's turn to die."

"Like a revolving door," Cameron said bleakly. "So

you think both women are already dead—that Cissy Cox watched Pauline Berger die, and in turn Mia Hale witnessed Cissy Cox's execution before she escaped? That's why she had Ms. Cox's blood on her?"

Eric thought of the families still holding out hope their loved ones might return home. "Yeah, that's what I think."

Cameron's eyes darkened. He started to say something, but the electronic buzz of his cell phone interrupted him. He looked at the device. "It's Lanie. I need to take this."

He stepped a few feet away, talking to his wife about an obstetric appointment. When he closed the phone a minute later, he said, "Lanie says to tell you hello. And that she's expecting you for dinner tomorrow night. We'd do it tonight but it's her dad's sixtieth birthday."

Eric nodded his understanding. "You've got a doctor's appointment?"

"It's a routine sonogram. The office called and asked if we could come in early. At four."

"Go," he said, glancing at his wristwatch. It was nearly three already. "Lanie needs you. I can handle some things on my own. For starters, I'm going to San Marco to see if I can speak with Ms. Hale today."

"We can schedule a formal meeting with her tomorrow, after we meet with the rest of the team. Why don't you get settled in at the rental?"

"I don't want to **wait**."

Cameron took out one of his business cards from the Florida Bureau, upon which Mia Hale's address and phone number were written. He handed it to Eric.

"The recordings…" He sounded uncertain, as if he wasn't really sure he wanted to know the answer. "Did you receive one of Rebecca?"

Eric fished in his pocket for his car keys. He thought of the days and weeks he'd waited, both dreading and needing to hear her voice a final time. He didn't look at Cameron as he answered.

"It was the only one that never came."

Allan Levi entered the fastidiously neat ranch house.

"Mother? I'm home," he called, closing the front door behind him. He noticed the interior was too warm, which wasn't surprising since Gladys was always claiming to be cold and tampering with the thermostat. At least her frugality kept the air-conditioning bills low. Carrying the white paper bag with *Walker's Pharmacy* printed on its side, he followed the television noise until he found her sitting at the kitchen table. Her gaunt frame wrapped in a floral housecoat, she was watching the small set on the counter, which she seemed to favor over the larger one in the living room.

"There you are." Allan bent to kiss the top of her gray head, catching a whiff of baby powder and White Shoulders cologne. He ignored the low warning growl of Puddles, her arthritic Chihuahua, who was curled into a dog bed on the floor nearby.

"I thought you weren't coming back," she accused. Her eyes remained glued to a religious talk show. "You've left me alone all day."

"You've been on your own for *three hours*," he corrected. "I had some errands to run. I told you that, re-member?"

"Did you get my medicine?"

He gave the bag a shake so the plastic pill vials rattled inside it.

"Humph. Took you long enough."

"I went into the city to get a television for repair. They're paying fifty extra for pickup and delivery."

Allan moved to the sink and washed his hands, taking care to scrub under his fingernails with a small, stiff-bristled brush before drying off with a paper towel. Then he sat in the chair across from Gladys. Depositing the bag's contents onto the table, he began the process of placing pills and capsules into the lidded, plastic case that helped him keep up with which medications she had to take and when. There were morning, noon and evening compartments for every day of the week. It was tedious, but he didn't mind the task so much. In fact, he rather enjoyed the order of it.

One red, one blue, one pink.

As he worked, he noticed Gladys had rolled her mobile oxygen canister into the kitchen. The tubing and cannula hung around her flaccid throat like a necklace, however, unused. His eyes slid to the counter. An ashtray sat next to the sink. "Have you been smoking again, Mother?"

"Shush," she said irritably, waving him off. "I can't hear my program."

"I didn't move all the way back down here to watch you blow yourself up." Allan frowned. He would have to talk to the cleaning woman—he knew it was that dirty Mexican whore sneaking cigarettes to her and at probably quite a profit. Normally, it would be enough to send him into a rage, but he reminded himself he had a lot for which to be thankful.

For starters, there could be law enforcement crawling all over the place right now.

He placed the last capsule into its proper slot.

"I'm going to my workshop," he announced, referring to the cinder-block building in back of the property, nestled among the tall pines.

"You spend too much time out there," Gladys criticized as he rose from the table. She finally looked at him, her watery blue eyes narrowing suspiciously in her lined face. From his vantage point, the droop to the right side of her mouth was clearly visible, a result of the stroke she'd suffered three years ago.

"I need to get started on that television—"

"Boy like you, with an expensive college degree I paid for." She shook her head, fretful. "And here you are. No wife or kids and not much of a job, if you ask me. 'Idle hands are the devil's playthings.'"

He felt his face heat. "I *do* work, Mother. I'm self-employed. And I take care of you now, too. That's a job in itself. I'll be back at five to make you dinner. We'll have spaghetti with meat sauce—how does that sound?"

Gladys remained sullenly silent. The Chihuahua growled again as Allan left through the kitchen's screened door. He slunk across the backyard and onto the beaten path through the copse of trees. The skeletal remains of a car went unnoticed. He had much to think about.

It had been two days of uncertainty, but he'd finally

begun to relax. *No one was coming.* According to her own newspaper, she remembered nothing at all. The potent drugs used to make her manageable and compliant had provided the very fortunate ancillary effect of erasing her mind. Allan ran again through his mental checklist, trying to figure out where he had been remiss. What careless blunder he'd made that allowed her to escape.

She had been so special to him, too.

Reaching the cinder-block building, he unlocked the door with his key, flipping on the overhead light as he went inside. Unoccupied. The redhead was rightfully gone, but *she* should still be here.

He'd first noticed her name bylining the articles on the missing women. *His girls.* Then a column had run that included her photo. He took a clipped copy from a drawer in his workbench and studied it. The window-box air conditioner behind him hummed. Here, he kept things as cool as he liked.

She was older now, of course. But even after all these years he had still recognized her. What were the chances he'd found her? And that she was a reporter, covering his…work. He didn't believe in coincidence. It was almost as if it were meant to be.

Allan's inner voice—the voice of reason—spoke.

She got away and you got lucky. It's too dangerous. You have to forget about her now.

Pick someone else.

He'd gotten rusty, that was all. Too much time spent trying to keep a low profile, until his darker urges had finally won out. *No more Mr. Sloppy,* he admonished himself.

The morning's paper had said the FBI's Violent Crimes Unit was being called in. That couldn't be helped now and truth be told, it made Allan feel important.

His lips formed a thin smile as he thought of Special Agent Eric Macfarlane and the bond they had shared.

3

For the first time in days, Mia felt somewhat at ease. Will had been right—the trip out had done her a world of good. Returning home, she sat in the passenger side of his Porsche convertible, feeling the warm breeze whipping her new, shorter hair. It was a blunt cut, just off her shoulders and about eight inches shorter than her usual style.

"A good haircut is better than Xanax," Will proclaimed, briefly studying her through the dark tint of his sunglasses as he drove.

"Thanks for lunch…and for everything else."

He shrugged. "I'm just using you to assist in my procrastination."

"The new book?"

"I missed my deadline. Again." He smiled, his dimples deepening. He and Justin had kept Mia entertained at lunch with their hilarious and at times ribald stories, and afterward the three of them had strolled along the scenic Riverwalk among the tourists and joggers until Justin had to leave for a meeting. It had been a distraction technique, she knew, but she deeply appreciated the effort.

"What happened to you this week, Mia…a lot of people wouldn't be able to get past it." He sounded serious for the first time since they'd headed out.

She sighed. "I just need things to get back to normal, that's all."

"What you *need* is a break from what you consider normal—writing about people inflicting violence on one another." He shook his head, his fingers loosely gripping the steering wheel. "Why don't you take some time off from all that? And I mean more than a few days—a real sabbatical. You've got Grayson Miller wrapped around your finger. He'd break his neck giving it to you, and *with* a paycheck, probably. I don't care what kind of shape the newspaper industry's in."

When Mia looked at him, he added, "You *do* know he's in love with you, right?"

She watched the scenery pass by, not wanting to think about Grayson in that way.

They entered San Marco Square with its endless supply of art galleries and cafés. Everywhere, people were milling about on the narrow, tree-shaded sidewalks. Traveling past the renowned giant statue of the three lions at the square's main intersection, they took a right and headed onto one of the side streets. San Marco was a diverse community, with multifamily apartment buildings and quaint, two-bedroom bungalows interspersed with enormous riverside mansions. Will and Justin had renovated a large, Tuscan-style manor on Alhambra Avenue accented by a terra-cotta, barrel-tile roof and graceful stucco staircases on the exterior. The former single-family residence now consisted of separate units on the main, second and third floors. Mia rented the mid-level unit and there was another tenant on top.

Parking in front of the building, they had just climbed from the convertible when a dark sedan pulled into the circular driveway behind them. A man in suit pants, a dress shirt and tie emerged. He was tall, even-featured and clean cut, somewhere in his mid-thirties, and Mia immediately summed him up as law enforcement. Her impression of him was confirmed when she saw the gun holstered at his waist.

Walking toward them, he presented his shield. "Ms. Hale?"

She felt a lump form in her throat. "Yes?"

"I'm Special Agent Eric Macfarlane. I'm with the FBI."

Self-consciously, she smoothed her windblown hair, her instincts speaking to her. "You're part of the VCU the paper mentioned this morning."

"Yes, ma'am." As he neared, he removed his sunglasses. His eyes were an unusual, moss-green color and reflected intelligence. "I was wondering if we could talk."

The ease she'd felt during the afternoon began to ebb. With a faint nod, she made the necessary introduction. "Agent Macfarlane, this is Will Dvorak, my neighbor and landlord."

"And *friend,*" he emphasized, a measure of protection in his voice. The men shook hands.

"Will Dvorak? The writer?"

"I'm surprised, Agent." Will was often recognized for his humorous and sometimes poignant essays on his awkward childhood and adolescence. His last book had been on the bestseller lists. "I wouldn't peg you for the type who'd read me. You're a little too butch."

Agent Macfarlane revealed straight, white teeth and a perfect smile. "My reading list is pretty diverse."

After another few moments of small talk, Will seemed satisfied she was in good hands. "Well, I've put it off long enough. I'm going inside to face the last twenty pages of my draft. Mia, sweetheart, if you need anything…"

"Thanks, Will." She waited as he retreated through the courtyard to his apartment on the ground level before returning her attention to Agent Macfarlane. "I've already spoken with one of the local agents, as well as detectives from the Jacksonville Sheriff's Office. I'm afraid there's not a lot more I can tell you."

"I've been briefed on the situation. And I'm aware of your memory loss." His eyes fell briefly to her bandaged fingers. "How are you, Ms. Hale?"

"I'm…fine."

His gaze was discerning. "You're a very lucky young woman."

"Compared to the other two women who were abducted, I would agree," she answered somberly, feeling a trickle of perspiration at her nape. It was a hot afternoon, especially for so early in the season. "We can go up to my apartment and talk in the air-conditioning, if you'd like."

He followed her upstairs. Mia wore cropped cargo

pants and a bare tank top, her outfit exceedingly casual compared to his businesslike attire. Unlocking the door to her apartment and disarming the security system, she dropped her keys and purse on a table in the foyer as he closed the door behind them. "Could I get you something to drink?"

"Water would be nice. Thank you."

From the kitchen, Mia could see him in the living room. He stood with his hands on his lean hips, looking around at her furnishings and the expanse of green park that was visible from the balcony.

"You have a nice place, Ms. Hale," he said as she approached and handed him the glass, ice cubes tinkling inside it.

"Please, call me Mia. And it's a fringe benefit of attending college with the building's owner. Will and his partner, Justin, rent to me for a steal."

"You and Mr. Dvorak are both writers—that's interesting."

"We met at the University of Florida, but Will ended up going the more creative route." Indoors, Agent Macfarlane's eyes were even more striking than she'd first realized, the mossy irises rimmed in black and accentuated by thick, sable lashes. His skin was golden-toned, his short brown hair nearly light enough to be considered dark blond. She indicated the couch.

"Please have a seat." Once he'd done so, she settled onto a nearby side chair.

He took a sip from the glass, then sat it on a coaster on the cocktail table in front of him. "I understand you'd been covering the recent abductions."

The irony of it washed through her all over again. Mia worked to keep emotion from her voice.

"I wrote two articles. One ran after Pauline Berger's disappearance a week ago. The second one ran right after Cissy Cox went missing. It was the same day that I…" She paused, twisting her hands together and placing them in her lap before completing her statement. "That I went missing, too."

"And your second article speculated on a connection between the disappearances?"

When she nodded, he asked, "Based on what?"

"Well, for starters, both women had family and friends, they led normal lives. They weren't engaged in any at-risk behavior such as prostitution or drug use, nor did they have any history of mental illness or previous unexplained disappearances." Mia looked briefly at her bandaged fingers. "Detective Scofield at the JSO also indicated that neither of the women's significant others were being considered as suspects. Two women like that, in the same metro area…they don't just simply vanish in isolated incidents so closely together."

His evaluating gaze remained steadfast. "And you have no idea how you ended up in a stolen vehicle?"

She shook her head, wishing she had the answer. "No. I woke up inside it next to the beach. That's all I know."

"The car was hot-wired. Do you think you could've done that?"

Her lips parted slightly, the unexpected question catching her off guard. She chose not to answer and instead stood and slowly paced the room before turning to face him again.

"You asked me how I am, Agent Macfarlane. The truth is…I'm having a hard time. I'm not used to being on the other side of all this. The one being asked questions." She swallowed. "I also don't understand why I'm the one standing here talking to you while those two other women…they're still…"

Mia briefly closed her eyes, her words trailing away. She was vaguely aware that he'd gotten up from the couch and moved to where she stood.

"Ms. Hale," he said quietly.

"Mia," she corrected in a soft whisper. Looking up into his face, she felt her heart beat harder. "Who did this?"

He released a breath, hesitating. "You need to understand that you're not just a victim. You're also a reporter. I have to factor that in."

"Off the record," she emphasized. "You have my word I won't write anything to jeopardize your investigation. I'm not even working at the moment. And as a victim I have a right to know, don't I? Agent Vartran, the detectives—they wouldn't tell me anything."

He looked at her for a long moment before speaking again. "I was over an investigation in Maryland three years ago. Five women were abducted. Their bodies turned up later with similar injuries as yours."

Their bodies. Meaning the women had all been murdered. "And did you catch the person responsible?"

His jaw tightened. "No."

"But you believe he's resurfaced here in Jacksonville, after all this time?"

"Based on the specifics of your injuries, it seems possible." He surprised her by lifting her hand and cradling it within his own as he studied the bandaged nail beds, her abraded wrists. Then he let her fingers slide from his and met her gaze again.

"I haven't read your articles on the abductions yet. I'm wondering, does your photo run with the byline?"

She shook her head. "But I do a column on Fridays. It's a police blotter roundup. My photo runs with that one. What does that—"

"If this *is* the same unsub, he's a sociopath and an extreme narcissist. You're an attractive female—he was probably flattered someone like you noticed his work. It could explain why he took you."

Mia thought of some faceless criminal circling her photo in the newspaper with a red pen. Stapling it to his bulletin board where he memorialized his victims. It sickened her. "The wounds to my hand and my stomach—he cut off my hair. Why?"

His gaze traveled to an impressionist painting over her couch, his expression making it clear he was still struggling with how much to tell her.

"I work a crime beat," she reminded him. "I can handle it."

"He pulled out your fingernails and cut off your hair as mementos," he said finally. "He considers himself a collector, but he can't keep his victims' bodies since they'll decompose. So he takes souvenirs that will last longer. Fingernails, hair, sometimes teeth, among other things."

Ice water moved through Mia's veins. Absently, she touched her abdomen through her top. He must have noticed the gesture, because he added quietly, "He also numbers his victims as a way to dehumanize them. He thrives on order and organization, as well as control."

She did the math, adding herself and the two missing women here to the five victims murdered previously in another state. The marking on her skin now made sense.

"Pauline Berger and Cissy Cox are already dead, aren't they?"

"We have no proof of that yet. There are no bodies. And for now what I've told you is speculation based solely on your wounds. Three years is a long time for a killer to stop, then start up again," he conceded. "We don't want any of this getting out unnecessarily or too early. I've already told you more than I should. My dealings with reporters haven't always been a positive experience."

Mia was aware of the delicate dance between the news media and law enforcement, and she'd always tried to conduct herself in an ethical manner. She touched his arm through his shirtsleeve. Her voice held a tremor despite her best effort. "I want this man caught, Agent Macfarlane. And I want…*I need*…to help those two women. I need to help them get back home if they're still alive, or at least bring some peace to their families if they're… not. That's the most important thing to me right now."

His shoulders were broad, and Mia could ascertain the fit, hard build of him under his dress shirt. He studied her for several long moments before speaking.

"What if you could regain some of your memory?" he asked.

She blinked. "I'm not sure I understand."

"There's some experimental, highly classified work being done that I've recently been made aware of." His words were speculative and careful. "It's a combination of drug therapy and hypnosis, but it's shown some usefulness in retrieving lost memories."

A small stone lodged inside Mia's chest. "How experimental, exactly?"

"The military has been using it with severely injured prisoners of war to help them recall certain key facts about their captivity, even when they were barely conscious for most of their ordeal. The theory is that the mind can register events—faces, voices, surroundings—even in an unconscious or altered state."

"Does it work?"

"The results so far have been mixed," he admitted. "And to my knowledge it hasn't been applied to drug-induced amnesia. But one of the pioneers is a practicing psychiatrist at the Jacksonville Naval Air Station. I have access to him."

She tried to process what she was being told. It sounded like something out of a sci-fi movie. "Are there risks?"

"If Dr. Wilhelm believes you're a candidate, he can discuss the risks with you. With both of us." He took a step closer. Although they were alone inside the apartment, his voice lowered. "If you decided to do it, I would be there with you, Mia. I'd want to hear any details you might be able to recall firsthand. My understanding is that when the therapy works, the memories can be vivid."

She felt the stone inside her chest grow a little larger.

"I—I'd like to think about it."

He nodded. "Of course."

Reaching into his shirt pocket, he handed her his business card. "Thank you for your time."

Mia accompanied him to the door. One hand on its knob, he turned again to face her. "You asked me earlier why you were here talking with me, while the other two women were still missing." He raised his shoulders in a faint shrug. "The reality is, I don't know. Maybe you were smarter or braver, or maybe he just got careless with you. *But you got away.* Those women didn't."

His eyes held a depth of emotion that surprised her. It was a step outside the cool, professional demeanor he'd exhibited so far. Once he had left and closed the door behind him, Mia continued standing in the foyer. She crossed her arms over her chest, the air-conditioning suddenly putting too much of a chill upon her skin. Mia still felt Eric Macfarlane's presence. What he had suggested was nothing she would have thought possible.

The memories can be vivid.

4

Eric had accepted Cameron and Lanie's offer to stay at a vacation rental property they owned a few blocks from Jacksonville Beach. The last unit at the end of a dead-end street, the bungalow was quaint and sun-weathered, and provided a roomier alternative to the sterile hotel rooms that were a regular part of his job with the VCU. Having unpacked and changed into a T-shirt, running shorts and tennis shoes, he stood on its concrete front stoop, for a time watching black skimmers and terns that flew overhead toward the ocean. The late day was rapidly fading into a warm, breezy twilight, causing the wind chimes hanging near the door to dance. Eric listened to their music as well as to his own spiraling thoughts.

It seemed strange to him that The Collector—if he really were here—could be looking at the same setting sun, feeling the same balmy zephyr as he did right now. That a sadistic killer could be out enjoying a seafood dinner at one of the beachside, family restaurants.

Even more absurd was the notion that he had somehow let an intended victim escape.

Mia Hale had been smaller than Eric expected—finely boned and slender, only a few inches over five feet. Seeing her injuries, he'd felt an instant protectiveness. Not to mention, the harshly lit photos from the E.R. hadn't come close to doing her justice. His physical attraction to her plagued him, creating a hard twinge of guilt.

Nearly three years had elapsed since Rebecca's death, allowing him to outdistance his grief, he believed. But it hadn't eased the agonizing sense of culpability he felt.

In a way, part of him had died with her.

Eric thought of the experimental therapy he'd told Mia about earlier. It was a long shot, maybe even a crazy one, but if she'd consent to it—if she could somehow recapture even a fraction of her lost memories—it could be the break he desperately needed. But it was also a lot to ask of someone who'd already been through unfathomable horror.

Days before her death, Rebecca had accused him of being a selfish bastard. Maybe he was.

Two joggers passed nearby on the intersecting side street. They reminded him of what he had come outside to do. He needed the exercise, needed to clear his mind. As he locked the door to leave for his run, he heard the insistent shrill of his cell phone coming from inside. Glad he hadn't set the bungalow's security system, he quickly let himself back in and checked the phone's screen, which read *Washington, D.C.* He knew the caller's identity from the number displayed. It was already after 7:00 p.m., but Special Agent in Charge Johnston was apparently still behind his desk at the FBI's Violent

Crimes Unit. Eric answered. He'd been both dreading and expecting the call.

The SAC wasn't one to mince words. "Your presence in Jacksonville is against established FBI protocol, Agent Macfarlane."

He rubbed his forehead. There was little point in dancing around it. "Yes, sir. I know."

"And your reason for bypassing the proper chain of command?"

Eric envisioned Johnston's smoothly shaved head, his muscular shoulders hunched tensely under his starched dress shirt as he pressed the phone to his ear. With forced patience, he said, "Because I knew you wouldn't allow it. I *need* to be down here. I know you can understand that—"

"What I understand is that you're far too close to this, Eric." Johnston's harsh tone receded somewhat, and his switch to a first-name basis and the familiarity it bestowed caused Eric's chest to tighten. "That's a recipe for mistakes to be made, son. Not to mention, you were on assignment *here*."

"Which is why I didn't bring Agent Crowchild with me—he agreed to step in as team lead," he explained, referring to his partner at the VCU. "I have the appropriate resources down here with the Florida Bureau."

Silence as heavy as a cinder block carried through the airwaves before Johnston spoke again. "Let me make myself clear. I do not approve of your participation in this investigation. In fact, I see it as downright dangerous, as well as an arrogant and self-destructive move on your part. But due to your connections within the DOJ, I've been overruled."

"I'm sorry. I didn't have a choice."

"I've known Richard Macfarlane for a long time— hell, I've known *you* since you were a boy. And I do sympathize with your situation. But I'm speaking with your best interests in mind. We have other, very capable agents who could have handled this. If this is the same unsub, you don't need to put yourself through—"

"With all due respect, sir, *I do*." Eric swallowed down his emotion and anger, the words thickening in his throat. "She was my wife."

After a while, Johnston gave a deep sigh of resignation. "It's out of my hands now. What have you learned so far?"

Eric filled him in on the facts of the case, although he left out the information about the experimental memory retrieval therapy being conducted at the nearby Naval Air Station. That confidential information had come from Eric's father, as well, and he saw no reason to raise the SAC's hackles any more than they already were.

"We're going to have a long discussion when you return," Johnston advised. "You've become one of my best senior agents, and you've never used who you are to your advantage. At least not until now. I don't like members of my team going over my head…even in tragic circumstances such as this. Good luck, Agent Macfarlane."

He heard the click as the SAC disconnected the phone.

Eric stood in place for several moments, letting the conversation sink in. He'd had the reprimand coming. Eric's father had warned him of as much but he'd still made the necessary phone calls for him within the U.S. Department of Justice.

His father had understood.

Eric held a master's degree in Criminology from the University of Pennsylvania. He'd graduated top of his class at the FBI training academy in Quantico and worked hard to join the ranks of the elite Violent Crimes Unit, where he'd been for the past five years. Despite his lineage, he had never once expected or asked for favors. Still, he believed he was doing the right thing this time. He owed as much to Rebecca, to see this through. He'd disappointed her as a husband but at least he could try to make things up to her in death.

The Collector had taken Rebecca as a way to get to him, to inflict hurt and prove his superiority. He'd been especially brutal with her, as her mutilated corpse had evidenced. At the memory, a lump formed inside his throat. Eric burned with the need to find him, to put him down like the rabid animal he was. This time, he took his cell phone with him as he locked and left the beach bungalow, needing the run more than ever.

"I'd like you to see a counselor," Grayson said, serious, as he leaned against the granite counter in Mia's kitchen. In his late forties, he was tall, with salt-and-pepper hair and wire-framed bifocals that made some of the newspaper staff think he looked a little like Richard Gere. "After what happened, it can't hurt to talk to someone. Your insurance would cover it. When someone experiences something like this, there can be residual effects."

Mia gave him a look as she placed leftover cartons of *pad woon sen,* shrimp curry and basil chicken in the refrigerator. She thought of the military psychiatrist Agent Macfarlane had told her about—in fact, she'd been thinking about it for hours—but she was pretty sure it wasn't the type of therapy Grayson had in mind. "I don't need to see anyone. I'm fine."

"What if I make it a condition of your coming back to work?"

Mia walked to where he stood. She took his wineglass from him and had a sip of the rich merlot before handing it back. "Grayson. I'm not traumatized because I don't remember anything."

"How long have I known you, Mia?"

She sighed, knowing he expected her to recount the story. "Six years. I was a kid fresh out of journalism school and you gave me my first job."

"That's right."

"If I recall, I got your coffee and picked up your dry cleaning for the first nine months."

He crossed his arms over his chest, chuckling. "You *worked* your way up. I had to see if you had the drive to back up that raw talent. I didn't plan on training you as a real journalist to have you run off to write for some gardening magazine."

"That wouldn't happen. I've never met a plant I couldn't kill within a week." She opened the refrigerator door again, frowning as she studied its contents. "Are you sure you don't want to take some of this food with you? Honestly, you brought enough to feed a small village—"

"Mia."

She turned around. He'd moved closer, and the levity that had been in his eyes earlier was gone.

"My point is that I *know* you, kiddo. I know how you grew up, how tough you had to be. It's okay if you want to be scared for a little while."

Mia considered his words. It would be so easy to cave in to all of this. Despite her earlier assurances, the real truth was that she felt like a spastic ball of nerves on the inside. But Grayson had a point; he knew her history, he was one of the few who did outside of Will and Justin. Where she'd come from, her difficult past—it had embodied her with a fighting instinct. From ages six to fifteen Mia had been bounced around the foster care system, and yet she'd remained strong. Giving in to her fears now wasn't something she wanted to do.

"I want to come back to work soon, Grayson. And I want to cover the missing-person cases. I want them back from Walt."

He shook his head. "I don't think that's a good idea. On a whole lot of levels."

"Just think about it, all right?" Deciding she needed more than a sip of his merlot, she poured her own glass and took it into the living room. Outside the balcony's French doors it was completely dark. Grayson had been late arriving due to a breaking news story, and they hadn't sat down to eat until nearly 8:00 p.m.

"An agent from the FBI's Violent Crimes Unit came to see me this afternoon," she mentioned as he entered the room behind her, glass in hand.

He gave her a look of interest. "Did you find out anything?"

Mia thought of what she and Agent Macfarlane had discussed—namely, the possibility of a serial killer from Maryland resurfacing in Jacksonville. She pressed her lips together, reminding herself that what she'd been told was off the record, a condition she herself had imposed. The juxtaposition of being a victim and a reporter was difficult, and she felt guilty for not sharing the information. But doing so would raise the likelihood of seeing it in tomorrow's paper. Mia understood the FBI's need to keep the speculation down.

She shrugged. "He mostly asked me the same questions as everyone else."

"What's the agent's name?"

"Eric Macfarlane."

Grayson raised his eyebrows. "No kidding? If I was a betting man, I'd lay a grand on that being Richard Macfarlane's son."

The name didn't register with Mia.

"Macfarlane's an associate attorney general for the Department of Justice—he's way up in the ranks. I read a profile piece on him in *Newsweek* last month related to the Ambruzzi hearings," he said, referring to a recent, widely covered political scandal involving the governor of New Jersey. "The guy's a real bulldog. The article mentioned he had a son serving in one of the Bureau's specialized units. Either way, I'll pass the name along to Walt, make sure he gets in touch with him."

He settled onto the couch for a time, catching Mia up on the daily travails at the newspaper before announcing he should get going. Twice divorced, Grayson lived alone and had a widely known practice of going to bed with the proverbial chickens in order to make it into the paper by his customary 6:00 a.m.

"Thanks for coming by," she said, walking him to the door. "But you really didn't have to."

"That's where you're wrong, Mia. I *did*." Grayson closed the scant distance between them, his expression solemn as he gazed at her. He swallowed nervously.

"I had to, for me," he said softly. Reaching out, he tucked a few strands of her newly shortened hair behind one ear.

Feeling her stomach give an awkward little flip, Mia whispered his name, uncertain as to what he was about to do. But he pressed a chaste, almost fatherly kiss against her forehead.

"I just feel fortunate to have you back, that's all. Almost losing you…it's given me a lot to think about."

She recalled what Will had said earlier that day. Eighteen years her senior, Grayson was her mentor, as well as her boss. He had given her the break she'd needed to advance from the lifestyles pages to crimes. Mia was one of only a handful of female reporters covering hard news at the *Courier*, not to mention the youngest by nearly a decade. Grayson's guidance, as well as his fondness for her, had played a big role. She cared about him, truly, but as a good friend.

He placed a finger under her chin. "Just think about the therapy thing, all right?"

She smiled weakly. "Think about giving me my assignment back."

After he was gone, Mia sighed and looked around her living room. Their two wineglasses sat side by side on the cocktail table. She left Grayson's where it was but picked up her own, taking it into the kitchen and refilling it. Liquid courage. She needed it for what she'd been planning to do.

Carrying the goblet, Mia went into the guest bedroom she had converted into a home office. Her desk was positioned near a large window, its lamp casting a soft glow. The police scanner on the columned bookshelf provided the background noise she needed to focus.

Sitting in front of the computer, she conducted an internet search on serial murders taking place in Maryland three years earlier, hitting the keys as best she could with her bandaged fingers. It didn't take her long to find what she was looking for. Within a short time, she'd pulled up a number of archived articles from newspapers in Maryland and D.C. Mia began viewing the stories in chronological order. Eric Macfarlane was mentioned in all of them and quoted in several as the investigation's lead. His grainy image appeared alongside one particularly substantial piece from the *Washington Post,* the photo taken at a news conference, according to the accompanying caption. In it, he looked serious and handsome—crisp, short brown hair and squared jaw—the perfect poster boy for the FBI.

None of the articles provided the detail he had shared with Mia, however. There was nothing about fingernails or hair being taken or numerals carved into the victims' flesh. The Bureau had done a good job keeping such pivotal facts confidential, and she realized again how far out on a limb he had gone in giving her such information.

Mia continued reading for the better part of an hour. Upon seeing the link to one of the last remaining pieces, she felt a shock run through her. The headline leaped out from the screen, something she hadn't expected.

FBI Agent's Wife May Be Serial Killer's Latest Conquest.

She clicked onto the link.

In a stunning twist in the serial murder investigation plaguing FBI and local law enforcement, Rebecca Macfarlane, age thirty-three, wife of FBI agent Eric Macfarlane, disappeared from the couple's Bethesda home on Wednesday evening. A Bureau representative who spoke on the condition of anonymity confirmed foul play is suspected based on evidence at the scene. Agent Macfarlane, part of the FBI's Violent Crimes Unit, is team leader on the case that so far involves the abduction and murders of four other women in the metro area. He is also the son of U.S. associate attorney general Richard Macfarlane. Agent Macfarlane has stepped down from the investigation pending the outcome of a three-state search...

She read the rest of the article. A follow-up story with a dateline of a few days later recounted the heartbreaking discovery of Rebecca Macfarlane's body.

Mia sat at her desk for several moments, coming to terms with the realization that Eric Macfarlane was even more invested than she'd realized. She wondered if his connections had allowed him to be reassigned to a case in which he had become very deeply, personally involved.

A burst of activity on the police scanner broke through her thoughts, the voice of a female dispatcher directing units to a waterside area at Yellow Bluff Fort Historic State Park. Mia knew the shorthand codes—the ten-fifty-five indicated a dead body. The location was the park's northeast boat ramp.

"Patrol units in the vicinity are requested for crime scene containment. Responding officers should be aware the site has been given federal jurisdiction..."

The state park was a half-hour away.

She wasn't supposed to be on the job. Not to mention, the abductions were no longer her assignment. Mia paced her office before heading back into the living room, driven by the need to know if one of the missing women had been found. The body could be anyone—an unrelated murder or even a fisherman who had fallen into the water and drowned. But the fact that the FBI was there increased the likelihood it was Pauline Berger or Cissy Cox. Locating her purse, car keys and JSO-issued press card, Mia set her security system and left the apartment.

She wasn't certain if her press credentials would have any credence with the Bureau, but she had to try.

Pulling her Volvo onto the darkened street, Eric Macfarlane's words echoed inside her head. *You got away. Those women didn't.*

5

The decomposing body of a female lay near the water in an unzipped body bag, shielded from view by a partially raised canvas. Eric stood nearby with his hands on his jeans-clad hips, his heart heavy as he squinted against the harsh mobile lights set up by Forensics. He breathed through his mouth, the stench nauseating. The corpse had been in the water too long to make a visual ID, but the wet hair matted to the skull was blond, and a portion of a tattoo on the right shoulder—a small, delicate butterfly—was still somewhat visible.

It was the same as the one Pauline Berger's husband had described.

If a numeral had been carved into the abdomen, it was no longer discernible since fish and other aquatic wildlife had been gnawing at the bloated flesh. But the fingernails were all missing, and he suspected the M.E. would find several teeth had been removed, as well. He looked out to where two men in wet suits and scuba gear were raking the floor of the St. Johns River, searching for evidence.

"A crabber with a spotlight found the body when he went out to check his traps," Cameron said, joining him near the boat ramp. He nodded in the direction of the crabber, an elderly looking African-American man who stood with several JSO deputies. The man appeared visibly upset by what he'd found.

"When's the last time he checked his traps?" Eric asked.

"He says two days ago."

A rope around the corpse's abdomen indicated it had been anchored with some type of weight to keep it from surfacing, but it had somehow broken free. Based on the decomposition, Eric estimated she'd been dead for about a week. The putrefaction was advanced but warm water tended to speed up the process.

"I'm guessing this isn't the original dump site, since the body's been moved downstream by the current," Cameron noted. "Still, it probably wasn't too far from here since the St. Johns has a decline of only about an inch per mile. It's one of the slowest moving rivers anywhere."

Eric's T-shirt was damp from the humidity and a mosquito buzzed near his ear. He looked around the crime scene, which was one of organized chaos. Squad cars from the Jacksonville Sheriff's Office blocked the entrance to the boat ramp's gravel parking lot, their lights flashing into the tar-black sky. Crime scene specialists went about their jobs while deputies controlled the area, waving on the civilian vehicles that had slowed out of curiosity on the adjacent road. Several FBI field agents were there, as well—men who Eric was supposed to meet officially the following morning. Detectives Boyet and Scofield stood nearby, conferring with the deputy who had been the first responder to the 9-1-1 call.

"We could drag the water upstream and see what turns up," Cameron suggested as they moved farther from the corpse. Behind them, the river glistened like wet obsidian. "We can have a larger dive team out here in the morning."

Eric nodded his assent. "I'd like to have deputies perform a grid search of the land around here, also. Until daybreak, keep the area sealed off."

"I'll coordinate with Boyet…" Cameron paused as he looked off toward the road. "I don't believe it."

Eric followed his gaze. Mia Hale stood on the periphery with two deputies, obviously trying to talk her way up to the barricade. He called, "Let her through."

Walking over, he took her arm and shuttled her a few steps from the crowd. "What are you doing here?"

"I heard on the police scanner—a ten-fifty-five with federal jurisdiction." Her brown eyes appeared pained as they moved from Eric's face to the raised canvas that sat about thirty feet away. He could see the shallow rise and fall of her chest. "Is it one of the missing women?"

"We don't have a positive ID yet," he said gently. "The body's been in the water for a while. We'll know more following the medical examiner's autopsy."

Mia held her press card in her injured hand, although a reporter for the *Jacksonville Courier* was already there. When she saw where Eric's gaze had fallen, she explained, "I'm not here in a professional capacity. I…just had to…"

She halted, her voice sounding frayed.

"Come inside." Eric placed his hand on her back, guiding her into the containment area. Allowing media to enter was rare, and he noticed Cameron watching as he escorted her closer.

"I—I need to see her."

He felt a wave of guilt as he allowed her to walk to the other side of the raised canvas. Eric let her take the remaining steps alone. She looked down and he saw her features go slack, her eyes filling with sympathy and horror. Retreating, she covered her nose and mouth with the inside of her right forearm in an attempt to defuse the odor.

"You really shouldn't be here, Ms. Hale," Cameron said, reaching her. Eric stepped in.

"I'll take her back to her car."

Cameron's questioning gaze met Eric's as he passed her over. Appearing pale, Mia walked stiffly beside him in silence, and he cleared their way through the dense line of deputies. The reporter from the *Courier* called out to her, but she ignored him and continued on until they reached an older-model Volvo that was parked farther down along the shoulder of the road. Eric observed a miniature Indian dream catcher hanging from her rearview mirror.

"The blond hair," she whispered. "It's Pauline Berger, isn't it?"

He didn't respond, instead asking, "Are you okay to drive home?"

Mia gave a faint nod. She still wore the skimpy tank top and cargo pants she'd had on earlier, although he noticed that she'd pulled her dark, glossy hair into a short ponytail. They were far enough from the crime scene that the faint chirp of cicadas could be heard coming from the woods. A van passed them on the side of the road with the call letters of a local television station printed on its side. Eric realized it was only a matter of time now before the story broke wide-open, before a reporter made the official leap from kidnapper to a serial killer at large.

"Are you going to give a statement to Walt?"

He knew she was referring to her coworker at the paper. "Agent Vartran spoke to him earlier. He confirmed only that a female body had been found."

She took a tense breath, appearing to gather her courage. "I want to try the memory retrieval therapy... I'd like to start as soon as possible."

The determination in her eyes was mixed with a vulnerability that made him feel guiltier. He'd known the feelings seeing the body would evoke, but he badly needed her help. "You're sure about this?"

"I want this bastard caught, Agent Macfarlane—"

"It's Eric," he said quietly. Their gazes held for a long moment, until he moved closer and opened the driver's side door for her. He briefly touched her upper arm, wanting her to know she would have his support.

"I'll contact Dr. Wilhelm at the NAS in the morning," he said. "I'll be in touch. Go straight home, all right?"

She nodded and slid inside the vehicle. Eric closed the door. He remained rooted in place until she had driven off into the night.

As a reporter, Mia had been exposed to dead bodies before, in countless photos as well as crime scenes where she had caught glimpses of death from behind the police barricades. But it was Pauline Berger's water-ravaged corpse that would remain branded in her mind forever. The woman's facial features had putrefied; her eyes were missing, the bones protruding from where her right cheek should have been. Mia's hands tightened on the Volvo's steering wheel.

It could have been me.

She wondered if Eric Macfarlane had seen his wife's body—desecrated, lying somewhere like discarded, spoiling meat. The possibility sickened her. As apprehensive as she was about the experimental therapy, tonight had made up her mind. If there was even a chance she could remember *something* that might be of use…

She traveled across the Fuller Warren Bridge headed back to San Marco. The St. Johns flowed beneath her, the same languid body of water that had given up Pauline Berger's remains on the other side of the city. As she passed under the bridge's steady sequence of overhanging lights, she glimpsed brief reflections of herself in the windshield. Even in the faint mirror image, she saw her mother's Spanish and Portuguese heritage tempered by her father's delicate Welsh genes. They were the only things her parents had ever really given her, other than life.

Mia also saw fear in her eyes and she tried hard to squash it down.

The traffic had been heavy on the bridge, but it began to thin as she made her way into San Marco. She turned onto Atlantic Boulevard, traveling past picturesque Balis Park with its fountains and moss-draped live oaks that comprised the heart of the square. White lights had been strung up around the vintage bandstand in preparation for a weekend arts crawl. At least here she was on familiar ground.

As she went deeper into the residential side streets, Mia noticed the headlights of another car trailing behind her. For a time they seemed to be the only two cars on the road. She didn't think much of it until the vehicle made all the same turns she did, three in all. Watching in her rearview mirror, she noticed that it seemed to keep a consistent distance even when she decelerated or sped up.

Her nerves were on edge, she knew that. Still, she tried to get a look at the vehicle, but it was difficult to make out much through the hard glare of its headlights. On Alhambra Avenue, Mia pulled into the shadowy, circular driveway in front of her apartment building.

The car never passed by on the street.

She felt a tingle of panic. Hulking camellia shrubs at the property's rim made it impossible to see if the automobile had turned off somewhere, or whether it had killed its lights and was sitting there, its occupant waiting for her to emerge. Despite the air-conditioning, perspiration broke out on her skin.

Will and Justin's residence was on the ground floor. Making an impulse decision, Mia pressed on the Volvo's horn and began flashing its high beams. As lights came on in the apartment in response, she saw a car go past. It was a compact, four-door sedan, dark in color. Innocuous-looking. Was it the one she thought had been following her? She couldn't tell for certain. Tall, swaying palm trees obscured the streetlight.

Startled, she cried out at the sudden knock on the driver's side window. Will peered at her through the glass, wearing a T-shirt and pajama pants. Black-haired Justin was behind him, dressed only in jeans and wielding a wooden baseball bat.

"Mia, what the hell?" Will pulled her from the car as she unlocked and opened the door.

"I'm sorry." Her knees felt shaky. "I…I thought someone was following me."

"Were they?" With a worried expression, Justin moved around the car and glanced out on the street.

"No. I mean, I don't know. I'm not sure." Mia passed a hand over her face, rattled and increasingly uncertain. "I went to a crime scene. I think I probably just spooked myself, that's all."

Will shook his head in rebuke. "Tell me you're *not* already back to work."

"No. And I don't want to explain it right now, okay?"

He and Justin exchanged a look. As the two men walked her upstairs, Mia glanced back over her shoulder. The night was quiet. Peaceful. Feeling skittery and foolish, she began to believe it really was only her overactive imagination.

6

The team meeting scheduled for Friday morning at the Florida Bureau offices in Baymeadows had been moved to the sandy riverbank of the St. Johns. Five hours later, however, neither the water nor land search had turned up anything of relevance. Eric watched as the deputies who had helped with the grid-by-grid walk-through began loading into their cars.

"The divers will be out here another two to three hours." Cameron approached from his car, a bottled water in hand. He'd been upstream overseeing the dragging efforts while Eric supervised activities in the more immediate area where the body had been found. Like the other agents, both men wore chinos and T-shirts in the humid conditions. Eric felt perspiration roll down his back, the sun hot on his shoulders. The team had been taking breaks under a tarp that provided shade, or by briefly ducking into their air-conditioned vehicles.

"Any word from the psychiatrist at the NAS?" Cameron asked. Eric had told him about the experimental therapy.

"Dr. Wilhelm can see Ms. Hale at three today."

"She's a trouper to go along with it."

Eric thought of the anguish he'd witnessed in Mia's eyes the previous night. He had been worried she might change her mind, but when he'd called her earlier that day about the scheduled appointment, to her credit she hadn't tried to back out.

"You're going with her?"

"I want to hear anything she might recall firsthand." He paused as a noisy group of sandhill cranes flew overhead. Several of the large, storklike birds were already fishing at the water's shallow edge. "Besides, I'm the one who asked her to do this and I don't want her to go through it alone."

Cameron checked his wristwatch. "You should get going, then. You'll probably want to shower and change first. I'll stay out here with the team to finish up the water search, at least for today. I figured a larger exploration out here was a long shot, but we'd be remiss not to do it. The problem is the river's just too damn big."

"Has anyone spoken to Pauline Berger's family?"

"We're withholding official notification pending the M.E. report. But unofficially we've already been in touch with next of kin and prepared them on the likelihood. I wanted to let them know before they turned on the news, heard about the female floater and put two and two together. Not to mention, the press are already speculating the body is one of the abducted women. No acknowledgment from us or the JSO, of course."

Eric had caught part of the local morning news prior to heading out to the river. He thought of the waiting families and it gave him a dull ache. "What about Cissy Cox's relatives?"

"We contacted her family as well and told them the body wasn't a match. It gave them some relief, at least for a little while."

He figured Cam was thinking about the same thing he was—the possibility that her remains were also out here, somewhere.

Cameron wore a baseball cap with the FBI logo emblazoned on it, and he lifted it from his hair to wipe his perspiring forehead. He moved to a lighter topic. "You still coming to dinner tonight?"

"Unless something changes with the investigation, I'll be there."

"Come around eight o'clock—I told Lanie we'd have to eat late. She's in a major nesting phase so be prepared for something extravagant." He smiled and shook his head. "She had issues of *Martha Stewart* spread out all over the kitchen when I got home last night."

"Agent Vartran? Agent Macfarlane?" A uniformed deputy strode toward them across the gravel lot. The man was heavily tanned, his already blond hair bleached nearly white by the sun. "I'm Deputy Hammond. Detective Boyet wanted me to let you know something that might be of interest."

They all shook hands. He pointed out to the two-lane road. "Last night, one of our men assigned to keep cars from stopping and gawking ran a few license plates, just for the hell of it. You never know when someone with an outstanding warrant might show up in the database, right?"

Cameron shifted his weight. "Anything come up?"

"Not last night. They were all clean." He placed his hands on his gun belt. "But one of the vehicles that came through here *was* reported stolen as of this morning. The owner's staying at one of the golf resorts in Ponte Vedra and hadn't used his car since yesterday afternoon. He only noticed it missing at around 11:00 a.m. today when he got ready to check out of the hotel."

"Which means someone else drove it through here last night." Eric understood why Boyet thought the information important. Along with the car Mia had been driving the night she escaped, it increased the possibility the unsub was using stolen vehicles for the abductions— eliminating any chance of being identified through license plates. Still, riding around in a hot car was a risk in itself. So was driving it past the dump site. But some perpetrators got off on seeing the turmoil they'd caused. Arsonists as well as murderers had been known to stand in crowds of onlookers, reliving their experience. If that were the case, however, Eric doubted the unsub had stolen another vehicle just to have a look. He probably had done it for a dual purpose. Like abducting another woman.

"What's the car's make?"

The deputy's silvered sunglass lenses reflected like mirrors. He swatted at a pesky fly. "Black Audi A4, turbo charge. We've got an APB issued for the model and tags."

Cameron's cell phone went off. He answered it, said a few words and then closed its cover. "That was Agent Olkarski upstream. The divers recovered plastic sheeting tangled around the leg of a dock. It has indentations consistent with the binding found on the body."

"Anything nearby on the river floor that might have been the anchor?" Eric asked.

"Two standard-grade cinder blocks with frayed ropes on them. Nothing distinctive. The ropes and sheeting could've come from any home improvement store in the area."

Eric stared out over the murky water. It wasn't the break he'd been hoping for.

Mia had expected a high-rise building comprised of steel and glass. Sterile, isolated corridors. High-tech fingerprint scans required to open solid metal doors. But Dr. Günter Wilhelm's office was located in an unassuming, one-story brick office complex inside the Jacksonville Naval Air Station base. She sat on a hunter-green-striped couch across from the psychiatrist's desk while Eric had taken the matching side chair. To her right, a large picture window provided a view of the adjacent naval hospital. The room was tastefully decorated and held the faint scent of pipe tobacco and citrus potpourri.

"Agent Macfarlane has apprised me of the investigation as well as your role in it, Mia," Dr. Wilhelm stated in a slight German accent. He was a fatherly looking man, with graying hair and a starched white lab coat. "You must understand there are no guarantees. The therapy has worked for only about thirty percent of the participants, and to varying degrees. A few of those have remembered large amounts of detail, but for most others it is far less."

Mia tried to wrench any anxiety from her voice. "If it's successful, what kind of things might I remember?"

"Possibly a visual image—a face or a location, a shred of dialog. It's difficult to say since every case is different. You'd also be the first patient I've worked with whose memory loss was induced by a chemical substance. I'm unsure of how it will affect the outcomes."

Nervous butterflies fluttered in her stomach. She tried to imagine what it might be like to actually see or hear something from those lost hours.

"What about the risks?" Eric asked. He was dressed in dark suit pants, a white shirt and tie, his suit jacket left behind in the car in deference to the heat.

"There can be physical side effects, although they're typically short-term. Some patients have reported a headache or dizziness for an hour or two after our sessions. In a few extreme cases, an elevation in blood pressure."

Mia toyed with her bandaged fingers. "What kind of drug is it, exactly?"

"In layman's terms, it's known as a *mental catalyst*. When used in combination with the right hypnotherapy, it makes it more possible to delve into untapped channels within the mind." Dr. Wilhelm smiled, a benevolent look on his face as he explained. "These channels hold memories we may not even be aware of. For example, a repressed childhood memory or something that might have happened when one was injured and unconscious, supposedly unable to hear or process thought. We've been able to prove the mind is capable of capturing event fragments even in such situations. The memories *are* there.

Tapping into them and bringing them to the surface is the real feat."

Mia said half-jokingly, "I'm guessing this catalyst *isn't* FDA-approved."

"You needn't worry overly—the drug is nonaddictive and has been tested in military clinical trials." He paused, clearing his throat. "However, its effect when used with hypnotherapy has proved to be potent, when it works. The memory captures can be quite vivid, which may be unsettling considering your circumstances, Mia. Not to mention, even once the drug has left your system there is a possibility of memory flashes."

"Memory flashes?" Eric asked.

"She may recall certain things outside of the session itself." The psychiatrist tapped his right temple. "Once the window is opened…"

There's no closing it. Mia looked at Eric and found his gaze on her. She hoped the tightness she felt in her lungs wasn't communicated on her features. It would be so easy to change her mind and retreat. But she thought of the rotting corpse that had been pulled from the water. She also thought of Rebecca Macfarlane. Whatever she remembered couldn't be worse than what those poor women had gone through. Sounding much braver than she felt, she asked, "How do we start?"

Dr. Wilhelm indicated a folder on his desk. "I received your medical records from your physician. You had a recent examination while you were hospitalized earlier this week and appear to be in excellent health. You've also signed the necessary waivers. Considering the urgency of Agent Macfarlane's investigation, there's no reason we can't start now."

"Let's do it," Mia said firmly, tamping down her anxiety.

He stood from behind his desk. "I'll go prepare the syringe. I'm going to try a relatively light dosage today and gauge its effect."

Once the psychiatrist had left the office, Mia stood and wandered over to the picture window. Jets taking off from the naval base were visible in the hazy afternoon sky, and she could hear their thunderlike roar. She felt Eric's presence behind her.

"Are you all right?" he asked.

She turned to face him, her heart skipping a beat as she realized his closeness. Mia smiled weakly up at him. "I guess I hadn't anticipated needles."

Despite her attempt at humor, he remained serious. "You don't have to do this—"

"I do," she replied. "And you need me to."

He stared at her, his intense, moss-green eyes searching hers.

"Thank you," he said, touching her upper arm. His fingers on her bare skin sent a tingle racing through her. He dropped his hand as they heard Dr. Wilhelm return.

"Once the drug is administered, we'll give it a little time to take effect and then we'll begin with some mind relaxation techniques," he said as he indicated the couch. Mia blanched at the small hypodermic needle he held. She'd never quite gotten past her childish fear of them.

She returned to where she'd been seated. Looking purposely away, she felt him tie the rubber tubing around her right biceps and then the sharp prick of the needle in the inside of her forearm.

"Why don't you lie down and close your eyes? Focus on slow, deep breathing." Dr. Wilhelm dimmed the lights in the room, then went over to lower the window blinds, choking out the bright afternoon sunlight. "Imagine you're sitting in a theater, all alone, facing a blank, white screen."

Smoothing down her sleeveless linen blouse over her cropped khakis, Mia settled herself on the couch. She felt a little foolish. Eric stood silently with his arms crossed over his chest, his features strained.

She gave him a final look, took a breath and closed her eyes.

"I'm sorry."

Eric glanced at her from behind the steering wheel. "Don't be. Dr. Wilhelm said it could take a few sessions to know if it's going to work. The good news is that you responded to the hypnosis. Not everyone does."

It was true; she *had* fallen under the psychiatrist's hypnotic suggestions. Mia had felt herself relaxing, being slowly drawn backward to the moment of her disappearance. It had all seemed so real. She recalled hearing the echo of her own footsteps on the concrete floor of the parking garage, the cheerful chirp of her car's key fob as she unlocked the door. She had been hungry and thinking about what to have for dinner as she slid into the driver's seat. But at that precise moment, the screen inside her head went blank. Dr. Wilhelm had taken her through that critical time span using various approaches, hoping she might recall seeing her abductor. None of them had worked. Her memory seemed to stop at the moment she closed the car door. He had mentioned the possibility of using a higher concentration of the drug during their next session, as a way to get past what he had called a *trauma block*.

"How are you feeling?" Eric asked.

Mia touched the injection site on her arm, which was a little sore. "I'm fine. No headache or dizziness."

"I want you to call me if that changes."

They were headed over the bridge toward San Marco. The late afternoon sun sat lower in the sky and cast golden dapples of light across the omnipresent river. It was slow going since they were caught in the Friday rush hour, with traffic inching along. She glanced at Eric's profile and thought again of the brief moment they seemed to have shared inside the psychiatrist's office. There was no denying she felt an attraction to him. Mia realized it only complicated her situation.

"I'm going back to work next week," she announced.

"Don't you think it's a little soon?"

"You sound like my editor." She tucked her hair behind one ear as she gazed out the window. "I asked for the abduction story back. He said no."

"Smart man."

Mia looked at him. "The *no* is temporary. No as in *not yet*. He wants me to handle smaller assignments for a while, but I'm hoping to convince him otherwise."

"I'm being honest with you, Mia. Your name on those articles already attracted this guy's attention once. Putting yourself back out there like that…" He shook his head. "It would be rare for someone like this to go after the same person twice, but he could see it as a challenge. It's just not a good idea."

His cell phone rang. Mia lapsed into silence, hearing only Eric's side of the conversation. Still, it was pretty clear what they were talking about. She felt her stomach clench as she thought of Pauline Berger.

"The M.E. made the identification through dental records," he said. "Two of the teeth were missing, however."

Mia closed her eyes, feeling a coldness creep over her despite the warm sun beating down on her through the windshield. She realized she'd referred to the investigation as an abduction case a few moments earlier. That had now officially changed.

A short time later, they pulled in front of her apartment building. Will's convertible was gone, although the third-floor tenant appeared to be at home judging by her Toyota Prius in the driveway.

"Wait there. I'll walk you up." Eric exited the vehicle. He went around to the passenger side and opened the door for her. It was something he'd done at the Naval Air Station, as well. Normally, she would scoff at such old-fashioned behavior, but it seemed to suit him as if it were second nature, something ingrained in his DNA. Mia was reminded of his family tree. She imagined private prep schools and cotillions, an Ivy League college education. It was a vast difference from her own background.

As they went up the steps to the building's second floor, she asked, "Are you going to speak with Pauline Berger's family?"

"Agent Vartran is on his way to see them, along with Detective Boyet and Detective Scofield."

At the top of the stairs, he took her keys and unlocked the door, pushing it open for her and then handing them back. "I'll pick you up at four-thirty tomorrow?"

Mia nodded, entering her pass code into the security system console as they stepped inside. Even though the following day was Saturday, Dr. Wilhelm had recommended another session within twenty-four hours. He'd suggested the late-afternoon time frame so he could get in a round of golf with some visiting military VIPs.

"I imagine Dr. Wilhelm doesn't schedule Saturday appointments for just anyone," she acknowledged softly, looking up into his face. Her searching gaze held his for several long moments. "I'm a journalist, Eric…I do research. I've looked into the Maryland investigation."

She saw the small lines of tension form around his eyes. Several beats of silence passed before he spoke. "Then you know why stopping this psychopath is so important to me."

After he was gone, Mia stood alone inside her apartment. She had believed it important for him to know that *she knew.*

She thought of Pauline Berger's husband and understood why Eric hadn't gone with the others to deliver the heartbreaking news.

7

The two little girls sat on a street curb nearly hot enough to burn the backs of their thighs. Mia felt sweat roll down her face and she wiped it away with a skinny forearm. Miss Cathy—as she made them call her—didn't like kids in the house.

There's a water hose out back if you're thirsty. You can come in at dark. Have dinner and wash up. No talking. Go to bed.

Mia felt a sickness in her stomach. She didn't like it here. Three days had passed since the lady who frowned and wore too much perfume dropped her off.

"Don't be scared, Mia," her new friend said, taking her hand. The girl had scraggly, reddish hair and was about her same age. There were a lot of kids who lived in the house. None of them were Miss Cathy's own children. Mia felt tears sting her eyes.

"It'll get better, you'll see."

A car came down the residential street, a powder-blue hatchback with a white racing stripe and loud engine. It slowed as it went past. The driver stared at them, turn-

ing his head to look for as long as he could. His face was in the shadows, but something about him made her want to run and hide.

The car stopped and began to back up.

Mia jerked awake on the couch. Sitting up in her living room, she ran a hand over her face, her heart thudding. The dream had been so real.

She hadn't thought of Miss Cathy's in years. She had lived there for only a few weeks, her first in a long line of foster care homes. But Mia didn't recall a red-haired girl ever being there or a man in a car at all. She wondered if Dr. Wilhelm's therapy session had confused her subconscious.

One thing was for certain; it had exhausted her more than she realized.

She'd lain down after Eric's departure, expecting to doze for only a little while. But apparently she had been asleep for hours. Outside, the sky had grown black, bathing the room in shadows. Mia stood and bumped her shin on the coffee table in her haste to get to a lamp. She'd never liked the darkness. She released a pent-up breath as soft light filled the space. Based in reality or not, the dream had brought back old memories she had worked hard to suppress.

Two days before her sixth birthday, the Florida Department of Family and Child Services removed Mia from her mother's home, relinquishing her into foster care. Luri Hale had been a mess, unable to care for herself, much less a child. Abandoned by her husband, jobless, given to binge drinking and interchanging bouts of mania and depression, she had made Mia's young

life a maelstrom of uncertainty. During Luri's up peri-
ods, their filthy apartment hosted an endless parade of
strange men. And when the crash—the corresponding
down period came—it was much worse. Mia was left
alone with her mother's drunken sobs and abusive out-
bursts.

The removal by DFACS came after Mia, dirty, barefoot, had been caught shoplifting food from a neighborhood grocery store.

Still, foster care had been a rough ride, with families
often taking children only for the modicum of cash they
brought in. And Mia learned quickly not to get too settled anywhere, since the following week or month might
mean a move somewhere else, including back home
whenever Luri regained custody of her before losing her
again. Because she refused to give up her rights, Mia had
been ineligible for adoption. Not that many couples were
looking for kids who weren't babies or toddlers, especially ones who weren't blond-haired and blue-eyed.

Mia knew Luri was still alive, living somewhere near
Brunswick, Georgia, an hour and a half up the coast. But
she never saw her, hadn't spoken to her in years. Even
now, she felt a sense of anger and loss for the family she'd
never had.

Wandering into the kitchen, she noticed the blinking
light on the phone console, indicating two new voice
mails. The phone's ringer was on low—had the calls
come in while she'd been asleep? She pressed the button
and waited for the first message. It was from Grayson,
who was checking in on her. He'd heard about the ID on

Pauline Berger's body, he said, and wanted Mia to call him back. Concern threaded his voice.

She *would* call him, soon. An image of the woman's corpse filled her head and sent a shiver running through her all over again.

Mia moved to the second message but was met with only silence—a good ten seconds of static-filled dead air before the voice mail system cut off the connection. She checked the caller ID screen, which read Unknown Caller. Zeroes were displayed where the number should have been. She received calls like that all the time, everyone did, and she hated that she was letting some telemarketing firm put her even more at unease. The draining therapy session, the strange nightmare—all of it had shaken her a bit. Mia realized it wasn't Grayson but Eric she wanted to call. She shoved away the impulse, however, not wanting to seem anxiety-prone and needy.

As she went to the fridge and rummaged through the Thai leftovers from the previous evening, her mind returned to the little red-haired girl. Even now, she could almost feel the child's thin fingers grasping hers, could see her clear hazel eyes.

It'll get better. You'll see.

Mia only hoped the dream-child was telling her the truth.

Eric had taken his beer out to the deck of Cameron and Lanie's house. The couple lived in St. Augustine, south of the Jacksonville area in a weathered, Craftsman-style waterfront home that overlooked the Matanzas Bay. The home had been built in the 1920s and passed down through three generations of Vartrans. A short distance away, the lighthouse on Anastasia Island was visible, its still-operational beacon glowing like a bonfire in the dark night.

"You know that thing's haunted," Lanie said, following his gaze as she came out onto the deck from the kitchen. She cupped the mound of her belly and eased down onto the step next to where he sat. Her blond hair lifted in the warm, brackish breeze. "As the story goes, the lighthouse keeper's young daughter drowned in the bay and her ghost can be seen on the observation deck from time to time."

Eric raised his eyebrows. "Do you really believe that?"

She smiled slightly, shrugging. "I've never seen her but it's good for tourism."

"Where's Cameron?"

"Doing the dishes for his poor, knocked-up wife. I thought I'd come out here and check on you."

Eric had found out at dinner that Lanie was due in early August, and she was having a baby girl. He had known Lanie for nearly as long as he'd known Cameron. During the years in which they'd been partnered, it had often been the four of them on weekends—Cameron and Lanie, Rebecca and himself. Cameron had served as a groomsman at his and Rebecca's wedding. Sitting on the deck with nothing but quiet and the water's dark beauty stretching out in front of him, he could easily understand why his friends had made the choice to return home.

"How are you, Eric?" Lanie nudged his shoulder with hers. "I mean, *really*. How are you?"

"I'm okay."

When she continued to gaze at him, concern on her face, he added quietly, "It's been almost three years, Lanie."

She pushed her hair from her eyes. "Time flies. We miss you. We miss Rebecca, too."

Eric took a sip of his beer.

"Even after Cam and I moved back home, Rebecca and I still kept in touch by phone. We talked every few weeks or so." Lanie didn't look at him as she spoke. Instead, she stared out over the water. "I know you guys were having problems. But she still loved you, Eric."

He sighed. He suspected she knew anyway. "We were getting a separation. Rebecca wanted it—I didn't."

His job had come between them. Bureau work was always demanding, but Eric's move to the VCU had only intensified the long hours and travel, as well as the pressure. The daily violence had worn him down more than he'd expected. Rebecca had always needed his attention, his time, and he hadn't been able to give it to her. At least not in the amounts she desired. Even if she really did love him, she had still wanted out.

"I let her down," he murmured, more to himself than Lanie.

"It's not your fault. Rebecca knew what she was getting into when she married a federal officer—"

"She didn't plan to die because of me."

Lanie fell silent. There really was no response she could give. Eric felt bad for the harsh edge to his words. Rebecca's murder had screwed him up, but he didn't need to take it out on someone else. After a few moments, he said, "Thanks for dinner, and for letting me stay at the bungalow. It beats the hell out of the Holiday Inn."

"Cam figured you get your share of hotel rooms without having to stay in one down here." Lanie played with her wedding band, sliding it up and down on her finger as she spoke. "We're lucky. His parents left him the rental property, and this house. The bungalow is a nice supplemental income, but it's in an older area of Jax Beach and usually doesn't rent out until the summer when everything else is full."

She hesitated. "I'm sorry we hadn't mentioned the baby before now. Called or dropped you a postcard or something. It's just that it's taken a while and with the miscarriage two years ago, I've been a little superstitious about talking about it."

Eric nodded his understanding. "You guys have a good life down here. You'll be good parents. Do you have a name picked out?"

"Rosalie Marie." She let out a small laugh. "It's horribly old-fashioned, but it was Cameron's mother's name. He's dead set on it."

"It's beautiful."

Eric had braced his hand on the thigh of his jeans, and Lanie covered it with hers. She gazed at him, her china-blue eyes serious. Even in the shadows, he could see faint sun freckles on her cheekbones.

"You deserve a good life, too, Eric," she said softly. "But Cameron thinks you're still not through punishing yourself."

He looked away and swallowed another sip of beer. Maybe when The Collector was dead or behind bars—

and he admitted he'd prefer the former—he'd be able to let go of the past. But not until then.

Both he and Lanie turned as the door to the kitchen opened. Cameron came outside. Eric got to his feet and helped Lanie to a standing position. Truth be told, she wasn't all that big yet but she was small-framed and her rounded stomach did make her seem a little off balance.

"Kitchen all done?" she asked.

Cameron nodded. He still had a dish towel slung over one shoulder.

"Do you want some dessert now? You boys can have coffee or another beer, and I'll be stuck with boring old herbal tea…" She halted, apparently catching the seriousness on Cam's face.

"We're going to have to take a rain check on dessert, babe," he said. His eyes moved to Eric. "I just got a call from Boyet. Another woman was reported missing an hour ago."

8

Eric and Cameron stood in the security office at Jacksonville International Airport, reviewing a digital recording with the facility's head of security. Anna Lynn Gomez, a twenty-eight-year-old flight attendant, could be seen in the grainy video. She was still in her uniform and rolling her suitcase across the concourse.

"No one appears to be following her," the heavyset security chief noted. He switched to a time-stamped recording from the parking garage. "And there's her Nissan Altima driving out of lot B at 11:28 p.m."

That had been Thursday night, and it was now in the very early hours of Saturday morning. Due to her work schedule, at first neither of Ms. Gomez's roommates had reported her missing, thinking her layover had been extended somewhere. But when she still hadn't shown up by Friday evening and failed to return messages left on her cell phone, they had grown concerned and contacted the local authorities.

Which meant she had already been missing for over twenty-four hours.

Eric watched as her car remained stopped at the parking attendant's booth on the video. Although it was hard to see clearly, she appeared to be alone. He thought of the stolen vehicle that had driven past the area where Pauline Berger's body was found on Thursday night. If the unsub had been out hunting then, it was possible he'd crossed paths with Ms. Gomez, who would have been headed toward the waterside suburb of Arlington where she rented a house with two other women. Eric considered several scenarios. She could've had a flat somewhere on the road, or stopped for gas or a late bite to eat. Any such event could have given her abductor an opportunity.

"The roads aren't enough—tell the JSO to check parking lots for her car between here and Arlington. Gas stations and restaurants open late in particular," Eric said as he and Cameron traveled back through the airport. Due to the hour, the terminal held only occasional patches of bleary-eyed travelers.

Cameron took his cell phone from his pocket. They stood in front of a closed Starbucks while he gave instructions to a Sheriff's Office dispatcher.

"Can we consider for a moment the possibility Ms. Gomez wasn't abducted?" he asked as they resumed walking. "You saw her on the video, Eric. She's pretty and young—maybe she's off with a pilot having hot sex at some beach resort. When we talked to her roommates, they acknowledged she can be impulsive, which I interpreted to be a diplomatic way of saying irresponsible. It's one of the reasons they waited so long to call."

"I hope that's the case." Eric *had* seen the flight attendant. Her petite frame and dark hair reminded him of Mia.

"But you don't think so."

"Do you?"

Cam shrugged. "Wishful thinking."

The disappearance of Ms. Gomez had made the Friday late-night news. Combined with the recent discovery of Pauline Berger's body, the media was hotly speculating on the presence of a serial killer in the metro area. The FBI would be making a formal statement in the morning, and Eric was working on getting a gag order in place prohibiting the press from talking about certain aspects of the investigation. Due to Mia's involvement, the *Courier* had already agreed not to publish specific details, but he couldn't count on other news outlets to have the same discretion. The order was being put in front of a judge at 7:00 a.m.

As they continued through a set of automated glass doors that led into the airport's parking garage, Cameron checked his watch. "I emailed you the M.E.'s report on Ms. Berger—it came through right after dinner. An analysis of the remaining skin tissue on the abdomen indicates a controlled, superficial laceration."

"In the shape of the number six?"

"Possibly. There wasn't enough tissue left to make a full determination. C.O.D. was most likely blunt force trauma. The skull was fractured. There were also several other broken bones."

Stopping at the elevator, Eric pushed the button. In Maryland, the unsub had killed his victims in multiple ways. Pauline Berger had apparently been beaten to death.

Eric wondered how long they had. If The Collector held true to form, Anna Lynn Gomez was still alive. She'd remain that way until he took another victim.

She'd barely slept after watching the late-evening news.

It was now after four on Saturday afternoon, and Mia stood in shorts and a tank top in the muggy shade of a live oak, waiting outside her apartment building for Eric's arrival. She had spoken to him only briefly that morning by phone. Even with the latest abduction, he had been intent on keeping their appointment with Dr. Wilhelm.

In fact, he'd said it was more important than ever.

Mia had come outdoors, thinking she would meet him there instead of him climbing the stairs to get her. Not to mention, she'd spent the sunny day inside so far, monitoring the television and police scanner for updates on Anna Lynn Gomez's disappearance. She needed some fresh air to clear her head.

A red Toyota Prius turned into the driveway.

"How are you, Mia?" Penney Niemen, the third-floor tenant, called as she turned off the car's ignition and slid from behind the steering wheel. Head chef at a popular vegetarian restaurant on San Marco Square, Penney was tall and willowy, with a mass of curly brown hair.

"I'm fine, Penney, thanks." Mia walked over to the car.

The other woman hesitated, then added awkwardly,

"Will and Justin told me about what…happened. That you're the unidentified woman on the news."

She glanced worriedly at Mia's bandaged fingers and abraded wrists. "I hope you don't mind—I know the press didn't release your name. But they thought I should be aware, living upstairs in the same building."

"It's okay," she assured her. "And it happened in the parking garage at the newspaper, not here."

"I still can't believe you managed to get away." Shaking her head, her curls bouncing, she lifted the car's hatchback to remove a bag of groceries. "It's like something out of a horror movie. You're incredibly brave."

Mia didn't feel that way. The truth was, she had checked her apartment's security system repeatedly last night and kept all the overhead lights on, something she wasn't proud of.

"They told me you were drugged. You really can't remember anything?"

"Not so far."

"It's probably a blessing. If that happened to me, I'm pretty sure I'd become a certified agoraphobic *and* a gun owner," Penney said. "They think he took another woman—a flight attendant—last night."

When they'd talked, Eric had told Mia the little he knew about Anna Lynn Gomez's disappearance so far. The FBI had released a statement that morning acknowledging that all four abductions, as well as Pauline Berger's murder, were believed to be the work of a single culprit. JSO deputies and federal agents were currently canvassing the city, looking for the missing woman's Nissan.

"Aren't you terrified this psycho might come after you again?"

"According to the FBI, it's uncommon for this type of serial offender to go after the same person twice," Mia said, recounting what Eric had told her. She hoped it would put Penney's mind at ease about living nearby.

"Still, you should be on your guard, Mia. I am. I've started carrying Mace." Penney closed the hatchback. Holding the groceries on one hip, she used her free hand to shield her eyes from the sun. "Look, I feel bad about not checking on you earlier. I've been working double shifts at the restaurant all week. And to be honest, I think all this has me a little freaked out. I live alone…"

"I understand." The two women didn't know one another all that well, anyway, mostly talking as they passed on the stairs to and from work, or attending the occasional party that Will and Justin threw. "I'm sure the restaurant keeps you busy."

"I'll bring you some treats—maybe some brownies?"

Vegetarian or not, Slice of Life was known for having some of the best pastries around. "Thanks."

The building had curving exterior staircases. Mia watched as Penney went up the stairs on the left and disappeared on the third-floor landing. A moment later, Eric's rental sedan pulled in behind the Prius. Mia came forward as he exited the car. He appeared tired, and she imagined he hadn't had much rest since another missing woman was reported.

"Any updates?" she asked.

He opened the passenger-side door for her. The car's air conditioner was running hard, battling the Florida humidity. "We located Ms. Gomez's Nissan an hour ago. It was in the parking lot of a Bargain-Mart off the Arlington Expressway."

The discovery eliminated any possibility that the young woman had just gotten a wild hair and gone off on her own free will. Mia felt a troubling disquiet.

Eric squinted at her in the strong sunlight. "Why would a woman stop at a place like that, alone, at nearly midnight?"

"Lots of reasons," she answered honestly. "Tampons. Emergency wine."

He seemed to appreciate her candidness. Touching her shoulder, he said, "We should go."

Placing a framed photo out of the way, Dr. Wilhelm perched on the edge of his desk in his office at the Naval Air Station. His face appeared a little sunburned from his golf outing earlier that morning.

"Did you experience any aftereffects from yesterday's session?" he asked Mia.

"I had a pretty vivid dream last night." She pressed her hands into her lap, aware Eric's eyes were on her, as well. "But it didn't really make any sense."

"Can you describe it?"

She released a breath. "I was a child, sitting on a street curb with a little red-haired girl. She and I were holding hands."

"And where were you exactly?"

"Outside a foster care group home." Mia felt exposed. She didn't like discussing her past, but she wanted to be truthful for the sake of the therapy. "I was in the system as a child. I lived at the group home for several weeks before being moved to a foster family. The dream's setting *was* real but I don't remember the girl being there at all."

"Did you and the other child talk in your dream?"

"She told me not to be scared. That things would get better."

Dr. Wilhelm nodded thoughtfully. "What else happened?"

"A car drove past us. A blue hatchback of some kind. It slowed down and then it started to back up—I woke up then. The dream was very brief."

"Did you see who was driving the car?"

Her chest tightened at the recollection. "It was a man but his face was in the shadows. I couldn't see him but he gave me a bad feeling."

She glanced at Eric and saw the concern on his features before looking back to the psychiatrist. "Couldn't this just be a run-of-the-mill, weird dream? Does it have to mean something?"

Dr. Wilhelm shifted his weight on the desk. "I think at the least it means you have the potential to be very receptive to the therapy. As you slept, your mind opened up, Mia. What was your experience like at the group home?"

"I hated it," she confessed. Head bowed, she stared at her bandaged fingers. "I was afraid and I missed my mother."

"So your mind took you someplace you didn't want to go. Which is exactly what we need to accomplish."

Mia looked up. "But the little girl wasn't real and I don't remember the event with the car, either."

"That's all right," Dr. Wilhelm said. He took a ball-point pen from the pocket of his lab coat and absently clicked its top up and down as he spoke. "While the dream *could* be a repressed childhood memory, my opinion is that it's actually emblematic. I think the man in the car is symbolic of your abductor. Your mind returned to a time when you were a child, when you felt most vulnerable, because it parallels the vulnerability you're feeling now as a victim."

It made sense, Mia admitted to herself. "What about the little girl?"

"Cissy Cox, one of the still-missing victims, is a redhead," Eric noted.

"So she was symbolic, too?"

"Possibly." Dr. Wilhelm rose from where he'd been seated. "What I want to do today is start by focusing on the moments leading up to your abduction again. I understand another woman was reported missing last night, so time is of the essence. As we've discussed, I'd like to give you a higher concentration of the catalyzing drug. That, combined with anything still in your system from yesterday, should help us tap into your memories."

Mia gave a small nod of consent. This time Dr. Wilhelm already had the syringe prepared and he walked to where she sat on the couch. She tried to distract herself from what he was doing by watching Eric as he paced the room.

"Lie down, Mia," Dr. Wilhelm instructed once he'd given her the injection. "This is a stronger dosage—you might feel some dizziness this time. I'll let you relax for a bit and then I'll rejoin you. Agent Macfarlane?"

"Please stay," she said softly to Eric. The psychiatrist nodded, closed the blinds and left the room.

Overhead, Mia heard the intermittent roar of military planes as they took off from the Naval Air Station's tarmac. Focusing on their sound, she reclined and closed her eyes, but opened them again when she sensed Eric sitting in the armchair next to the couch. He leaned forward so that he was closer to her, his elbows resting on his knees. A frown creased his forehead.

"I appreciate what you're doing," he murmured. "I want you to know that."

Mia placed her hand on his forearm. He'd rolled up the sleeves of his dress shirt, and she felt the hard sinews under his warm skin, the faint sprinkling of male hair. "I'm going to try to do better this time."

His expression appeared tense. "Whatever happens, it's all right."

Her fingers grazed his wrist, and then she closed her eyes.

As she lay in silence, Mia felt a warm fuzziness spread through her, the sensation much stronger than the day before. She wasn't asleep, but her body felt relaxed and buoyant, as if she were floating on the ocean or in a backyard pool. She wasn't aware of Dr. Wilhelm reentering the room, but she heard him speak.

"Let's go back to the night in your newspaper's parking garage," he suggested in a calm tone. "It's late and you just filed your story. You're headed home. Tell me what you see, Mia."

"My car," she whispered, concentrating on the steel-and-concrete deck surrounding her. It was as if she really were there, but at the same time she remained tethered to Dr. Wilhelm's voice. "I'm parked in the last spot on the first row."

"Are you alone?"

"Yes."

"What are you doing?"

"I'm…walking. I have my keys." Just like the last time, she felt the hard shape of the key fob in her hand. Mia pressed the device and it gave a bright chirp in response. Opening the Volvo's door, she tossed her purse inside and slid onto the cool leather seat.

"Are you inside the car now?"

She nodded. "I'm…looking in my purse for my cell phone. I'm going to order takeout on my way home and—"

Her heart lurched, scalded by surprise and fear. An arm curled tightly around her throat, yanking her backward against the headrest and cutting off her windpipe. She tried to get free, tried to scream but nothing more than a few breathy gasps escaped her. She couldn't breathe. Her fingers clawed at the hard, corded vise choking her and she felt a sharp stab of pain in the side of her neck. Within seconds it became harder to fight. Her hands felt heavy and uncoordinated, then dropped limply to her sides on the car seat. She wanted to blow the Volvo's horn or set off the panic button on the key fob dangling from the ignition switch, but she couldn't gain control of her fingers. Her pulse pounded in her ears.

The shadowed form behind her smelled faintly of

aftershave. Only his eyes were visible in the rearview mirror. She felt a kiss against her right temple.

"Hello, Mia. You're even prettier than I imagined."

9

"Mia?" Dr. Wilhelm repeated. "Can you hear me? Tell me what's going on."

Eric dragged a hand through his hair, watching as her eyelids fluttered and her head rolled weakly from side to side. She'd stopped talking, instead gasping for air. "You need to pull her back—"

The psychiatrist raised his hand in a silencing gesture. "Listen to me, Mia. Whatever's happening right now, I want you to distance yourself from it. Go back to the empty theater we've created and focus on the white, blank screen. Can you do that?"

He made the request twice before she seemed to obey, her breathing eventually slowing and her body releasing its tension. "You're safe here, all right? We're going to rest in the theater for a little while. Let the blank screen fill your mind. Don't think of anything else."

He got up and went over to his desk. Eric followed him over.

"Is she okay?" he asked in a low voice. His eyes fell

on the blood pressure kit Dr. Wilhelm extracted from his credenza.

"I'm going to monitor her BP as a precaution. But the therapy is working, Agent Macfarlane. You *were* aware the memories were going to cause some discomfort."

Eric knew he needed to relax and let the doctor do his job. He just hadn't expected his protective instincts to kick in quite so hard. Eric looked again at Mia. She lay on the couch—no longer moving, her eyes closed. Her lips were slightly parted and her sleek, dark hair spilled across the striped cushion underneath her head.

"You're going to feel a slight pressure on your upper arm," Dr. Wilhelm advised in a soothing tone as he returned to the chair beside the couch. Gently, he slipped the cuff onto Mia's slender biceps. "It's nothing to worry about."

Taking the reading, he gave a nod to Eric, an indication her blood pressure was in an acceptable range. "Tell me what happened after you got into your car, Mia. There's no need to go back there. Just tell me about it from where you are now."

They waited for her to speak. She took a fragile breath, her eyes still closed and her voice soft and dreamlike. "There was a man hiding in the backseat…he stuck me with a needle."

"Did you see him?"

She shook her head faintly. "Only his eyes. In the rearview mirror. They were blue, I think. He was wearing latex gloves."

Which would explain why there were no other prints inside the stolen car Mia had used to escape. Eric felt disappointment that she hadn't gotten a better look at the unsub. He had apparently used an injectable, dangerous cocktail of liquid Rohypnol and GHB. It would have been potent and fast acting, much more so than if it had been simply laced into a drink at a bar or nightclub.

"How old do you think he might have been?" Dr. Wilhelm prodded.

"I'm not sure. But he had crinkles around his eyes."

"Did he say anything?"

"That I was prettier than he'd thought." Her breath hitched, and her hands clasped and unclasped on her stomach. "I...I don't remember anything else."

"You're doing very well. I want you to rest some more, all right?" Standing, Dr. Wilhelm motioned Eric to the hallway where they could speak more openly.

"We can take this further before the effects of the drug begin to recede—as you know, we don't have a lot of time. Each session gives us only a few minutes of peak access. The choice is yours, Agent Macfarlane. We don't want to overtax her in a single session, but due to the higher concentration of the catalyst she was given this time, we'll have to wait a few days before trying again. I advise you to use this session to your fullest advantage."

Eric stared at the partially closed door. He thought of Anna Lynn Gomez. The decision squeezed his lungs. "Keep going."

Back inside the office, Dr. Wilhelm once again settled into the armchair next to the couch. Eric stood tensely nearby, his arms crossed over his chest.

"We're going to leave the theater for a little while again. The man who was hiding in your car *took* you somewhere, Mia. You were drugged and things will be hazy. But I need you to look through that veil and tell me what you see, and what you hear. Maybe you're in another car or an unfamiliar place. Maybe the man is there with you. Take your time…"

Her silky lashes formed half moons against her cheeks, and her small, rounded breasts lifted and fell with her shallow breathing. She frowned in concentration for what seemed like a long time.

"I—I don't know where I am," she whispered. "My head hurts and—"

Her hands twisted suddenly, fear punctuating her words. "Oh, God. My wrists…they're tied to a table!"

Eric thought of Mia's excised fingernails and hoped she wouldn't have to relive that torture. Anxiety gnawing at him, he paced a few steps before returning.

"I'm right here with you," Dr. Wilhelm reminded. "Try to remain calm. Look around and tell me what you see. It's very important."

"I…I'm in a room with cinder-block walls." Her voice shook. "There's a peg board with tools hanging on it… and pliers on the table in front of me."

Eric's nerves felt raw.

"There's plastic sheeting up on the walls. I…" She stopped speaking. Her throat convulsed, her breath growing more ragged.

"What is it, Mia?" Dr. Wilhelm asked. "Is the man with you?"

"I—I don't see him. But there's a woman. She's tied up on the other side of the room. She's gagged and she's staring right at me. She's hurt and…" A terrified sob escaped her. "Oh, God, I hear someone outside the door. I think he's coming back!"

Dr. Wilhelm spoke to her, trying to control her panic, but she cried out and sat bolt upright, bucking and slapping at him as he attempted to force her back down on the couch. Eric launched forward to help.

"Mia, listen to me. It's Dr. Wilhelm. We're going back to the theater now. To where it's safe—"

"No!" She convulsed and opened her eyes, drawing in deep gulps of air as if she had been underwater too long. Perspiration glistened on her skin. She'd clearly wrenched herself from her hypnotic state.

Eric's jaw clenched, his pulse thrumming.

"Don't sit up. Try not to talk yet." Dr. Wilhelm reinflated the cuff still on Mia's arm, waiting as the system got a reading. "Her BP's quite elevated. The drug's effect is starting to diminish or else she wouldn't have been able to pull herself out. I think we've gone as far as we can for today, but we've made quite a breakthrough."

Mia looked up at Eric, her brown eyes shimmering with tears.

"I saw Cissy Cox," she whispered.

It was headed into early evening, the blue sky slowly fading. There were no other cars in the driveway in front of Mia's apartment. Eric put the sedan into Park. Cutting off the ignition, he glanced at Mia.

She sat in the passenger seat, eyes closed and head leaned back against the headrest. Her hands lay motionless in her lap. He swallowed.

He didn't want to wake her. She'd fallen asleep almost

as soon as they had driven off the naval base. Clearly, the therapy session had drained her physically as well as emotionally. Feeling tired himself, for a time Eric stared through the windshield at the building's stucco-and-stone courtyard with its wrought-iron fencing and lush foliage. A wave of frustration washed through him. Mia had been to hell in the space of two hours and they had nothing to show for it. No physical description of the unsub, no clues as to his location. Dr. Wilhelm had reminded him to be patient. The therapy had worked, but they could only go at the pace her mind would allow. Even more, what she witnessed, the scenes her mind latched on to— it was like spinning a roulette wheel.

He didn't want to put her through those horrible hours again, but he realized that as long as she was willing it was exactly what he'd have to do. Too much was at stake.

"Mia?" he asked softly. She stirred at his voice, blinking at him hazily.

"I fell asleep," she murmured in realization.

"Stay there and I'll come around to help. You were a little wobbly leaving Dr. Wilhelm's office—"

"I *saw* her, Eric. Cissy Cox was there, still alive. What if she still is?"

Eric had unfastened his seat belt, but at her words he remained seated. He sighed and turned toward her, noting the downward curve to her pretty mouth and her anxious expression. He said as gently as possible, "Based on the killer's M.O., she's already dead."

Her eyes held hope. "But you can't be sure."

He couldn't bring himself to tell her that in all likelihood she had witnessed Cissy Cox's murder. In fact, he suspected that if she hadn't pulled herself out of her hypnotic state when she did, she might have had to relive it all over again.

"He has another woman now. We can still help *her*." With the engine off, the cool air inside the car's interior had begun to diminish. Exiting the vehicle, Eric went to the passenger side and opened the door. Mia got out, her slender form wavering a little as she stood. Eric steadied her, his hands clasping her upper arms. "Still dizzy?"

"I'm okay," she said, although her eyes didn't share the same confidence as her voice. Her pupils were still dilated and that worried him. He'd taken Dr. Wilhelm's word for it that the drug used in the therapy was safe, and he wondered now if he shouldn't have pressed for more information before getting her involved.

Don't get personally attached. It was a primary rule within the Bureau, one ground into every agent beginning with basic training at Quantico, but Eric realized he didn't seem to be paying much attention to protocol these days. Aware of her need for independence, he said, "I believe you, but I'm going to hold on to you up the steps anyway. Either that or I'm carrying you up. Your choice."

She didn't argue. They made their way across the courtyard and up the stairs, Eric keeping a careful, protective hold around her shoulders in case another wave of dizziness hit. At her door, he took her keys to unlock it. They stepped inside the apartment and Mia gave him her pass code so he could disarm the security system.

"How are you feeling, other than the vertigo?"

She shook her head. "I'm angry with myself. If I'd just stayed under a little longer…"

"Don't beat yourself up. What you did today took a lot of courage."

"He was coming back. I could've seen him—"

"Remember what Dr. Wilhelm said. Your mind knows how much it can process at one time. You can't force it."

Mia didn't appear convinced. She briefly ran a hand over her eyes.

"Let's get you to the couch, all right?" He helped her to the sofa in her living room, then sat next to her.

"You don't have to stay and babysit me."

Based on the missing Porsche outside, Eric suspected that Mia's friend, Will Dvorak, wasn't home. He thought of her admission during the therapy session, about her spending time in foster care, and he wondered if she even had any family to rely on. Other than Will, there didn't appear to be a man—a significant other—in her life.

"I'm going to make a few phone calls. I need to check in with Agent Vartran. But I'm not leaving, Mia." He looked into her eyes. "Not until I think you won't end up facedown on the floor if you try to get up on your own."

Her fingers clung to his. Eric didn't pull away. They had been touching one another a lot, and he'd rationalized that it was due to necessity and the sheer emotion of the situation. Their shared need to find and stop a killer. But he also knew himself well enough to understand how drawn he was to her. He hadn't felt anything like it in a long time. The realization was unsettling.

"If you need some privacy to talk, you can use my

office," she said. "It's down the hallway, the first room on the left."

Eric nodded. Withdrawing his fingers from hers, he stood. He watched as she placed one of the sofa cushions on her lap and with a sigh, hugged it to herself. The slanting, dying sunlight that came in through the balcony doors made her appear even more fragile to him.

Her office was efficient and tidy—a laptop sat on the desk, a comfortable-looking love seat, shelves filled with neatly lined books and a police scanner with the volume turned low. There was also a framed degree on the wall from the University of Florida, indicating she'd graduated with honors, as well as several framed photos. In them, he recognized a younger version of Mia, performing in a graceful dance troupe. A small brass plaque underneath one of the photos read Jacksonville Inner-City Ballet.

She was full of surprises.

Lingering among her personal possessions, he moved to a more recent, candid snapshot that sat on the desk. In it, Mia had much longer hair, nearly halfway down her back. Wearing a bathing suit top and denim shorts that revealed her slender, tanned legs, she stood on a pier with Will Dvorak, dazzling blue water and a setting sun behind them. Eric scanned the rest of the room. He noticed that none of the displayed photographs had anyone in them who looked like family—no smiling images of proud parents or siblings with similar dark hair and pale olive skin.

Again, no obvious boyfriend, either. Strange, considering her beauty.

Figuring he'd done enough snooping, Eric made his phone calls.

Fifteen minutes later, he reentered the living room. Mia remained seated where he'd left her. He had half expected her to have fallen back asleep.

"Is there anything new on Anna Lynn Gomez?" she asked.

Eric shook his head. "I spoke to Agent Vartran. The Florida Bureau and JSO have a task force meeting set up for tomorrow morning to restrategize."

"On a Sunday," she noted, looking up at him. "No rest for the wicked, so no rest for law enforcement, either."

"Something like that." He came closer. "How's the dizziness?"

"A little better."

"Are you hungry?"

"Not really."

Eric suspected she hadn't eaten in a while, her nerves deadening her appetite. Having an empty stomach probably wasn't helping with the light-headedness. He sat back down on the couch, broaching the topic that had been on his mind. "How long were you in foster care?"

"A while," she replied quietly.

"What about your parents?"

"My father left when I was four years old. He was in the military. He met my mother overseas and brought her back to the States. I don't really remember him." She shrugged, smoothing her fingers over the cushion she still held. "My mother, Luri, wasn't much of a mom. She had some mental issues—bipolar disorder that she wouldn't take medication for—as well as a drinking problem. Child Services to the rescue…"

Eric heard the cynical edge to her voice. He knew enough about the system to suspect where Mia had ended up—bounced between group homes and private residences, a new place every few months. Probably not feeling very wanted anywhere.

"You hot-wired the car you escaped in, didn't you?"

"It's possible," she admitted. "A guy in one of the homes I was in had a history of car theft. We hung out and he taught me some things. I know how to."

He now understood why she'd evaded the question when he had asked her the first time—she didn't want to reveal that part of herself. But the therapy sessions had forced it into the open. Eric wondered how Mia had managed to come through such a tough, grim childhood. She'd graduated from college, she held down a demanding job. He wanted to know more about who she was, but didn't want her to feel he was prying.

"Depending on what's in your pantry, I'm going to make you dinner. Or we'll order takeout, but you need to eat."

She gazed at him, her brown eyes soft. Unable to help himself, he touched her face.

"It's going to be okay, Mia," he murmured.

To his surprise, she settled her head against his chest. Eric wondered if she could hear the heavy thudding of his heart.

10

The reclaimed memories had overwhelmed her. Leaning against Eric's chest, Mia felt safe and protected. She closed her eyes, reveling in the feel of his big hands stroking her back. The gun on his hip cut into her side but she ignored it, giving in to the indulgence of being close to him, if only for a little while.

After several long moments, she pulled away and uncertainly met his gaze. His eyes had darkened. He swallowed hard.

"I'm going to see about that food," he said hoarsely.

Sliding his fingers over the soft skin of her forearm, Eric got up and went into the kitchen, leaving her on the couch. Mia curled onto her side. She drifted in and out of sleep, lulled by the sound of running water and the occasional rattle of a pan or the close of the refrigerator door. She felt overly emotional, and having his presence in her apartment was like a soothing balm on her frayed nerves.

"Mia?"

She awoke sometime later to the sound of his voice

and realized her catnapping had turned into a full-on slumber. He leaned over her, and she wondered how long she'd been out. How long he'd been watching her sleep.

"How are you feeling now?"

"Better, I think. No more dizziness," she said as she slowly moved to a sitting position.

"That's good. Do you want to eat?"

She got to her feet, testing her steadiness. Much of the light coming in from outside had died away, but Eric had turned on a few lamps and there was a warm glow emanating from her breakfast nook. Mia wandered into the cozy eating area and saw he was true to his word. He'd prepared a pasta carbona with linguine, bacon, some fading parsley from the refrigerator's vegetable drawer, and cream. The scent was heavenly. He'd also put out a beer for himself and a goblet filled with ice water for her. As Eric pulled out her chair, she noticed he'd abandoned his tie somewhere as well as his holstered gun. His shirt-sleeves were rolled up, the top buttons of his dress shirt open, and she could see the white cotton of his T-shirt at his throat. He sat across from her and dished pasta onto her plate.

"I can't believe you made a meal out of the pathetic scraps in my kitchen. This looks really good."

"I like to cook—it relaxes me." He added quietly, "I used to do it for my wife."

At his words, she felt a pang of compassion. One of the online articles had included Rebecca Macfarlane's photo. She'd been blonde and fashion-model pretty—an interior designer by trade, according to the piece. Mia figured they had made a striking couple.

"How long were you married?" she asked tentatively.

"Five years."

Then you know why stopping this psychopath is so important to me. Mia recalled the intensity of his statement the day before.

As they ate, they moved to easier subjects, including Mia's pending return to the *Courier* the following week. They also talked about the next session with Dr. Wilhelm that had been scheduled for Tuesday, the earliest the psychiatrist would agree to another round of the catalyzing drug. The prospect of going back under hypnosis caused a ripple of anxiety to run through her, but she was determined to return to that room and remain there long enough to see her abductor's face.

Eric had stressed to her that he believed Cissy Cox was dead. But in her memory, she'd been alive and breathing, squirming against the ropes that bound her to a hook in the cinder-block wall. Was it possible Mia herself had escaped, but left the other captive woman behind? She couldn't imagine doing something so terrible.

"You all right?"

She nodded, shoving down her thoughts.

Once they were done with dinner, he stood and began clearing the table. "I've got this. You should rest."

"I'll help. With everything going on, you couldn't have gotten more than a few hours' sleep last night." She picked up her plate but he reached for it, bringing the two of them face-to-face.

"Eric…I appreciate dinner, and you staying with me."

"It's the least I can do," he said, serious. "I'm the one asking you to relive a nightmare."

"May I ask you a question?" She set the plate back on the table and searched his eyes. "What frightens you? I mean, these psychotic, sadistic men you pursue—"

"You write about them," he pointed out.

"Most of the time I report on drug-related shootings and bank robberies. Domestic violence that ended up as a homicide. They're bad things but they're not like this." She felt a rush of nerves just talking about it. "What you chase at the VCU is *pure evil,* Eric. These men are monsters that live for the thrill of torture, of having someone under their total control. It's not about money or a crime of passion. These animals have a sadistic need to inflict pain and fear. They live for it."

His gaze was sincere. "I *am* afraid sometimes. I'd be a fool not to be. But I'm more afraid of letting them continue to roam free so they can keep killing. Keep taking other people's loved ones."

He was thinking of his wife. For a brief moment, Mia wondered what it must have been like to be loved by him. She thought of the solidness of his body as he held her a short time earlier.

Eric moved closer to her, his voice low. "I understand if you're scared, Mia. And I've told you, we're in this together."

Her throat dried with need as she gazed up at him. She craved more of his hands on her, she realized. Unable to help herself, Mia touched his shirtfront. The air seemed charged around them as they stared at one another. But a hard knock at the door shattered their connection. Eric clasped the back of his neck with one hand and stepped away. She went to the foyer, her face hot. Looking out through the peephole, she swallowed a sigh and opened the door.

Grayson swept into the apartment like a storm tide. "Jesus, Mia. Don't you return messages anymore? I've called you twice already today. I was starting to worry."

"I'm sorry. I've been out." She hadn't told Grayson about the sessions at the NAS, mostly due to the strict need for confidentiality. But as her boss, he would need to know eventually, since he would be aware of her comings and goings from the newspaper. She'd have to trust him.

"Where've you been? It's Saturday night. Don't tell me you had a date—"

He stopped speaking, seeing Eric standing in the entrance to the kitchen. Mia made the introductions.

"Grayson Miller, this is Agent Eric Macfarlane with the FBI. Eric, Grayson is executive editor of the *Jacksonville Courier*."

Clearly taken by surprise, Grayson stepped forward and the two men shook hands. "You're here due to the recent abductions and murder, Agent Macfarlane."

"I am." He looked at Mia. "And I should probably be going."

"Anything new on the Anna Lynn Gomez disappearance?"

"Unfortunately, no. Nothing beyond her car being found earlier today, which the news channels are already reporting. Agent Vartran with the Florida Bureau is overseeing an ongoing canvas of the area where it was found. I'm on my way there now." He walked to the granite pass-through counter and retrieved his holstered gun, clipping it back onto his waist. To Mia he said, "You're sure you're all right?"

She nodded. "I'll take care of the kitchen."

"Call me if you need anything." Their eyes held for a bare second before Eric moved to the foyer and let himself out. Mia felt a tingle of disappointment. She turned to Grayson again, his gaze on the table that had obviously been set for two.

"Good-looking guy," he noted.

Mia pressed her lips together, aware his curiosity was piqued. He noticed Eric's silk tie that had been left draped over one of the bar stools, and he made a point of folding it neatly before placing it on the counter.

"Did I walk in on something?" His tone remained casual although she noticed a tightness around his mouth, something she'd witnessed before in the newsroom when the pressure got high.

She went to the table, planning to finish clearing the dishes. "We just had dinner."

Grayson said nothing. He shoved his hands inside his pockets, his eyebrows raising faintly.

"It's not what you think. And I need to tell you about something confidentially."

"Confidential as in off the record?"

"I need to talk to you as a friend, not a newsman. I need your discretion."

She told him about the experimental therapy.

Eric stood outside the apartment building, his cell phone pressed to his ear. He hadn't yet gotten into his car and as he listened to Cameron, he stared up at the light emanating from Mia's windows.

"Ms. Gomez used her credit card inside the Bargain-Mart at 11:58 on Thursday night," Cam told him. "She can be seen leaving on security footage from inside the store's vestibule, but not outside. Store management concedes there's a camera blind spot in the parking lot of about fifty feet to the left of the front entrance."

"That's the route to her car?"

"You got it."

Eric pinched the bridge of his nose. "So the guy's either lucky or he's familiar with the camera range."

"We're running background checks on store personnel now, as well as employees of the company that installed the CCTV system four years ago. I interviewed the store's security team myself—no red flags. By the way, Ms. Gomez's purchase was found in a Dumpster behind the building, still in the bag with the receipt."

"What did she purchase?"

"Chewing gum and tampons. Why?"

"No reason." The night was humid, and a warm breeze ruffled the fronds of the palm trees lining the property's front. "I'm on my way there, all right?"

"How did the session with Ms. Hale go?"

Eric briefly filled him in, then disconnected the call as Will Dvorak's Porsche convertible pulled into the driveway.

"Agent Macfarlane," Will said in greeting as he got out. An Asian man exited the passenger side, and he introduced him to Eric as his partner, Justin Cho. After a moment, Justin excused himself and went into the ground-floor unit.

"Are you coming or going, Agent?" Will asked.

"Going, actually."

"I see Mia has a guest." He indicated the car parked next to Eric's.

"Grayson Miller—we met upstairs." The man seemed nice enough, although Eric had detected a territorialism when he'd discovered Mia wasn't alone. He was pretty sure most editors didn't check in on reporters at their homes on Saturday nights, and he wondered how far their relationship went outside the workplace. He realized he didn't like the idea of it being more than a supervisor-employee situation. Miller was too old for her.

"I know you and Mia are close—"

"She's told me about the mad scientist experiment at the naval base," Will remarked drily, although his gaze was somber and direct. "As her friend I advised her not to do it."

Eric released a breath. At least someone was looking out for her well-being.

"I may sound overprotective, but Mia's been through a lot. And I'm not just talking about the past week. She's had a hard life. I understand you have a major investigation on your hands, but be careful with her, Agent Mac-farlane. The abduction took a bigger toll on her than she'll ever admit." Will bid him good-night and began to walk through the courtyard, but Eric's request halted him.

"Tell me about her mother."

Turning, he looked surprised. "She mentioned Luri to you?"

"Indirectly. She told me about growing up in foster care."

"That's something she rarely talks about." Will returned to where Eric stood. He shook his head. "Luri Hale had Mia on a yo-yo. She would clean up her act long enough to get her back, then start the cycle of neglect and abuse all over again. Mia was in and out of the system for years, but she was always eventually sent back to Luri—the courts are big on the biological rights of the mother and keeping families together. Mia's hell continued until she was granted emancipation at sixteen."

"Her mother didn't object to the petition?"

"She didn't have a choice." He hesitated as if trying to decide how much more to divulge. "Luri was beautiful and there were lots of men around. Men she accepted money from on occasion for favors."

Will paused again. "She attempted to…prostitute her own daughter. Mia threatened to go to the police if she didn't sign the court papers."

The information was shocking. Mia had said her mother was bipolar, but Eric couldn't accept that as an excuse. He thought of someone that young being out on her own. "Does she have other family?"

"Justin and I are it."

He frowned. "Your concerns are noted, Mr. Dvorak—"

"Please, *Will.*"

"I don't want to put Mia through any more hardship. I promise I'll do everything I can to minimize the impact on her, but we *need* her help. Women are dead and another one's life is at stake. In the meantime, what I was going to ask is that you keep an eye out for anything suspicious around here."

He nodded. "Of course. She told you about the car, right?"

"What car?"

"It was two nights ago. Mia was returning from a crime scene, I think, and she thought someone was following her. She made a commotion out here in the driveway so Justin and I would come out."

Eric thought of the unsub out hunting that same night. "Did you see the vehicle?"

"No. Mia decided she'd freaked herself out and imagined the whole thing. Maybe she did. She was embarrassed about it, but also pretty shook up. I realized then how much all of this is getting to her."

A short time later, Will said good-night and went inside. As Eric opened the door to his car, his gaze returned briefly to the building's second floor. He wondered why Mia hadn't told him about the possibility she'd been followed. The nighttime breeze had died away, leaving a dead quiet around him.

He couldn't shake the feeling it was the calm before the storm.

11

A crushed sleeping pill in her evening tea ensured Gladys would sleep through the night. Allan made a practice of giving it to her bedside, in a chamomile blend with honey that masked any unpleasant aftertaste. By ten o'clock, she was typically snoring like a logger, giving him freedom to do whatever he desired without the guilt trips or prying questions.

He felt no remorse about it, really. He was a good son who'd come home to care for her.

Besides, Gladys needed her rest.

Tonight, he had retired to his workshop in the pine-woods. He sat at the metal-topped table, pill bottles lined up in front of him like attentive schoolboys. Allan scanned them until he found what he was looking for—the one with *Rebecca* printed neatly on its label. Mastering the childproof lid and tipping the vial sideways, he gently tapped the amber plastic until its contents spilled out with little plinking sounds.

Ten perfect ovals. He felt a thrill course through him. One could tell how well a woman took care of herself by simply looking at her nails. As a boy, Allan had read this bit of wisdom in a ladies' fashion magazine. And Rebecca Macfarlane's nails *were* exquisite. French manicured, delicate half moons with pristine white at their tips. Each one filed and buffed to faultlessness. He ordered them on the table according to size, reliving his conquest.

Agent Macfarlane had been on the news that morning, giving an official Bureau statement. Allan watched it with Gladys over breakfast. Or at least *he* had watched it—she'd been too busy complaining about the oatmeal he had prepared. Even in the stifling Florida heat, Macfarlane had appeared cool and composed, handsome in a well-cut, dark suit. He'd aged somewhat over the past three years, but if anything he only seemed more settled into his looks. The faint lines fanning from the corners of his eyes revealed he had his battle scars. Allan liked knowing he'd been the one to put them there.

Ad victorem spolias. To the victor go the spoils.

Picking up the vial again, he tapped it a little harder and two white, enameled kernels at the bottom fell out. Pearly molars. No cavities, of course. She had also taken exceptional care of her teeth.

Allan touched all the remnants of Rebecca once more before carefully sliding them back into the vial and returning it to his collection. His eyes moved across the labels in front of him, bearing the others' names. The last one said simply *Mia.*

He shook it once, heard the thin, disappointing rattle inside it. A sullen curve formed on his mouth.

Mia was an acronym, he'd realized. *Missing in action.*

A muffled moan rose above the hum of the window-box air conditioner, capturing his attention. Good. She was coming around. He'd timed the drug so she would be waking now, when Gladys and her flea-infested mutt were snoozing and his night was only beginning. He enjoyed spending time with his girls.

"I hope you had a pleasant sleep."

Anna Lynn Gomez blinked at him, her dark eyes glassy and filled with fear. It had been so easy to strike up a conversation with her in the parking lot.

She struggled—gagged, helpless, her bloodied hands bound above her head and shackled to a hook in the cinder-block wall. Allan had only taken four nails so far. He liked to space the extractions out, giving them both something to look forward to.

He picked up a hammer from his workbench, gripping it in his right hand for emphasis. Her stifled cry in response gave him satisfaction. He snacked on her terror like junk food. "I'm going to free you for a little while— to eat and take care of necessities. You understand what I'll be forced to do if you misbehave?"

He'd made her a turkey-and-Swiss sandwich in the kitchen, which sat on the workbench on one of Gladys's fine china plates. No paper. It was the least he could do. "I hope you're going to have more of an appetite tonight. You have to keep up your strength—you're only hurting yourself by being finicky."

Anna Lynn's throat convulsed. She was pretty enough, but at the end of the day she made a poor substitute. An inferior replacement for the petite brunette he'd had in mind. Finding her again had made him think life was more than just a series of unrelated, random events. And then she'd slipped through his fingers.

Allan untied his captive.

"I do have *some* good news for you, my dear," he said as the young woman shrank from him. "If things work out, you're going to be getting a roommate soon."

12

It was just after eight on Sunday morning. Eric stood in the Bureau offices, a large corkboard behind him bearing an investigational time line and the missing women's photos. The briefing room held two-dozen sheriff's deputies, detectives and field agents.

"The man we're looking for is Caucasian, probably a college graduate, although it's likely he's never held a career position due to his disdain for supervision and authority," Eric said, hitting the highlights of the VCU's behavioral profile. "While he's a loner socially, he has the ability to present a temporary, superficial charm that's aided him in getting close to some of his victims. He's also highly organized and compulsively neat, something that carries into his personal grooming."

"The women so far haven't been raped?" The question came from another agent.

Cameron answered. "Medical exams of the bodies, both in Maryland and here in the case of Pauline Berger, have been negative or inconclusive, the latter due to tissue destruction caused by environmental factors. The rape kit completed on the escaped abductee last week showed no evidence. No semen, bruising or trauma."

"Maybe he just never got around to it—she got away first," a detective commented as he poured coffee into a foam cup from one of the carafes placed around the room.

"It's believed the unsub lacks any real sexual interest in women," Eric explained. "Still, he objectifies them and enjoys playing God over them—it makes him feel dominant in a world he otherwise feels unimportant in."

"If he's not into sex, why take just women?"

"They're smaller and easier to control, for one. It's also possible he has some latent hostility against a female in his life, probably an older relative who held power over him in childhood."

The detective took a sip from his cup. "Most serial killers are between eighteen and thirty-two. What about this guy?"

Mia had recalled seeing the unsub's eyes in her rear-view mirror. Eric said, "I'm estimating he's older. Early to mid-forties. The reality is that he may have been killing for a while, maybe even for most of his life, but with enough time between murders to stay under the radar. It's his recent spree behavior and increasingly compulsive need to repeat patterns—taking specific souvenirs and numbering his victims—that have put him in the VCU's spotlight."

The discussion moved to investigative field strategies, including a crackdown on area chop shops in hopes the unsub had been using the operations to unload stolen cars. As the group dispersed a short time later, Eric spoke briefly with Detectives Boyet and Scofield before joining Cameron in the hallway.

"Deputies are in the abduction area, handing out flyers with Ms. Gomez's photo," he said. "It's also running on electronic billboards along I-95."

"Prepare for false sightings," Cameron noted cynically as they went down the corridor. He checked his wristwatch. "We've got interviews continuing at noon."

Eric nodded, knowing he was referring to workers at the Bargain-Mart, as well as technicians from the security company that had installed the store's cameras. Background checks were ongoing, but so far no one stood out.

"In the meantime, one of the vice detectives mentioned a pawnshop on Union." Cam sidestepped a group of deputies conversing in the lobby. "A guy there named Big Al has been known to receive stolen electronics, including GPS systems and high-end stereo equipment from cars. I'm going to drop in on him. Want to come along?"

"You think it's open?"

"Seven to seven, seven days a week." He stopped in the elevator bay. "Let's go by my office first, though. I need to grab a few files."

Cameron's third-floor office had a large window with a view of the plaza and parking lot below. Eric waited as Cameron went to his desk, pausing at his stacked inbox. Flipping through its contents, he frowned. "When the hell did this come in?"

He held up the small, bulging envelope carefully by

one edge. The neat handwriting on the package's front gave Eric a bad sense of déjà vu. It was addressed to him.

He had wondered when they would begin to arrive.

"It must've come in with yesterday's mail." Cam shook his head. "The Saturday admin staff probably dropped it off in here when we were out. That's not protocol—they should've called."

"Do you have gloves?"

He located a box of latex gloves in a credenza and handed over a pair. Eric put them on and took the envelope, not that he expected there to be any prints. He sat and opened it, sliding out the thin, palm-size device nestled in Bubble Wrap.

"You're sure it's not rigged to explode?" Cameron sounded as if he were only half joking.

Eric removed the wrap from around the digital recorder. It was the cheap kind, only worth about twenty dollars and available at any mass-retail chain or office supply store. He had four more just like them, stored in the VCU evidence room back in D.C. He drew in a tense breath and clicked the play button.

Hearing the tinny voice emanating from the recorder was like stepping back into a nightmare.

"It looks as though I've brought you all the way down to sunny Florida, Agent Macfarlane. As long as you're here, I hope you're taking the opportunity to enjoy our beaches and local attractions," the man on the audio said. "I trust you've been well, although I'm sure the past few years have been rather *difficult* ones for you…"

Anger and emotion tightened Eric's throat as the man chuckled, obviously enjoying himself.

"I never had a chance to tell you how sorry I was for your loss. I considered sending a sympathy card, but they can be so trite. Please accept my condolences now. She was a lovely woman...I'd know, wouldn't I?"

He heard Cameron's soft curse beside him.

"Well, now that we have that awkward business out of the way, shall we move to the matter at hand?"

The recording lapsed into dead air before the unsub spoke again.

"What is your name?"

A female answered, her voice quavering. "I—I told you. It's Pauline...Pauline Berger! Please don't hurt me anymore! I—I just want to go home."

She sobbed. "I have children! If it's money you want, my husband's well-off—he'll pay you!"

As she continued to plead, Eric felt Pauline's hysteria wrap around him. There were sounds of movement, struggling, on the audio. His heart began to beat harder.

"No, please!"

He heard her last, terrified protests, her words becoming thick and garbled as something was stuffed into her mouth.

A short time later, the muffled screams began.

Déjà fucking vu.

"Jesus," Cameron whispered roughly.

Eric passed a hand over his eyes, forcing himself to continue listening as Pauline Berger was savagely beaten. The recording went on for several more minutes, a frenzied cacophony of choked sobs and shrieks drowned out by a cloth or ball gag. He had never been sure which one, at least not until Mia's memory recall.

The final sound of something heavy, hitting hard against bone, sickened him. Then Pauline was silenced, the recorder picking up only the man's heavy breathing and a diffused, faint whimper. Eric's trained ears could make out the sound of another female in the background. He knew what to listen for by now. He shut off the device and stood.

"An audio tech can amplify the sound in the background, but it's Cissy Cox," he said hoarsely. "He had her watching."

Cameron's face appeared ashen. "Based on your theory, Pauline Berger was dead before you even arrived, Eric. How—"

"The recording was made previously. He put in the intro after the fact and mailed it."

Cameron stared worriedly at him. "As soon as he learned *you* were down here."

He didn't have to say more. The recording eliminated any last shred of doubt that the unsub here and in Maryland were one and the same. Eric rubbed the back of his neck.

It was clear The Collector wanted to pick up where they'd left off three years ago.

Another dream had awakened Mia, a replay of the one she'd experienced two days earlier. In it, the little red-haired girl had clasped her hand as the blue hatchback cruised past them on the neighborhood street. And just like before, Mia had bolted awake when the car began to back up. Dr. Wilhelm had called the dream emblematic—a comingling of her childhood trauma with the more current one she'd endured. Being careful with her injured fingers, she slid on a pair of denim cutoffs over the one-piece swimsuit she wore.

Whatever it was, she just wanted the disturbing vision to stop.

Locking her apartment and heading downstairs, she tossed her beach bag into the Volvo and climbed in after it. The decision to head to the beach had been an impromptu one. The sand and rolling waves, the seagulls fishing along the shore—it always had a calming effect on her. Not to mention, the other Sunday beachgoers would ensure she wasn't alone. It seemed like a good way to spend her last day before returning to work.

Mia had watched the morning news. Unfortunately, there had been no updates on Anna Lynn Gomez, and she wondered if Eric was still in the task force briefing he'd mentioned the previous night. She glanced at the striped canvas bag on the passenger seat, which contained her wallet and a water bottle, suntan lotion, a paperback she'd been reading and her cell phone. She wanted to call him. But she instead switched on the car radio.

Leaving San Marco, she had intended to take one of the roads stretching eastward to the coast, then travel south until she reached Vilano Beach, which was a bit farther down but was the one she preferred. Her thoughts swarming, however, she drove on autopilot until she realized she was headed in the exact opposite direction—inland, not southeast but northwest. A pang struck her hard in the chest as Mia realized where her subconscious was guiding her. She struggled with whether to continue following its lead.

Even more, she wondered if she would even be able to find the old house.

Driving up the interstate for nearly ten miles, she got off at the Edgewater exit, aware of the general area where Miss Cathy's foster care home had been located. The recent dreams made its image—white siding and black shutters, an overgrown magnolia tree in the front yard—especially vivid. She also remembered that Miss Cathy's had been close to a school as the children would sometimes pass the day there on its playground.

Tourists were encouraged to avoid certain areas northwest of the city. Some neighborhoods had fallen into disrepair, and it wasn't an area for sightseeing. Mia's experience with crime scenes meant she was relatively comfortable going into questionable territory. Still, she worried about the wisdom of this particular journey but kept driving, her eyes scanning the residential street signs for something that might stand out to her. A few minutes later, she felt her stomach dip as she saw the chain-link fence that enclosed the playground she recalled. It appeared unused and unkempt now, with its merry-go-round and seesaw peeking out through tall weeds. The school itself was closed, a no-trespassing sign on its redbrick front. She was close. Her heartbeat began to speed up.

Three streets over, the two-story house with a wide front porch loomed in front of her on a corner lot. The magnolia was still there, although half of it was brown and dead, and the home itself appeared abandoned. The black shutters were gone, the windows boarded over. An ominous gang symbol marred its peeling siding.

Mia parked the car against the curb. She sat and stared at the structure for several long moments, emotion welling inside her.

Face your fears.

Taking a breath, she grabbed her canvas bag and got out, walking up to the front lawn. It was more dirt than grass now, and patches of overgrowth remained where Miss Cathy's flower garden had been. Broken beer bottles were scattered on the porch. Mia felt a coldness despite the heat of the midmorning sun on her bare shoulders.

Why *had* she come here? Maybe she was still attempting to make some sense of the unsettling dream. Trying to prove to herself the red-haired girl never existed. But standing in the neglected yard, all she felt was foolish and alone. A sense of betrayal and abandonment, as strong as it had been when she was a child, fell over her. Mia took another long look at the dilapidated house, then turned back to her car. The sound of a barking dog came from farther down the street, and sirens wailed not too far off in the distance.

Reaching the curb, the air left her lungs.

The powder-blue hatchback rolled slowly past her, its engine rumbling and exhaust pipe belching black smoke.

This isn't real, she told herself, trying to control a sudden wave of dizziness.

The car stopped and began backing up. Mia's heart pounded in time with the vibrating bass beat of its radio. A male hand protruded through the open driver's-side window, dangling a doll with yellow hair. The vehicle came to a halt again, its brake lights glowing red on the street.

Mia felt the thin fingers loosen that had somehow become intertwined with hers. The little red-haired girl's face was filled with delight. She pulled away and began walking toward the car, entranced by the doll. Mia remained frozen on the curb. The man was luring her. He was going to take her. The child moved closer.

"No," she whispered. "Don't—"

She screamed at the hard tap on her shoulder. Whirling, she stumbled backward, the eerie vision dissolving like mist.

"Give me some money, lady?" The junkie's eyes were bloodshot in his sweat-streaked face. He smelled like garbage. "I got kids at home. They need to eat."

He gazed at her, hopeful and jittery, advancing a step closer. His eyes roamed her bathing suit top. Mia reached into her bag, grasping a loose ten-dollar bill. She shoved it into the man's skinny chest and hurried away on wobbly legs.

"Hey! What's your rush, baby? We can hang for a while—"

She slammed the Volvo's door closed and locked it. Hands trembling, Mia started the engine and peeled away from the street. She'd been wrong to come here. As she drove, her eyes flicked to the Indian dream catcher swaying from her rearview mirror. She tore it down and shoved it into the glove box.

13

"Welcome back," Grayson announced, striding toward Mia as she entered the newsroom on Monday morning. Her coworkers—reporters, copy editors, web masters and photographers—echoed the salutation, gathered around a tray of bagels and pastries that had apparently been laid out in her honor. Putting an arm around her shoulders, he escorted her over. "We're just glad to have you back, kiddo."

Mia accepted the staff's well-wishing as they made a grab for the food and carried it back to their respective desks, ready to get a jump on the day's assignments. However, she didn't miss the sympathetic looks and curious glances at her still-chafed wrists and bandaged fingers, reminding her that she'd been the recent watercooler topic. Grayson handed her a paper cup filled with orange juice.

"Get settled in and come see me in my office," he said.

"New haircut?" Walt Rudner asked pointedly, his mouth full of cream cheese and onion bagel, as Grayson departed. Balding and bearing a generous paunch, he was the senior reporter who had taken over the abduction stories in Mia's absence. "Was that by choice or necessity?"

She gave him a hard look, causing the typically gruff reporter to spit cream cheese as he chuckled. "C'mon, Mia. The task force has a gag order on us. I can't write about the specifics, but I know enough JSO detectives to hear things. Like the hair and fingernail fetish this freak has."

He nodded to her midsection. "I also understand he has his own perverted take on the Dewey decimal system."

Mia's face grew hot. Walt could be an insensitive lout. "What do you want?"

"Information? Look, I know you supposedly don't remember anything about what happened to you, but I'm betting you've got some special insight into the investigation." He wiped his fingers on the pocket of his sports coat. "For starters, I saw Agent Macfarlane escorting you past the crime scene tape at the boat ramp on Thursday night—the same tape meant to keep the rest of us lowly scavengers on the outside. What gives?"

"I wasn't there as a reporter," she said quietly.

"So it was a social visit? I noticed you got an *up close and personal* with Pauline Berger. Or what was left of her."

Mia bristled. She'd picked up a Danish pastry but dropped it into the trash, her appetite gone. "You're an ass, Walt."

"And you're too tangled up in this. Which is why you're not getting the investigation back. I know you asked Miller for it. Normally you get what you want around here, but not this time."

She'd started to walk away, but she turned to look at him.

Shrugging his thick shoulders, he wolfed down the rest of his bagel. "Not my decision. Go ask him."

Stopping by her desk in the bull pen, she plugged in her laptop, then shoved her purse into one of the drawers. Mia traveled through the newsroom to a row of glass-walled offices occupied by senior editorial and management staff. Grayson had the large corner room, giving him a panoramic view of the St. Johns River below. Mia knocked on the door. Glancing over the top of his bifocals at her, he motioned her inside. She entered and sat across from his desk.

"How did the parking garage go this morning?" he asked, concerned.

"It went fine."

"We should've had someone from security meet you and walk you up. It couldn't have been easy going back there—"

"I'm *fine*, Grayson," Mia assured him, although in truth the garage had taken some courage to navigate, even in daylight. "I just want to get back to work."

He nodded. "All right. I'm sending you to the county courthouse. They're arraigning D'Angelo Roberts on vehicular homicide charges this morning."

Mia had heard about the arrest. D'Angelo Roberts was a former NFL star who had moved to the upscale Ponte Vedra beach community. Over the weekend he'd crashed his Ferrari with an underage female passenger inside, killing her. Toxicology tests indicated a high level of cocaine in his system, as well as the girl's. It wasn't a horrible assignment—it could even be considered a rather choice one considering Roberts's high profile. But it was a far cry from the recent abductions and Pauline Berger's murder.

"Walt tells me I'm not getting reassigned to the investigation."

"You know Walt—he's marking his territory. He thinks the serial murder investigation's going to earn him a Pulitzer."

"Is he right?"

"About the Pulitzer?"

Mia didn't find it amusing. "About me not getting back on the story."

When Grayson failed to answer and instead glanced at his computer screen, she added, "Have you told him about the therapy I'm undergoing at the Naval Air Station?"

"Did you ask me not to?"

"Yes. That information's off the record—"

"Then I didn't." He removed his eyeglasses and laid them on the desk. "Although as executive editor of this paper, I should be making it a top story. I knew this victim-reporter thing was going to get complicated."

Mia sat rigidly. "If I wasn't a victim, you wouldn't know about the NAS sessions anyway. I agreed to confidentiality and only told you because it may require me to be away from work."

"I *thought* you told me because we're friends." He stood and walked around to the front of his desk. Sitting on its edge, Grayson peered at her, lowering his voice. "Look at you, Mia. You're trying like hell to act tough, but my guess is you're barely holding it together. You don't need to be covering the Anna Lynn Gomez abduction or any other part of the investigation right now. Trust me, okay? I'm watching out for you. You're not ready."

Releasing a breath, she thought of the hallucination she'd experienced outside the abandoned foster care group home the day before. She'd wondered if it was one of the memory flashes Dr. Wilhelm had warned her about. But that would require the memory to be *real*.

"Just take the D'Angelo Roberts arraignment, all right? I want something online by this afternoon. No later than two."

With a faint nod, she got up and left Grayson's office, ignoring Walt's chortle as she went past his cubicle. Returning to her desk, she entered her network password so she could log on to the internet to update herself on the vehicular homicide investigation before traveling the short distance to the Duval County Courthouse. As she worked, Mia tried to ignore the rock song that had been on nearly constant replay in her head all morning. She was all too aware of where she'd heard it. In her vision, the same rollicking INXS song had been booming from the blue hatchback's speakers. Even now, the heavy thud of its bass seemed to throb inside her chest. On impulse, she did a quick web search on the lyrics and discovered the song had been number one on the play charts in 1987.

It was the same year she had lived at Miss Cathy's.

The added bit of realism caused her to bite her bottom lip in thought. But last night, Mia had searched online for news articles on a female child abducted out of the foster care system in Jacksonville twenty-five years earlier, unable to get the image out of her head. After nearly two hours of looking, she had come up empty.

Maybe Dr. Wilhelm really *was* right. The car's driver, the red-headed girl—they were all symbolic of her current situation. Maybe Grayson had been right, too, when he'd said she was barely holding it together.

Seeing him leave his office and head in her direction, Mia switched the computer screen to the information on the vehicular homicide case. Either way, she couldn't keep thinking about it now. She had work to do.

Eric and Cameron returned to the FBI offices no better off than they'd been two hours ago. A woman jogging on the Southbank Riverwalk had been accosted earlier that morning, spurring a frantic call to 9-1-1. Task force members had sprung into action, but after searching the area and finding the male subject based on the woman's description, the consensus was that it was a case of aggressive panhandling and not an abduction attempt.

"How's your hip?" Eric asked as they crossed the parking lot, which had already reached the temperature of molten lava. Cameron had taken a fall as they tried to capture the fleeing perp.

"I'll live," he said, grimacing. "It's my suit pants I'm not so sure about."

The recent abductions and murder, as well as media talk of a serial killer, were wearing on the public's nerves and creating a heightened sense of anxiety. A growing number of incidents were being reported—suspicious cars cruising parks and neighborhoods, believed sightings of the missing women. It was a lot for task force members to sift through.

A cold blast of air-conditioning met them as they pushed through glass doors and entered the building's lobby.

"I'm going to the restroom to clean up." Cameron indicated the grass stains on his knees. "I'll meet you upstairs."

Eric went ahead to the reception desk, his security clearance badge in hand.

"Agent Macfarlane."

He turned to see a stout, middle-aged man with dark hair and tan skin moving toward him. It was Anna Lynn Gomez's father. He and Eric had spoken before, just hours after his daughter's disappearance had been reported.

"Mr. Gomez—"

"Where's my daughter?" He spoke in a heavy accent, his eyes wild and pain-filled. "She's been missing for over three days! What are you doing to find her?"

"Everything we can, sir," Eric assured him. "We've gotten her photo out to the public and we're following up on every lead—"

"It's not enough!" He stepped closer and jabbed a finger into Eric's chest. Alcohol emanated from his breath. "My Anna's out there somewhere and you're in here not doing a damn thing! Do you know what might be happening to her? She could end up like that Berger woman!"

Eric's face infused with heat. In his peripheral vision, he could see other agents advancing. They would treat the man as a threat and he didn't want that to happen. He braced himself as Gomez gave him a small, angry shove.

"It's okay," Eric told the closest agent who already had his hand on the butt of his gun. "You're going to have to calm down, Mr. Gomez. Now. Look around you. This isn't the place to be out of control. We can go into the conference room and talk—"

"Enough talking! Do your job! Get my little girl back!" Tears formed in his red-rimmed eyes. "She was the first in our family to go to college! A beautiful young woman with a bright future and now…" He let go of a sob. Overcome with frustration and grief, he shoved Eric harder this time, forcing him back a step. Two field agents intervened, grabbing Gomez.

"Take him home," Eric instructed quietly, a dull ache inside his chest. "He shouldn't be driving."

"You don't give a damn about my daughter!" Gomez struggled as the agents escorted him out. Looking over his shoulder, he remained focused on Eric. "Big man with the VCU! You've got no idea what it feels like to have someone taken from you!"

Cameron returned from the restroom in time to witness the last of the chaos. "Was that Victor Gomez?"

Eric didn't respond. He watched as the two agents put the man in back of a sedan to take him away.

It was after dark by the time Eric returned to the bungalow in Jacksonville Beach. He let himself in using his key and deactivated the security system but chose not to turn on the lights. Instead, he stood in solitary darkness, his mind heavy and tired. They were no closer to finding Anna Lynn Gomez or her abductor.

You've got no idea what it feels like to have someone taken from you.

The pain-filled declaration—the sheer irony of it—had stuck with him, competing with Pauline Berger's muffled screams inside his head. With a sigh, Eric divested himself of his gun, wallet and shield, laying them on the coffee table beside his cell phone before wandering into the kitchen. He wasn't hungry, so instead he extracted a beer from the refrigerator and opened it. Taking a long sip, he stared out between the vertical blinds on sliding glass doors that led to a rear deck. Flimsy light from a streetlamp slanted across its bleached wood planks.

Anna Lynn was still out there somewhere, still alive. She would stay that way until The Collector took another woman. He wanted to find her more than he wanted his next breath, but he also knew they were running out of time.

He drank from the bottle again, letting in the memories he'd managed to stave off until now. Victor Gomez's anguish—his grief—had summoned them, taking him back to a cold February morning. The sky iron-gray and spitting snow, it had been his own day of reckoning.

You don't want to see her, Eric.

Bobby Crowchild, Eric's partner at the VCU, had attempted to hold him back from the shallow grave on the undeveloped lakeside property. He'd grabbed Eric by his coat, trying to talk some sense into him. Bobby's breath fogged in the icy air, his face lined with sympathy.

Listen to me. Don't. You don't want to remember her like this.

He hadn't taken any heed. Throwing off Bobby's grip, Eric had pushed through the overgrowth, frozen grass and leaves crunching under his feet. A sea of grim-faced Bethesda police officers and federal agents parted for him. No one but Bobby dared block him.

Rebecca lay in a ditch. Refuse had been brushed partially away from her corpse by the recovery team. The decomposition was limited due to the winter's consistently frigid temperatures, but the stomach-turning odor of death still hung in the air.

Twigs and leaves were tangled in the blond hair that spread out on the ground.

She'd been mutilated and strangled.

Eric had literally dropped to his knees, the sight knocking his legs out from under him. On the ground beside her, he'd choked on his grief and guilt, tears flowing from his eyes. As much as he'd tried to prepare himself following her abduction, he hadn't been ready. The pain had been so intense that for several seconds he considered taking out his gun and putting a bullet in his brain before anyone could stop him. Vaguely, he recalled Bobby's hand on his shoulder. Bobby guiding him, half carrying him out of the woods and putting him in back of a Bureau car.

Victor Gomez was wrong about him. Eric was no stranger to grief. He knew exactly what pain felt like.

He pulled himself from the reverie before he drowned

in it. Returning to the living room, Eric picked up his cell phone. He stared at its screen for several long seconds before hitting its auto dial, then closed his eyes as he heard the call going through.

"Eric?" Mia asked after the second ring. She must've seen his name on her caller ID.

"I...wanted to check in," he said, voice raspy and uncertain. He hadn't seen or talked to her since Saturday night, since his rather hasty departure after Grayson Miller had shown up at her home. "To see how things went on your first day back at work."

She sounded genuinely happy he'd called. He listened, drinking in the animation in her voice as she told him about the media frenzy surrounding D'Angelo Roberts's arraignment that morning. She also relayed Miller's continued refusal to put her back on the abduction stories. He was grateful for that, at least. She was already in this far too deep.

"Eric, are you all right?"

He heard her concern through the airwaves and realized she'd picked up on his melancholy. He rubbed his forehead. "I'm fine."

"Did something happen in the investigation?"

An image of a sobbing Victor Gomez being ushered from the lobby appeared in his mind. "No. There's nothing new. It's just been a long day."

"You should go to the beach," she suggested. "You're staying a few blocks over, right?"

He nodded. "Yeah."

"At the risk of sounding New Agey, the ocean at night can do wonders. Sneak some beers and sit in the cool sand, watch the crashing waves for a while. It can give you a whole new perspective."

"Do you ever do that?"

"Not lately—not at night, I mean. But before my life went crazy, I used to."

He smiled faintly at the thought of a federal agent being hauled in by the local police for drinking on a public beach. However, the image of Mia at the shore, the rough winds blowing her dark hair, enticed him.

They talked awhile longer, mostly about the therapy session scheduled with Dr. Wilhelm at the Naval Air Station for the following afternoon. Eric remained hopeful she might remember something that could be a turning point in the investigation.

"Are you dreading it?" he asked.

"It helps to have you there with me."

He swallowed, feeling bad for what he was putting her through. A few moments later they wished one another good-night. Eric disconnected the phone, and listened to the clatter of wind chimes outside the bungalow.

14

Pain brought her to a ragged consciousness, radiating up from her fingers in hot, pulsating waves. Dr. Wilhelm's voice, faint and far off in her head, reminded her of her mission.

"Mia, can you hear me?"

"I'm here," she whispered, fighting back fear. "I'm in the room again."

Something restrained her movement. She looked down, tugging in reaction. Her wrists were bound with thin rope to a metal hook in the table. Two raw, bloody wounds throbbed on her left hand where her nails should have been. An icy chill slid up her spine as panic set in. She was in her underwear—her stomach was bleeding, too. Mia bit back the scream on her lips. She had to stay focused.

"Are you alone?" Dr. Wilhelm asked.

Her eyes darted around the room. "I—I think so. But I'm so dizzy."

"Try to take in your surroundings. Look for something that might indicate where you are. I'm right here with you…"

But was he? He was becoming increasingly harder to hear, as if he were on shore and Mia was adrift on a raft being pulled rapidly out to sea. Soon his voice became lost in the roar of blood in her ears and the sound of her own tattered breathing.

A pair of pliers lay on the table in front of her. Small, pale discs she recognized as her own fingernails were next to it. Her stomach turned. *Oh, God.* Forcing herself to look away from the grotesque sight, she scanned her prison. The walls were comprised of gray cinder block, and plastic sheeting hung up around the frigid room. She worked to gain control of her sluggish vision, aware of something on the floor, mostly hidden behind one of the sheets.

Someone lying facedown.

"H-hello? Can you hear me?" There was no response, no movement. Mia knew in her gut that it was Cissy Cox. Desperate to free herself, she twisted against her binds until her wrists began to bleed. Tears of frustration and terror filled her eyes. She had to get to Cissy and help her. *Damn it, Mia! Think.*

She couldn't loosen the ropes holding her, but could she move the table? She focused on the clawlike tongs protruding from the peg board on the nearby wall, holding various tools. If she could push herself to it—if she could get hold of the hedge shears or a pointed spade—she could possibly use it to fray her binds. Mia stood shakily and began shoving the heavy table the few feet to the wall. Muscles straining, she prayed no one could hear its legs screeching against the slab floor as she inched it slowly closer.

Finally reaching the peg board, she rammed the table against it, cursing under her breath as the hanging tools swayed and bumped but didn't fall. She repeated the process, banging it repeatedly. A tool dropped, bouncing off the table and crashing uselessly to the floor. A minute later another fell, a blunt hand shovel that wouldn't slice butter. Mia's hip bones bruised as she continued rocking and pushing.

At last a pair of small pruning shears fell. She stilled, incredulous as it landed only an inch from her fingers. Stretching for it, the ropes tightened painfully around her wrists until the shears were within reach. Her breath coming in cramped waves, she turned the tool awkwardly and worked its blade between her skin and the tethering rope, using it to saw at her restraints.

What seemed like an eternity later, she let out a sob as her binds gave way.

Without the table to steady her, Mia realized the full extent of her light-headedness. Stumbling toward the human form, she slipped and fell, striking her jaw on the edge of a workbench. Black spots danced in front of her eyes. Trying to get up, she slipped again, unable to gain traction on the wet concrete. A cloying metallic odor hung in the air. Blood. She was crawling in it. It was coming from the body behind the sheeting, leaking slowly toward a grate in the room's center.

Dread nearly closing her throat, she continued on hands and knees to the motionless form. Cissy lay on her stomach, limbs sprawled like a rag doll. More blood pooled underneath her and matted her red hair. Mia gagged as the room spun. *It wasn't supposed to be like this.* When she'd last seen Cissy, she had been bound and frightened but very much alive.

With trembling fingers, she felt the lifeless wrist for a pulse. She rolled the woman over, emitting a horrified cry as she came face-to-face with her open but unseeing eyes. Her throat had been cut. It gaped open, grinning at Mia like a second mouth. Heart seizing, she scrambled backward in the gore until she reached a patch of dry concrete. She screamed for Dr. Wilhelm, begging him to pull her back.

Her voice echoed off the cinder-block walls. There was no response.

Adrenaline pumped through her veins. She had to get out of here—had to find a way out or she would be next.

Managing to stand, Mia went to the door and twisted its handle. Locked. The noisy hum of the box air-conditioning unit caught her attention. It filled the room's only window…the only other possible exit. Staggering over, she shoved repeatedly at the appliance and the plywood boarding that kept it wedged inside the window frame. Sweat dried on her skin as she worked in its icy blast, applying all of her weight and weeping with relief when the boards finally dislodged. The heavy unit fell to the ground with an electrical crackle from the outlet. *Freedom!* The rain outside the window created a blanket of white noise. Mia hoisted her shaking body up and out, landing on dank, wet moss beside the air conditioner. Her energy exhausted, she lay there for several seconds, panting and trying to gain her equilibrium enough to run.

Go, Mia. Now.

Tall pine trees surrounded her, soaring into the black night. Forcing herself up, she took a wavering path through the rain toward the front of the building. As she reached it, an angry shout came from somewhere in the distance. The sound of heavy feet traveling in her direction sent her into flight. *Run...run!* She fell on the slick earth before getting back up and taking off toward a shadowed car parked on a gravel path. To her acute surprise, the car wasn't locked.

Mia dove inside and slammed the door, locking it behind her. She wiped her hands, slick with rain and blood, on the passenger seat. Shaking, nearly hyperventilating, her fingers searched clumsily over the ignition switch. There were no keys. Her heart dropped into her stomach. She felt frantically under the dashboard and found several wires already dangling, their copper insides exposed.

A fist slammed onto the windshield in front of her, making her scream. A man's face, contorted with rage, loomed inches from hers. His lips curled back in a snarl as he cursed and pounded on the glass with such force Mia feared it would break. Her trembling fingers twisted the wires hanging from the dashboard's underbelly. He bellowed as the engine rumbled to life.

Mia lurched the vehicle forward, its tires slipping and flinging up pebbles from the makeshift road. Rain beat on the car's roof and distorted the windshield. Shrouded car skeletons whipped past as she skidded and veered drunkenly up the path. Dizzy, her field of vision narrowing, she worried she might pass out. But she pressed her foot on the accelerator, finding the possibility of dying inside warped metal preferable to her fate in the cinder-block cell she'd left behind.

"Mia? Mia!"

She came awake with a strangled cry, gasping for air and her heart pumping like a trapped animal's. Dr. Wilhelm sat on the edge of the couch beside her. His hand was on her shoulder, keeping her down. The blood pressure cuff was back on her arm, and her clothing was damp with perspiration. He shook his head worriedly at the reading.

"Too high." He looked at Eric, who stood nearby, his face drained of color, his eyes fixed on Mia.

She felt a wave of vertigo so strong she thought she might be sick.

"We couldn't get you back," he said hoarsely.

A drop of crimson fell onto her khakis. Her bandaged fingers were bleeding.

"I don't understand how I managed to escape," Mia said in quiet disbelief. She rubbed her hands over her upper arms, causing Eric to turn the air-conditioning down in the car as he drove. "I was drugged, dizzy…"

"People do extraordinary things to survive." He studied her profile as she stared out through the windshield, aware of the shock her memories had caused. They'd remained at Dr. Wilhelm's office for over an hour, waiting for Mia's blood pressure to drop and her light-headedness to ease. "What you did *today* was pretty remarkable, too."

It had also scared the hell out of him. Mia had somehow lost contact with Dr. Wilhelm. She'd writhed and sobbed as she lay on the couch, ignoring his urgings to retreat from whatever was happening to her. It had been all Eric could do not to take her into his arms and shake her awake. But instead, he'd stood helplessly by, watching as she relived a nightmare she would be better off never remembering.

Mia had relayed the things she'd seen. The cinder-block building hidden in the pines, the stripped cars along a gravel road—it gave them something to look for. Even more important, she had briefly seen the unsub's face through the car window. Eric had already contacted Detective Boyet, asking to have a sketch artist meet them at Mia's home. He didn't think she was up to traveling into one of the stations.

"He just looked so average." She shook her head at the recollection. "I wish there was something about him that was specific—like a big nose, or a scar or mole."

Eric agreed some distinguishing characteristic would be helpful, but it wasn't uncommon for a serial killer to be an everyman, someone who didn't raise a potential victim's suspicion until it was too late. More of them came closer to looking like Ted Bundy than Charles Manson. It was also problematic that the rain had blurred his image. Still, even a vague description was better than nothing.

They traveled on the bridge toward Mia's home. The Tuesday afternoon was fading, turning the St. Johns into a golden, glinting sea as the sun lowered on the horizon. Glass-windowed, downtown high-rises glimmered at the water's edge as sailboats and speedboats darted along. Mia seemed lost in the scene, but Eric suspected the wheels in her mind were turning.

"You were right," she admitted softly. "Cissy Cox *is* dead."

Eric said nothing.

"The first time I saw her during the therapy session on Saturday, she was in the room with me, alive." Mia looked at him, her eyes haunted and confused. "But this time..."

"I believe you witnessed her murder, Mia. It's part of your missing memory." His fingers tightened on the steering wheel as he spoke, filling her in on the grim theory about The Collector ritualistically forcing his newer abductee to watch as he murdered the woman he had taken before. He also told her about the digital recordings evidencing the practice, each one delivered to him by mail. "Your memory today skipped to *after* she was already dead."

"I hope I never remember seeing her be killed," she whispered. Her face had paled.

Eric hoped the same thing. But there was always the chance of it since beyond Dr. Wilhelm's initial suggestion, Mia's mind could roam anywhere during the hypnotic session. The next time, the plan was to try to take her back to the point of escape in the car, with the anticipation she might see a street sign or highway marker that could narrow down the location where she'd been held prisoner.

If there *was* a next time. Dr. Wilhelm had confessed the drug dosage was one of the highest he'd ever given, but it had gotten Eric the results he needed. Whether the psychiatrist would agree to administer a similar amount again—and whether Eric would even want him to—was uncertain. He didn't want to put Mia in danger, and her blood pressure elevation during the therapy was worrisome. But Anna Lynn Gomez was still out there, and so was a killer who would hunt again. At the least, they would have to wait several days to allow the drug to pass through Mia's system before attempting another session.

He parked the car outside the apartment building and went around to the passenger side, opening her door. She was still a little unsteady, and he helped her out so they stood face-to-face. Eric lightly clasped her shoulders.

"You okay?"

She seemed profoundly saddened by what she had recalled. Her voice held a faint tremor as she looked up at him. "I guess I just needed her to be alive."

The drawing completed, Eric returned to the living room after walking the sketch artist to the foyer. Mia stood looking silently out through the French doors that led onto the balcony. Beyond her, the sky had turned to complete darkness. Eric bent to pick up the sketch, which lay on the coffee table. She'd been right; the image was pretty generic. The unsub could be almost anyone. Early to mid-forties, slightly receding dark hairline and average features. Still, he'd get the drawing scanned and distributed to the local authorities, and to the media outlets, as well. It could run that night on the late news. He anticipated the media would ask *how* the drawing had been possible. It was a question he didn't plan on answering. If pressed, he'd tell them a witness to Anna Lynn Gomez's abduction outside the Bargain-Mart had emerged. He didn't want the unsub thinking that any part of Mia's memory had returned.

"How are you holding up?" He returned the sketch to the table as she turned to face him.

Mia ran a hand through her dark hair. "I'm not dizzy anymore, just tired. But I'm a little afraid of going to sleep."

The bad dreams she'd been having. The vulnerability he saw on her features tugged at him. "You can call me, Mia. Anytime, for any reason. Even if you just want to talk. I need to get the sketch out, but I can come by later—"

"Did you hold out any hope of getting her back?" she asked, voice soft. "Your wife."

Several heartbeats passed before he spoke. He shifted uneasily, wanting to tell her the truth. "Based on the killer's M.O., I thought he'd keep Rebecca alive until he took another woman…I thought I had more time."

He paused, feeling the old guilt grab hold. "I didn't know she would be his last victim. He killed her within a few hours of taking her, according to the M.E.'s report."

She winced. Her eyes reflected sympathy. "You must have loved her very much."

Eric released a breath. "Things weren't good between us. We were in the process of separating."

"I'm sorry—"

"I'm sorry she didn't leave me sooner." A hard edge slipped into his voice. "If she had, she'd still be alive."

Mia laid her fingers on his arm. "You couldn't have

foreseen her abduction, Eric. You had no idea he would go after her."

He stared into her soft brown eyes. On impulse, he lifted his hand and allowed his thumb to stroke over her jaw, the bruise there barely visible now. Her lips parted as she stared up at him. She seemed so delicate, like an oleander that required special care. But he reminded himself Mia was stronger than that. She'd managed to escape a killer bent on her torture and death.

"I should go," he rasped. "If you need me…"

She gave a faint nod as he took a reluctant step back. Picking up the sketch before heading to the door, he wondered whether she would call him and if she did, how much longer he would be able to fight the growing attraction between them.

15

A recent lightning storm had finally taken out Karen Diambro's antiquated laptop. The electronics store's going-out-of-business ads in the Wednesday newspaper proclaimed savings of fifty percent or more, so she figured it was worth a shot to see if it had one within her budget. As she cruised the crowded aisles perusing the display models, however, she realized just how little she actually knew about computers.

"You don't want that one," a man remarked as she tried out the keyboard on a sleek-looking number. Karen looked at him. He was tall with slightly receding dark hair and blue eyes behind horn-rimmed spectacles.

"I don't?"

"The manufacturer has a reputation for service issues and overseas technical support." He indicated a different laptop. "Now *this* one's an excellent brand. It also has a better processor and you're paying only a little more."

The screen was smaller than what she had in mind. She pointed at another model. "What about that one?"

It seemed clear he didn't think her second choice was

a great selection, either. "I'd go for the best hardware you can afford. That one's cheaper because it's already obsolete. You can upgrade the processor and memory in a year or two, but it will end up costing you almost as much as buying a new computer."

Karen arched an eyebrow. "Do you work here or something?"

He smiled and stepped out of the way of a shopping cart being pushed past. "No, but I probably should. Electronics are a hobby of mine. I'm Allan, by the way. I hope you don't mind the advice. I'm rather passionate about computers."

She shook the hand he extended and smiled back. "Karen. And actually I appreciate it. There's not enough salespeople in here to go around."

"They're all kids, anyway. A few know their stuff, but most will just tell you what you can read yourself off the back of the box." They talked awhile longer about the laptop he'd recommended before Karen decided to purchase it, even though it was still more than she had planned to spend. Removing one of the boxes from a shelf beneath the display model, he loaded it into her cart.

"Thanks for the help," she said, slipping her dark hair behind one ear.

"You'll enjoy it." Her gave her a congenial nod and strolled off.

Karen felt disappointed their conversation hadn't gone further and he hadn't asked for her number. He was clean-cut—her type—and she noticed he wasn't wearing a wedding band. As she waited in line at checkout, a

banner overhead announcing All Sales Final, she glanced
around for him in the store. She spotted him in the television department, looking at one of the flat-screens. She
needed a new television, too. Karen considered being
bold and asking him for more advice, but it was her turn
to pay. After placing the purchase on her credit card, she
rolled her shopping cart out of the store. It was already
dark outside but overhead lights illuminated the parking lot. The box the laptop came in was big but didn't
weigh much, so she put it in the backseat of her Chevy
Impala and got inside. She drove off, mentally calculat-
ing how much she would have to pay on her credit card
each month in order to have the new computer paid for
by the end of the year. Since the divorce, money had been
tighter and she was working to keep down her debt.

She lived just south of the city. Taking Phillips Highway, eventually she drove into what was known as Old
Mandarin, with its stately homes on the river and ancient,
moss-draped live oaks. Karen loved the old-world, Southern elegance, although she herself lived in one of the
area's newer suburbs comprised of much smaller, cookie-
cutter tract homes. Traveling on a side street, deep in
thought, she realized with a start the traffic light in front
of her had turned yellow. She braked abruptly to avoid
running a red light. Her head bobbed forward as she both
heard and felt the crunch as another car bumped her from
behind.

Great. Karen looked in the rearview mirror and saw
a man getting out of a new-looking Infiniti SUV. In her
mind she heard her husband's voice—now her ex—
reminding her to take safety precautions. *Stay inside*

and roll your window down just a crack. Keep your cell phone in hand. Her stomach somersaulted in surprise as she recognized the approaching male. She opened the door and got out.

"Karen?" Allan shook his head in surprise. "I'm so sorry. I don't believe this."

"You were following me?"

He appeared perplexed. "What? No! I was just on my way home. What a coincidence and an unfortunate one, I'm afraid. Do you live around here, too?"

She walked around the back of her car to assess the damage. The rear bumper had a large dent and hung slightly askew. The SUV was less impacted. A few cars passed around them on the dark, quiet street.

"This is all my fault," he fretted. "I have insurance."

"Maybe we should exchange information?"

He nodded. "Let's get our cars out of the way first before we cause another accident."

Looking around, he pointed to a nearby waterside recreation area with a playground and basketball courts. It had a parking lot that was dimly lit and shrouded by trees. "We could go over there."

The suggestion made Karen a little uncomfortable. She'd really just met this man, and she still wasn't certain she believed him about not following her from the store. They were miles away from the shopping plaza now.

"What street do you live on?" she asked.

"Morning Dove Lane."

She recognized the name. It was two streets over from the school her son attended. He *did* seem to know the area.

"I really am embarrassed about this." Hesitating, he made a small, helpless gesture with his hands. "To be honest I've got a lot on my mind and wasn't paying attention. I'm recently divorced and I'm still having some trouble adjusting. My wife…she left me for someone else."

"I'm sorry." Karen felt a rush of empathy, thinking of her ex-husband's twenty-four-year-old secretary. The *new* Mrs. Diambro. Absently, she touched the faint indentation on the ring finger of her left hand where her wedding ring used to be. Even after the divorce was final, it had taken her months to stop wearing it. She stepped back as another car careened around them on the street.

"Maybe we really should get out of the way." He indicated the nearby lot again.

Consenting, Karen returned to her car and drove it into the empty recreation area with the SUV trailing behind her. Maybe their fender bender really was fate. With a nervous release of breath, she turned off the engine and took a quick glance at her reflection in the rearview mirror, wishing she had on some lipstick, before getting back out. Allan was already walking toward the car. The lazy croak of bullfrogs came from the nearby water, and several large moths circled the streetlamp in front of the public restrooms.

"Do you have kids?" she asked.

"A son. He's with his mother this week."

"Does he go to Jason Creek Elementary?"

He shook his head. "He's in private school."

She felt another fleeting wave of apprehension, aware their cars were blocked from street view by the trees.

Ducking back into her car for her purse, she pulled out her wallet to retrieve her ID and insurance card. Straightening, she turned and met Allan's gaze. He'd moved a little closer, and her eyes flicked to his right hand. He was casually trying to hide something. Karen was a pediatrics nurse. She approached small, frightened patients in the exact same way. She saw it then. He was holding a syringe, and in the faint glow of light she suddenly realized his hand was encased in a latex glove.

"What...?"

Dropping her wallet, she stumbled backward and threw herself into her car, but he wedged his body in the door, keeping her from closing it. Karen screamed and lunged for her cell phone inside her purse. She felt the sharp sting of the needle as he plunged it into her thigh. She kicked at him as he dragged her out, his hand covering her mouth and muffling her cries. Karen elbowed him hard, heard his *oomph* of surprise. Breaking free, she tried to run but her legs felt suddenly heavy and uncoordinated and she ended up sprawled face-first on the asphalt. Whatever he'd injected her with was strong. Her frantic pulse pounded in her ears.

He flipped her over and towed her by her upper arms to the waiting SUV. She felt little flares of pain as loose gravel on the lot cut into her bare calves. She tried screaming again, tried wriggling loose of his tight hold, but her body no longer responded beyond a few weak mewls and flails.

Last night's evening news...the FBI sketch of the man who'd been abducting women...it all came together in her increasingly muddled head. Terror turned her lungs to stone. He hoisted her into the front passenger seat of the SUV with a hard grunt. Karen's head lolled on her shoulders. He used the seat belt to keep her in place.

"You're a nice woman, Karen," he purred, brushing her dark hair back from her clammy cheek. "But if you don't mind me saying so, you seem a little desperate."

He took her hand and studied her fingers, frowning. The last thing she saw before blacking out was Allan heading to her car and removing the boxed laptop from the backseat.

16

The doll dangled from the driver's-side window, its gold hair shimmering in sunlight. Mia stayed on the curb while the other child approached the hatchback. The male voice coming from inside the car was barely audible, wrapped in the radio's pulsating beat.

"Hey, sweetheart, look what I have. Don't you want it?"

The doll waggled enticingly in the hot, sluggish air. Sweat beaded on Mia's brow and her heart began to beat harder. This wasn't...right. She watched as the little red-haired girl inched shyly closer.

"Tell your friend it's okay. She can come, too."

Cuddling the doll now, the child grinned and looked back, motioning excitedly to Mia as the door creaked open behind her. Within the space of a breath she was snatched up in hard, corded arms, her skinny legs kicking in midair. A hand clapped over her mouth, stifling her cry. The eyes that met Mia's were clear and cold... and hungry. Her knees felt shaky. She took several steps back, nearly tripping on the curb. The girl was stuffed inside, the door slammed closed and the hatchback peeled away, tires screeching on the sleepy neighborhood street.

Mia stared at the bedroom's white ceiling as she waited for the frantic pace of her breathing to slow. She had seen the car's driver in her nightmare this time, but he hadn't really been a man at all. More of a rangy teenager, with a shock of dark hair and wearing a white T-shirt and jeans. But his *face*...

It was a much younger version of the man in the sketch.

Although the night-light cast a soft glow, Mia sat up and turned on the bedside lamp. The alarm clock indicated it was after two in the morning. Shoving away the sheets, she got up and paced the room, arms wrapped around herself. She once again contemplated Dr. Wilhelm's theory that the dreams were merely symbolic of her recent trauma. That premise made even more sense now, since in this latest version the face of her abductor had been transposed onto the man in her nightmare.

Still, something kept stubbornly whispering to her the dream could be real.

She hadn't found anything to support such an idea, however. No articles about children abducted from foster homes in Jacksonville, either recently or twenty-five years ago. But there was one additional place she could check, she now realized—the newspaper's microfiche archives, stored in a basement room known as "the morgue" since it was a burial ground for old news clippings, most from decades back. She had forgotten about it until now, since pretty much all research these days was done online. The problem was, she wasn't sure if the film even still existed. Much of it had been disposed of several years earlier and the archive manager laid off. Newspapers, even the larger ones, were all undergoing hard times.

When she went into work in another few hours, she would find out if the archives were still intact. Or she could go now. Mia felt restless and couldn't sleep anyway, the troubling dream nagging at her like a sore tooth. Making a decision, she showered and dressed, then took off for the paper in the early-morning hours.

Pulling her Volvo into the building's parking garage, she felt a trickle of nerves. She'd braved the decks several times since her abduction, but this was the first time she had navigated them with no one around—no other cars or people walking through, and in an eerie blanket of darkness. Mia prayed it wouldn't set off some terrifying flashback.

She parked close to the glass-door entry that led to the building's lobby, her heels echoing off the concrete walls and her skin prickling as she hurried through the shadows. Sliding her employee ID card through the after-hours entry system, she let herself inside.

The newspaper offices were empty; the lights lowered at the chrome-and-glass reception desk. Mia walked past it, down the corridor and into the newsroom, flipping on the harsh overhead fluorescent panels. She placed her purse inside her desk drawer and locked it, then headed to the elevators.

Getting off on the windowless basement floor, she

gasped as she nearly collided with Ronnie, one of the evening janitors, who seemed just as surprised to see her.

"What're you doin' here, Miss Hale?" The African-American man with graying hair frowned as he checked his watch. "It's the middle of the night. You got some kind of breakin' news story?"

"I'm just looking for something. An old article, actually."

"You're here all by yourself?" He shook his head. "You think that's a good idea, after what happened?"

"Probably not." Mia felt sheepish, aware of his wisdom. "Ronnie, is the morgue still down here?"

"Uh-huh. What's left of it, anyway. Door's locked, though. I don't think anyone's been in there in a long time."

"Can you let me in?"

He fished into his trouser pockets, withdrawing a massive key ring. Mia waited as he rifled through it before finding the right one. "C'mon."

She followed him to the end of the hall. He unlocked a metal door. "I was just leavin', but you want me to stay down here with you? This ain't a real morgue, but it still gives me the creeps."

"Thanks, but I may be down here awhile. I'll be fine."

Ronnie gave a polite nod and departed. Mia turned on the light. Tall filing cabinets lined the walls, and there were several antiquated microfiche viewers sitting on desks in the middle of the room. She went to the cabinets and began looking. Multiple decades were missing, but to her relief the year she was interested in was still among the remaining film. She pulled out the entire section, which consisted of a stack of acetate sheets upon which the newspapers were imaged, page-by-page and reduced to thumbnail size. With no searchable index, it could take hours or even a full day to scan through all the headlines, she realized dejectedly. She figured she could at least eliminate the ones from the winter months, since in her dreams the heat had been sweltering.

Mia took the film over to the closest viewer, plugging the cord into the electrical outlet and wiping dust from its acrylic screen. Beginning with the microfiche marked *April 1987-week one,* she inserted the first sheet into the slot and focused it. She began scanning the headlines, turning the viewer's knob to see each page.

Some two hours later, she stopped to rest her strained eyes. Frustrated and feeling foolish, she wondered again if the whole thing was a waste of time. *Dr. Wilhelm believes the dreams are just that...dreams.*

Another half hour had passed when she placed the film marked *June 1987-week two* into the viewer. She began scanning the pages of the daily editions. When she reached page two of the paper dated Tuesday, June 11, she felt her heart drop into her stomach:

Child Missing from Foster Care Group Home.

A little girl named Joy Rourke had vanished without a trace.

It hadn't even made the front-page news.

Mia sat at her desk as Eric read the printout from the newspaper archives. She had called him a short time earlier, waking him to tell him what she'd found. Outside the newsroom windows, the morning sky was still dark and only one or two other early birds had made it into work.

"Why wouldn't I tell someone?" she asked, confused and unable to hide her upset. "A little girl was taken right in front of me, the article proves it. It happened at the same group home where I stayed until I was placed with a foster family. I never said a word. I never even remembered it until—"

"Until you started the memory-retrieval therapy." He finished her statement, his voice still a little husky and sleep-roughened. His eyes were sympathetic. "You were a six-year-old child yourself, Mia. Torn from your mother and home just days earlier. And the only friend you'd made was abducted off the street. You were *traumatized*. Your mind couldn't process anything else, so it shut down and repressed what you saw."

She rubbed a hand over her tired eyes. Eric's rationale failed to lessen her guilt. If she had given a description of the hatchback and teenage boy she'd witnessed taking Joy Rourke all those years ago, she might have been able to help her. She shook her head, still in disbelief that she'd somehow shut out the terrible event. While she had awaited Eric's arrival, she'd gone through later issues of the archived newspaper, but so far had found no additional articles. "I wonder what happened to her. Whether she was ever found."

"Now that we have a name, I'll contact the Sheriff's Office and see if they can come up with any files. It was a long time ago, though." Eric dragged his fingers through his short hair. He'd taken only enough time to put on jeans and a T-shirt, and his jaw held a bluish hint of stubble. Even in the current situation, Mia realized she felt the same hard attraction to him.

"Dr. Wilhelm was wrong about the dreams," she said quietly. "They weren't symbolic at all. They were real."

"They could mean a lot more than that, Mia."

She didn't respond. Eric lowered his words. "It means there's a possibility this guy's connection to you is deeper than we thought."

Mia rose from her desk, fidgety and nervous. She'd told him that in her latest dream, Joy Rourke's kidnapper appeared to be a younger version of the man who had abducted *her* in present day. Until now, the assumption was that Mia had been taken because she'd gained The Collector's attention by writing about the recent kidnappings. But what if he'd also known her to be the same little girl who had witnessed him taking another child off the street all those years ago? The possibility put goose bumps on her skin.

"I need coffee," she murmured, seeking an escape.

She went into the staff kitchen. No one had started the coffeemaker yet, so she busied herself with filling the carafe with water and placing a packet of grounds into the filter. She didn't have to turn around to know Eric had followed her.

"Look at me," he ordered softly. When she finally turned to face him, he asked, "What time did you get here this morning?"

"I don't know, three-thirty, maybe. I couldn't sleep and I remembered the clippings archive in the basement."

"So you came here alone, in the middle of the night."

She stiffened at the censure in his voice. Mia gave a small nod.

"That can't happen again. You were already taken once, right out of this building's parking garage."

"I'm not going to live in fear, Eric. And you said yourself it's rare for someone like this to go after the same person twice—"

"Will Dvorak told me a car might've followed you last week. Did it?"

"No. I mean, I don't know." Mia sighed, realizing she wasn't sure what she thought anymore. "I think I probably just spooked myself. Seeing Pauline Berger's body had me rattled."

"Why didn't you tell me?"

"Because I wasn't sure…and I didn't want you to think I was some panicky—"

"Mia." He whispered her name. When she tried to pull her gaze from his, Eric's fingers caught hers. Something in the air shifted around them, and she felt her heart beat a little harder as he bent his head closer to hers. His intense eyes held a seriousness that made her throat ache.

"I don't want anything to happen to you. We need to start taking some precautions. Especially if your dreams were really repressed memories and the unsub knows you from before. We also need to alert Dr. Wilhelm about this."

Mia chewed her lip. She just wanted all of it to go away.

"Is there anything else you remember about Joy's abduction?"

"Just that he used a doll to lure us—"

"Us?"

"He tried to get me to come to the car, too."

The shrill of his cell phone pierced the air. Eric looked annoyed. He dug the device from his jeans pocket and answered, pacing a few steps away as he talked. Mia tried to concentrate on the hiss and glug of the coffee-maker behind her, but she heard enough of the conversation to fill her with dread. After a few moments, he closed the phone.

"I've got to go meet Agent Vartran. A car was found south of the city at a waterside recreation area in Mandarin. A woman's wallet was on the ground underneath it with an ID inside, her purse still in the car. Deputies were sent to the home but no one's answering."

He didn't have to say more. The possibility it was another abduction took the air from her lungs. She clutched Eric's arm.

A noise outside the kitchen interrupted them. Grayson gripped his briefcase in his right hand and a Starbucks Venti-size coffee cup in the other. Mia wondered how long he'd been there and how much, if anything, he'd overheard. He acknowledged Eric's presence with a curt greeting and retreated to his office.

"I've got Walt headed to Mandarin," Grayson said as Mia entered his office a short time later. Behind him, the gradually lightening sky suggested a morning rain, and cars with their lights aglow were visible traveling over the St. Johns into the city. "I roused him out of bed and told him to get his ass down there."

So he *had* overheard that much. "I'm here now. Let me cover it—"

"I don't need two reporters down there." He peered sternly at her over the tops of his bifocals. "Speaking of, did Macfarlane share any other information with you about this? Do you know the woman's identity?"

She shook her head. "No."

"Any eyewitnesses or security cameras in the area?"

"I don't know that, either. You were standing outside the door. You heard pretty much everything I did."

"Let's say you *did* know. Would you tell me if he asked you not to?"

Stifling a sigh, she closed the office door to give them some privacy. "What's this about, really, Grayson?"

He shrugged and took a sip of coffee. "I need to know where your allegiances are, that's all. You say you want this investigation back, but not only do I think you're not ready emotionally—I also think you'd be more concerned about keeping Macfarlane's confidence than reporting the news."

She wasn't sure what to say. The truth was, her deepening relationship with Eric had created a complicated tightrope. It was one she still believed she was capable of walking, however.

"I heard you telling Macfarlane someone tried to get you into a car." Grayson's eyes held concern. "Who the hell were you talking about? Did this psycho come after you again?"

"No. It's nothing like that."

She knew she was being evasive. Mia noticed the familiar lines of tension on Grayson's face. She wanted to confide in him, tell him about her dreams and the things she'd learned as part of the experimental therapy with Dr. Wilhelm. Admit to him it was she who had provided the vague sketch of the suspect now being circulated by the media. But he was a newsman, first and foremost. She couldn't forget that. It was bad enough that he knew about the sessions without giving him the details of them, too.

"Damn it, Mia," he muttered irritably, removing his glasses and tossing them onto the desk. "I don't like the idea of Macfarlane using you. The Feds can be just as ruthless as the men they're chasing."

She lifted her chin indignantly. "He isn't *using* me. And for what it's worth, he agrees with you that I shouldn't be covering the investigation."

"Of course he does. He's spending time with you and if you were working the case that would create an obvious conflict of interest."

When Grayson said nothing more, Mia started to leave. Her steps halted, however, as she heard the creak of his desk chair. He came around to face her, blocking her exit. "Have you slept with him?"

"What?" Mia stammered, caught off guard. "No."

"But you *are* attracted to him. It's obvious he's attracted to you. I saw the way you two were huddled up in the kitchen."

She felt her face heat. "I don't think that's—"

"Any of my business?"

"No," she said plainly, meeting his gaze. "It isn't."

Grayson's jaw hardened, and he appeared pained. Their eyes remained locked until he shoved his hands into his pockets and returned to familiar territory. "I sent you an assignment by email, kiddo. Best get to it."

Dismissed, she walked back to her desk, a lump in her throat. She didn't like whatever had just happened between them.

17

The morning mist had turned into a steady downpour. Eric stood beneath a covered picnic pavilion about twenty feet from Karen Diambro's Chevy Impala. Rain pounded on its roof, and he watched as a wrecking service prepared to tow it to the Bureau's lab for processing. The Impala had a dented rear bumper, raising suspicion that a fender bender had been the ploy that got the woman to pull into the isolated area.

"Ms. Diambro's a nurse—she didn't show up for her shift at Children's Hospital this morning," Cameron said as he ducked under the eaves, stamping water from his shoes. "We got hold of the ex-husband, too. He's with his new wife and Ms. Diambro's son—they're in New York at a business conference."

With the ex-husband out of town, it eliminated a possible suspect in the woman's disappearance and increased the probability The Collector had taken another victim. If that were the case, it also meant Anna Lynn Gomez had run out of time. Thinking of Victor Gomez, Eric felt guilt pool inside him.

"There's a receipt for a laptop inside the vehicle," Cameron noted. "It was time-stamped at 8:16 last night."

He hadn't seen a box in the car. "Where's the computer?"

"Good question. Either her abductor took it as a bonus, or someone else happened along and helped themselves."

Several news vans were parked on the road adjacent to the recreation area, although deputies in rain slickers were keeping the media from getting any closer. Additional officers were conducting a checkpoint at the nearby intersection, asking drivers if they had witnessed anything unusual, including a minor traffic accident, in the area the previous night.

"You want to fill me in on these retrieved memories of Ms. Hale's?"

Eric had started to update Cameron earlier, but with this latest missing person, it had taken a backseat to canvassing the waterside park. "Like I said, she's been having nightmares, something the naval psychiatrist said to expect. But there's been a recurring dream about her watching a little girl being kidnapped. Until now, the psychiatrist thought it was purely symbolic of her own recent abduction trauma."

"But it's not?"

He told him about the archived news article from 1987, confirming a child named Joy Rourke actually *had* disappeared from the same foster care home where Mia herself had been living. "It was no nightmare, apparently. It looks like the therapy brought out a repressed memory from her childhood, as well."

Eric paused, knowing that what he was about to say, if

it were true, was a game-changer. "Mia believes the male she witnessed abducting Joy Rourke twenty-five years ago was a younger version of the man she saw through the car window the night she escaped."

"The same suspect who's in our sketch?" Cameron appeared skeptical. "That's some pretty out-there stuff. And even if the child abduction *was* real, isn't there a chance Ms. Hale's subconscious got confused and inserted her present-day abductor into the scene?"

There was always that possibility, and it was one Eric had already considered.

"The perp tried to abduct *both* girls," he said. "Mia got away."

The significance wasn't lost on Cameron. "Attempting to have two females under his control at once does sound like our guy's M.O."

The only difference was that he'd graduated to taking women at some point.

I hope you're taking the opportunity to enjoy our beaches and local attractions. It was something The Collector had said on the Pauline Berger recording… the way he said it made Eric suspect he was a Florida native, a prospect made even likelier if he was indeed the child abductor in Mia's memory. It was possible he had relocated to Maryland for a time but for whatever reason had now returned home. The tow truck started up with a roar, the yellow light bar on its cab flashing and its oversize wheels rolling forward through a large rain puddle as it pulled the Impala from the lot. Regardless, if Mia *had* actually witnessed him taking the child

all those years ago, then Eric feared she was no passing fancy.

"So we have one abduction in Jacksonville twenty-five
years ago. A child," Cameron recounted, his thoughts
apparently on the same wavelength as Eric's. "Then the
unsub goes dormant for over two decades before starting up again in Maryland?"

"He could've lived a normal life for a long time, until
some stressor kicked off his killing drive again." Eric
also recounted his theory from the recent task force
meeting. "Or, he could have stayed under the radar for
years by taking victims infrequently or choosing women
who weren't likely to be missed, like prostitutes or run-
aways. He's only gotten the FBI's attention because of
his recent spree behavior and the similarities of the victims' wounds."

"The numbers carved into their skin and the missing
fingernails and hair—"

"Indicative of an increasing compulsion." He paused
before adding, "I think we should consider protective
measures for Mia Hale."

"You think she needs it?"

"I'd rather be safe than sorry."

Cameron shrugged. "You can ask for it. But the reality is this guy hasn't made another move on her. And
a dream she's been having isn't much justification for
soaking up police resources."

"Agents?" A forensic technician approached, holding
a clear evidence baggie that contained a syringe. "It was
in the trash receptacle near the restrooms."

"Well, at least he picks up after himself," Cameron

grumbled. He turned to the tech. "See if we can get any prints off of it—make it a rush job, okay?"

Eric released a breath. He'd left the syringe behind this time. Its presence all but confirmed that Karen Diambro was The Collector's newest victim.

"What does Ms. Diambro look like?" he asked, dreading the answer.

"Her hospital ID badge was in the glove box," Cameron said. "Mid-thirties. Dark hair and eyes."

The unsub had changed his preference for variety. His last two abductions were both brown-eyed brunettes. Substitutes for the one who got away? Tense, Eric peered out through the heavy curtain of rain.

Cameron's cell phone rang and he answered, placing his hand over his free ear to better hear the caller. A few seconds later he disconnected the phone, his features somber.

"That was the office. Another package arrived for you in this morning's mail."

Eric closed his eyes as he listened to Cissy Cox's muffled screams.

He sensed Cameron pacing behind him as they waited for the inevitable to play out on the recording. This time the audio included no personal message or taunt. The Collector had forced the woman to state her name, and then he'd gone directly to the business of torturing her. An eternity seemed to pass before the knife slitting her throat—based on Mia's regained memory—had cut off her agonized shrieks. The only remaining sounds on the recording were the unsub's heavy panting and a very faint, terrified mewling.

It was Mia in the background.

She had been there—tied up and gagged, helpless, witnessing everything. As he listened, Eric realized his own breathing had grown strained. He hoped like hell the memory of what she'd seen would never resurface.

"Sick bastard," Cameron muttered. He came around to the desk where Eric was sitting, his face as gray as the afternoon sky outside the office window. "Even without a body we need to notify the family."

A knock sounded at the door.

"Agent Macfarlane?" Jeremy Hatcher, a tall, dark-complexioned rookie agent assigned to the task force, stood in the threshold. His eyes flicked to the digital recorder. He cleared his throat. "Forensics couldn't find any prints on the syringe. But I did the cross match you wanted. There's something you should see."

He stepped inside and handed over the computer print-out. Before returning to the office, Eric and Cameron had visited the consumer electronics store where Karen Diambro had shopped the night before. While there were no security cameras in place, the manager had agreed to provide a listing of in-store transactions occurring in the same time frame as Ms. Diambro's—customer names only, excluding credit card numbers. Eric had assigned Agent Hatcher the task of running any male customer names on the list through an offender database. Flipping through the printout with Cameron looking over his shoulder, he stopped at a name circled in red pen. "What was he in for?"

"Battery and false imprisonment. That was ten years ago, but—"

"Good job, Hatch," Cameron said.

"There's more. The guy lives in *Callahan*."

Eric glanced at Cameron, who filled him in. "It's a fairly rural area northwest of Jacksonville. It could be a match for Ms. Hale's description of the wooded area where she was held captive."

The man's record, combined with his presence at the consumer electronics store the same night as Karen Diambro, made him worth talking to. Eric rose from the desk. "Let's go."

The split-level house sat on a secluded cul-de-sac. It appeared in dire need of maintenance, with a crumbling stucco facade and missing window shutters. The front yard was more dirt than grass and a rotting, split-rail fence ran partially around its perimeter. An old dog, asleep in the day's heat, was chained to a cinder block at the edge of the property. Going up to the stoop, Eric rapped on the door as Cameron, Hatcher and another agent stood alert nearby.

He called the man's name. "FBI! Open up!"

The door creaked slowly inward and an older woman with graying hair in a long braid peeped out. "What do you want?"

"We're with the FBI, ma'am. We want a word with—"

"He ain't here," she snapped in a phlegmy voice. A second later the sound of a slamming door came from the back of the house.

"He went out through the back!" Eric drew his gun.

The team dispersed, with he and Cameron heading left around the house and the other agents traveling at a rapid pace in the opposite direction. At the edge of the woods behind the house, a black-haired male wearing jeans and an undershirt ran into a dense coverage of trees.

"FBI! Stop!"

The fleeing man discharged his gun, the shot cracking in the air and echoing.

"Son of a bitch!" Cameron intoned through gritted teeth, ducking instinctively as they kept going.

The rain had stopped, but the overcast day was muggy and hot. Eric gave a signal to the other agents, instructing them to travel around behind a detached garage to the right. Cameron went left again as Eric continued on the direct path behind the shooter. Running, he could see the occasional white flash of the man's shirt ahead of him as he darted through the semitropical undergrowth and trees. Steam rose from the wet ground, attesting to the humidity. A branch hit him in the face, stinging his cheek.

The man fired again and he heard the whiz of a bullet as it passed close by. With a curse, he continued in hot pursuit, his lungs burning and heart pounding. He was gaining on the man, could hear his labored breathing and grunts of exertion. Up ahead, a plane of water was visible through the trees, as well as a dock. Eric entered the clearing seconds behind the suspect, who was headed toward a moored fishing boat in hopes of escaping.

"FBI! Drop the gun!"

The man spun, weapon poised.

Eric didn't halt. He moved steadily closer, remaining

in shooting stance. The man's finger twitched on the trigger, its barrel aimed directly at him. The other agents had caught up, advancing on both sides.

"Put the gun down or they'll put you down," Eric warned.

"Fuck!" the man finally yelled in frustration, realizing he was cornered. He lowered the gun and let it fall to the ground with a thud, then raised his hands in surrender.

"On your knees! Now!" Cameron stepped forward and shoved the man to the dirt face-first. He kicked the weapon away. "Hands behind your head! Gordon Clark, you're under arrest!"

Eric bent slightly forward to catch his breath. Holstering his gun, he ran a hand down his face, his palm coming away with sweat and blood, probably from the branch.

"You all right?" Cameron asked, studying him. Eric simply nodded in response.

A short time later, he stood in the house's unkempt yard as the handcuffed arrestee was put in the backseat of one of the Bureau cars. The man's muscular shoulders were slumped, his scraggly hair concealing his face. Meanwhile, the woman—apparently his mother—stood in her housecoat on the patio, railing at the agents.

"It's not him," Eric said quietly, as much to himself as anyone. The area behind the house was wooded, but there were no stripped cars along a winding gravel road. No cinder-block building with a low-slung metal roof like the one Mia had described. Instead, the house's cheap, detached garage was painted brown and had a rusted metal pull-up door.

"You're basing that judgment solely on Ms. Hale's recollection?" Cameron asked. "She was stoned out of her mind—"

"I'm basing it on my gut."

One of the other agents emerged from the house. They had no warrant but had gone in anyway under exigent circumstances, in case Karen Diambro was stashed somewhere inside. The agent shook his head. A cursory search of the garage had revealed the same discouraging results.

Cameron looked at the car that contained the suspect, his eyes narrowing. "Either way, this dickhead must be up to something or he wouldn't be running from us."

They were just spinning tires here. Clark wasn't The Collector. One look at the untidy surroundings and the man's slovenly appearance—uncombed hair, grease-stained wifebeater—and it had been clear to Eric he wasn't the man they were looking for. Which meant both he *and* the unsub could have been shopping at the same, soon-to-be-defunct electronics store on the same night. It sent a chill through him thinking how much evil there really was in the world. He made a mental note to call his sister in Maryland and tell her to be safe.

"You could've gotten yourself killed back there, you know that?"

Eric released a breath. He'd been expecting it, had seen the reprimand in Cameron's eyes earlier. At least he had waited until they were out of earshot of the other agents. He avoided his gaze. "I was doing my job."

"You should've waited for the rest of us before stepping into that clearing and advancing. The guy had a direct shot at you—"

"Which he didn't take."

"Jesus Christ, Eric," Cameron whispered roughly, shaking his head.

Hatcher approached. Judging by the look on his face, he was clearly still enthralled with his first foot chase.

"Did you at least see anything in the house?" Eric asked.

"We know why he was bargain hunting for computer equipment now," the rookie agent revealed. "He forgot to shut down his screen before hightailing it into the woods."

18

Mia sat on the couch in her apartment, attempting to lose herself in a crisp glass of sauvignon blanc. Despite the fact that she'd been up since the early-morning hours, she still felt too wired to sleep. The discovery that Joy Rourke had really existed, her tense words with Grayson—all of it continued to weigh on her. As did the repeated news reports on Karen Diambro's disappearance. With a sigh, she glanced at the laptop on the coffee table in front of her. She'd been working on a story about a recent string of downtown muggings for the paper's online edition.

Violence was everywhere, it seemed.

At the knock on the door, she tensed. It was after 10:00 p.m. and she knew Will was out at a Chamber of Commerce cocktail party with Justin. She went cautiously into the foyer and looked through the peephole. Eric stood on the landing. Mia disarmed the security system.

"What happened?" she asked, her eyes going to the angry scratch on his right cheekbone as he stepped inside. He had changed from the jeans and T-shirt she had seen him in earlier that day.

"It's nothing. I hope it's not too late?"

"No…I'm just having a glass of wine."

He handed her a manila folder. "It's Joy Rourke's file from the JSO. I made copies for myself, but I wanted to bring you the original."

Taking it, Mia bit her lip. The folder had yellowed with age. She followed him into the living room. "What does it say?"

"It's a cold case, basically. The child was never found. It took Detective Scofield most of the day to find the file. The detective who led the investigation has been retired for years."

A renewed sadness bloomed inside her chest. "I only found the one article about her in the archives. I guess no one cared much about a missing foster kid."

His eyes were sympathetic. "It was twenty-five years ago. Things were different then. There were no child advocates or AMBER alerts."

"And there was no family to fight for her or demand that someone do something," Mia said. She opened the file and saw that Joy Rourke had no living relatives. Her mother had died of a drug overdose, and the state had been in the process of moving her from the foster care group home to an orphanage. Taking it to the table, she scanned through the contents, stopping at what appeared to be a school photo. A shiver ran through her as she stared at the thin-faced girl with a missing front tooth and mop of reddish hair.

"Oh, God, it's really her," she whispered. "The little girl I've been dreaming about."

He'd come to stand next to her, and she felt his hand on her shoulder. After a long moment, Mia replaced the photo and closed the file, deciding to review it all more thoroughly later. She couldn't handle the raw emotion of it now, and she wanted to concentrate on Eric.

"You look tired," she noted, concerned. "Would you like something to drink?"

"A beer would be great."

Mia went into the kitchen and got him one. He thanked her and took a long swallow from the bottle. His tie had been loosened, and she noticed a few drops of dried blood on the collar of his dress shirt.

"Is there any update on Karen Diambro?"

"No," he admitted, adding somberly, "but I received the recording of Cissy Cox's murder this morning."

An image of her slit throat filled Mia's head, as did the sickening sensation of slipping in her blood. She heard a tightness in his voice as he continued. "There was a second female in the audio's background. She was gagged, but—"

"It was me." Her stomach flip-flopped uneasily.

Eric put the bottle down and moved closer. "I've stepped up the police presence in your neighborhood, Mia. That's about all I can do for now. If it were up to me, I'd have you under protection."

She shook her head, not wanting to be made a prisoner. "He hasn't come after me again."

"Maybe not, but if it's true you witnessed this bastard's first abduction years ago, you're special to him.

And I meant what I said this morning. You have to start being more careful."

The seriousness in his eyes nearly made her flinch. Desiring a change of subject, her fingers rose to gently touch the scrape on his face. He still hadn't answered her question from earlier. "How *did* this happen?"

"We had a lead this afternoon, a possible suspect in the latest abduction. The guy even lived on a wooded property like the one you described."

"But it wasn't him."

Eric shook his head. "It took a shoot-out and a foot chase to confirm that, though. He isn't the unsub, but he *is* into child pornography. Underage females—some of them barely teenagers. He had camera equipment and images on CDs, plain brown envelopes for mailing."

Mia felt ill. She recalled a recent newspaper statistic indicating there were more than a thousand registered sex offenders in Jacksonville alone. "Do you know who any of the girls are?"

"He wasn't exactly forthcoming. We went into the home without a warrant—we had to—but the evidence was in plain sight. My gut tells me what we found will be admissible in court."

"Good," Mia said.

"His attorney will probably still try to get it kicked out. Regardless, he's being charged with fleeing authorities and aggravated assault. That's enough to get him a prison term."

The thought that he'd been so close to danger was unsettling. She took his hand. "Come with me? I want to clean up that scratch before it gets infected."

He allowed her to lead him into the hall bathroom. She knelt, searching under the vanity for the basket that held first-aid supplies. Mia was vaguely aware of how her tank top rose above her yoga pants, exposing her lower back as she reached into the cabinet. Standing, she placed the basket next to the sink. "Tell me that's not a bullet graze."

He laughed softly. "It was a tree branch. But a sinister one."

"You're tall and I'm…not," she remarked, looking up at him. Taking the hint, Eric sighed and sat on the edge of the vanity so she could reach him more easily.

Filling the basin with warm, soapy water, she wet a washcloth and wrung it out. Mia stepped between his legs, her heartbeat increasing a little as her body brushed his. Carefully, she pressed the cloth against the cut, letting its warmth sink into the wound. Eric closed his eyes as she worked, his brown lashes thick against his high cheekbones. Mia studied the elegant planes of his face unobserved. He was classically handsome—straight nose, full, masculine mouth and strong jaw. His skin was flawless. She could imagine a younger version of him gracing a poster for some Ivy League college.

"There," she whispered a bit shakily, applying a small amount of antibacterial ointment to the cut with the tip of her pinkie. "All done."

Eric's eyes opened, his gaze heated as it traced over her features. They were so close she could feel his breath playing over her skin. Mia's throat went dry as they stared at one another. Then his right hand closed around her slender wrist, slowly drawing her even nearer to him, so that their bodies touched. She saw him swallow, uncertain. More than anything, Mia wanted his mouth on hers, she realized. Their breathing seemed timed together as she made the first move, tilting her head and softly pressing her lips to his. He returned her kiss, gentle at first and then with an increasing fervor, deepening it and taking control. Settling more fully against him, every troubling thought in her head was swept aside, replaced by a lustful tightening in her core.

Eric released her wrist, his right hand cradling the nape of her neck. Mia's arms looped around his neck, her fingers threading through his hair. She felt his hands move to her waist, skimming under her tank top so that his fingers lay on her fevered skin. As they continued kissing, he stroked the small of her back and up her sides. He lightly cupped her breasts, his thumbs brushing over her gentle curves. Heat radiated from him, and she felt his male hardness, insistent. Mia ground herself against it, lost in the sensual thrill.

"Mia," he murmured as he reluctantly pulled his lips from hers. She tasted his jaw, the hollow of his throat, her fingers working at a button on his shirt. "Mia."

Gently, he took hold of her arms. Disappointment wound through her and she felt a flush rise over her skin. He appeared just as shaken, his breathing erratic. He briefly laid his forehead against hers.

"I should go."

"You don't have to," she offered quietly.

Eric gazed at her, appearing torn. He caressed her face and she closed her eyes, not wanting him to see the raw need she suspected shone there.

After he was gone and the security system reinstated, Mia stood in the solitude of her living room, unable to stop thinking about what had happened. He'd left her unsatisfied, wanting more. The place seemed far emptier without him.

Being alone was something she'd never minded. In fact, after a youth spent in and out of foster care, sharing a bedroom with one or more other girls, having no place that was just hers—sometimes not even a bed—she relished her privacy and space. Tonight, however, Mia ached from the isolation. She wondered whether it was Eric's sense of propriety that had stopped him from taking things further, or if he was still grieving for his late wife after all the time that had passed.

Have you slept with him yet?

Grayson's prying question had delved more deeply into her desires than she'd cared to admit.

She was single by choice—she'd dated, had casual affairs, but in the end she had never really trusted another person with her heart. Her mother had made it difficult for her to put her total faith in someone.

Eric could break through her armor, she realized.

Leaving her wineglass on the table next to his unfinished beer, she picked up the case file on Joy Rourke. It wasn't ideal bedtime reading, but she had to know more. Guilt tugged at her. Whatever had happened to Joy was in many ways her fault. She flipped through the folder's contents, a dull pain inside her chest.

The little girl whispered to her, her gap-toothed grin a ghost in Mia's head.

"What are you thinking about?"

Cameron sighed. He lay next to his wife in bed, staring up at the ceiling. "How did you know I wasn't asleep?"

Lanie had turned onto her side to look at him, her head propped on her elbow and her face in shadow. "Um, no snoring?"

"That's ridiculous," he said softly. Sitting up on the edge of the bed facing away from her, he ran a hand over his face. "I don't snore."

"You keep telling yourself that." Lanie sat up as well, although the growing mound of her belly meant it took her a little more time. Behind him, she burrowed her face against his bare back, kissing his shoulder blade. "Something's on your mind, Cam. You've been quiet all night. Is it the case?"

The bedroom's grainy darkness was like a velvet blanket, disrupted only by the moonlight spilling in through the sliding glass doors. Tomorrow morning would come early. Maybe he would try a glass of warm milk. If that didn't work, a shot or two of Jack Daniel's.

"Yeah, it's the case," he said finally, not wanting to reveal much more. He liked to keep his personal life a separate thing from the Bureau. Lanie, the baby on the way after a long time trying, their cozy house on the waterway—these were the things that kept him grounded and sane. He smiled faintly as she rose onto her knees and shifted behind him. She kissed the side of his neck, then massaged his tense shoulders. Cameron couldn't imagine what it would be like to lose her. Merely entertaining the thought made it difficult to breathe.

"I know you don't like telling me about the investigation," she murmured. "You don't want to infect me with the ugly stuff and I appreciate that. But I have a television. I know what's going on and that it's bad."

Cameron hung his head. He was a federal agent; *he'd seen things*. But this newest menace went beyond anything he had ever experienced. Even now, Cissy Cox's stifled cries and the slow agony of her death tore at his insides. At the VCU, he suspected such horror was routine. He had no idea how Eric dealt with it, day in and day out. How he listened to those women's screams without being hurtled back to the brutal murder of his own wife. The killer's intent in sending the audios was clearly to keep torturing Eric, as well.

"We went out to talk to a possible suspect today," he said finally. "The guy took a shot at us and fled."

"God." Lanie's hands stilled and she moved to the edge of the bed to sit beside him. She brushed her honey-blond hair from her eyes. "Was anyone hurt?"

"No, but it's a miracle. Eric took off after the guy. None of us could keep up with him—he was a sprinter in college, you know." Cameron shook his head. "No backup and nothing between them. Clearly against protocol. They had their guns drawn on each other and Eric kept moving in, refusing to take cover or back down."

"You know how much he wants Rebecca's killer. Maybe he wasn't thinking clearly—"

"That's the thing," Cameron said, looking at her. "Eric knew practically from the moment we got there we had the wrong guy. But it didn't keep him from taking the risk."

He rubbed his tired eyes. "I brought him in on this. Maybe it's too much."

"He got caught up in the heat of the moment and made a bad call. Eric's been through a lot but he's solid."

Cameron hoped that was true.

Wearing only pajama bottoms, he stood and went to the window, looking out at the languid waterway behind their home. Somewhere out there, Karen Diambro was being held prisoner. Based on Eric's theory, Anna Lynn Gomez was a corpse by now, a deteriorating shell waiting to be found, identified and claimed by her loved ones.

"Come back to bed." He realized Lanie stood beside him. She ran a hand up his arm. "I get lonely without you."

Turning to her, he placed a lingering kiss against her lips, his fingers intertwining with hers.

"I can't sleep," he whispered.

"Maybe I can help you with that."

Cameron allowed her to lead him back to their rumpled sheets, vowing never to take for granted what he had been given, not for a minute. He thought of Eric and the different paths they'd taken, how each of them had been dealt a very different hand.

He had taken Mia's suggestion to heart.

Eric stood on the beach, his shoes and socks left

behind at the wooden steps leading onto the sand. It was late, and the darkened, roaring sea spread out in front of him, whitecaps visible as waves crashed along the shore. Two teenagers, a boy and a girl, walked by hand-in-hand. They glanced curiously at his dress clothes, the gun on his hip, before hurrying past.

He'd come out here to think, to deal with his spiraling thoughts. He should be focusing on the investigation—the lead weight of responsibility on his shoulders—but his mind remained on Mia.

She had kissed him. It had been all Eric could do not to take things further. He felt desire for her so sharp it created a near physical hurt inside him. But those feelings came layered with a heavy guilt. He had a job to do and she was a complication he could ill afford. He thought of Rebecca—what she'd gone through because of him. Mia was a salve for his wounds he very possibly didn't deserve.

The cell phone in his pocket rang, pulling him from his internal sparring. Eric looked at the number on the phone's screen. He considered not answering but then accepted the call.

"Hello, Dad," he said quietly.

"The investigation's getting coverage on the national news," Richard Macfarlane remarked in his typical direct manner, no salutation given. "What's happening down there?"

Eric released a breath, his chest tight. He wondered how much he knew. "He took another woman last night."

"That's two since you were brought on to the case. You need to catch this bastard, Eric. Now."

"Yeah," he rasped, gazing off toward the lights coming from a line of multistory hotels not too far off in the distance. "I know."

"Your mother saw Clarissa Garner yesterday at the club," he said. "Awkward situation. Clarissa still won't speak to her, of course. She has to use a cane to get around now, poor woman. Charles was with her…"

Eric closed his eyes as he listened to his father talk about his former in-laws. They'd had Rebecca late in life; they had lost their only child. Both Clarissa and her husband, Charles, had refused to acknowledge Eric at their daughter's funeral, which he had interpreted as a direct accusation. He hadn't protected Rebecca, hadn't loved her enough to keep her safe. She was dead because of the enemy he had created.

"What's your game plan, son?"

"Quite honestly, Dad, I don't know. I'm taking one day at a time. We're looking into every lead."

A long moment of silence stretched between them. It was clearly not the response his father had wanted. Richard Macfarlane was known as a tough nut to crack within the upper echelons of the DOJ. It was what made him a force to be reckoned with in his job. "I've taken some criticism for putting you on the case. But I know what this means to you. To Rebecca and her family, too. You have to put this dog down."

Eric heard the unspoken directive. *Don't disappoint me. Make me proud.*

They talked awhile longer, with Eric asking after his mother and sister, Hope, who was younger by seven years and working on her doctorate in Art History at

Georgetown. The remainder of their conversation was perfunctory, an almost obligatory, even formal exchange between father and son. Richard loved him, Eric believed that, but he was uncomfortable with emotion and he set the bar high for his eldest.

"Be careful, Eric."

Good hunting. Godspeed. The airwaves went dead. He returned the phone to his pocket and stared out at the tumultuous body of water awhile longer, his heart heavier than before.

19

"Two canoeists hiking down to Black Creek found it." The park ranger was still chalk-faced under his uniform hat. "One of 'em went off trail to take a piss and stumbled over the grave. Hell of a start to a Saturday morning."

Eric followed his gaze to the two young men who sat huddled on a downed tree trunk a few dozen feet from the parking area. Their canoes and backpacks lay nearby. Although Jennings State Forest was outside of their Duval County jurisdiction, Detectives Boyet and Scofield were there as well, talking to the local police. Workers from Forensics and the M.E.'s office moved around the cordoned-off crime scene.

"The fella with the ponytail thinks he stepped on her." The ranger added with a grimace, "You know, *squish*."

Cameron frowned. "Didn't he notice the smell?"

"We've got a lot of wildlife out here—raccoons, otters, alligators—he just thought it was a dead animal until he saw a hand sticking out of the brush. Hey, is this one of those abducted women out of Jacksonville?"

Eric didn't answer. He had arrived a few minutes behind Cameron, who lived closer to the latest dump site. Dread sat heavy in his stomach. Karen Diambro had been missing for over two days, but he already knew the body located by the canoeists wasn't hers.

He left Cameron talking to the ranger and moved past the crime scene tape to the makeshift grave, although it was more of a natural, shallow ravine than a hole someone had dug. Tree limbs and brush had been used as cover. One of the forensics techs was busy taking photographs.

Eric stared down at Anna Lynn Gomez. He wiped his mouth with the back of his gloved hand, his throat tight with anger and guilt. Wild animals had gotten to her, not to mention the impact of the Florida heat that had sped up the deterioration process. Bugs crawled over the badly bloated corpse. It was hard to imagine the flight attendant had only weighed a hundred and fifteen pounds. The release of gases inside the body had caused blisters to form on the skin. Despite this, a crudely carved number, *nine,* remained partially visible.

Eric couldn't look away. Her fingernails were all missing. Flies buzzed around the rotting carcass.

Cameron joined him. Based on the white smear under his nose, he'd taken time to borrow vapor rub from one of the techs in an attempt to mask the stench. "He won't make it official until autopsy, but the M.E. suspects she died by hanging, due to pinpoint hemorrhaging and horizontal bruising around the throat—the line's too high for manual choking. He rolled the body earlier and there's an inverted V indentation on the back of the neck indicating where the noose was pulled tight by the vic's body weight."

Based on the low ceiling of the room Mia had described, there wouldn't have been much of a distance for a hanging victim to fall. Which meant The Collector had probably placed her on a chair and then taken it out from under her. Eric looked briefly over the sloping, moss-covered ground, heartsick. Death in that manner would have taken a while, the asphyxiation gradual. He tried not to think of Anna Lynn struggling, suspended in midair for her killer's pleasure.

He pushed emotion from his voice. "As soon as we're done here, I'll notify the family."

"Do you think that's a good idea? Victor Gomez already unloaded on you once. Why don't you send the detectives—"

"I'm going," he said tightly. "I owe her father that much."

"Then I'm going with you. That's nonnegotiable, Eric."

A tech who had been combing over the forest floor near the gravesite captured their attention. He held up the butt of a marijuana joint in an evidence bag. "We've got something."

"That's not the killer's." Eric nodded discreetly at the two guys seated on the tree trunk, who were exchanging nervous glances with one another. He guessed they'd attempted to calm themselves while waiting for the ranger service, or it was why they'd been off trail in the first place. His own nerves felt splintered. He was merely chasing dead women, left behind like a trail of stale breadcrumbs for him to find.

There had to be a break in the investigation soon.

Forty-five minutes outside Jacksonville, Mia drove along the Atlantic Coast, heading north into Fernandina Beach.

Bypassing the historic downtown district, she traveled past hotels and high-rise condominiums until the buildings became older and incrementally smaller, eventually morphing into a long line of private beach homes. A few minutes later the Volvo's GPS indicated she had reached her destination. She came to a stop in front of an aged beach cottage with a covered observation deck on the roof. Tall clumps of sea grass bordered the property, and a whimsical painted-wood sign on its gate announced it as The Captain's Roost.

Mia took the yellowed folder from the passenger seat. The sultry breeze lifted her hair as she exited the car, bringing with it the scent of seawater and suntan oil from vacationers on the shoreline. She went to the front porch and rang the doorbell.

"Up here," a booming voice called. Shielding her eyes, she squinted up to the deck. Retired JSO detective Hank Dugger was not what she had expected. Far from frail, even robust, he leaned over the deck railing, his eyes bright under a thick head of silver hair. "Take the stairs around back."

Smoothing her khaki shorts, Mia headed up the steps. Green outdoor carpeting covered the deck floor, and a corner bar made out of old dock timbers displayed an impressive collection of liquor. A battered rattan couch and chair set were arranged nearby under a canopy of netting woven with seashells. Jimmy Buffett sang from a pair of speakers mounted to the wall. She extended her hand, which he shook.

"I'm Mia Hale. We spoke earlier by phone?"

The retired detective had deep crinkles around his blue eyes. He remained handsome despite the sun damage to his tanned skin. "Back in my day, reporters didn't look like you, Ms. Hale. If they did, I might've been a little more cooperative."

"Call me Mia." She judged Hank to be somewhere in his mid- to late sixties.

"Can I get you a drink? How about a rum and Coke?"

"I have a long drive back to Jacksonville. Just the Coke would be great."

As he poured their beverages, Mia noticed the view from the deck. Even though the house was nothing fancy—more of a beach shanty, really—the view was breathtaking. Seagulls fished and took flight on the shore, and vacationers' umbrellas provided pops of bright color along the pale sand. Just beyond them the green ocean waves rolled and crashed into foam.

"You can see the old lighthouse to the left," he noted, handing Mia her drink. Indeed, it stood on a faraway sandbank, a red-and-white candy stripe swirling up its length.

"You have a nice place, Detective."

"I worked for thirty years and bought this property when it was still affordable. And I'm not a detective any-more, thank God. Call me Hank." He peered at the folder

Mia had set on the low table in front of the rattan couch. "Is that it?"

When she nodded, he said, "I'll be damned. I'm surprised they haven't cleared all that out by now."

"Apparently it was buried in the JSO records room. I understand it took a while to find."

His eyes held interest. "And they passed it over to a reporter, just like that?"

Mia hadn't been completely forthcoming with the retired detective in their earlier phone conversation. "I *am* a reporter with the *Courier*. But my interest in the case is more…personal. I think I might've known Joy Rourke as a child. We were both in foster care, in the same group home at the same time."

Hank nodded thoughtfully as he regarded Mia. Taking a sip of his drink, he sat on the couch and indicated she should do the same, then leafed through the file. As he read, Mia noticed the sign over the bar.

This Property Guarded by Smith & Wesson Three Days a Week. You Guess Which Three.

Based on her impression of the man beside her, she wasn't completely sure it was tongue-in-cheek.

"Yep, these are my reports—I can tell because the space bar on my typewriter had a tendency to stick." He shook his head nostalgically. He'd retrieved a pair of bifocals from the pocket of the Hawaiian shirt he wore and perched them on his nose. "Crying shame we never found this kid. My partner, Carl Witherspoon, and I worked the case. Carl died a few months ago. Throat cancer."

"I'm sorry."

Hank grunted, still scanning the file. His gaze returned to Mia. "How can I help you, exactly?"

"I'm wondering why the Sheriff's Office closed the investigation."

"As best I remember, we ran out of leads and were assigned elsewhere—"

"Didn't a child's disappearance merit more time?"

He frowned. "It wasn't my decision. JSO detectives in those days were handling nine, maybe ten cases at once. Probably a lot more than that now with the city's budget cuts and the jump in crime. Like I said, I'm glad to be retired. It's not like it used to be. These days you look at a perp the wrong way and get your ass sued."

"You said you followed up on all the leads regarding Joy's disappearance—no one stood out to you?"

He sighed. "We talked to neighbors, the group home director and caseworker, even the children who were residing there. No one claimed to have seen anything. The little girl didn't have any relatives, and those are typically the first suspects when a child goes missing out of state custody."

Mia scrubbed her hands over her thighs, ill at ease. She wondered if Detective Dugger and his partner had spoken to her back then and what, if anything, she'd told them.

He must have noticed her disquiet, because he leaned forward and added, "I know this girl seems special, but you need to understand that over two thousand children a day are reported missing in this country, whether a noncustodial family member or a stranger takes them, or they just run off of own their accord. We did what we could given the resources, but eventually we turned the information over to the FBI. They keep a file on missing children. If I recall, the NCMEC even put her face on billboards for a while, but none of the calls that came into the hotline panned out."

"The NCMEC?"

"The National Center for Missing and Exploited Children. You say you knew this girl?"

"Not well," she admitted.

Draining the rest of his drink, Hank placed the empty tumbler on an end table. He handed the file back. "I wish I could tell you more, but it was a long time ago and my memory's not as sharp as it used to be. 'Course, that's why God invented notepads."

Mia tilted her head. "I'm not sure I understand."

"What you read in that official file are just summaries—the forms and paperwork required by the job, rolled up to an executive level so the top brass doesn't have to waste time reading through everything. Most of my real thoughts on cases I kept in a spiral-bound notepad. Probably went through hundreds of them over my career."

"Do you still have them?"

Chuckling, he slapped the arm of the couch as he stood. "Pardon my French, but does a bear shit in the woods?"

The cottage was comfortable and quaint, with a country-style braided rag rug in the living room and well-worn furniture. A television set was blaring a Tampa Bay Rays baseball game. Mia followed Hank through the kitchen into a rear bedroom that now appeared to be used as a study. As he rummaged in the closet, Mia noticed framed photos that indicated grandchildren and possibly also a wife. But there was no other sign of a female presence in the house. Her heart tightened as she wondered if Hank was a widower.

"Here it is." He pulled out a cardboard box labeled 1985-90.

"I can't believe you still have all those," Mia said as he shuffled through the collection of notepads, most of them looking as old and dog-eared as the cold case file she held.

"I'm a pack rat, young lady. Old habits die hard. And once upon a time I considered writing my memoirs." He finally located the notepad he was looking for and handed it to her. "You're welcome to my notes, Mia. If you can decipher my chicken scratch. I can't guarantee anything in there will make sense after all this time, but who knows. Like they say, the devil's in the details."

"Thank you. I'll be sure to return it."

"I'd say don't bother, but if it brings you out to see me again, all right." He gave her a wink. "Next time, wear your bikini, though."

As he walked her to the door, Hank handed her several coupons for free margaritas at a bar where he worked part-time at the Fernandina Harbor. "My pension's good, but bartending gives me a chance to get out and knock off the dust."

"You're hardly dusty, Hank." She touched his arm. "And you should consider writing your memoirs again. I suspect you have some stories to tell."

They said goodbye. Her purse strap over her shoulder, Mia returned to her car with the cold case file and notepad.

The devil's in the details.

It wasn't exactly what the idiom meant, but she wondered if something in the detective's notes might be useful in discovering more about Joy Rourke's abduction. Flipping through the thick notepad, she noticed Hank's tendency to fill up every inch of space. There were notations running along the margins, thoughts and observations written in a loose scrawl, phone numbers as well as names. She shook her head, smiling faintly at the jumble. Starting the engine, she turned on the radio and pulled onto the highway. But the good mood the feisty Hank had put her in soon dissolved.

The lunchtime news report stated that a body believed to be that of Anna Lynn Gomez had been found.

20

It was the worst part of the job and one that had been required of Eric too many times over the years. He'd fully expected Victor Gomez to rail at him, even take a swing at him. But the man had simply crumpled to the floor, his shoulders heaving with silent sobs. Behind him, his wife and remaining daughter had clung to one another, their cries filling their modest home.

Eric wished Gomez *had* hit him. Physical pain was preferable to the responsibility he felt. There had been nothing he could do but hoarsely offer his condolences and leave the family alone with their grief.

Entering the rental bungalow, he removed his holstered gun, the darkening sky a purplish bruise through the window behind him. The Saturday had been one long blur of unpleasantness, beginning with the discovery of the body and search of the surrounding areas, ending with the grim autopsy proceedings. Eric had attended alone, sending Cameron back to the office to file reports. In between, there had been a news briefing and another tense call with SAC Johnston. His muscles ached from the stress collecting in them all day. Mia had left a voice mail message on his cell phone, but there had been no time to get back in touch.

He looked out as Cameron's car pulled in front of the property, the arrival giving him a sense of foreboding. His partner had been anxious to get home on a weekend night.

"What's up?" he asked, meeting him at the door.

Cameron looked troubled as he entered. He carried a too-familiar white envelope. "It was in the office mail."

The padded envelope turned Eric's heart sideways. He hadn't expected the recording of Anna Lynn to arrive so soon.

"I...listened to the beginning of it," Cameron said. "I know how hard the Gomez family hit you today. I thought if there was nothing useful on the recording I'd hold it until tomorrow."

"You did the right thing to bring it. I should hear it now—"

"Eric." Cam's eyes held his. He hesitated, swallowing hard. "You don't understand... It's not Anna Lynn Gomez."

Realization slowly hit him. Eric felt his world spin a little.

"When I realized what it was, I thought about not giving it to you. But she was your wife..."

He had stopped hearing him, Cameron's voice drowned out by the buzz building in his ears. Neither man wore investigational gloves. Not that it mattered— he'd been through this too many times before. There would be no prints. Eric took the already opened package. He recalled the painful wait three years ago for the recording that never came, the awful anticipation its own form of torture.

It was here now. He worked to find his voice. "How much did you listen to?"

"Enough to realize it was her." Cameron stepped closer, his expression earnest. "You don't have to do this. I'll take it and listen to it for you—all of it. Let me do that as your friend. This guy's messed you up enough."

Eric shook his head. "No."

"Then I'll stay while you listen. You can come home with me tonight. Lanie can have the guest room ready. You shouldn't be alone—"

"Go home, Cam," he said quietly.

Cameron remained standing by, uncertain. After a while he said, "I'll call you in the morning, all right?"

Eric had moved to the pedestal dining table in a corner of the living room. He lowered himself to one of its chairs and placed the envelope in front of him, his eyes fixed to his name and the neat, hand-printed address on the envelope's front. For a brief time, he thought Cameron had already left, but then realized he'd only gone into the kitchen. Returning, he set a glass and a bottle of single-malt Scotch on the table. Where exactly it had come from, Eric wasn't sure.

"When this place isn't rented out, I use it when I need some time to myself." Cameron briefly clasped Eric's shoulder and then departed.

A short time later he heard Cam's car start up and drive away. Eric sat in heavy silence before sliding the recorder from the packet. Then he poured a generous drink and drained it, feeling its slow burn down his throat and into his stomach. Gathering his courage and taking an uneven breath, he pressed Play.

"What is your name?" The Collector demanded.

Something broke loose inside him as he heard Rebecca's voice for the first time in nearly three years. She stated her name, her words too thin and high, pinched tight with fear.

"And who is your husband, my dear? His full title is desirable."

"Special Agent Eric Macfarlane," she replied on a sob. Eric felt his muscles go weak.

"You understand why you're here?"

"P-please! I—I just want to go home. I've got nothing to do with this—"

He startled at the sound of something slamming down, possibly a fist onto a table. "Silence!"

Rebecca whimpered. Eric ran his fingers over his face. Dread nearly closed his throat, perspiration breaking out on his skin.

"He'll be receiving this audio. If you have a message for him, now is the time. I won't give you another opportunity."

The recording picked up her ragged breathing. "Eric? Please, help me! He's insane! He's going to kill me if you don't stop him!"

"He can't save you, Rebecca. What I'm giving you is the chance to say goodbye."

She cried out. "N-no! Please! Don't do this! You don't understand—we're not even together anymore—"

"Very well. No goodbyes necessary, then." A tone of

resignation carried in his voice. Eric knew what came next and he swallowed thickly. Rebecca's frantic pleas were stifled as she was gagged.

Her torture began. Eric clamped a hand over his eyes at the sound of her muffled screams. Pitch-blackness washed over him, pain blinding him as he forced himself to keep listening, to keep breathing. His mind flashed to Rebecca's decimated corpse and the unspeakable things the sick, fucking bastard had done to her.

So many knife wounds.

An eternity later the screaming stopped as she was strangled to death. He could hear the unsub's grunts of exertion as he pulled the cording tight around her throat until she was asphyxiated. This time, there was no other woman discernible on the audio. Only The Collector, obviously aroused by what he had done.

"That was for *you,* Agent," he panted.

Eric sat immobile for a long time after the digital recorder had clicked off. He wiped his eyes and had another drink, hoping to numb the acute pain that tore at him. But he couldn't escape the hard truth. Rebecca had been taken because of him. She'd died afraid and in agony, hating him and begging for him all at once. He had failed as her husband and as her protector.

Lost in fresh grief and self-recrimination, he was well into his fourth glass of Scotch when there was a knock at the door.

"Go away, Cam," Eric warned under his breath, hearing the faint slur to his words. A glance at his watch indicated almost two hours had elapsed. The last light had leaked from the sky a while back. He rubbed a weary hand over his features, trying to pull himself together. The knock came again, more insistent this time.

With a curse, he got up a little unsteadily on his feet and swung the door open.

He hadn't expected Mia. He hadn't seen her since Wednesday night when they'd made out like a couple of teenagers. She stood on the porch, dressed in shorts and one of those skimpy tank tops she was so fond of. Her brown eyes were wide and questioning, her dark hair sleek and glossy as it grazed her tan, bare skin. Frowning, Eric peered down the darkened street. She was alone. Going around at night by herself with the angel of death running loose. He grabbed her wrist and hauled her inside.

"We talked about this," he said hoarsely. "You shouldn't be out by yourself."

She appeared taken aback by his tone. "I wanted to see you. I…heard about Anna Lynn Gomez."

He briefly squeezed his eyes closed. He hadn't given her the rental property's address. "How'd you find me?"

"Jax Beach isn't that big. I drove around until I saw your car."

He dragged a hand through his hair, thinking he should call the JSO and arrange for a deputy to tail her home. He was in no condition to drive. "This isn't a good time, Mia."

She glanced around the room, then back at him, concern on her pretty features. "I can see that. What's going on?"

When he didn't answer she took a tentative step closer. Laying her palm against his chest, she peered up into his eyes, her voice soothing and soft. "You're upset, Eric. Whatever it is, whatever's happened, let me help you, all right?"

He'd been carrying so much heaviness and guilt for so long. He had *been* alone for three long years in a self-imposed exile. Eric stared at her. More than anything, he wanted to forget for just a little while, to let go of the crushing pain. He needed her, needed someone to keep him from drowning. Tangling his fingers in her silky hair, he drew her to him. He pushed the door closed with his foot. His head lowered, his mouth tender and rough against hers all at once.

Mia felt the hard bruise of his lips, his need.

He was hurting—she'd been able to tell that much by his reddened eyes and disheveled appearance. His mouth on hers tasted of fine Scotch. She should push him away, *tell him not like this,* but instead she responded as he deepened their kiss, his tongue exploring, his mouth demanding more from her.

This was wrong. She should stop him, frame his face with her hands and ask him again what had happened. But she knew instinctively that right now what he needed was her submission.

It was something she was willing to give.

He pressed her backward, his mouth still on hers, his breathing heavy and labored. The wall solidly met her shoulder blades. He pinned her there with his body, his lips eventually leaving hers to travel a wanton path down her throat, over the delicate line of her collarbone. Eric cupped one of her breasts, massaging. Heat raced to her core. He pulled the thin strap of her tank top downward. His mouth, hot, covered her hungrily through the thin lace of her bra. Head back, eyes closed, she arched into him.

He stilled, then raised his head and looked into her eyes. In them, anguish and desire warred with one another.

"It's okay," she whispered, caressing his face, giving him permission to go on.

He took in a shaky breath. Then slowly, he drew the top over her head, his fingers unhooking her bra and sliding it down her arms, his mouth returning this time to her bare breasts. The stubble on his jaw was an erotic sensation, dimmed only by the feel of his mouth closing over one nipple, sucking, his teeth rasping sharply over the tightened bud until she thought she might die from the pain-pleasure of it. As he shifted to feed at her other breast, she pulled his tie loose from his collar and dropped it onto the floor, her shaking fingers moving to the buttons on his shirtfront, undoing them, her hands seeking him out. His skin was heated and fevered, his chest hard and covered only by a light sprinkling of crisp hair. He tugged impatiently at the snap on her shorts, then shoved them down until cool air met her thighs.

Her clothing abandoned on the floor, he lifted her easily, coaxing her legs around his lean hips. For a moment she thought he might take her against the wall. But Eric carried her past the sofa and down the hallway. His erection rubbed against her, making her wetter, tighter with need. Mia kissed his jaw, clinging to his shoulders as they entered a small, unlit bedroom. He laid her on the comforter, undoing the straps of her heeled sandals and letting them fall to the floor with twin thuds. Her panties went next. Mia stared up at him, the handsome, serious planes of his face submerged in shadow as he removed his shirt that already hung open, then disposed of his pants and boxers. He lay down alongside her, his long, masculine fingers stroking over her body as he devoured her breasts again, making her moan and writhe.

She stilled as his touch moved to the flat plane of her stomach. Even in the midst of their passion she hadn't forgotten the scabbed numeral—The Collector's mark, his forever claim on her. Eric's brow furrowed as he looked at it. She cupped his face, gently tugging his gaze back to hers.

Don't let him come between us.

Mia rolled onto her side, kissing him full on the mouth, wanting to take away the dark thoughts. Her hand moved to his hardened member, gripping him, pumping him, until he could take no more. With a strangled cry, he rolled with her until he was on top of her again, his breathing shallow and labored.

"I want to be inside you," he rasped, his voice melting her.

Mia felt the hard weight of his body as he positioned himself over her. She gasped, losing her breath as he entered her in a single, deep thrust. He was large, and she felt her body stretching to accommodate the size of him. Throat arched, she gripped his shoulders as he drove into her, until he captured her wrists, pinning them against the bed's coverlet on either side of her head.

"Look at me, Mia," he urged huskily.

Her eyes fluttered open at her name. Staring into her face, his strokes gentled and slowed. They found a rhythm. She wrapped her legs higher around him, inviting him even more deeply inside her as his mouth recaptured hers. He rode her until she was half out of her mind, until she was begging for more and his thrusting became faster and more urgent again. Mia felt her own climax approaching as his teeth nipped at her throat.

"Ah, God," he uttered finally, coming hard. Mia cried out at nearly the same time, her inner walls clenching around him. Panting heavily, he burrowed his face into her shoulder, spent.

A short time later, she lay beside him, having covered them both with an extra blanket from the foot of the bed. Eric's breathing had slowed and deepened. He was beautiful, unguarded in his slumber, the pain and tension from earlier gone from his face. She suspected he'd had enough to drink to give him a headache in the morning.

Sleep, Mia thought, watching him as she wondered again what had upset him. She slid her fingers through his short, thick hair. *Just sleep.*

They hadn't talked after their encounter. There had been no promises or pronouncements of feelings and emotions. Mia had been his escape from something— she understood and accepted that.

She wondered whether to spend the night or slip away under cover of darkness. Whether he would want her there in the morning. Feeling restless and uncertain, she rose carefully so as to not wake him, then padded from the darkened bedroom into the cottage's no-frills living area with its faux leather couch, low end tables and television in an entertainment armoire. The place was tidy but minimalistic, ready for the use of vacationers. They had left the lights blazing. Nude, Mia closed the curtains.

At the table, she filled the glass tumbler with a generous portion of Scotch. As she sipped, her eyes studied the digital recorder. She suspected what it contained. Another woman's final screams as she was tortured and murdered. Was it Anna Lynn Gomez? Was that what had shattered him so?

Mia's journalistic intrigue called to her. But something told her she didn't want to listen to the audio, didn't want to invade Eric's life in that way. His trust was more important to her. He would tell her about it if he chose. She stayed in the living room until she finished her drink, trying to decide whether to go.

Her need for him won out, however. Mia returned to the bedroom and slipped back under the blanket, settling next to him. She took comfort in his warm, smooth skin and steady breathing. He had turned onto his side in his sleep, and she pressed her lips against his back, closing her eyes.

She prayed neither of them would have regrets.

21

The shrill of a cell phone from somewhere outside the bedroom woke her. Mia heard Eric's voice, low and barely audible as he spoke with whomever had called. Sitting up, she blinked sleep from her eyes. Pale morning light leaked between the window blinds, reminding her of her nudity and her clothes that had been left elsewhere in the bungalow. Climbing from bed, she slipped into the wrinkled dress shirt Eric had discarded the previous night.

He sat at the table outside the kitchen, wearing jeans and a white, V-necked T-shirt, his feet bare and hair rumpled. An open bottle of aspirin was on the table in front of him. She waited in the hallway until he finished his call.

"Something with the investigation?" she murmured, feeling vulnerable as she came forward, her arms crossed against her chest. Eric's gaze fell over her, causing heat to infuse her face.

"That was Cam...I mean, Agent Vartran." He offered

no details of the conversation. Despite the sleep she knew he had gotten, he still appeared tired.

"How are you feeling this morning?"

"Like shit," he admitted. "There's coffee in the kitchen. I'm afraid I don't have much else here."

The digital recorder that had been on the table was now placed out of sight, she noticed. "Coffee's good."

In the small, galley-style kitchen, an automatic coffeemaker sat on the Formica counter, and she looked through the pinewood overhead cabinets until she found a partial set of chipped earthenware mugs. The coffee she poured was dark, as if it had been made hours ago.

"There's no milk or sugar. Sorry."

Mia turned. Eric stood in the doorway. She merely nodded and took a sip from the mug.

"I have to go in a little while," he said. "We have a task force meeting this morning."

Another Sunday meeting. Mia wanted to talk, to tell Eric about the case notes Hank Dugger had provided—she'd already started going through them—but now didn't seem like the time to bring it up.

"I understand." Placing the mug on the counter, she added, "And I should probably go find my clothes and start my walk of shame before it gets any lighter outside."

"Hey," he whispered as she moved past, turning sideways in the narrow entranceway to get through. Mia stilled and looked up at him. His striking, moss-green eyes appeared serious and troubled.

"I don't take what happened between us lightly...I want you to know that." His voice faltered. "It's just been a long time for me, that's all."

"You were upset."

"And a little drunk." He clasped the back of his neck, sounding sheepish.

"I'm pretty sure you're not someone who drinks to excess often," she noted softly. "There was probably a good reason."

He released a breath. But he still didn't reveal to her whatever had been the source of his pain. She stood there, wearing only Eric's shirt, her legs bare and their bodies nearly touching.

"I'm going to go," she said, briefly laying her fingers against his chest. "You can take a shower and get where you need to be."

Eric paced the oriental area rug in the psychiatrist's office. It was late Monday afternoon and clouds were visible through the large picture window. The rapidly graying sky suggested a building thunderstorm, a common occurrence in the subtropical Florida climate.

"I'm concerned about continuing the therapy," Dr. Wilhelm said from behind his desk, his fingers templed in front of him. He spoke not to Eric but to Mia. "While your outcomes have been remarkable, not just under hypnosis but also with regard to the repressed childhood trauma you've recalled, I'm worried by your adverse reaction to the drug dosage required to access your memories. Your blood pressure rose significantly last time and took a while to bring under control. That's a potentially dangerous situation."

Mia sat on the couch and seemed to contemplate what

he had said before she spoke. "Karen Diambro is still missing. She's probably still alive. I'd like to try again."

Her dark-lashed eyes slid to Eric. "What do you think?"

He frowned. He believed she was close to making a breakthrough—on the verge of seeing or hearing something significant that could lead them to the unsub. But he didn't want it to come at too high a cost to her. "Dr. Wilhelm, may I speak to Mia alone?"

The psychiatrist hesitated, as if he expected Eric to railroad a decision in his absence. He stood, however, and retreated from the room.

"You don't have to do this," he said once they were alone.

Mia stood and walked to him. Her eyes held his. "You don't have any leads and we both know Karen Diambro is on borrowed time. As soon as another woman goes missing—"

"I don't want you doing this for *me*."

Hurt flickered over her features. When she spoke, her voice sounded strained. "I'm doing it for the women he murdered. And for the ones he *will* murder if he isn't stopped."

Thunder rumbled in the distance, and the view outside the window had gotten darker. Eric sighed. Despite her willingness, he couldn't shake the feeling that he was using her. Just as he had two nights earlier to blot out his pain. Even now he recalled her soft skin, her taste. He'd been drunk, but not too drunk to remember every inch of her slender body. He worried that he'd treated her like a one-night stand—the sex had been too hard and too fast. She deserved better, deserved to be more than a distraction from the mess that had become his life. Their growing closeness was a complication.

"I signed a waiver when I began the therapy," she reminded. "Neither you nor Dr. Wilhelm would be held responsible if something happened—"

"I don't give a damn about *liability,* Mia. I care about your safety." He took a few steps away and raked a hand through his hair, torn by his indecision. He knew how much was at stake here.

"Let me try again," she urged.

A short time later, they called Dr. Wilhelm back. Eric stood by tensely as he once again prepared her to be put under hypnosis. The tubing around her upper arm, the injection, the lowered lights and the psychiatrist's subdued voice as he spoke to her—he watched all of it much as a witness watches a death row execution. He knew it was for the common good, but it did little to quell his unease. Since Mia's time under hypnosis was limited, they had previously discussed the best strategy for the session, which was to try to take her back to the point of her escape.

"I need you to return to the car you drove away in, Mia. The silver Acura," Dr. Wilhelm stated gently once it appeared the drug had taken effect. He sat in the wing chair, which he'd pulled up next to the couch where she lay, her eyes closed and breathing slow and deep. "You've already escaped that terrible room, but you need to get far away. You're twisting the loose wires under the dashboard to start the engine—you know how to do it."

She didn't speak for a long time, almost appearing

to be asleep. Then Eric's heart skittered as she suddenly jerked. "He's banging on the window! It's going to break!"

"Then you have to go, now. Put the car into Drive. Is it moving?"

"Y-yes. But I'm so dizzy. My vision's blurred." Her voice trembled. "Oh, God, I think he's following me!"

"He's not," Dr. Wilhelm promised. "Just keep driving and tell me what you see."

"It's dark and it's raining so hard. I'm swerving on the road! I—I can't help it."

"Are there street signs?"

"I—I can't read them. Trees are blocking the streetlights and I'm going so fast…"

"Just keep driving." Dr. Wilhelm exchanged a look with Eric, who stood close by. He realized again what a feat Mia had accomplished in getting away without wrecking the car and killing herself or others in her drugged state. It had been blind luck, literally.

"I'm on an interstate," she said a short time later, voice still shaky. "I don't know how I got here."

"It's all right. The interstate should be well lit. Look for signs."

A jagged streak of lightning lit up the office window and thunder rolled overhead. Eric heard the patter on the roof as the storm broke. At least it was raining in Mia's memory, too, decreasing the chance of it being a distraction. The interstate was her best chance of seeing something useful.

"I-95 North," she murmured. "That's what the road marker says."

He felt a sense of triumph. It wasn't a pinpoint location, but it narrowed the geographic area down. Wherever she'd been held, it was south of Jacksonville. Mia had apparently traveled up the interstate before turning east somewhere and driving onto the A1A that ran along the coast. He recalled the broken fencing at the site where she'd finally veered off the road outside Atlantic Beach.

"Keep looking," Dr. Wilhelm prodded. "There might be an exit sign or a billboard. Tell me anything you see."

She fell silent again. But something had changed. She began to squirm, her head lolling fitfully from side to side. Worried, Eric looked at Dr. Wilhelm, who leaned over her, alert to her stress. "Mia? What's going on?"

She sobbed, her breath quickening. Her hands fisted at her sides.

"Mia, you must listen to me. Tell me what's happening." Already, he'd begun inflating the blood pressure cuff on her arm.

"I'm back in the room again. Oh, God. He…he has a knife!"

A coldness slid down Eric's spine. They'd been warned this could happen—she could start out following Dr. Wilhelm's suggestion, but her subconscious might wander elsewhere, to other memories more deeply entrenched.

She trembled harder, her voice breaking. "No! Please!"

Eric felt his pulse pound. "Bring her out of it. Now."

"It's not that simple." Dr. Wilhelm glanced up at him, then returned his attention to the digital screen on the blood pressure unit. He frowned and shook his head.

"Bringing her out too quickly could make her BP go even higher."

Eric watched helplessly as she continued to thrash on the couch, her breathing growing more ragged. He should have never let her do this.

"Remember the theater where you're safe, Mia?" Dr. Wilhelm said, trying to regain control. "I want you to go there now. Replace what's going on around you with the blank theater screen. Stare at its whiteness. It's cool and quiet there. Serene. The door's locked so no one can come in. No one can hurt you—"

She screamed, her back arching off the couch. Blood rushed to Eric's face. He knew what was happening, what the bastard was doing to her. He was carving the numeral into her skin. "Bring her out of it!"

Mia's anguished cries were punctuated by broken sobs and gasps for air.

Dr. Wilhelm clapped his hands sharply in front of Mia's face. "Wake up, Mia! You have to come back now!"

On his third attempt at jolting her awake, she sat upright, wheezing. Her face had a bluish pallor that scared the hell out of Eric. He took her by the shoulders.

"It's all right, Mia. You're back. You're safe."

Tears streamed down her cheeks. Blood from the scabbed cut on her stomach seeped through her white top. Dr. Wilhelm got another read from the device, then yanked the cuff off her arm. "Her BP's skyrocketed. One-sixty over one hundred. We need to get her to the E.R., now!"

"I—I can't breathe." She clutched at her chest.

"Jesus," Eric whispered under his breath. He lifted Mia into his arms and carried her out into the downpour.

22

Eric stood as Dr. Wilhelm entered the waiting room in the naval hospital's E.R.

"She's stabilized," he announced. "Her blood pressure's coming down and they're giving her oxygen."

Relief slumped his shoulders. "Is she going to be okay?"

"A beta-blocker was administered to combat the hypertension." He paused as the hospital intercom crackled to life overhead, paging a doctor to the surgical ward. "Her arterial blood gases are also within an acceptable range now. They're going to keep her a few hours for observation. If the second round of tests comes back normal, you should be able to take her home."

Eric shifted his stance to let a military family pass by. His clothes were still damp from the downpour outside. "What happened, exactly?"

"In layman's terms, we've taken the drug dosage too high. It sent her adrenal glands into overdrive. She went into a fight-or-flight reaction she couldn't come down from, causing the hyperventilation and prolonged spike in her BP." He shook his head, his expression grave. "If it went on any longer she could've had a heart attack."

Eric stared down the corridor where the trauma staff had taken her. He hadn't wasted time getting her into a car, instead carrying Mia from Dr. Wilhelm's office across the parking lot to the adjacent hospital. As soon as the E.R.'s electronic doors had slid open, she'd been plucked from his arms and strapped to a gurney, then rolled away to one of the exam bays. That had been nearly an hour ago.

"I understand the urgency of your situation, Agent Macfarlane. But I don't recommend continuing the memory-retrieval therapy, especially not at the current dosage level. Unfortunately, it's the one required to access her memories."

Eric nodded, a dull ache in his chest. "Can I see her now?"

"Of course. She's in the fourth exam bay. The hospital's tight on bed space, so they don't plan to move her to a room unless she has a relapse. If anything like that happens, I've asked to be called."

Bidding him good-night, Dr. Wilhelm walked past the admissions desk and out into the graying haze of early evening. It had finally stopped raining outside and steam rose from the asphalt at the E.R.'s entrance. Eric chastised himself for letting Mia attempt the therapy again. He wanted the unsub badly, but not like this. Even now, he could still hear her strained gasps as he traveled with her across the parking lot.

He'd have to find another way.

Eric left the waiting room, heading past hospital workers and patients waiting for treatment. He went down the hallway until he reached the windowed exam bays. The curtains were closed and lights lowered in the one Dr. Wilhelm had indicated. Eric knocked softly on the door. A stern-faced nurse on her way out stopped him, but he presented his shield and she allowed him to enter.

"She needs to rest," she pointed out before pushing her cart away.

Wire leads from the heart monitor snaked under the neckline of Mia's hospital gown. The machine beeped nearby. A pulse oximeter was clipped to the index finger of her right hand, and an oxygen cannula had been adjusted under her nose. He swallowed hard, feeling a surge of protectiveness. She appeared small and pale under the gurney's sheets. Eric stepped next to it, causing her eyes to flutter open.

"Sorry. I didn't mean to wake you."

"I wasn't sleeping, just floating." She sounded groggy. "Valium, I think."

"You gave me a scare," he said quietly.

"But we know he's somewhere south of Jacksonville now. If I'd stayed with the memory a little longer—"

He hushed her. "Let's not worry about that."

She could've had a heart attack. His insides twisted at the prospect.

"The carving on my stomach...it started bleeding again." She placed her hand on the sheets over her abdomen, puzzlement in her voice. Mia looked up at him with glassy eyes, probably caused by the medication. "The same thing happened before...only last time it was where he pulled out my nails."

It was some kind of strange phenomenon. But to Eric, it only underscored the realism of Mia's experiences during those sessions. She really *was* reliving those lost memories, not just viewing them like someone passively watching a slide show of past events. He regretted the torture she'd been put through all over again, forced to endure a psychotic killer cutting into her.

"I got a better look at him this time."

"We can update the sketch in the morning."

"I'm sorry," she murmured.

Frowning, Eric brushed her dark hair back from her forehead. "What do you have to be sorry for?"

"I wanted to remember something that might make this finally be over."

He pulled a stool beside the gurney and took Mia's hand. It was unclear to him how someone so delicate-looking could also be so brave. He studied her scabbed nail beds, then brought her fine knuckles to his mouth and kissed them, his eyes somber.

"Think you could bust me out of here?" she asked half-jokingly.

He wanted to make certain she was all right. "Not a chance. We're staying until they release you."

It was nearly eleven by the time they returned to Mia's apartment. She felt tired and still a little woozy from the sedative, but also appreciative of the close watch Eric had kept over her. He hadn't left her bedside at the hospital except to make a few necessary phone calls. Once they had gotten her release papers, he'd carefully guided her into his car to take her home.

"You're a dancer."

Mia turned to see him holding her worn pair of ballet slippers. He stood in the doorway to her bedroom, having followed her down the hall, worried about her steadiness on her feet. The ribboned slippers had been hanging from a hook on the front of the door. It was a rather childish decoration, out of place with her more chic furnishings, but she liked having the shoes where she passed by each day.

"I also saw the photos in your office," he admitted. "You made a pretty ballerina."

She felt herself blush at his comment. Mia took the slippers from him, her fingers pensively gliding over their pale satin. "I got started as a teenager, a little late, but I had promise. I trained with the youth program at the Jacksonville Inner-City Ballet. I ended up getting a minority arts scholarship to the University of Florida. It's how I went to college."

"I'm impressed."

Her thumb worried at one of the slipper's frayed toes before she laid them on the distressed wood of her bureau top. "Don't be. I blew out my knee as a junior, ending my scholarship."

"But you still managed to finish school."

"It took a while since I was working two jobs— waitressing and doing a paid internship at the Gaines-ville newspaper, but I made it."

"You amaze me, Mia," Eric said, taking a step closer. His eyes were sincere. "Especially considering all you've been through…"

His words trailed off, but she knew what he was thinking. That given her background she could have ended up with no education or career. Worse, she could have followed her mother's path, sustained by welfare, accepting money from men for sexual favors. Luri Hale might not have walked street corners, but the nameless men she picked up in bars still looked upon her as a whore.

"I've been on my own since I was sixteen," she said, thinking of the night Luri had come home with two men. *One for her and one for her little girl,* she'd said in her thick accent, a gleam in her eye that suggested she was back in her manic phase. When Mia refused to go into the bedroom with the stranger, Luri had slapped her and said he was willing to pay two hundred dollars, money they needed for rent. She shouldn't be so high-and-mighty.

Mia had run from the apartment. She'd gone back to it only once after that, to pick up her clothing and her few possessions, and to tell Luri she wanted to be free of her forever.

"Well, I wasn't *completely* alone," she conceded, her voice soft. "One of the dance instructors, a woman named Delora Vance, took me in. She gave me a room in her house until I finished high school. Delora had this creaky old Victorian in the Springfield Historic District that had been in her family for generations. She helped supplement the stipend for independent living I'd gotten from the court, and I got the university scholarship with her help. I'm not really sure what I would've done without her."

"Are you still in touch with her?" Eric asked.

Mia shook her head, still feeling Delora's absence.

"She's dead now. She was robbed and shot outside her home four years ago."

Springfield was returning to gentrification, but at that time it had still been a haven for crime. "I covered the investigation for the paper. A fifteen-year-old gang member killed her for fifty dollars. Before that I saw her fairly regularly, though. I used to go to her place for dinner on the last Sunday of every month. Usually Mayport fried shrimp or barbecue pork, Delora's specialties, and always with sweet tea."

"I'm sorry," he said, somber. "Do you ever dance anymore?"

"I teach during the summer at one of the nonprofit urban centers downtown. I like to introduce it to children who otherwise might not get the chance." *Kids like me,* she thought. "The classes start after school's out for summer. Three nights a week I'm surrounded by cute little girls in pink tights."

Eric studied her. "I'd like to see that. You with all your miniballerinas."

She smiled wanly, knowing it was unlikely to happen. When the investigation was over, he would return to D.C. It was true what she'd said tonight. More than anything, she wanted to remember something that would put an end to the violence. To help Eric finally capture the man who had caused him so much grief. But she couldn't help it— thinking of his departure made her feel hollow inside.

Afraid he could sense her melancholy, she lowered her gaze. Her hand went to her blouse, which had rusty droplets of dried blood on its front. She recalled why she'd come to her bedroom. "I'm going to change."

He moved back to the door. "I'll be just outside."

They hadn't talked about what had happened between them at the bungalow, not since their awkward morning after. "You don't have to stay, Eric. It's late and I'm really okay now."

"I'd like to spend the night." His hand remained on the door frame, steadfast. "I don't think you should be alone. Not tonight."

Mia thought of The Collector's knife cutting into her. The memory was enough to rattle her all over again.

"It was before he took my nails," she said in recollection. "My wrists were tied over my head and bound to a hook in the wall. He sat in a chair in front of me, taking his time…"

She shook her head in disbelief, unable to control the tremor in her voice. "The whole time, he was humming some tune, like I was a piece of wood he was carving on."

Eric's eyes darkened.

She found him in her office, looking through Hank Dugger's notepad.

"They're from the retired detective who handled the Joy Rourke abduction," Mia said as she entered, wearing a soft pair of print pajama bottoms and fitted T-shirt. She'd also taken a shower, her dark hair damp. "I went to visit him on Saturday."

"He gave you his notes?"

"I told him I might've known Joy when I was in foster care."

Eric had pulled his dress shirt free from his suit pants,

and she noticed his jacket and tie were draped over the back of her desk chair. His shield and gun in its holster were also nearby, on the bookshelf next to several reference journals and an old *AP Stylebook* she'd had since college journalism courses.

"Have you found anything in them?" he asked.

"Not so far. It's mostly the same information as in the cold case file, although some of the detective's personal thoughts and observations are included along with the facts. I've been trying to locate people he talked to during the investigation, but there are a lot of names and it was twenty-five years ago. Some are dead, or moved or are just generally hard to find. I worked on it Sunday, and a little today at the paper between assignments."

Still studying the notepad, he took it to the love seat. Mia sank down beside him and pointed to one of the names on the list, a man who had lived across from Miss Cathy's. "His house would've been in the best position to see something that day. He died a year ago, I found out."

"Keep looking," Eric said. "We have task force members going through the JSO file, but if someone stands out to you or raises any flags, let me know."

She nodded, although she realized it was a long shot. Hank Dugger and his partner had worked the case thoroughly, it seemed.

"Would you like something to eat?" she asked.

"I had a bite at the hospital cafeteria when I was making calls. What about you?"

She shook her head, stifling a yawn.

"What I'd *like* is for you to get some rest." He released

a breath as he looked at her. "If anything had happened to you tonight, Mia, I wouldn't be able to forgive myself."

"I'm in this by choice. Today got a little rough, but next time—"

"There won't be a next time." The resolution in his voice left no room for argument. "Dr. Wilhelm believes it's gotten too dangerous. I won't risk your health again."

He touched her face. "I also think you should take tomorrow off from work."

"I don't need to. The E.R. doctor said I'm fine."

His eyes held hers. Then he kissed her, a soft pressure against her lips that made Mia yearn for more. Their lovemaking two nights ago had been hard, desperate, but tonight it was clear he was treating her as a fragile thing. He gently wrapped his arm around her shoulders, pulling her to him as he sat back and continued reading through Hank Dugger's notes. The room's lighting was soft, with only the sofa lamp and the fluorescent glow of the computer warding off the darkness. Her eyelids heavy, the sedative still in her system, Mia laid her head against his chest.

Sometime later, she awoke in her bedroom, tucked in under her goose down comforter. She vaguely remembered Eric rousing her and taking her to bed. The nightlight cast a blue, hazy glow. He lay next to her, his arm across her stomach as he slept. His breath played against her hair. She let herself take temporary comfort in his presence, feeling safe and protected in his embrace.

I don't take what happened between us lightly. I want you to know that.

Mia sighed softly in the darkness. But in the end,

what did that really mean? *He was drunk and hurting that night,* she reminded herself. *And when his work is done here, he's going to leave.*

No matter how adult and sophisticated she believed herself to be, she also understood the real truth.

She was setting herself up for a fall.

23

The indentation in the now-vacant pillow beside her was a reminder she hadn't slept alone. Shutting off the alarm clock's drone, Mia pushed the covers back and padded to the kitchen, following the scent of freshly brewed coffee. She found Eric there, already dressed in his clothing from the previous day.

"Good morning," she mumbled sleepily.

He didn't respond. Instead, in a quiet voice, he asked, "Why didn't you tell me about this?"

"Tell you about what?" Rubbing her eyes, she came closer. The Tuesday edition of the *Jacksonville Courier* lay open on the granite countertop. He must have retrieved it from her doorstep while she was still in bed. As her vision focused on the headline at the top of page two, she felt her drowsiness evaporate: Investigating VCU Agent Has Personal Ties to Jacksonville Killer.

"I didn't know about this." Mia scanned the article. Walt's byline was at the top, but the italicized line at the bottom of the column made her heart beat harder with anger. She was listed as a contributing journalist, along with a reporter from *The Washington Post.* "And I didn't contribute *anything.*"

Eric ran a hand through his hair, clearly caught off guard by the article.

"My name on there is some kind of editorial mix-up—"

"It's a profile piece," he pointed out. "I thought you had to be interviewed for something like that."

"Not always," Mia admitted. She forced herself to slow down and read the article more thoroughly. It made the connection between the recent murders in Jacksonville and the ones in Maryland three years earlier, something the local press had already reported. But this time, the bistate killings were simply a backdrop for a story on Special Agent Eric Macfarlane, the investigation's lead. It was all there in print—the details of his wife's gruesome death at the hands of the serial killer, his familial connections within the Department of Justice that had allowed him to remain on the case.

> *Two days after being abducted from the couple's Bethesda home, Ms. Macfarlane's mutilated corpse was discovered in a snow-edged ravine near the Rawlings Lake community. According to FBI and police reports, Agent Macfarlane identified his wife's remains at the scene...*

Mia's stomach clenched. Eric didn't need the spotlight on him right now, no more than it already was. Three women were dead in Jacksonville and a fourth missing.

He didn't need anyone recounting his tragic past or questioning his suitability to do his job.

"I have to go," he said, not looking at her. It was predawn, still dark outside. "I need to go by my place to shower and change."

She trailed him to her office. "Eric, I had nothing to do with this."

He didn't seem angry, just distracted. He took his wallet, shield and holstered gun from the bookshelf, clipping the latter items to the belt at his waist. "If you did, you were just doing your job. You're a reporter, Mia, and everything in the story is accurate—"

"Please believe me. I wouldn't blindside you."

With a sigh, he turned to face her. He studied her for several long moments.

"I believe you," he said finally. "I'll arrange for the sketch artist to meet you at the paper this morning. Be careful, all right?"

A few moments later, she locked the apartment door behind him. Mia stood in her pajamas, wondering if he really *did* believe her or if he'd just wanted a nonconfrontational escape. Reporting was her job. She'd confessed before that she had done research on him. Along with her name attached to the article as a contributor, it had to create some real doubt in his mind.

Despite his composed demeanor, she knew Eric was reeling. His painful history had been brought front and center, splashed onto the *Courier*'s pages. And while it was true the information was already in the public domain, rehashing it now seemed both unnecessary and a disruption to the investigation. Returning to the kitchen, she made a cup of coffee and took it back to the bedroom, anxious to dress for work.

Arriving at the newspaper an hour later, she headed to Grayson's office. He was behind his desk, his bifocals perched on top of his salt-and-pepper hair as he loaded his laptop into its travel case. Mia stepped inside and closed the door behind her.

"I need to talk to you."

"Sorry." He zipped the bag closed and placed its strap over his shoulder. "I've got to run."

"Where are you going?"

"To a publishers conference in Boston. I'm chairing a panel on social media. My flight leaves in three hours. I just came in to pick up a few things. I emailed you an assignment—a mugging near Jacksonville Landing early this morning. The fourth in two weeks."

The destination was a popular venue on the St. Johns, comparative to Miami's Bayside. Locals and tourists alike frequented it.

"This one got pretty violent," he continued. "The victim's been hospitalized at St. Vincent's. See if you can talk to him, and to the detective who caught the case at the JSO. Keith Berkman is serving as chief editor in my absence—"

"Why was my name on Walt's piece as a contributor?"

Grayson walked from behind the desk. "You mean the one on Macfarlane? It must've been a copy edit mistake. Walt's probably pissed. He hates sharing credit."

"Why didn't I know the profile was being written?"

"Why should you? It wasn't your story." He side-stepped her and opened the door.

"You shouldn't have run that piece."

"Walk me to my car, Mia?"

She accompanied him through the newsroom in silence. It was still early enough that only a handful of other staff members had shown up, most of them sitting at their desks and nursing their coffee as they checked email and phone messages. Grayson didn't speak until they had traveled through the lobby and into the parking garage. He stopped at his car to open the trunk and dropped the laptop case inside.

"Now, want to tell me why that story shouldn't have run?" He kept his voice low and controlled. "The last time I checked, we were in the news business. Eric Macfarlane *is* news. He's got a pretty, murdered wife and a daddy who's third man from the top at the DOJ. The family wants justice and Macfarlane's got the clout to defy FBI protocol. The story has high stakes, raw emotion and nepotism within the federal government. We'd be fools *not* to tell it."

"He wasn't even interviewed."

"It wasn't necessary. The reporter from the *Washington Post* who covered the Maryland murders provided more than enough background." He closed the trunk. "I've got to go."

"You put me as a contributor on the profile, didn't you?"

Grayson didn't answer. Instead he said, "I'll be back this weekend. We can get together for dinner and finish this discussion."

Mia shook her head, upset. "No."

"It's a *business* dinner," he clarified. His face had reddened somewhat, and he snatched his glasses from the top of his head and stuffed them into his shirt pocket. "We have some things to talk about—things I'd rather not discuss in the office. I'll send you an email with the time and location. Now I suggest you get yourself over to St. Vincent's. The guy's a tourist and he's leaving town as soon as he's discharged…maybe as early as today."

She stood there as Grayson started the car and pulled it from the parking space. The sedan's taillights glowed red in the still-shadowy confines of the concrete deck until it turned the corner and headed down to street level. Mia rubbed a hand over her eyes, hating the tension that had developed between them. Although she disliked his methods, she realized Grayson was right.

She'd lost her objectivity where Eric was concerned.

Like the other law enforcement surrounding the metal warehouse, Eric wore a Kevlar vest, a protective measure that was also nearly unbearable in the midday Florida heat. Gun drawn, he exchanged a glance with Cameron as the Sheriff's Office squad commander gave the silent signal to move. The deputies swarmed, several Bureau agents among them, traveling over dirt and gravel and keeping low to the ground. The warehouse's inhabitants scattered as officers burst through its front door.

"Sheriff's Office! Get down! Get down!"

Through the chaos, Eric zeroed in on an African-American male cowering behind a car that was up on blocks, something concealed in his grip. "You! Let me see your hands! Now!"

The man took off through a back door, sprinting outside and into a large maze of industrial-strength shelving that held an abundance of car parts and scrap metal. Eric ran after him through the narrow passages, yelling out orders to halt. The shelves were piled so thickly it was impossible to see anything but the path forward and the fleeing man's dreadlocks a dozen feet ahead of him. Rounding a corner, Eric felt an explosion of pain as something hit him square in the chest. He fell backward, his gun skittering out of reach.

A different male—this one Hispanic, with long, scraggly hair and a beard—stood over him, wielding a metal exhaust pipe. He raised it, preparing to swing it down like an ax. Writhing on the ground from the blow, Eric flinched, lifting his forearm in defense.

"Drop it!"

The pipe froze in midair. Detective Boyet's hulking form filled the space between the shelving, his gun aimed. "I got no problem blowing you away, asshole!"

With a vicious curse, the man dropped the pipe as the detective advanced.

"You all right, Macfarlane?" Boyet's eyes and gun remained steady on the perp.

"Yeah." Winded, Eric had trouble forcing the word out. He reclaimed his weapon and used the shelving to pull himself up. The air had been knocked from his lungs and his chest hurt when he drew in a breath, but he was pissed off more than anything. Perspiring, he squinted against the hot ball of sun. "The other one got away."

"No matter. This one's the big kahuna," Detective Scofield said, appearing from the other end of the maze with her gun trained.

"Remy Martinez," Boyet growled, spinning the man around and kicking his legs apart to be frisked. "You're under arrest."

Eric and Cameron stood with the two detectives outside the JSO interview room. The chop shop sting had netted eight arrests.

"Twelve cars a day are reported stolen in Jacksonville. Stoner Jesus in there has probably had his hands on half of 'em." Boyet nodded toward the glowering perp. Handcuffed, Martinez sat on the other side of the two-way observation mirror.

"Stoner Jesus?" Cameron asked.

"You know, long hair and beard. He also stinks of weed."

"This is the biggest operation we've busted to date." Scofield had gotten a recent haircut, her blond hair shortened into a gamine pixie-style that suited her athletic frame. "If the unsub's selling the stolen cars he uses in the abductions, Martinez might've done business with him. Word is he has two dozen hoods on the street, jacking for him regularly. The JSO infiltrated the ring with an undercover detective."

Eric had been notified that morning of the pending sting, and he'd wanted to take part. He turned at the sound of footsteps. A deputy approached with a sheet of paper.

"Here's a copy of the updated sketch you were waiting on, Agent Macfarlane. Hot off the printer." He handed it over.

Eric looked at the more detailed description Mia had

provided to the artist. She'd been right—she was able to give a bit more detail. The unsub's features were better defined, particularly his weak chin and arched brows. The eyes, however, remained as clear and cold as in the first sketch. Eric thought of Mia being at his mercy. "Let's get this redistributed."

"How's your chest?" Scofield asked.

He realized he'd been absently pressing his hand against the sore spot. "It's fine."

"Vests don't do much for blunt force trauma," Boyet pointed out. "You're lucky he didn't crack your sternum with that pipe."

He was luckier still the detective had shown up when he did, Eric thought. "Do you mind if I go in alone?"

"Be our guest. As far as we're concerned you can close the blinds and get some payback."

Eric left Cameron with the detectives. He went inside the interview room, shutting the door behind him. Despite the handcuffs, Martinez leaned back in his chair, his posture cocky and defiant. He fought the urge to kick the chair's legs out from under him.

"Have you bought stolen cars or parts from this man?" Eric asked, laying the sketch on the table in front of the arrestee.

Martinez's eyes barely flicked over the drawing. "No."

"You're sure? We've got you cold for auto theft and operating a chop shop, not to mention assaulting a federal officer."

"And me knowing this guy would change any of that?"

"If it leads to an arrest, it might get you a better prison to spend the next ten to twelve in. I hear Bakersfield is a hellhole, which is where you're probably headed without intervention."

Martinez peered up at Eric through stringy hair, then took a more thorough look at the sketch. "Yeah, I think I know this dude. He comes around once in a while. *Hijo de puta.* Snooty son of a bitch but he brings in nice parts. Real top-line stuff."

Eric felt a flare of hope. The chop shop was located south of Jacksonville, putting it in the right proximity. "Do you know his name?"

"No name and no contact information. Sorry." He grinned, revealing a gold front tooth. "That's how I do business, *Holmes.*"

A short time later, Eric stepped back into the hallway. The detectives were gone, but Cameron was still there, finishing up a call on his cell phone.

"What did you find out?" he asked once he'd closed the device and returned it to his pocket.

"The unsub's sold high-end auto parts to Martinez before. Most recently, pieces from an Audi a little over a week ago."

"Which would match the stolen car that went past the boat ramp the night Pauline Berger's remains were found." Cameron fell into step beside Eric as they headed to the building's lobby. "I'll make sure the team inventories any pieces that might've come from that car and dusts them for prints. But you saw the size of the operation—it could take a while. Anything else?"

"Unfortunately, no. It's a no-names, no-questions-asked kind of business." Although the interior of the car Mia had escaped in had been free of prints, there was still a possibility he'd left some on the Audi parts he had taken into the chop shop. Eric doubted he'd worn gloves to transport them. If he had a record and was in the system, it could be the break they needed. For Karen Diambro's sake, Eric hoped it came before another woman went missing. "We need to make it look like Martinez's shop is still operational and put surveillance on it in case our guy comes back."

Cameron grunted his agreement.

"Who was on the phone?"

"The M.E.'s office. The toxicology report's back on Ms. Gomez. Same mix of Rohypnol and GHB in her bloodstream."

Eric frowned as he pushed through the JSO lobby doors that led to the outside. Anna Lynn's funeral was tomorrow. He planned to attend, out of respect to the family and to supervise the other agents who would be watching the crowd of mourners to see if anyone matching the sketch was in attendance.

"Martinez hit you with a pipe?"

"It's nothing. He surprised me behind the warehouse."

Cameron shook his head but didn't give him a lecture. "You're sure you don't want to go by the E.R. and get an X-ray?"

"I don't need one."

He stopped, halting Eric, as well. The sultry, peaceful breeze coming in from the river was at odds with the blare of car horns and radios on the busy downtown street. "Are you going to bring up the article or should I?"

Eric had wondered how long it would take Cameron

to ask about it. They'd covered everything else—the previous afternoon's therapy session and Mia's adverse reaction to it, as well as her memory of driving on the interstate somewhere south of the city. But the profile piece that had run in the *Courier* hadn't been discussed, the proverbial elephant in the room. Although no one had mentioned it to him directly, he'd seen the glances at the Bureau offices that morning, and also at the JSO meeting held prior to the raid. If anyone had been unaware of his personal ties to the investigation, they knew about it now. Although Boyet was characteristically stone-faced, Eric had seen sympathy in Detective Scofield's expression. It bothered him.

"Mia Hale contributed to the article," Cameron noted.

"She says she didn't."

"Then why would her name be on it?"

Eric thought of Grayson Miller. It was possible he knew about their relationship and was trying to drive a wedge between them. He believed Mia hadn't known about the profile—her surprise had been too genuine. But what had happened still underscored the fact that she was a reporter, not to mention a victim. And he was sleeping with her.

He'd never veered off the course of professionalism before.

"You and Ms. Hale have gotten pretty close." Cameron peered out over the busy street. "I just think you should keep your guard up, that's all."

24

Richard Macfarlane sat behind his polished walnut desk on the sixth floor of the Robert F. Kennedy Department of Justice Building in Washington, D.C. He looked up from his paperwork at the intercom's buzz on his phone console.

"Sir?" The female administrative assistant's voice came through the speaker. "SAC Johnston with the Violent Crimes Unit is here to see you."

He masked a sigh. The visit wasn't entirely unexpected. Colin Johnston hadn't made an appointment, and he considered feigning a meeting or an important phone call. But instead he removed his reading glasses and briefly pinched the bridge of his nose. His policy was to address unpleasant matters head-on. "Send him in."

A moment later the door to his office opened. The SAC entered, his bearing as ramrod-straight and his physique as hard as it was twenty-two years ago when they had served together in the first Persian Gulf War.

"Colin," Richard said, standing. He reached over the desk to shake hands. "How are you?"

"Good."

"Maggie?"

Johnston had been divorced for years. Maggie was his daughter, who Richard recalled as being a happy, blond-haired child.

"She's married now, with a baby."

"Time flies." He shook his head in disbelief, then indicated a supple leather wing chair across from his desk. "Please, sit down."

Johnston cut directly to business, handing him a document. "It's from the *Jacksonville Courier*. It ran this morning. I thought you'd want to see it."

"I already have," Richard said impassively, returning his eyeglasses to his nose. He glanced briefly at the article before setting it aside. "I received it by email a little while ago. It's unfortunate. Eric can handle it, however."

"Can he?"

He gave him a hard stare. "He's my son."

Johnston was quiet for several moments, seeming to weigh his words. "You're my superior here, Richard. I understand that. We also go back a long way. But I don't agree with Agent Macfarlane's placement on the Jacksonville assignment. I've been against it from the beginning, as you know. This article isn't good press for the Bureau. Going against protocol to place an agent on a case who's clearly got a personal involvement—"

"He's got three women dead down there and one still missing. That's Eric's biggest problem. Not some damn newspaper exposé." Richard stood from behind the desk and went to look out the large window onto Pennsylvania Avenue. Outside, the afternoon sky was a cloudless, cerulean-blue, a perfect spring day. The white froth of cherry blossoms was visible on the trees lining the federal plaza below. Taking a calming breath, he released it. "He just needs a little more time, Colin. He deserves to be the one to bring the bastard down."

"Is that his ego speaking or yours?"

He turned, shoulders rigid. "What if it were your daughter? Maggie? You wouldn't want justice?"

"No one's saying there won't be justice. We have other, very qualified agents, you know." Johnston rose and walked to the window to stand beside him. "Have you thought about what this might be doing to him? I had a concern after Rebecca's murder that he might resign, or at least move to a different, less stressful unit. The VCU has one of the highest turnovers in the Bureau. We had an agent spiral out of control and commit suicide just last year—"

"And you think my son might be on a ledge somewhere?" Richard laughed, a choked sound.

Johnston frowned. "What I'm saying is the VCU is a pressure cooker. The unsub's already wreaked havoc in his life—"

"Which is why he's going to get the son of a bitch this time," Richard said, feeling a rise of emotion in his chest.

"Despite his connections within the department, Agent Macfarlane's always been his own man." Johnston paused. The overhead panel lighting reflected off his smoothly shaved head. "I've respected him for that. But he's put himself in a sensitive position. Not to mention, the unsub clearly enjoys proving his superiority—"

"Superiority? Hardly."

"Eric's special to him, because of who he is... *your son*. This maniac needs to feel powerful. Think about that."

Richard's mouth formed a grim line. He returned his gaze to the window. "He already murdered his wife. What else can he possibly do?"

Johnston lowered his voice. "Just don't make this about you, Richard. I know you hate to lose."

He bristled. He didn't just hate to lose, he *refused* to. "Until Eric does something to warrant otherwise, he stays."

When it was clear he had no other comment, Johnston turned to leave.

"Semper fidelis," he said in quiet defeat, then closed the door behind him.

Richard repeated the motto in a rough whisper even though the other man was already gone. Johnston was a good man. He'd been a good marine officer, under his command. Only to himself, in a moment of weakness, did he admit his advice was sage.

He looked around the large, well-appointed corner office afforded to him by rank. Family photos were lined up on the credenza behind his desk in tasteful, sterling-silver frames. Richard had been told on more than one occasion that he was too hard on his son. Eric had followed in his footsteps within the DOJ because he wanted to please him... and also because law enforcement and justice were in his blood.

Opening the credenza's drawer, he removed another framed image. Eric and Rebecca's wedding photo. He'd put it away after her death. Even now, he felt a sense of loss for what might have been. He had known about their pending separation, and that Eric hadn't wanted it. But he also knew it hadn't lessened the responsibility he felt over what had happened to her.

Emotions were a dangerous thing in the field. They could get you reprimanded, or they could get you killed. He swallowed hard.

Still, he stuck by his decision.

It was nearly dark by the time Mia returned to her apartment. Temporarily deactivating the security system long enough to come inside, she kicked off her shoes in the foyer, her feet tired. Late that afternoon, the JSO had announced the arrest of two suspects in the downtown muggings, requiring her to attend a news briefing and revise her article before filing it with the paper. She was glad, however, the men had been caught. The hospitalized tourist she'd spoken with was a mess. He'd suffered three broken ribs and a deep laceration on his scalp requiring sutures. All for his wallet and iPhone. He'd told Mia he hadn't resisted, but the men had beaten him anyway.

At least now they were off the streets. The suspects were being arraigned in the morning. Mia would be in the courtroom for their hearing.

She had ordered delivery at the paper while working, eliminating the need to rustle up dinner. Going into the bedroom in search of more comfortable clothing, she slowed at the sight of her rumpled, still unmade bed. Absently, she ran her fingers over Eric's pillow, wondering how the day had fared for him. She checked her voice mail from the nightstand phone. No messages. There had been none on her cell phone, either.

He owes you nothing, she reminded herself.

After changing into shorts and a T-shirt, she went into her office and sat on the sofa, picking up Hank Dugger's notepad as a distraction. She began leafing through the pages again, starting at the spot where she'd last left off. As she read, Mia was again struck by the notion that Hank seemed to have a fear of white space. Nearly every inch of paper was covered with commentary, with some of it running vertically up the paper's edges when he'd run out of room at the bottom. And while the comments were interesting—a few cynically humorous, even—she still saw no areas the investigation had overlooked.

She had just turned on the television for company when someone knocked at the door. Putting down the notepad, Mia went to the foyer, cautiously peering out through the peephole. Will stood on the landing. It wasn't who she had been hoping for.

"What's wrong?" she asked as soon as she opened the door and saw his face.

"It's Justin's mother." He came inside. "She took a bad fall."

It was upsetting news. She'd met Sonya Cho just a few months ago when she'd come to Jacksonville to visit during the winter. Despite being in her seventies, she had seemed agile and robust. "Is she going to be all right?"

"It's too early to tell. Her hip's broken, and apparently she was on the floor for some time before anyone found her. Pneumonia's set into her lungs. Justin's fallen to pieces—he's packing to go up there now. They're very close, you know. I've become quite fond of Sonya myself."

"Sit down," Mia told him. "I'll get you a glass of wine."

She rejoined him in the living room, bringing them both a glass of merlot.

"Justin's an only child, so he'll have to make arrangements for her care should she no longer be able to live alone. Heaven knows she won't leave Chicago—we've discussed it with her before. At the least, we'll have to stay up there until we can get a handle on the situation."

Of course Will was going with him, she realized. Justin needed him there. "Is there anything I can do while you're gone? Anything that needs looking after?"

"We're flying out tomorrow morning." Will added hesitantly, "I can change the plane reservations to *three* of us."

It took Mia a few heartbeats to understand what he meant. She shook her head. "Will, I can't go with you. I have work."

"You can take some time off. You've said yourself Miller isn't giving you the choice assignments, anyway." He worriedly shook his head. "I just don't feel right leaving you here, not with everything going on. I've seen the squad cars driving by on the street. I think having Justin and me downstairs gives you some security. Penney on the top floor is never home—you'll be here all by yourself."

"I'll be fine."

He looked at her doubtfully, then sighed. "You *do* seem to have Agent Macfarlane at your disposal."

Will paused as if she might have something to tell him. He'd probably seen Eric's car parked outside overnight. But the truth was, Mia wondered if Eric would ever be inside her home again. If the memory-retrieval sessions were truly over, it was possible whatever was between them had come to an end, too. The therapy had made it necessary for them to spend time together. With that gone—and with the recent tension over the profile on him in the *Courier*—there was a very real possibility this morning had been the culmination of what they'd shared.

"You all right, sweetheart?" Will asked.

"I'm just worried about Justin's mother, that's all."

He stayed long enough to finish his wine, and then Mia walked him to the door. Part of her wanted to cry on his shoulder. Will was her friend and confidant—he'd always been there for her. But he seemed overwhelmed by his current situation and she didn't want to add to his burden with her own problems.

She hugged him goodbye and wished him a safe trip.

Closing the door and reactivating the security system, she stared up at the vintage iron chandelier that hung in the foyer. Mia dimmed its glow but didn't turn it off— she'd been keeping the lights on all night lately. She and Will had gotten the fixture at a junk shop downtown, the store's owner claiming it had been salvaged from one of the famous old bordellos on Ward Street. Regardless, it reminded her of their friendship and better times.

Returning to the living room, Mia picked up their wineglasses. She took them into the kitchen and washed the crystal stems by hand. As she dried the second one, however, she felt an inexplicable tingle at her nape. Someone walking over her grave, as the old saying went. She turned. Her breath left her lungs, the wineglass shattering on the tile at her feet.

The Collector held a knife gripped in his fist. Mia let out a choked cry. She tried to scramble away, but her fear-clumsy legs crumpled beneath her.

And then he was gone.

It took several moments to realize it had only been a vision. Another *memory flash* like outside the foster care home that day. Still, she couldn't stop the frantic thudding of her heart. Her shin was bleeding—she'd cut herself on the broken glass.

Picking herself up from the floor, tears of frustration welled in her eyes. But she wouldn't call Eric. Her pride and independence wouldn't allow her to.

She had to handle this alone.

25

Pulling to a stop under the columned portico, Mia got out of the Volvo and handed the valet her keys. She had dressed for the five-star resort on Ponte Vedra Beach in an ice-blue silk sheath dress and heeled silver sandals. It was Saturday and she'd received an email from Grayson that morning, instructing her to meet him at the hotel's main restaurant at 8:00 p.m.

Eric, however, had been maintaining his distance. He'd called once to check on her but had kept their conversation brief and impersonal. Mia hadn't pushed.

Entering the upscale lobby with its marble floors and tiered chandeliers, she tried not to dwell on it. She yearned to see him, but she had learned a long time ago one couldn't force something to happen simply by obsessing over it hard enough. *He's busy with the investigation,* she reminded herself.

Still, with each passing day her heart had grown a little heavier.

At the restaurant, she gave Grayson's name and the hostess escorted her inside. Like the resort, the dining room was posh, with starched linen tablecloths and glowing centerpiece candles. The tinkling sound of a piano came from the adjoining bar.

Mia wasn't certain what to expect—she'd had meals with Grayson before. But the majority of those were eaten with chopsticks from take-out cartons, or accompanied by draft beer in a paneled barroom overlooking the EverBank Field stadium where the Jacksonville Jaguars played. Those times had been comfortable, enjoyable. The atmosphere here seemed off for what he had classified as a *business* dinner.

He sat at a table beside a long window that provided a dramatic view of the darkened ocean, and he stood as Mia and the hostess approached. Pulling out a chair for her, she noticed he wobbled a bit before reclaiming his own seat. He indicated the empty crystal tumbler in front of him.

"Have the waiter bring another vodka tonic."

"And you, ma'am?" the hostess asked.

"Pinot grigio."

He waited until they were alone. "You look great, kiddo."

She toyed with the small clutch purse in her lap before placing it on an empty chair at the table. "I didn't have much choice. This is hardly a blue jeans, shrimp-in-the-shell kind of place."

"I've been traveling all week for the damn newspaper," he grumbled. "Let them pick up the tab."

Mia was aware of the faint slur to his words. She wondered how many drinks he'd had before she arrived.

Grayson appeared tired and tense, the lines deeper on his face than she remembered.

"Are you all right?" she asked quietly.

Before he could answer, they were interrupted by the arrival of the waiter, who had their drink order and gave a rundown on the evening's specialties. Once he was gone, Grayson asked, "Now where did we leave off on Tuesday? Right...you were reaming me out for that piece on Macfarlane."

"I'm sorry for that," she admitted. She didn't want to argue again, especially not here. Besides, she'd thought about it and realized he was right. "I was surprised by the profile, that's all. Sometimes I forget you're my boss, Grayson. I was out of line to question you and I should've left my personal feelings out of it."

"Everything in the article *was* accurate," he pointed out.

"With the exception of my being a contributor."

"Like I said, mistakes happen. Damn copy editors." His blasé comment suggested again it hadn't been an error. She studied him as he took another sip from his drink.

"So what's this about? You said you wanted to talk to me away from the office."

"Can't we just enjoy ourselves for a little while?"

Mia held his gaze until he spoke.

"The *Courier*'s having issues," he said finally. "Our circulation's declining and we're losing subscribers."

None of this was new information in the digital age. Most newspapers and magazines were experiencing similar difficulties as readers moved to other sources—

television and the internet especially—to get their news. Still, Mia had thought a recent paring down of staff, combined with an increased emphasis on ad revenue from the paper's online edition and social networking initiatives, had evened things out.

"How bad is it?"

"We may have another round of layoffs."

She felt butterflies in her stomach, wondering if that was why he'd brought her here. "Does that include me?"

"I hope not," he said carefully. "But that's up to you."

The waiter returned to their table. Neither of them had glanced at the menu yet.

"Could we have a little more time?" she asked.

With a small bow, the man retreated. Mia returned her attention to Grayson. "I don't understand."

He took another long sip from his drink, ice cubes clinking against the crystal. "You're a good reporter but you're still young and learning, Mia. You have the potential to be great—I've always believed that. I want to continue investing in you."

"But something's changed?"

"*You've* changed." He raised his shoulders in a shrug. "Maybe it's the abduction. I can't imagine what it must be like to deal with something like that—the lost hours, realizing how close you came to… Sometimes I have a hard time dealing with it myself. I care about you, Mia."

He reached across the table and took her hand.

"I care about you, too, Grayson," she said, feeling a little uncomfortable. After a moment, she gently slid her fingers from his. "You *know* that. But I still don't see what you're driving at."

He frowned as he looked into her eyes. "I thought you had the fire in your gut. That you *wanted* to be a journalist."

"And I don't now?"

"Goddamned if I know," he muttered. "Lately you've been distracted, missing time from work, running around like some smitten kitten after Macfarlane. It's not who you are."

Mia felt her face grow hot.

"That's not fair," she argued. "You're the one who told me to take a few days off, remember? And I've been asking for my previous assignment back. You keep refusing me, telling me I'm not ready for it—"

"Then *prove* to me you are. Prove it and I'll take Walt off the whole thing. You just said yourself you haven't been objective." Turning, he caught the passing maître d' and asked for another drink.

"Don't you think you've had enough?"

"I've been drinking since you were in diapers, Mia. Don't monitor my alcohol intake," he snapped. The reprimand stung. "I want to do a piece on the memory-retrieval therapy you've been undergoing at the Naval Air Station. You've got information, details, no other media outlet has access to. Not to mention the whole sci-fi aspect—"

"I can't—"

"You can. I've got one of my reporters smack-dab in the middle of the year's biggest story and you're as tight-lipped as a priest. I want details on what's been going on—"

"We've discussed this." She strove to keep her voice calm. "I agreed to confidentiality. That's off-limits."

"Like Eric Macfarlane? The paper's not supposed to cover *him,* either." His eyes narrowed inquisitively. "What is it, Mia? Hero worship? You're frightened and vulnerable and he has a badge and a gun? That gets you off?"

She'd been twisting the linen napkin in her lap, but she stood and dropped it on the seat. Her insides knotted with irritation, she picked up her purse. "If I'm being laid off, I'll get by. Good night, Grayson."

"Mia, sit down. Mia!"

She heard him calling her name, but she kept walking as quickly as she could in the suddenly ridiculous evening sandals. Anger and humiliation tightened her lungs. Was he *threatening* her? Telling her she had to divulge confidential details about the therapy in order to keep her job? Maybe he just wanted her to prove that her allegiance to him outweighed whatever she'd had with Eric. A bellhop held the door for her in the hotel lobby. She went outside, noticing there were several people waiting in line for the valet service to retrieve their cars.

She needed time to collect herself. Mia bypassed the line and headed toward the beach. Stopping at the boardwalk, she bent to undo the straps of her shoes. Leaving them on a concrete ledge, she walked barefoot down the short flight of stairs and onto the resort's pristine white sand. Moving to the shoreline, she closed her eyes against the warm, briny breeze and reminded herself to breathe.

She'd never known Grayson to behave like this.

"Mia." A minute later, she turned at the sound of her name. He was walking toward her, his dress shoes sinking into the sand.

"Christ," he said when he reached her, shaking his head. "That wasn't me in there."

"I don't know what to say. If you're that unhappy with my work…"

"No." Grayson clasped her upper arms. His face appeared pale in the moonlight. "You've been through hell and I've been acting like a total shit tonight. Taking my problems out on you. I'm sorry."

He let go of her and briefly laced his fingers behind his neck, cursing under his breath. "I've been in the newspaper business for twenty-six years. It's my life. It's all I've got and things are getting harder every day. It's making me insane…"

He paused, swallowing hard as he looked at her. "I'm also in love with you."

Her lips parted slightly, her throat going dry.

"I've *been* in love with you for a long time," he said hoarsely. "I just never had the guts to tell you. And then I almost lost you."

Mia stared at him, her heart beating hard. Grayson was eighteen years her senior, but she had never thought of him as old. He had always been just *Grayson* to her. He was her friend, her mentor, even a father figure. She'd known he was fond of her. But Will had been right; she should've taken his feelings for her more seriously.

"After the abduction, I realized I had to do something. I had to put my stake in the ground. And then this FBI agent arrives…" Inebriated, sliding his hands into his pockets, he stumbled a little in the sand as he looked out at the crashing waves. "I see the way you look at Macfarlane. The way you talk about him and defend him. *I know you,* Mia. You've never acted like that about any man, as far as I can recall."

He shrugged weakly. "The green-eyed monster rears his head. *He* was the one talking to you in there."

"Grayson…" She shook her head as she struggled with what to say. "You know I would never want to hurt you…"

He laughed, his eyes sad. "To quote Bob Marley, 'Everybody's going to hurt you. You've just got to find the ones worth suffering for.' I already know you don't feel the same way about me."

Vacationers strolled in front of them, including a man and a woman, arm in arm. They stopped to kiss, the waves' foam floating around their bare ankles. Mia looked away, the act of passion playing out in front of them making their conversation even more awkward.

Grayson continued. "The Macfarlanes are loaded, you know. Old money. It beats the hell out of me why any of them went into public service. Eric Macfarlane should be sailing around on a yacht somewhere, not down here, watching autopsies on dead women. Or stealing you."

"Whatever was between us…I don't think it's going to work out," she confessed softly.

Grayson considered her statement. "Then he's a damn fool."

"You shouldn't be driving. Can I give you a ride home?"

"I'll call a cab or get a room. I might not be done

drinking yet." He took a deep breath and let it out with a resigned sigh. "But now you know. Hopefully I won't remember the ass I made of myself tonight."

"Grayson, please don't go."

She fell silent, watching as he lifted a hand to silence her and then walked carefully away, trying not to stagger so that he might maintain some last shred of dignity. He headed back up the stairs to the hotel.

Like the sand she stood on, the world seemed to be shifting under her feet. Her heart hurt for Grayson, for his unrequited love and the crack in their relationship that could probably never be fully repaired. She wondered again if she would be on the chopping block if and when more staff was let go by the paper. Without him in her corner—if she'd lost his friendship—it was possible.

None of this was fair.

Looking up at the black sky, she thought about the past few weeks of her life. It all seemed so surreal— escaping a serial killer, then getting involved with the federal agent assigned to hunt him down. She held her purse, her phone inside it. More than anything, she craved the sound of Eric's voice. She'd become addicted to it, she realized. But she didn't call. Instead, she sat on one of the resort's chaises lined up on the beach. Mia dug her toes into the cool sand, feeling tired and contemplative, unsure.

Night had fallen over the San Marco neighborhood like a heavy blanket.

Allan crouched inside an older model Mercedes, well hidden by the heavy, drooping branches of a weeping

willow on a nearby property. He had been there for over
two hours. In fact, he had watched her leave earlier that
night. From where he sat, she'd looked so lovely in her
new hairstyle and pale blue dress. But it had been too
early in the evening then, too many cars and passersby.

Now, however, traffic had begun to die down on the
residential street.

He fidgeted, gathering his courage. For weeks, he'd
been telling himself to forget her. Trying again would
be too dangerous. But his desire for her had only gotten
stronger and the brunette divorcée was starting to lose
her appeal. She'd become an obsession to him.

If he were really going to do this, now was the time.

His heart began to beat a little harder.

Exiting the Mercedes, he closed its door with a soft
snick. He stole across a lush lawn, then climbed through
a line of shrubs until he stood near the building's Tuscan-
style courtyard, still out of reach of the streetlight. *So
close.* He'd been watching the place for a while now and
he knew when no one in the three-level structure was
home. The men who lived in the ground-floor unit had
departed with suitcases days ago.

He had thought about waiting for her in the darkened
recesses of the courtyard, but it was too open and there
were too many paths for escape. Allan needed her closed
off and cornered. He looked upward to her apartment.
She would hurry cautiously across the patio from her
car, but up there at her door, she would think she was
home free. Safe. He could overpower her. It would be
a long way to get her to the Mercedes, but if she were
unconscious he could carry her down, leave her behind

the gardenia bushes and bring the car over to pick her up. He would only have to time it against the squad car that conducted a drive-by on the half hour. Besides, she probably only weighed a hundred and ten sopping wet. He'd moved televisions that were heavier.

The deputies had gone past just a few minutes ago. Waiting for the residential street to be devoid of cars, he slunk up the staircase on the building's right side, keeping against the stucco wall so that he remained in shadow. Up here, there would be no escape for *him*, either, he realized. His plan would have to play out, no matter what. Throat dry, he glanced at the wedge of moon above him.

It had already occurred to him she might not come home alone. He had seen her in the company of Eric Macfarlane before. Which was why Allan had brought his gun as a precaution.

The level of danger was both nerve-racking and exhilarating.

On the landing, he unscrewed the bulb inside the antique bronze sconce next to her door. The light, hot against his fingers, sputtered out, leaving him in darkness. To the left of the apartment, there was a space underneath the stairs that rose to the building's top level. It presented the perfect crevice in which to hide. He would wait for her to insert her keys into the door and then he would advance, let her glimpse his face before her world went black. His memory conjured up an image of Mia as a skinny, forlorn child, her large brown eyes fearful as she backed away from him on the street. He wanted to see that same fear in her eyes tonight. He believed in closing the loop. It was an anomaly that she'd escaped him twice now.

It wouldn't happen a third time.

As he waited for her, he allowed his fantasy to play out in his mind. His big hand over her mouth to keep her from screaming, the sharp jab of the needle and the feel of her body as it sagged in his arms. Allan realized he had half an erection at the prospect of total power. The sickly sweet scent of gardenias in the courtyard wafted up to him.

Some time later, headlights illuminated the street in front of the building. Then the sound of a car slowing and pulling into the driveway below. Quickly, he stepped farther back into the stone-black cove and rubbed his latex-clad fingers together in anticipation.

His nerves zinged. Only one car door slammed. Good. She was alone. It was all falling into place. He took the filled syringe from his pocket and removed the safety tip, his pulse pounding in his ears.

Come to me, little girl. You won't cheat your destiny again.

26

Allan felt as tense as a coiled spring, his muscles quivering. The hair on his forearms prickled as her shadow passed by him on the darkened landing. She held a box, its white cardboard luminescent in the thin slant of moonlight.

She wore flats, not heels.

Something was wrong.

Too tall, the head capped by a mass of curly brown hair. Not the sleek bob he'd expected. His heart stopped. *It wasn't her.*

"Mia?" the woman called as she knocked on the door.

He made out the words printed on the box. Slice of Life. He recognized the name—that hippie eatery in San Marco Square. It was the third-floor tenant who drove the red Prius and never came home before midnight. What was she doing here now? She tilted left and peered between the window blinds into the lit apartment, then turned. Allan pressed himself against the stair's underbelly, trying to soak into the blackness. *Go away.* Her gaze fell to the ground. His shoes. Visible. She dropped the box, a frightened squeak emitting from her mouth. Then she was stumbling, making a mad dash for the stairs, starting to scream louder.

Panicked, Allan lunged after her. He had to shut her up before lights started snapping on all over the neighborhood. His gun was equipped with a silencer he'd bought from a spy store online, but it was tucked into the back waistband of his pants. The needle was faster, already poised. He jabbed it into her neck. But before he could push the plunger, she broke away. He made a final grab for her, snarling, catching her wrist and whipping her around at the top of the steps. Off balance, she fell headfirst, plummeting down the staircase, her body gaining momentum and tumbling over itself in a sickening series of thuds. Cursing, Allan hurried down the stairs. She lay at the bottom. Her left arm was twisted at an awkward angle, undoubtedly broken. Her nose was broken and bleeding, too. Blood from her badly scraped leg leaked onto the concrete.

He hadn't accounted for this.

Unable to help himself, he stopped to gawk at the damage. Her eyes slowly fluttered open. To his mild surprise, she was still alive. Her mouth worked soundlessly until a moaning keen came from her throat. Allan knelt and put his hand over her mouth, silencing her. The gardenias hid them from street view.

He couldn't take this one—she was too damaged. Nor was she who he'd come for. Leaning over her, he peered into her dazed eyes. He let go of her mouth and cradled her face between his palms, his thumbs hooking into the soft skin under her jaw.

"Shh."

"P-please," she begged, voice garbled. Blood from her nose dripped down her face, making a mess. "Don't kill me!"

She *knew* him. Even with the horn-rimmed glasses he had taken to wearing instead of his contacts. The damned sketches. He wondered again about the unnamed witness the news had reported.

She began to cry out for help.

This woman had ruined everything. Even if he hid the body, the blood staining the courtyard would attract attention. And a neighbor could have heard her and be on the way now. His plan, his daring—all of it wasted. She wasn't even supposed to be here. Anger surged inside him as she wailed again.

"Shut up!"

With a forceful grunt, he slammed the back of her skull onto the concrete and felt it bounce. She fell silent. He did it again—three, four times—until he was breathing heavily with exertion. Blood bloomed slowly behind the woman's head, soaking into the thick, brown curls. The light in her eyes had faded, and her jaw had gone slack. He had to get out of here. Rising, he wiped a shaking hand over his mouth and dove back through the shrubbery toward the car.

Mia turned into the driveway, her mind still on the disastrous dinner with Grayson.

She had driven home barefoot, her sandals on the passenger seat next to her clutch bag. Even now, the ocean's scent lingered in her hair and on her skin. Granules of sand still clung to her calves and feet, between her toes. She'd lingered on the beach, lost in her thoughts, until the trail of passersby had begun to thin and it no longer seemed safe to remain alone.

She got out of the car and pressed the key fob to lock it, then walked toward the courtyard. Penney Niemen's Toyota Prius sat in the first parking spot. At least she wasn't the only one in the building tonight. Still, Mia increased the pace of her steps, aware of the shadows and the fact that Will and Justin were out of town.

As she turned past the line of gardenias at the courtyard's entrance, she slowed. Something lay in shadow at the base of the stairs.

Penney?

She dropped her shoes and purse. Tiny pinpricks of fear traveled over her as she rushed forward. Penney's body was sprawled out, one foot still on the bottom step, her curly brown hair spread out like a halo on the concrete.

"Oh, God! Penney!"

She reached her, falling to her knees. Penney gazed blankly upward. The blood pooling around her head glistened darkly in the streetlight's filmy glow. Mia let out a strangled cry, aware she was kneeling in wet crimson. Blood was everywhere—Penney's face, her legs. Her surroundings spun as she was hurtled back to a cinderblock room and another dead woman staring up at her.

"Someone help me! Please!" Her plea echoed off the courtyard walls.

Despite the tremors racking her body, Mia felt for a pulse at Penney's neck. Nothing. She recognized the small particles and glimmering globs stuck in her beautiful hair. Skull fragments and bits of brain matter—she'd seen it before in crime scene photos of a convenience store clerk shot at point-blank range. She gagged reflexively, the fact that she'd had nothing to eat or drink the only thing stopping her from vomiting.

Too shaken to stand, Mia crawled to her purse. Somehow, she managed to close her trembling fingers around her cell phone and dial 9-1-1.

"Operator. What's your emergency?"

Her voice sounded unfamiliar to her own ears. "I'm at 1211 Alhambra Avenue. Please hurry! There's been an accident, a woman's dead!"

An accident. Even as she said it, she felt a wave of certainty that this was more than a freak fall down the stairs. She shivered uncontrollably. How long ago? The body, the blood—they were still warm.

"You're certain the person is deceased?" the female operator asked. "Have you attempted CPR?"

She looked back at Penney. Tears blurred her vision.

"She's dead. There's no pulse. Her head's..." Mia couldn't finish the statement. The words caught in her throat. "She's dead."

27

"Thanks for letting me know."

Downbeat, Eric ended the call with the Bureau's fingerprint specialist. Steering the car, he closed his cell phone. Parts from the stolen Audi recovered earlier that week had turned up prints, but none was a match in the FBI's biometric database other than those of the chop shop operators. Which meant that The Collector—if his prints were among those on the parts—had no prior arrest record, eliminating any chance of identifying him that way.

He traveled over the Main Street Bridge, its neon-blue lights and the glittering nighttime cityscape reflecting onto the dark waters below. Eric had been south of Jacksonville looking into a lead in the rural Bayard community. It hadn't panned out. On his return into the city, he had driven past San Marco. For several minutes, he'd considered turning into Mia's neighborhood, but he had been deliberately putting some space between them.

You and Ms. Hale have gotten pretty close.

Cameron's observation echoed in his head. He had

been a widower for nearly three years. It was natural to desire physical companionship. But Mia was more to him than that, and that was what was dangerous. Above all else, he was here seeking a killer. A woman, very possibly still alive, was missing. His rational self told him he couldn't afford distractions or further emotional entanglement in the investigation.

Eric sighed. He shouldn't have kissed Mia, shouldn't have slept with her. But that didn't stop him from wanting her right now.

Seeking a diversion from his thoughts, he used his cell to call Cameron, wanting to update him on the dead end with the prints. He got his voice mail, however. Eric was in the midst of leaving a message when another call beeped through. The screen read JSO Dispatch. He switched over and answered. A male operator's voice reached him through the airwaves.

"Detective Boyet asked me to alert you, Agent. An emergency call came through about ten minutes ago. The location is a residence at 1211 Alhambra Avenue."

At the address, Eric's blood ran cold. San Marco was only a few miles back but he was still on the bridge, headed the opposite way. "What was the nature of the call?"

"Report of a dead body. First responders are on the scene."

His heart dropped.

"Male or female?"

"Sorry, Agent. That's all I know."

Please don't let it be her. Traffic on the four-lane bridge traveled in two directions. He had to get back there. Disconnecting the call, Eric made a sharp U-turn, his tires screeching as he left the northbound lane and cut across the median into traffic. Cars heading south swerved and honked. Panic bearing down on him, he punched the car's accelerator to the floorboard, zigzagging between vehicles. He tried calling Mia's cell phone. No answer.

He said a fervent prayer to a God he hadn't talked to in years.

Eric's mouth had gone dry. He passed a hand over his eyes and told himself it could be someone else—others lived there. But Mia was the one who'd recently escaped a killer. She was the one with a possible connection to him that went back to her childhood. He berated himself for not trying harder to set up some kind of formal protection, not pushing something through despite Mia's resistance and the refusal from the local Bureau head.

He couldn't lose her like this, too.

As he drove, Eric forced himself to think past the choking fear. The unsub would have taken her, wouldn't he? He would have wanted time alone with her. Killing her at the scene wasn't his M.O.

Unless something had gone horribly wrong.

The car careened through traffic as it sped through San Marco Square.

Reaching the residential street, the sight in front of him gutted his insides. Lights from a half-dozen squad cars and an ambulance stained the black sky. Eric stopped his sedan in front of the building and got out, leaving the door open. Pushing through a gaggle of neighbors being contained at the edge of the scene, he flashed his shield at the deputies in charge.

More officers were milling about in the driveway, but the courtyard had been cordoned off with crime scene tape. A body lay on the ground, blocked almost entirely from view by a man and woman. Although they weren't facing him, he could tell it was Boyet and Scofield.

Eric moved forward, his knees weak. He could see only the body's lower limbs. Shapely calves and slender, delicate ankles, legs splayed out on the concrete. Female. *God, no.* He couldn't breathe. Boyet turned and began walking toward him, his broad shoulders and girth further obstructing his line of sight. "Macfarlane—"

Eric kept going, shrugging free of the man's hold on his shoulder.

"It's not her," the detective called.

He stared at the dead woman, at the mass of curly, blood-soaked hair and pale skin. Eric felt dizzy with relief. He briefly closed his eyes, trying to pull himself together.

"Who is she?" he managed to ask, voice hoarse.

"Third-floor tenant. Her name's Penney Niemen." Scofield was dressed casually, in jeans and a Florida State University T-shirt. She wore her shield on a chain around her neck. "At first glance it looks like a fall down the stairs. Skull's split open, pretty badly, based on the blood and brain matter. We're waiting on the M.E. to roll her to get a better look."

"Where's Mia?"

"She's here—she made the 9-1-1 call. She came home tonight and found her." Boyet indicated the corpse. "Between this and Ms. Hale's abduction, I'm thinking this isn't the luckiest building to live in."

He looked around the confusion, searching for her. His gaze fell on a squad car at the far end of the property. It was parked on the opposite side of the driveway under the gnarled limbs of the live oak. The light bar on the vehicle's roof was flashing, its rear door open. A shadowed form was in the backseat. Eric worked his way through the horde of deputies as a van from the medical examiner's office rolled to a stop in front of the building.

Seeing him, Mia climbed out and ran barefoot into his arms with a sob. Her blue cocktail dress was stained with blood. Eric held her, letting her cry against his chest. The feel of her trembling against him was nearly his undoing.

"It's okay," he whispered, stroking her hair.

"Penney's dead. I—I came home and she was lying there…" Her voice was muffled. "This was my fault. He was here for me."

He hushed her, holding her more tightly. The moss-draped tree branches shielded them somewhat, but at the moment he didn't care if they were witnessed. Nothing mattered except that she was alive.

"Agent Macfarlane? We've got something." A forensics tech motioned Eric to an ornamental concrete planter that ran parallel to the base of the stairs. Walking over, he peered into the dense foliage. A hypodermic syringe sat in the dirt.

"Get a photo of that and bag it," he instructed. It appeared the syringe had been lost in some kind of struggle on the upper level, dropping into the plants below.

"The barrel's still full," the tech noted. "He never got a chance to inject her."

Boyet came down the staircase, one latex-gloved hand on its wrought-iron railing. "Ms. Niemen must've stopped on the second-floor landing to deliver a package to Ms. Hale. It's still up there along with her purse—a box from that vegetarian place in San Marco Square."

"The deceased was the head chef," Eric said, recounting what Mia had told him. He'd already been upstairs once to survey the scene. One of Penney Niemen's shoes had also been left on the top step. "She'd probably just gotten off work for the night."

Boyet scratched his cheek. "There's an area under the stairs that would make a perfect hiding place. I bet the perp was waiting up there."

Eric still felt shaken. If the upstairs tenant hadn't arrived first, Mia would be dead or vanished, instead of upstairs in her apartment with Detective Scofield. He looked to the victim, although she had since been placed inside a body bag. The concrete was still a mess, however. Darkened blood and gore remained.

"You think she was pushed, or she fell trying to get away?" Boyet asked. He'd been elsewhere when Eric had spoken with the M.E. called out to the scene.

"Either way, the examiner believes the damage to the skull wasn't caused by the fall alone," he said. The skull had been shattered, the damage diffuse and indicating more than one strike. "The blood spatter analyst concurs with the assessment."

Boyet frowned. "Where's Agent Vartran?"

"I've been in touch with him by phone. His wife's

pregnant, they had a Lamaze class tonight. I told him I'd cover things here."

Boyet left to give instructions to the deputies, who were still keeping out the neighbors as well as the news teams now at the scene. As Eric again scanned the crowd of bystanders looking for a match to their sketch, he glimpsed Walt Rudner's jowly face. He was conversing with one of the deputies, trying to glean details. The task force hadn't yet released the dead woman's identity, and Eric wondered if Rudner was more interested in getting the story or finding out if his coworker was the one inside the body bag. Knowing what he did about the reporter, he suspected he knew which one.

Turning, he carefully sidestepped the blood at the stairs' bottom and went up to Mia's apartment. Lights glowed from its interior, the door wide-open.

He entered, his dress shoes sounding on the wood foyer that opened into the living area. Detective Scofield stood in the room with her arms crossed over her chest. She appeared out of place in Mia's feminine surroundings.

"Ms. Hale is down the hall, speaking with the building's owner by phone. He's in Chicago on a family emergency," she said. "He's willing to fly back into town if needed."

Eric nodded. "How's she doing?"

"She's a mess, understandably. First, this psycho kidnaps her and she manages to escape him, then she finds out he came back looking for her tonight and killed one of her friends instead."

"I'm going to talk to her," Eric said.

"I'll go back down, then."

He stopped in the bedroom doorway. Mia had changed clothes. The bloodied, ruined cocktail dress lay crumpled at the foot of the bed. She now wore cropped jeans and a soft, scoop-necked summer sweater. When she realized his presence, Mia brought the call to a close.

"Agent Macfarlane's here, Will," she murmured. "I have to go."

She disconnected the phone, her eyes red. "Is she still down there?"

"The M.E.'s office will be moving her soon." He took a step closer, touching her. "Can you pack a bag? You can't stay here tonight."

She didn't argue. Eric held her gaze. "This changes everything, Mia. He's made a direct attempt to kidnap you again. You need to be under protection."

"So it definitely wasn't an accident."

"It's unlikely, based on the damage to the skull. We also found a syringe in the courtyard."

Anguish flashed on her features. The scene below was gruesome, and he could only imagine her stumbling over the body by surprise. Being alone with it while she waited for help to arrive. It occurred to him she hadn't called him, hadn't sought out his help.

"Take me to a hotel, all right? I don't want to be any trouble to you—"

"Mia," he whispered. "I'm sorry I've been out of touch."

She looked up at him. Her pretty features were without accusation. "You don't trust me anymore. After the profile piece, I don't blame you."

Unable to help himself, Eric touched her cheek. His

chest hurt as he realized how close he'd come to losing her. Keeping his distance seemed unimportant now.

"I trust you," he murmured.

Tears built again in her eyes.

"I can't leave…not until they take Penney away." She shook her head, her voice breaking. "I can't see her like that again, knowing I caused this."

28

He didn't take her to a hotel. Eric held the strap of Mia's overnight bag on one shoulder as he unlocked the bungalow door. She had said little on the drive over, instead sitting mostly in stunned silence. As they entered, he turned on the lamps in the living area, filling it with pale light. He watched Mia closely. She wandered the room, her arms crossed against her chest as if warding off some coldness around her.

"You're still in shock." He slid the bag to the floor. Remembering the half-empty bottle of Scotch, he went into the kitchen and poured a glass. Returning, he pressed it into her hands. "Drink this."

Obediently, she took a sip. Eric led her to the couch across from the curtained windows. Then removing his holstered gun, he sat next to her. She appeared sad and distressed.

"Penney was from West Virginia," she finally said in a subdued voice, speaking after several long moments. "A small coal mining town that's pretty much died out. Her dream was to live in Florida near the beach."

"Were you close?"

She shook her head. "Not really. She worked nights and weekends. Restaurant hours. We talked in the driveway sometimes—I was getting home from work when she was leaving. I'm not even sure why she was home tonight. Saturdays are usually late shifts for her. I've been keeping my lights on in the apartment lately, but why didn't she notice my car wasn't outside?"

Lost in thought, she stared into her nearly empty glass, head bowed.

"Do you want something to eat? We can call for delivery."

"No, thanks."

"Mia." Leaning closer, he tucked the shimmering curtain of her dark hair behind one ear to better see her face. "It's going to be okay."

"I don't even know how to reach her family. Someone needs to—"

"We're notifying next of kin. It's being handled."

She looked at him, her dark eyes searching his. "Why would he come after me again now? It's been three weeks. He's taken two other women—"

"Two other women who *looked* like you," he pointed out somberly. "The unsub had a specific cycle in Maryland. A blonde, a redhead, a brunette, then a blonde again. I believe he was starting a similar pattern here until you escaped him. Since then, he's been fixated on petite, dark-haired women. But I think he realized no one else could satisfy him."

She closed her eyes at his statement. Eric knew she didn't want to hear it, but he had to make her understand.

"It was a real risk coming after you again. You were bound to be more cautious after already being abducted once, not to mention the increased police presence in your neighborhood. But I think ever since he discovered you were the little girl in foster care who saw him taking another child, he's wanted you."

"For his collection?" Her voice was strained.

Eric hesitated. "I think he recognized you from the beginning—your name, your photo with the news column on Fridays. You became a *crime reporter,* Mia. This guy's an egomaniac. He probably thinks you chose your career because of what you witnessed all those years ago. He believes he made you into who you are today."

"Maybe he did," she said tensely. "Joy Rourke's abduction has been locked in my subconscious all these years. So has he, apparently. What if all my life, everything's been heading into a confrontation with this monster?"

"I won't let that happen. I'm going to make sure you're protected from here on out. Will you be able to sleep?"

She shrugged. "I don't know. I'll try."

"I can pour you another Scotch if you think it'll help."

Mia didn't respond to his offer. Instead, her gaze remained questioning. "The night I came here and you'd been drinking...you never told me what had happened."

The night they'd made love, if one could call it that. Eric clasped the back of his neck, thinking of how out of control he'd been.

"I received the audio of Rebecca's murder that night. It was mailed to the Bureau office here in Jacksonville," he said quietly. He wanted honesty between them. Eric swallowed at the admission, recalling how the recording had cut him to the bone. "He'd never sent it until now. He kept it for nearly three years, waiting for the right time to wound me again."

As she listened, Mia laid her fingers on his forearm.

"Anna Lynn Gomez's body had been found that morning and I'd gone to break the news to the family. It was a lot to handle in one day. Getting the recording caught me off guard." He shook his head in recollection. "Hearing Rebecca's voice again, begging me to help her…it brought everything back."

"Are you still in love with her?" she asked, her eyes pained.

He had been, deeply, at the time of her murder. His heart had since been able to slowly let go of her, but not the guilt.

"I still feel responsible," he said. "I always will."

"Eric, I'm so sorry."

After all that had happened to her, *she* was trying to comfort him. Even if he'd had no way of knowing The Collector's plan to take Rebecca, Eric sure as hell should have been better prepared for what had happened tonight. Things were going to change regarding her safety. Mia was headstrong but hopefully tonight had frightened her enough that she wouldn't fight him.

It was late, well after midnight.

"I need to get a shower," he said. "You'll be okay for a few minutes?"

She gave a small nod. Still, she appeared fragile, as if she might shatter like china if handled too hard. He ran his fingers through her silky hair. Then he rose from the couch. Checking the lock and setting the security system at the front door, he went down the hallway.

The hard rain stung her skin like pellets. He was gaining on her, his shoes slapping over wet ground.

Run faster! He's going to kill you!

Stumbling over tree roots, she fell headfirst onto pine needles and moss. A flash of lightning illuminated the dark forest. She saw him coming toward her. He was rangy, six feet at least, black hair plastered to his skull by the storm. A knife was gripped in his fist.

Get up. Get up!

Running again, the grainy image of a car appeared to her up ahead in the downpour. She reached it and grasped the door handle, her heart seizing. Locked. No! She jerked at it, sobbing and frantic. Pounding on the window, she tried to break the glass. He was in the clearing now, advancing too fast. Terror choked her as she took off again but he caught her, his hand sinking into her sodden hair and yanking her roughly back.

Mia fought blindly, struggling to break free of the hard arms around her.

"Hey…hey." She heard Eric's low voice. "I've got you. It's all right."

She realized she was in a bed, being held against his bare chest. She stopped fighting. Her heavy breathing punctuated the darkness, her heart still pumping hard. Mia's body went limp with relief.

"It was a bad dream," he whispered. "That's all."

He sat on the mattress edge, dressed only in jeans.

A thin slant of light spilled from the bungalow's living area into the bedroom. Mia recalled she'd gone to bed, suddenly bone-tired, while Eric had stayed up to check email and file a report.

"I heard you crying out," he said.

"I was back in the woods…I was running from him." She ran a trembling hand over her face. "But the car was locked this time."

She blinked back tears, hating the weakness she felt. "I couldn't get away."

Gently, Eric tilted her chin up, lifting her eyes to his. "It was a dream—not a flashback this time. You *did* get away. You escaped."

His features were drenched in shadow, but she could still make out the hard, handsome planes of his face. All of it came rushing back in on her…Penney…the reason she was here with him. Eric stroked his hand over her back. She wore a short, cotton gown she'd brought from home.

"I'm afraid," she admitted.

Eric kissed her forehead, then her lips, a slow but featherlight touch of his mouth to hers. He smelled clean, like soap, from his shower. "I'm right here. I'm right outside."

It wasn't enough. The nightmare, Penney's death— all of it had heightened her emotions. She needed to feel alive. Connected to someone. His mouth remained just inches from hers. She slowly arched her back and kissed him, their contact more lingering this time. Responding, Eric's hand cupped the back of her head as Mia's fingers slipped through the still-damp hair at his nape. She heard his low grunt, felt the kiss deepen, his tongue mingling with hers.

When he finally pulled back, his breathing had grown shallower, his expression hungry but unsure.

"You've been through a lot tonight," he said hoarsely. "Maybe we shouldn't…"

For just a little while, she needed the world to fade outside of their darkened bedroom. She wanted to lose herself in the taste of him, feel him inside her again. His body could distract her from the nightmare that had become her life.

"Please, Eric," she murmured. "I…I need this. I need you."

She saw him swallow. Releasing a breath, his palm cradled her face, his thumb softly stroking over her bottom lip and his eyes staring into hers. Then his hands moved to the lace-edged hem of her gown. He slowly drew it over her head. She wore only panties underneath, a thin satin thong. The cool air on her suddenly hot skin made her shiver.

Her nipples hardened instantly at his touch. Eric kissed her again before lowering his head and suckling first one breast and then the other, his mouth lavishing the attention she craved. She moaned as his teeth gently imprisoned one tender bud, his expert fingers slipping inside her panties and finding her slick wetness at the same time. He stroked her, building her heat.

She needed him now. Mia clasped his erection through the coarse denim he wore and felt a tremor run through him.

Clumsily, she worked at the buttons of his jeans. When

she had the top one undone he took over for her, sitting back against the headboard and freeing himself. Reaching into the nightstand drawer, he took out a condom, something he'd purchased since their last encounter. As he readied himself for her, Mia stood from the bed, removing her panties, sliding them down her thighs to the floor. His eyes, dark with desire, followed her movement. Then she returned to the mattress, her hands braced on his broad shoulders as she climbed onto him, straddling his seated body. Closing her eyes, she slowly sank down onto his length. He gave a low hiss in response, his head falling back.

"Ah, God, Mia," he whispered, voice rough.

Eric's mouth took hers again, his hands holding her narrow waist. She remained still for a long moment, getting used to being filled so fully by him. Her breasts pressed against his chest, and they kissed until they were both gasping for air.

Her forehead pressed briefly against his, and then she began to move.

There was no sound in the room except for their cramped breathing and the rhythmic creak of the mattress.

"Kiss me again," Eric demanded huskily. Mia lowered her mouth to his as she rode him, their passion embodied in the feel of his lips against hers. He nipped at her bottom lip, lapping at the hurt with his tongue and causing Mia to groan in response. It made her want more of him, made her drive down on him more deeply, over and over. A tightening sensation built in her core that only got stronger with each rise and fall of her body onto his, until she was so close to coming that his name escaped from her lips, her fingers catching in his short hair. Instinctively, he knew when she'd reached the point of no return. Mia gasped as he moved forward with her, pinning her onto the bed with his hard frame. He took control then, thrusting into her as she climaxed around him.

He came seconds after her, his body shuddering with his own release.

Afterward, Mia lay on her back, her dark hair spread across the pillow. Eric had turned onto his side facing her. She felt his eyes studying her, and she ran her fingers over the corded sinews of his forearm, feeling the light sprinkling of crisp, male hair on his skin. The room around them was black except for a silver shaft of moonlight reaching through a gap in the curtains.

"I hate the dark," she whispered. She paused before confessing the reason. "My mother used to lock me in the closet when I was small."

When he spoke, his voice was low. "I can turn on the bathroom light."

She shook her head. "I feel safe with you."

He pulled her closer, turning her so their bodies were spooned together. His breath felt warm against her hair. Her hand covered Eric's on her stomach, his fingers brushing over the scabbed, reddened numeral on her skin. Like her nail beds, the wound was healing. But the carving would leave a scar. It was a part of who she was now.

Mia thought about what he'd told her earlier, about hearing his wife's last moments on the digital recording that night. The same man who hurt her had brutalized him as well, although in a different way. He was broken, like her.

I'm in love with him.

She accepted that emotion, even as she understood there were no promises between them. All they had was now.

29

A clock in the shape of the sun hung on the wall of the bungalow's kitchen. Eric glanced up at it as he heard a car pull into the crushed-shell driveway outside. Peering through the small, curtained window above the sink, he sighed. Mia was still asleep, so he went to catch Cameron before he knocked.

Cam carried the Sunday newspaper, which he tossed onto the table as he entered. Walt Rudner's byline was beneath the front-page headline: *Jax Serial Killer May Have Claimed Another Victim*.

"It says a syringe was found at the scene matching the unsub's M.O. We don't have labs back on the contents yet and they're reporting it," he grumbled before heading into the kitchen.

Nor had the task force made an official statement yet, although a news briefing was scheduled for later in the day. Eric scanned the article, which gave Penney Niemen's name as the deceased and listed the apartment building's address. He thought of the deputies and forensics techs who had worked the scene. One of them had shared information about the syringe with Rudner, evidence that linked the unsub to last night's death. He continued reading, his frown deepening as he reached the third paragraph.

> *Although an autopsy has yet to be conducted, a preliminary examination by the Duval County Medical Examiner's office indicates the likelihood of foul play. An earlier victim, the only woman believed to have escaped the serial killer dubbed The Collector, resides at the same building where the suspicious death occurred, suggesting she may have been the intended target.*

At least the article hadn't given Mia's name, maintaining some modicum of privacy.

"The building's been all over the television this morning," Cameron said as he returned with a mug of coffee from the kitchen. "I'm guessing you put Ms. Hale somewhere else for the night."

Eric released a breath. He might as well tell him now. "She's here, actually."

Cameron's gaze flicked to the bedroom's closed door. "Then I'm going to assume you slept on the couch."

"Let's go out on the deck." He didn't want Mia overhearing their discussion. Stopping at the coffeemaker on the kitchen counter, he refilled his own mug he'd left next to the sink. A sliding glass door took up much of the room's rear wall. Unlocking it, he pushed through the vertical blinds and went outside with Cameron behind him. It was still early, and the air outside was warm but not yet uncomfortable. A wood fence enclosed the small backyard, beyond which a few weathered beach houses could be seen on the posterior street.

"I want a watch put on her. We've got justification now. And I also want to use this place as a safe house," Eric said.

Cameron leaned against the deck railing. "Why not just assign a detail to her apartment?"

"You've seen the building—it's huge. The courtyard, verandas and staircases—there are too many places to hide and too many points of entry. It would take six or seven uniforms to properly secure it. This place is small and contained. We can put a single unit right out front."

"And where will *you* be moving to?" he asked pointedly.

"I'll be here with her at night. With the limited resources we have, it makes sense."

Lips pressed together, Cameron looked over the yard with its mixture of grass and sand. In the far corner, a rope hammock hung between one of the fence posts and a scrubby grapefruit tree. "You never did have much of a poker face, Eric. How long have you been screwing her?"

Seagulls flew overhead, cawing as they headed to the ocean. His face heated. "It's not like that."

"You care about her."

"Yeah," he said quietly. "I do."

The admission must have given Cameron pause, because for once he was without a rebuttal. Eric had an idea of what was on his mind, however.

"Look, before you start, I don't need a lecture on protocol. It's been drummed into my head since I was a rookie. 'Don't get involved—'"

"I don't give a damn about protocol. I'm not your supervisor." Cameron placed his mug on the railing. "And let's set aside the fact that she's a reporter—"

"She's been taken off the investigation."

"You're my *friend,* Eric." His concern appeared genuine. "This psychopath *wants* her. Last night proved it. What if he gets to her, too?"

Like Rebecca. Eric felt sick at the thought. "We're not going to let that happen. She's going to end up dead if she continues running around Jacksonville by herself. It's by sheer luck she's not the one lying on a slab in the M.E.'s freezer right now."

Cameron checked his watch. "Speaking of, we've got the Niemen autopsy at eleven and the news briefing at two-thirty. They're also going to want an update on the Karen Diambro abduction—not that we have anything new to tell them—as part of it. In the meantime, I'd like to go by the crime scene."

Eric nodded. "We'll take Mia with us. She's going to need to pack some things. Afterward, I can have a deputy bring her back here and stay with her until we can make a more formal schedule."

He glanced through the glass doors into the kitchen. Mia stood at the coffeemaker, her back to them, unaware of their presence. At least she was dressed. When Eric had left her in bed that morning, she'd been gloriously naked. He'd yearned to make love to her again, but he knew she needed to rest. Her sleep had been fitful last night, at best.

"Give me a few minutes to talk to her alone, all right?"

He left Cameron on the deck. Mia turned abruptly when she heard the door's glass panel slide open, her face pale.

"I'm sorry." He came into the kitchen, placing his mug on the counter. "I didn't mean to startle you."

"I didn't know you were outside." She held her own coffee mug in both hands, cupped between her palms. Faint, violet shadows smudged her eyes.

"I got milk," he said. "In the fridge—"

"Is that Agent Vartran?" she asked, seeing Cameron, who had apparently taken the opportunity to make a call. He paced the deck's cedar planking, his phone to his ear. A blush stained her cheeks, and Eric figured she was wondering how much the other agent knew about them.

"Yeah. We have some things to do. But we're going by your apartment first."

Misinterpreting, she set the mug on the counter. "Just give me a few minutes to pack up, all right?"

"Mia." He gently caught her wrist, halting her retreat. "You don't understand. I'm not…dropping you off. Agent Vartran and I think you need to stay here for a while. I'd like you to come with us and get some more of your things. Whatever you need."

Her lips parted slightly as she looked at him. "For how long?"

"Until we catch this guy." Eric went with her into the living area. "I'll be with you at night. During the day or when the investigation calls me away, we'll have a JSO squad car right outside."

"Why can't we do this at my apartment?"

"The unsub knows where you live. He can't come after you again if he doesn't know where to find you. Besides, resources are limited and it will take less men to protect you here than at your building."

"Today's Sunday. What about tomorrow? I have to go to work."

"You may have to take some time off."

"I can't," she said. "I won't. I'm already in trouble with Grayson."

"I'll talk to him—"

"That's not a good idea." Mia rubbed a hand over her eyes. "The *Courier*'s considering more layoffs. I need to be there and be productive. After the investigation's over, I have a life I'll need to get back to. And I'll need my job. If you haven't heard, they're hard to come by in the newspaper business these days."

Stress was visible on her features. The past several weeks had been a disruption, he knew. It rankled him that Grayson Miller was putting additional pressure on her right now.

"We'll figure something out, all right?" He stepped closer, sliding his hands over her arms in a consoling gesture. "Even if that means giving you an escort to and from work."

She didn't appear happy about the prospect.

"Do you trust me?" he asked in a low voice.

Mia gave a faint nod. Eric turned as he heard footsteps in the kitchen. Cameron came into the living area.

"Ms. Hale," he said in somber greeting, then shifted his attention to Eric. "I just got off the phone with Sco-field. She got a heads-up—Karen Diambro's ex-husband is talking to the media. He's complaining the task force isn't doing enough to find her. The segment's going to run on the evening news."

He shook his head, irritated. "We've been busting our asses looking for her, with men working overtime. We're doing all we can. I don't know what else he expects."

Eric released a breath, feeling the heavy weight of responsibility on his shoulders.

"He expects us to find her."

Crime scene tape still cordoned off the apartment building's courtyard, appearing out of place among its serene, gurgling fountain and stone benches. Two deputies, a male and female, remained stationed at the front to keep out the unauthorized. Flashing his shield at the officers, Eric placed a reassuring hand against the small of Mia's back as they entered.

"I guess I don't have to ask where the body was found," Cameron commented under his breath. A cleanup crew was at work, one of them using a pressure washer at the base of the stairs to remove Penney Niemen's blood from the concrete.

Eric noticed Mia had turned her head away from the scene.

"I'm going upstairs, if that's okay," she said.

He motioned to the female deputy. "Go with her, please."

The cleanup crew halted their work long enough for Mia and the officer to slip carefully past them and climb the steps to her apartment. Concerned, Eric's eyes followed them up to the landing.

"So tell me how this went down."

Eric walked Cameron through the likely scenario of what had taken place, culminating in the deceased's skull being repeatedly bashed against the concrete, based on the M.E.'s initial assessment. He pointed out the planter at the base of the staircase. "The syringe was found over there, the needle upright in the dirt like a dart. We figure it was lost in the struggle on the second-floor landing and ended up falling into the planter."

Wearing sunglasses, Cameron glanced around the courtyard and building. "I see what you mean. There's a dozen different places around here for someone to hide. It would take a platoon to seal it down."

"There's a set of staircases on the building's rear, too. It's basically a duplicate image of the front, although the courtyard in back has a swimming pool."

"Nice place," Cameron noted.

"Mia said the current owners renovated it from a single estate home into three units. It was built in the 1920s by a gangster who made a fortune bootlegging alcohol."

"So the crime tradition continues."

A media van pulled up across the street, at a respectable enough distance that it wouldn't likely be chased away by the deputies on guard. The agents watched as a cameraman got out of the van's side door and began setting up. A blonde female in a fuchsia suit, probably a reporter, accompanied him.

"Even if Ms. Hale isn't staying here, the unsub won't know that. We need to set up a watch," Cameron mentioned. "What about last night? Did anyone survey the bystanders?"

"We circulated the most recent sketch to law enforcement on the scene." Still, the place had been chaos, with cars passing by on the street and neighbors gathered in groups on the adjacent lawns. Eric had even gone into the crowd himself, searching for someone matching the unsub's description.

A member of the cleanup crew went past, wearing earplugs attached to an iPod as he hummed along with his music. Carrying a trash bag, he was picking up refuse left behind by the emergency responders—foam coffee cups, cigarette butts and wrappers from medical supplies. Eric noticed the back of the man's blue jumpsuit was emblazoned with a business logo and the name Bio-Clean, Inc.

"A civilian group?" he asked.

"It's an outsource firm contracted by local law enforcement for crime scene cleanup. We use them—so do the JSO and local arms of the DEA and ATF, on occasion. It's cheaper than keeping a crew on payroll and paying benefits. Of course, you big-timers at the VCU probably have your own people."

Eric failed to respond to Cameron's lighthearted dig. Instead, he was thinking of the Bargain-Mart where Anna Lynn Gomez had been abducted two weeks ago. Security cameras had caught her image in the store's vestibule as she left with her purchase, but not outside the building. The store had admitted to a camera blind spot of approximately fifty feet to the left of the entrance—something some of its employees and technicians from the company that installed the CCTV system knew about. However, all of them had turned up clean.

"The Bargain-Mart," Eric recounted. "When you ran background checks on employees at the company that put in the cameras, did you ask about outsourcers?"

"No," Cameron said. "They knew it was an abduction investigation. They would've mentioned it if they used outside support."

Still, he dug into his pocket for his cell phone. It was a long shot, Eric realized, but cable carriers and phone companies sometimes used service contractors to augment their full-time employees. What if the security company did, too?

A short time later, Cameron snapped the phone closed. "I got their answering service. Someone from management's supposed to call me back."

Another news van pulled up, this one daring to park against the curb directly in front of the building.

"I've got this," Cam said. He walked away, shouting orders to the driver. Eric turned and went up the stairs. Once inside the apartment, he sent the female deputy back down. He found Mia in her office. She wasn't packing, but instead stood staring out through the large window that overlooked the pool and patio below. Nearby, the outstretched branches of a live oak, heavy with Spanish moss, shaded the lawn.

"What're you thinking about?" he asked, coming to stand behind her. He gently clasped her upper arms.

"Will and Justin had an oyster roast at the pool, just last month. They strung up paper lanterns and little white lights everywhere. They even hired an acoustic guitarist…" Mia shook her head, her tone reflective. "Penney was there. She brought a date. So much has changed since then."

"We're going to catch him, Mia. It's only a matter of time."

She turned to face him, her brown eyes haunted. "How many more women have to die before then? I'd like to try the memory-retrieval therapy again, Eric. Maybe I'll remember something key. You said yourself you thought we were close. Let me do it for Penney—"

"You can't. It's gotten too dangerous."

Her chin tilted up a fraction. "I'm willing to take the risk."

He ran his fingers through her hair, his voice low. "I'm not. I'll find another way."

They held each other's gaze until Mia's cell phone rang inside the purse she'd laid on the desk, its ring tone a popular Maroon 5 melody. She went over to check it, frowning as she peered at the screen.

"It's Grayson," she said. "I need to take this."

Eric left the room, giving her privacy to talk. He went into her bedroom, noticing that she'd at least put her laptop in its case and had her suitcase open on the bed's goose down comforter. Like the rest of the apartment, her bedroom had a vintage style, with distressed wood furniture and a rustic, bronze chandelier hanging over the bed. The closet door was open, and he smiled faintly at the disarray of clothing, shoes and storage boxes inside. A night-light—a stained-glass butterfly in hues of soft purple and blue—was plugged into an electrical socket nearby. Thinking about what Mia had revealed to him last night after they'd made love, he took it from the wall. Carefully wrapping it in one of her T-shirts, he placed it in the suitcase's side pocket.

"Everything okay?" he asked as she entered the room.

"Grayson overslept. He just now heard about what happened."

She appeared anxious and sad. Swallowing a sigh, Eric tucked his hands inside his pockets. He hated that he was asking her to leave her home, but his gut told him it was necessary. She needed to be somewhere the unsub didn't know about, out of his reach.

"If I stayed here, he might come back. You could have men outside, watching—"

"We will," Eric stated. "But I still want you somewhere else."

Although the front door of the apartment had been left open, someone rang the doorbell. Figuring it was Cameron, Eric said, "Go ahead and get packed, all right? If you forget something, I can send someone back for it."

He went down the hallway and motioned the other agent inside.

"The general manager for the security company just called," Cameron told him as he walked from the foyer. "He says they use only their own staff to install the systems. They're thoroughly background-checked, as we already knew. But they *have* used freelance repairmen in the past when they were backlogged. Most of them came through a temp agency downtown. He apologized for not mentioning it earlier—he said it slipped his mind since it's been well over a year since they needed any additional help. Business is down with the economy."

The blind spot in the camera range at the Bargain-Mart niggled at him. It could have been just sheer luck, but there was a chance Anna Lynn Gomez's abductor had known about it because he'd worked on the system at some point. "We'll need to get the paperwork on whoever the agency sent out."

"I'll get on it," Cameron said. He looked around the apartment. "She's got good taste."

Eric couldn't stop thinking about what had happened here last night and how close Mia had come to being in the bastard's grip once again. How much time had passed between his departure and her arrival home? He estimated no more than a half-hour and possibly much less.

Considering their shared past, he felt certain The Collector would take extra care in harming her.

If he got another chance.

30

"There isn't enough mayonnaise on this," Gladys complained, pushing the plate away. Petulant, she added, "And I don't like dill pickles. I like sweet gherkins."

"We're out of the gherkins, Mother. I'll go to the store later." With forced patience, Allan took the turkey and rye and spread another thick layer of mayonnaise onto the sandwich. He sat the plate back in front of her on the table with a testy clank.

Peering suspiciously between the slices of bread, she frowned. "There's no cheese, either."

He went to the fridge and pulled out a wrapped slice of American. It was processed—not even real food—but it fit Gladys's childlike palate. He tossed it onto her plate. "I'm in a mood today. You'd be wise not to push me."

She snorted, unimpressed, as she unwrapped the cheese with bony fingers. "What're you going to do? Go hide in that little building of yours?"

Dismissively, she turned up the volume on the small television, shifting her attention to a Sunday afternoon worship program. A minister with a silver pompa-

dour and pinstriped suit bellowed from the pulpit, rant-
ing about demons and dark temptations. Allan wasn't
hungry, so he put the turkey and mayo back into the
fridge, the rye into the bread box. As he carefully swept
crumbs from the counter, his mind returned to the cat-
astrophic events of the previous night. He'd planned so
carefully, conducted surveillance on the apartment building for days before making his move. All of it wasted,
now. The woman on the top floor wasn't even supposed
to be home at that hour. He recalled the repeated, dull
thud of her head on the concrete. Her price for interven-
ing with fate.

His anger still simmered, however.

"It wouldn't hurt *you* to go to church," Gladys noted
once the pipe organ had started up on the television,
accompanying a robed choir. "You might meet a good
woman and do something with your life."

Shutting her out, Allan closed his eyes, envision-
ing Mia at his mercy. It was meant for him to have her.
There was simply no other reason for her to have come
back into his life. He imagined hurting her, tasting her
fear. But the fantasy didn't last long. Gladys broke into a
coughing fit, rocking in her chair as she choked on a bite
of sandwich. Little bits of turkey and bread flew from
her wrinkled mouth. Patting her back, Allan handed her
the glass of milk he'd poured for her earlier.

"Drink this, Mother."

Finally the coughing spasms subsided. Irritable, she
shooed him away and went back to watching the strut-
ting minister as she ate. Her jaw clicked with each masti-
cation, and he noticed a glob of mayonnaise on the front

of her housedress. There was another gelatinous drip
oozing down the tubing of her oxygen cannula. The Chihuahua stood by her chair, begging in his high-pitched
whine. Allan seethed. She was a thankless old woman.
He'd moved three states away—lived here for almost
three years now—caring for her. Gladys should *worship*
him, not treat him like some kind of impotent failure. He
thought again of what he'd done to the curly haired bitch.
Was that the work of a weak man?

He didn't think so.

Allan returned to the sink, tamping down his annoy-
ance as he prepared to marinate chicken for the evening's
dinner. Ritualistically soaping his hands under the faucet's scalding stream, he looked up as something outside
the window caught his attention. Lupita, their so-called
housekeeper, was skulking through the backyard, her
ample hips jiggling in her stretch pants.

She headed into the pines toward his workshop.

Allan quickly dried his hands on a paper towel and
stomped out through the kitchen door, its screen banging.

"I need my pills," Gladys called after him.

Eyebrows clamped down over his eyes, he marched
across the lawn in Lupita's wake. It was one of her days
off—she wasn't even supposed to be here. The backyard ended at the thicket of trees, which ran parallel to
the makeshift gravel road. He traveled into the woods,
taking the same beaten-down trail as the housekeeper.
A few hundred yards out, the dull gray of cinder blocks
and the body of a stripped car peeked out through the

foliage. As he approached, he could see Lupita, knocking on the door.

"Meester Levi?" she called in her thick, peasant accent. "You in there?"

He slowed, staying just outside the clearing. The woman knocked again, then twisted the door handle. Allan felt himself vibrate with anger, his hands balling into fists at his sides. She had been clearly instructed never to come down here.

Wait. See what she's up to.

He took a step farther back into the woods as she looked carefully around. Then she slunk to the side of the building, to the lone window that held the air-conditioning unit. The top pane was covered from the inside with heavy butcher paper, so she bent over, attempting to peek through the half-inch space between the unit and wooden planks used to keep it wedged into the window frame. Fury exploded in Allan's head, the hard thrum of his pulse propelling him forward. He grasped the housekeeper by one flabby arm and spun her around as she gasped loudly.

"What do you think you're doing?" he roared.

Her eyes went wide, her mouth gaping open in surprise. *"Meester* Levi! I—I was just looking for you!"

"You were snooping!"

"No, I—"

"Why didn't you come to the house?"

"If Miss Gladys sees me, she expects me to stay. You're always down here. I thought—"

As Allan crowded her she took a step back, her thick shoulders meeting the building's exterior wall. He was breathing hard, his fingers still biting into her upper arm. "You were told never to come down here! This is my private sanctuary! What are you looking for?"

She cowered, her face growing as white as the laundry hanging on the line in the backyard. "I—I came to get paid! You owe me for two weeks—my son, he needs the money, today!"

Allan stared at her, every nerve in his body crackling with vehement hatred. He thought of pounding Lupita's thick skull against the ground, too, watching it split open like a ripe melon. He came to the very edge of doing it. But he knew her son would come looking for her. Instead, he punched a hard finger into the center of her chest. Her heavy bosom bounced.

"You *never* come down here again, you hear me? *No aquí!*"

She shook her head. Tears filled her eyes. "No, sir, I understand. Please…"

Lupita cried out as he blocked her attempt to creep away. Allan placed one hand on the cinder-block wall above her head, not through terrorizing her. His breath fanned her face. "If I ever catch you down here again, I'll hang you and skin you alive."

She whimpered. He reached into his back pocket. Extracting his wallet, he pulled out several bills, cash he had from a recent repair job. He threw them on the ground, watching as she bent, sobbing, to pick them up. Doing so, she rose and scrambled away, bumping her plump hip against the front of the partially disassembled car he had up on blocks. When she believed she'd reached a safe enough distance, she spat on the ground and screamed, "You're crazy! I quit!"

Allan watched her go. His rage was a living thing now, a snake coiled up inside his belly. Lupita was like kindling on a fire that had been building since his failure last night. He *had* returned to the crime scene briefly, and he'd witnessed something that struck a chord. Mia running into Eric Macfarlane's arms. He'd held her like a lover.

If they were together, taking her would be doubly sweet.

She was his missing number eight. The little girl who'd witnessed his maiden voyage.

She belonged to him.

He drew in several deep breaths, trying to bring his spiraling thoughts back under control. As long as he was down here, he might as well be productive.

Going to his van parked on the gravel, he opened its back doors and felt a blast of hot air from its interior meet his face. Then taking out the keys to his workshop, he let himself inside, leaving the entrance open. A short time later he exited again, a mass wrapped in plastic sheeting over one shoulder. He dumped it into the van's back with a heavy thump, then slammed the doors closed again.

Allan relocked the building. Wiping perspiration from his face with the back of his forearm, he felt a sense of loss that no one had been around to witness his power. He'd wanted Mia tied up and watching. Knowing she would be next. But he'd needed the release too badly last night.

He didn't have much time until the body began to stink.

Allan walked back up the wooded trail so he could give Gladys her pills and marinate the chicken. After dinner, under the velvet blanket of darkness, he would head out to dispose of the remains and prowl the night.

31

A squad car with two sheriff's deputies inside sat in front of the bungalow, in a wide berth of sand on the street's shoulder. Parking his vehicle in the driveway, Eric walked over to it. The driver's-side window lowered as he approached.

"Everything okay tonight?" he asked.

"It's been quiet, Agent," the young deputy behind the steering wheel responded above the roar of the unit's air conditioner. Eric glanced at the halo of light emanating from behind the bungalow's closed curtains.

"You need us to stay?"

"No. I'll take it from here. Good night."

The deputies nodded and pulled away, leaving him standing under a starless evening sky. A hard breeze blew in from the ocean, ruffling the line of tall pampas grass that grew along the driveway and suggesting rain. It had been a long day, punctuated by Penney Niemen's autopsy and the continued canvassing of Mia's San Marco neighborhood. No one, however, claimed to have witnessed anything, although one neighbor admitted to hearing what he thought might have been a scream. Eric went up to the bungalow's stoop, knocking and announcing himself. Momentarily, he heard the muted beep of the security keypad inside. Opening the door, Mia wore denim shorts and a smocked top, her hair pulled into a short ponytail.

"Is there anything new?" she asked, appearing tense. Eric entered, and then closed and locked the door behind him.

"Just that the M.E. gave confirmation on Ms. Niemen's cause of death. But you probably already heard that on the news."

Her expression indicated she had. The segment had also included the interview with Karen Diambro's ex-husband. Eric had watched at the FBI offices along with Cameron, feeling defensive as well as culpable. Because the truth of it was, no matter how hard they were trying, they had so far been unsuccessful in coming up with a suspect. The Bureau, JSO and Duval County District Attorney's Office were all feeling an increasing juggernaut of pressure.

"You look tired, Eric. Are you hungry?"

He realized it had been hours since he'd eaten. "Yeah, I am."

"We'll have to order takeout. You know about the dismal state of the kitchen pantry." She offered him a weak smile. "Maybe the deputies escorting me from work tomorrow can be talked into taking me by the grocery store."

"It's late. You didn't have to wait for me to eat."

"I wanted to. There's a place on Jax Beach that has good fried oysters and shrimp. I think they deliver."

He gave a nod of agreement. As she went to look up the restaurant's number in the out-of-date phone book in the kitchen, Eric's cell phone rang. Its screen identified Cameron as the caller.

"Someone from the temp agency finally checked their messages and got back with me," he said through the phone. "The guy was hedging—it sounds doubtful they've checked backgrounds thoroughly on people they've sent out on jobs. I told him we need the paperwork, including job applications, for anyone used by the security company for maintenance or repairs over the last three years."

"When will we have it?"

"He asked me to give him until end of day tomorrow. He said they had a computer meltdown a few months ago with no disaster backup plan, but he has paper files that he has to find and cross-reference."

Eric ran a hand through his hair. He wasn't as concerned about criminal records, especially since none of the fingerprints on the car parts had been a match to those in the FBI database. But what he did want to know was whether anyone on the list had lived or worked in Bethesda, Maryland, or the surrounding areas during the same time as the murders occurring up there.

"Did he estimate how many people we're talking about?"

"Ballpark? Twenty to thirty."

"Give him until two tomorrow and not a minute later,"

Eric instructed. "In the meantime, we can file for a sub-poena to produce in case he fails to deliver."

As he completed the call, Mia returned from the kitchen. "I placed the order. Oysters and shrimp with cocktail sauce, hush puppies and coleslaw. It'll be here in thirty minutes."

Thinking of all the fried food, he shook his head. "I've got to make time for a run."

Mia walked over to him and laid her fingers against his shirtfront. "I don't know. You seem in pretty good shape to me."

Despite his fatigue, her nearness stirred him. He lifted her hand and kissed the inside of her wrist. "As delicious as it is, not everything has to be breaded and deep-fried, Southern style. In Maryland we have crab cakes—sweet lump meat, a little bit of mayonnaise for a binder, and a hint of Old Bay. Maybe I'll make them for you some-time."

Sometime. A shadow in Mia's eyes told him that her thoughts paralleled his. If it were possible to imagine a day when all this might be over, it would also mean something far less pleasant, as well. He belonged to the VCU, and she was established here in Jacksonville, with a career and a life. They would have to discuss how, or even if, they could go further in a relationship. It was something he didn't want to think about now.

"How bad was it here today?"

She shrugged. "A little like being an animal in the zoo. Cooped up in here with the deputies watching from outside. They kept coming to the door every half hour to check on me, like I was thinking about sneaking out the back."

"Were you?"

"Maybe a little."

Eric worried she wasn't joking.

"I went over Hank Dugger's notes again. I've been through them so many times I'm pretty sure I can recite entire pages from memory at this point." She shook her head. "No matter how much I want it to, nothing stands out. It looks like he and his partner really did do a thorough investigation on Joy Rourke's disappearance. Just like he told me, they eventually ran out of people to talk to and were assigned to more active cases."

He could sense Mia's frustration. At least letting her go into the newspaper would give her something to focus her nervous energy on.

"The interview with Karen Diambro's ex-husband had to be tough," she remarked softly.

"It didn't help," he admitted. Eric looked into her eyes. There was nothing more he wanted than to have some downtime with her and try to decompress. If they slept together, he would still need to make up a bed on the couch. The deputies would arrive early the next morning to escort her to work and he wanted it to appear that there had been no impropriety. It felt dishonest, but it was necessary. Law enforcement could gossip like schoolgirls. He didn't want Mia being talked about in that way.

"Will called me," she said. "He got back tonight—he left Justin in Chicago. He said an unmarked car showed up out of nowhere when he pulled into the driveway. He had to show them his ID."

Which meant the field agents assigned to the property's surveillance were on top of things, Eric thought. "He didn't have to come back for the investigation. Any routine questions we have for him or Mr. Cho as the property owners could've been answered by phone."

"He knows. I think he just feels horrible about what happened and not being here." A few strands of hair had escaped Mia's ponytail and she brushed them from her face, her expression pensive. "He spoke with Penney's family. They're taking her back to West Virginia to be buried as soon as the body's released, despite her wishes. She wanted to be cremated and have her ashes scattered here on the ocean, but they don't seem to care."

Eric recalled Rebecca's funeral service and burial, as well as the pain-numbed days that had followed in their wake. As bad off as he'd been, her parents had been worse, emotionally distraught and looking for someplace to lay their anger. Most of it had been directed onto him.

"Burials are for the family," he said. "They may need it in order to let go."

"Will says they're very religious. They never approved of Penney's lifestyle. Not being married and living so far from home, all by herself in a large city…maybe they were right."

He studied her, aware of the survivor's guilt she felt knowing she'd been the intended target. "What happened isn't your fault, Mia."

She appeared doubtful. "I just need to do something—"

"I know."

"Will's going back to Chicago later this week. I want to see him before he leaves. Privately."

He nodded his understanding. "I'll make it happen."

Taking her hand, Eric led her to the couch where they sat side by side. He placed his arm on the cushion behind her. Mia looked up at him, her dark eyes filled with yearning. Eric lowered his mouth to hers, their kiss lingering. Then with a small sigh, she laid her head on his chest as they waited for their food to arrive. Above them, rain began to thud on the bungalow's roof, making the small living quarters seem cozy. Eric leaned his head back on the couch. Tomorrow and whatever it might bring would come soon enough.

"He wasn't supposed to call you," Mia said as she stood in Grayson's office the following morning.

"Well, he did. And even if he hadn't, I would've made the same decision. From here on out, you're on the news desk, kiddo. You field calls, monitor the police scanner, assign out the smaller stories and assist with editing, but you're officially off the street."

She sighed, realizing it made the most sense. She couldn't have two deputies following her around the city while she tried to do her job. Since her abduction she hadn't been allowed to operate at full capacity, anyway. But being officially relegated to the news desk felt like another step down.

"I'm sorry about all this," she offered. "I know it's an inconvenience at the least—"

"Close the door."

Feeling a wave of dread, she did as told. Grayson removed his glasses and rubbed his eyes. He looked tired and a little hungover, the lines deeper in his face. Mia wondered if his drinking binge had extended over the remainder of the weekend. She felt responsible.

"Don't take this as a punishment. The fact that this guy came after you again changes everything, Mia. Macfarlane's one-hundred-percent right about keeping you underground until this psycho is caught. You're to stay in the newsroom. We can use you there."

She started to say something, but thought it better if she just listened. Grayson clearly wasn't done. He cleared his throat, uncharacteristically subdued.

"I realize our relationship's changed, too. After what was said on Saturday night, we probably won't be able to go back to where we were before. That's my fault." He appeared pained and lowered his voice. "But I still wouldn't be able to live with myself if anything happened to you, Mia… I think I've made how much I care about you embarrassingly clear."

"I just want things back like they used to be," she murmured, wistful.

"And I wish I hadn't gotten drunk and acted like a jackass. Or spilled my guts to you. But I did. I can't forget that." There was no malice in his words or expression, just sadness and a bit of chagrin.

She couldn't help feeling sorry for him. "We'll get through this."

Grayson didn't comment, however. Through the window behind him, she noticed the sun had already begun to burn off the remaining clouds from last night's rainstorm. It was supposed to be another beautiful day, but all she felt was gloom.

"You can start by fact-checking Clarkson's piece on the drive-by shooting in Brentwood." He returned his attention to his computer monitor. "I want it online ASAP."

Sensing she'd been dismissed, Mia left his office. She passed Walt Rudner, who was leaned back in his desk chair, its frame creaking under his considerable girth as he yakked on the phone. Upon seeing her, he lowered his tone, but Mia had already heard enough to know he was talking about her deputy escort to work. They'd driven the squad car into the parking garage, then walked her into the newspaper lobby through the enclosed rear entrance to draw as little attention as possible. Mia had been instructed to call when she needed to leave the building. She'd also heard Eric telling the deputies to make sure they weren't followed.

It was a strange way to live.

She collected her things from where she normally sat in the maze of cubicles that held the features reporters. Her new responsibilities would transfer her to one of the desks up front, facing the newsroom. She'd just gotten settled in when Walt brushed by, shoving his thick arms into his blazer as he lumbered toward the lobby. He had the look of a hungry jackal that had just been told a rabbit dinner was about to be served.

"What's going on?" His excitement made her uneasy.

"I just got a tip. A dead female. The Feds are involved."

32

The body had been dumped behind a tire store in a slightly run-down section of Old St. Augustine Road on the city's south side. Eric stood with Cameron as the M.E.'s office conducted its examination.

"Internal temperature is consistent with the outdoors," an attending physician said, kneeling beside the body. He removed the thermometer that had been inserted into the liver, another affront to what was left of Karen Diambro. "Combined with the stage of rigor mortis, I'd say she's been dead about thirty-six hours. The pattern of burn marks suggests she was hooked to some kind of electrical device and repeatedly shocked. I don't know if it was a form of torture or the C.O.D., especially considering the other wounds to the body—there's a lot to choose from here. That's all I can tell you until I get her on the table."

Eric thought of the agony the woman had endured, as well as the little boy now left without a mother. In addition to the grim burns and extensive bruising, the underwear-clad corpse held other, more familiar markings—the numeral ten carved into the stomach and ten raw, open wounds on her fingers where nails should have been. He looked away, trying to keep a handle on his anger and emotion.

The morning was heating up, the sun already creating little shimmies of heat off the parking lot asphalt. JSO deputies were holding back the crowd that had gathered on the sidewalk to gawk. Detectives Boyet and Scofield were in front of the hastily strung up crime scene tape, talking to the tire store's owner, who had found the body when he arrived for work.

"He didn't even attempt to hide this one. The employees park back here," Cameron said as they took a few steps away.

It was a notable deviation. The others so far had been well concealed in nonurban areas. In fact, the body of one of the victims—Cissy Cox—had yet to be recovered. But it was almost as if this one had been left where it would be quickly found. The damage to the body was the worst so far.

"The foiled abduction on Saturday night could've served as a stressor, which would explain the change in M.O.," Eric theorized. "A guy like this doesn't like to mess up. He took his anger out on Ms. Diambro. Maybe he wanted us to see what he'd done as a way to reassert his power."

"What about his fixation on having his next victim watch?"

"That plan failed and he was too irate to control himself." Eric was all too aware the next victim was supposed to have been Mia. "He was geared for the kill and couldn't delay his gratification any longer."

Disposing of the body here had been a significant risk. Eric had been on this area of road before and it was well populated, even at night. The unsub had driven his vehicle around back and unloaded the body, not even bothering to stash it in the nearby metal Dumpster. His eyes searched the tire store's brick exterior but he saw no surveillance equipment, only a clearly displayed sign that stated No Loitering.

"Check the dry cleaners next door and the quick print across the street for security cameras—maybe they got something," he instructed a passing field agent.

A news van had shown up on the street, parking in front of a line of stubby palmettos. It had the same call letters as the television station that had run the interview with Ms. Diambro's ex-husband. The body's discovery would certainly mean its replay today. Eric prepared for a new wave of criticism.

"Agents? We've got something."

They returned to the body, watching as the physician extracted something from the mouth with a long pair of medical tweezers. "It was stuffed into her throat. I almost didn't see it when I made the oral exam."

It appeared to be a folded piece of white paper. Eric realized what it was. A business card, flecked with blood and still wet with the victim's saliva. He felt a jolt as the physician carefully opened it to reveal the familiar insignia and black typeface.

Eric A. Macfarlane, Special Agent. Federal Bureau of Investigation, Violent Crimes Unit.

Cameron shook his head as the pale-faced physician held out the card.

"Bag it," Eric murmured. The card wasn't one of his current ones. The design was several years old. He suspected the unsub had gotten it from Rebecca's purse. He'd kept it all this time as a souvenir.

"So what's your take on this?" Cameron asked a few minutes later. The crew from the M.E.'s office had turned the body over to complete their exam, revealing the mottled lividity marks where blood had settled after circulation had ceased. Once they were done, it would be Forensics' turn to get a better look. They'd go over the body for other clues—fibers from rope or carpets, human hairs not belonging to the deceased.

"My take is that he's going to want another captive soon—"

"I'm talking about *you,* Eric. He rammed your card halfway down her throat. You don't consider that some kind of challenge?"

"No more than sending me recordings of dead women," he said quietly.

"You know what I think?" Cameron looked out over the crowd of onlookers before returning his gaze to Eric. "I think this guy's escalating and Karen Diambro's corpse was nothing more than a gift box for holding a message to you. You're an obsession to him."

Eric didn't respond. Instead, he was thinking of the past two days. So far they had a high-risk abduction attempt gone awry, the beating death of Penney Niemen out in the open, and now the poorly hidden corpse of another victim, dumped in a high-traffic locale.

"We've learned something, at least," he said. "When

this bastard gets angry he loses control and takes bigger risks, which increases the chance of us catching him."

"So what do we do?"

"We piss him off."

It was late afternoon, and pretty much everyone on the *Courier* staff who wasn't on an immediate deadline had gathered around the flat-screen in the newsroom.

Mia stood among them, her arms crossed over her chest as she watched the televised press conference. Eric faced the cameras behind a microphone-heavy podium, giving an update from the Bureau building's lobby on the identification of Karen Diambro's body earlier that day. He appeared solemn, his tone authoritative as he provided a statement prepared by the joint task force.

Much of the information wasn't new to her, since Walt had returned from the crime scene a few hours earlier. Mia herself had fact-checked his article, which had already been posted online and was slated for the paper's Tuesday print edition. But it was what *hadn't* been included in the story that truly sickened her. Walt had talked to the deputy who had been first responder to the 9-1-1 call from the tire store, and he'd described the heinous injuries to the body. Mia's heart ached for the Diambro family. She also felt for Eric and the pressure he had to be under.

On the television, a buzz broke out among the reporters in attendance as he opened the floor to questions. The queries came at him at a dizzying speed, but he fielded each with clarity and brevity.

Ms. Diambro's ex-husband has been critical of the

investigation. What is the FBI's response now that the body has been found?... Is it true the killer has been in touch with you, sending audio recordings made of the victims prior to their deaths?... Agent Macfarlane, your own wife was believed to be a victim of the same killer in another state three years ago. What led him to Jacksonville, and should you be heading up the investigation, considering your personal involvement?

The last question had come from Walt, who was at the press conference. He was off camera, but Mia recognized his gruff voice. Eric had made no public comment following the profile on him that had run in the *Courier* the previous week, but he spoke now.

"Based on key evidence, we're confident that the perpetrator of five murders in Maryland three years earlier is the same man currently at work here in Jacksonville," he said. "As you know, the FBI's Violent Crimes Unit is called in when serial crimes—namely homicides—cross state lines or when other law enforcement agencies request assistance. It is the VCU's belief the subject of this investigation is in actuality a Florida native who lived in Maryland during the time frame the murders there occurred. For whatever reason, he has since returned to his home state and after a period of dormancy, is now operating here."

He paused, preparing to answer the second part of the question. Several cameras flashed, and Mia realized her heart had begun to beat harder.

"My late wife, Rebecca Garner Macfarlane, was the fifth and final victim in Maryland. I offer no commentary on that other than to give my sincere assurance that I will capture her killer, and the killer of nine other women to date."

The lobby exploded with follow-up questions, but Eric nodded to an Asian-American female in the first row who Mia didn't recognize as a local journalist.

"Agent Macfarlane, can you give a profile of the man dubbed The Collector?" she asked.

"We have a physical composite provided by an unnamed witness we've shown before, which should be appearing again on camera right now." As he spoke, the screen switched to the more recent sketch Mia had worked on with the artist.

"The unknown subject is Caucasian, early to mid-forties, approximately six feet tall with a slightly receding, dark hairline. He's average-looking and unremarkable in appearance," Eric emphasized. "Psychologically, he is an extreme narcissist with a highly inflated sense of self-worth. While arrogant, he's a severe underachiever in all aspects of his life—financially, socially and emotionally. He is single and unemployed or works at a low-paying job, and has few to no friendships. We also have reason to believe he is asexual or may have latent homosexual tendencies. The abductions and murders have not been sexually motivated, and he is thought to regard women as inanimate objects he can overpower and control. In fact, dominance is the one thing that gives him stature in a world he is otherwise largely incapable in."

The television screen returned to Eric. "If you believe you've seen the man in this sketch, or know his whereabouts, I urge you to call the task force hotline."

The number appeared at the bottom of the screen. More questions were shouted from the floor, but he took a step back and another member of the task force came forward to conclude the conference. Mia felt a chill fall over her. The artist's sketch had captured her abductor perfectly, right down to the coldness in his eyes. It was disturbing to see it again.

"You all right?"

As the others dispersed and headed back to their desks, Mia turned to find Grayson studying her. He'd slipped out of his office at some point and joined the group watching the news conference. "You're as white as my shirt."

"I'm fine."

He lowered his voice. "You provided the sketch, didn't you?"

Mia hesitated, then gave a faint nod.

"Impressive. The memory-retrieval sessions must have worked to some extent—at least until you had to stop." He lifted one hand and added, "*And I know,* it's something we're not allowed to report on. I'm keeping the promise I made you. No matter what I said this past weekend, the sci-fi stuff at the NAS stays off the record."

"Thank you," she said softly. She felt a small flare of hope that some part of their friendship might be salvageable, after all.

Grayson was called away and Mia went back to the news desk, drawn by the ringing telephone. As she answered it, her thoughts remained elsewhere, however. She'd been on the brink of discovering something key during those sessions, she was certain of it. Her abductor's face, the cinder-block building in the woods, her flight on the interstate south of Jacksonville. What else might she have remembered?

She understood the danger. But if she'd been allowed to continue, both Penney and Karen Diambro might be alive right now.

33

"If the Bureau doesn't work out, you might have a future in television," Eric quipped to the rookie agent who'd posed as a reporter during the news conference— a way to make sure the right question was asked at the right time. He went past her, heading toward the elevator bay as journalists continued filing from the building's lobby.

"Do you think he saw it?" Cameron asked as he caught up to him in the corridor.

"If I know this guy, he continually scans the media for any mention of himself."

"Well, if you wanted to piss him off, calling him an 'asexual underachiever' in front of the entire city should do it."

Arriving at the elevator, Eric pushed the up button. Normally, psychological profiles remained internal to the team. But if the unsub could maintain his current state of anger, he might continue to take flagrant risks and make a mistake that would get him caught. Goaded or not, Eric felt certain he would attempt to take another woman soon. With the frustration of the foiled abduction, he wouldn't be able to go for long with no one in captivity.

"We're putting extra men on surveillance in Ms. Hale's neighborhood tonight," Cameron said as the elevator doors slid open and they entered. "Just in case your press conference got him riled up enough to try to visit her again."

Eric checked his wristwatch. Mia would be back at the bungalow soon and under the watch of two armed deputies. If anything *did* go down in San Marco tonight, at least she wouldn't be there. He'd been second-guessing himself about allowing her to go into work, but he figured it was better than her pacing a hole in the beach house's floor. She'd left him a voice mail earlier, unhappy about his call to Grayson Miller, which she had asked him not to do. He would deal with the consequences of that later. Eric had wanted to be sure Miller understood the situation and didn't send her out to cover a story. Keeping her alive was more important than keeping her job.

"What about the security camera on the building next to the tire store?" he asked as they entered Cameron's office.

"I had Hatcher go through the footage from the dry cleaners. The camera angle is off. The perp drove in through the side entrance, not through the parking lot. We've got a shadow entering at just past midnight, but you can't get a make on the vehicle. It's out of range. With our unsub, it might've been stolen, anyway." Cameron went to his desk and sat in front of his computer.

"We did get the employee paperwork from the temp agency a little while ago. It came through while you were preparing for the press conference."

"Any red flags?"

"I'll print it out for you. As I suspected, the agency's records are sloppy. The guy basically emailed digital images of approved job applications for anyone they sent out for small electronics repair over the last several years. He's unsure which workers were used to service the security firm's clients, though—he says that information was part of the computer files they recently lost."

Which meant there would be a larger number of workers to look at, Eric thought. "Did they do background checks?"

Cameron gave a sardonic grunt as the printer in the corner of the room rumbled to life. "His idea of security clearance is asking applicants to check a box if they've ever been convicted of a felony."

Eric went to the printer and began leafing through the pages being pushed out.

"I already ran through them on-screen. No one has previous work history for companies in Bethesda or the surrounding areas. At least no one claimed to. But it might be worth the time to cross-reference the names with the Maryland and Virginia DMVs. See if anyone ever had a driver's license up there." Cameron glanced at the clock on the wall. "It's nearly six. They're closed now but I can do it first thing in the morning."

"You should get going," Eric said. He took the printed sheets and put them in his briefcase. "Don't you and Lanie have an appointment?"

"Yeah, and traffic's hell getting back to St. Augustine this time of day." Heading to the door, he retrieved his suit jacket that hung from a peg on its back. Sliding into it, he said, "What about you?"

"The hotline's been lit up like a pinball machine. Every other civilian in the metro area thinks they've seen the unsub now that we've recirculated the sketch." False sightings were common whenever the media put out a photo or artist rendering of a suspect, even when it had been shown before. "I'm going to stick around and see if any of the calls are worth looking into."

"We've got field agents for that."

Eric gave a faint nod. "I know."

"Hey." Cameron hesitated, serious. He stood just outside the office's threshold. "Start watching your back, Eric, all right? You don't know how this guy's going to react to what you said about him today."

Cam was a good friend—they'd been close during their years at the Bureau. It felt like decades ago and yesterday all at the same time.

"Go drive your wife to Lamaze class."

Once he was gone, Eric moved to the window. Looking out over the building's plaza, he released a breath, feeling the stress he carried in his shoulders. At the parking lot's perimeter, a line of tall palm trees swayed in the early-evening breeze. Cars exited onto the main road, workers heading home to families and loved ones. It was unsettling to know this lunatic was out there among them. Waiting for another chance to strike.

Walt Rudner's question about his personal ties to the investigation had been harder to answer on camera than he'd expected. Maybe it was having his emotional laundry aired in a public forum, but it had hit Eric like a fist, reminding him all over again how much he wanted justice for Rebecca's murder. How responsible he still felt for her death.

He thought of Mia. He wouldn't let someone else he cared about end up like that.

It had been a long and frustrating Monday. Mia sat in the backseat of the squad car as it pulled discreetly from the newspaper's parking garage, heading in the direction of the Fuller Warren Bridge.

The sun had begun to settle over the St. Johns, and she caught glimpses of its dappled waters as the vehicle traveled along Riverside Avenue, heading past Memorial Park with its massive live oaks and the renowned bronze sculpture that served as its focal point. Inside the park, people on blankets and folding chairs dotted the expanse of green lawn. Musicians were setting up for an outdoor evening concert. Mia longed for the time when she could have attended such an event freely, without concern for her safety or the need to be escorted by armed deputies. She'd taken her former world for granted.

If you believe you've seen the man in this sketch, or know his whereabouts, I urge you to call the task force hotline...

Eric's request at the press conference that afternoon had been so earnest. He'd appeared tired, and she realized there were limits to endurance, even for someone as strong and capable as him. She closed her eyes, trying to diffuse the image of The Collector that was still inside her head.

In the front seat, the two deputies had been engaged in enthusiastic conversation about Florida pro football teams, but the one in the passenger-side seat turned to her. He had a square, chiseled face and blond hair in a bristled crew cut.

"It's a no-go on the grocery store detour, Ms. Hale," he said, sounding apologetic. "Agent Macfarlane doesn't want you out, not even with us. Once we get you back to the beach house, you can make a list and we'll send someone to pick up whatever you need."

Mia nodded, unsurprised. "Did Agent Macfarlane say when he might be back tonight to take over?"

"No, ma'am. I figure he's going to be tied up for a while—the press conference today and the appeal made to the public probably brought out all the crazies."

Feeling a wave of anxiety, she wondered about the likelihood of a particular *crazy* being among them.

The squad car traveled onto the traffic-congested bridge. Mia stared out over the water. She'd made this trip back and forth to the downtown for years. When they reached the other side, however, she knew there would be a deviation. They'd be taking a different path—not into San Marco but heading east on Beach Boulevard until they reached the Atlantic Ocean. She'd be tucked away in a weathered beach house not unlike the hundreds of others nestled near the shore. With a sigh of resignation, she rested her head on the back of the seat. In the front, the two deputies had lapsed back into their trash talk, one-upping each other with increasingly disparag-

ing comments about the athletic prowess of the Jacksonville Jaguars and Tampa Bay Buccaneers.

Neither noticed the dented black van that remained
several cars back on the congested road. The one that
had been lagging behind them since leaving the newspaper's parking garage.

When the squad car turned onto the dead-end street
leading to the bungalow, the van continued on its path
on the A1A, heading southward along the coast.

34

It seemed strange how some things became so quickly familiar, like the crunch of shells on the driveway outside. Mia lay in the bungalow's single bedroom when the sound caused her head to lift from the pillow. Pushing back the sheets, she moved to the living room. Headlights at the property's border were visible through a small gap in the closed curtains. She watched as the squad car that had been on duty pulled onto the road and drove away.

A few moments later Eric entered, his tie loose around his neck and his briefcase in hand. He locked the door behind him and reset the security system, canceling out its high-pitched beep.

"Did I wake you?" he asked, concerned. "It's after midnight."

"I wasn't really sleeping." Barefoot, she moved closer, wearing a camisole top and pajama shorts.

"We had a lot of calls come through the hotline after the press conference." He placed his briefcase on the table. Head bent and brow furrowed, he opened it, shuf-

fling through papers until he found whatever he was
looking for. "None of them turned out."

She wanted to say it was all right, but Mia knew it
wasn't. She was aware of what preoccupied his mind.
With Karen Diambro dead, The Collector would be hunting again. Maybe even tonight.

"Are you hungry? Because the deputies had groceries
delivered—"

"No," he admitted. Clasping the back of his neck, he
rubbed at the knotted muscles he found there.

"Eric, you need to get some rest."

He shook his head. "I'm too wired right now."

"Let me help you, all right?" Taking his hand, Mia led
him to the couch. It still had sheets tucked neatly into its
cushions, a pillow at one end. The bed he'd made to make
it appear they weren't sleeping together. Eric looked at
her, his moss-green eyes inquisitive as she told him to sit.
But he removed his holstered gun and did as instructed
while she went into the kitchen. She returned with a beer.

"Thanks." He took a sip from it, stretching out his
long legs and putting his feet on the coffee table. Mia
walked around behind him. Wordlessly, she began to
massage his shoulders and the back of his neck. After
several minutes of her ministrations, Mia felt him take
a deep breath and release it. She continued her rhythmic pressure, squeezing, feeling the play of firm muscles
under his skin.

"You're good." His voice was a low rumble in his
chest.

"Then maybe I'll have an alternative career when I'm

let go from the paper." She made the statement without rancor, however.

"I know you asked me not to call Miller—"

"I understand why you did it. I'm not upset."

"Come here." Eric turned and looked at her, his soft demand causing her stomach to flip. She released his shoulders and allowed him to slowly draw her down onto his lap. She laid her head on his shoulder.

"Sometimes I feel everything bearing down on me so hard I can't breathe," he confessed. "Knowing I was coming here to you tonight…it was the one good thing I kept holding on to all day."

Mia's lips brushed his collarbone through his dress shirt. "What if I'd been asleep?"

"Then I would've just watched you. It would be enough."

She thought of the press conference and the pain that had been visible on his features as he spoke of his late wife. What he did was vital, she knew, and yet so draining to the soul. She wondered again how he kept his head above water and didn't succumb to the strong undertow around him.

He finished his beer.

"I might be ready for bed, after all," he mused huskily. "But I wasn't thinking of sleeping just yet."

Mia looked up at him. Eric's lips lowered softly to hers. Her fingers grazed his hard jaw, the faint stubble there causing an erotic thrill to travel through her. As their mouths tasted one another, she undid his already loose tie with her fingers, sliding it from his collar.

"We could make love here." He nibbled at her neck. "At least the couch would look used."

"I prefer the bed."

He gave a low grunt. "Me, too."

They rose from the couch and Mia gazed into his handsome face. She noticed his expression had changed, his eyes more serious. He stroked his thumb over her cheek, appearing to struggle with voicing whatever was on his mind. "I don't know what's going to happen with us, Mia…but I want you to know I care about you, deeply."

"I know," she whispered.

"I'm going to get a shower, all right?"

She remained in place as he went into the bathroom. In the doorway he turned briefly to look at her, and Mia could see the well-defined lines of his body silhouetted against the hall light. His broad shoulders and hard chest, narrow waist and hips. Emotion mingled with the desire she felt. *I don't know what's going to happen with us.* It was an uncertainty they shared.

When he entered the bedroom a short time later, she was already nude and under the sheets. She noticed he had brought both his cell phone and service weapon with him. Although the security system was on, she was aware of the danger that existed outside their safe haven.

She raised herself onto one elbow as he removed his boxers and got into bed, turning to face her. He caressed the gentle curves of her body, cupping one small breast, the brush of his fingers instantly hardening her nipple. For a time they simply stared into one another's eyes. Then Mia kissed his throat, his collarbone, her fingers threading through the sparse hair on his chest. The night-light she'd found inside her suitcase, wrapped in one of her T-shirts, cast the bedroom in a soft, bluish glow. Even now, that one simple gesture from him tightened her throat with gratitude.

He readied himself for her, rolling on a condom, and she sighed at the welcome weight of his body over hers. His mouth captured her small gasp as he entered her, his hands tangling in her hair. She blinked hazily up at him as he began to move inside her. Their bodies were still so new to one another. Mia reveled in the way he filled her, in the way his languid strokes brought her to a fever pitch, until she was breathless and whispering pleas against his ear.

She loved his own ragged gasp as he came inside her.

A short time later, she skimmed her fingers through his hair as he slept. She'd become his refuge, she realized, from the lethal shadows he chased.

Mia said a fervent prayer to keep him safe.

It was early morning, the sky still gray outside.

She was already showered and dressed, awaiting the arrival of her deputy escort. Wandering the small living area, a cup of coffee clasped between her palms, Mia could hear the water running behind the closed door of the bathroom.

Eric's briefcase sat open on the table. She slowed next to it, unable to *not* look. A series of black-and-white photographs peeked out at her from beneath his paperwork. Despite the sense of foreboding that fell over her, she placed her cup on the table and picked them up, feeling her stomach clench at nearly the same time.

She barely recognized Karen Diambro.

In the crime scene images, her nearly nude corpse lay on black asphalt, swaddled in plastic sheeting. Enough of it had been pulled away to reveal the full extent of desecration, however. Mia swallowed past the lump in her throat. Her mind flashed to the same type of sheets that had been strung up inside the cinder-block room where she herself had been held captive only a few weeks ago.

The body was battered. Bruised. Odd burn marks marred the torso, as did the numeral carved into the skin. One hand was splayed over her breasts, its fingers bearing five gruesome holes. Even with Walt's warning, the sight shook her. She'd heard the police terminology for it before: overkill. The brutality inflicted caused tears of anger and empathy to burn behind her eyes, the images far more personal to her than any she had seen before on the job. She flipped slowly through the rest of the photos. Karen Diambro had been petite, with dark hair and brown eyes like hers.

I was the lucky one. I escaped.

Anna Lynn Gomez and Karen Diambro were substitutes for me.

The images brought the harsh reality home.

She couldn't let this psychopath continue—she had to do whatever she could to help, didn't she? The water stopped in the bathroom. Mia buried the photos back underneath the papers.

"Everything all right?" Eric asked a short time later. He'd emerged from the bedroom, wearing suit pants and a blue dress shirt. He struggled with his tie. Mia walked over to help him. As she pulled the silk through and tightened the knot for him, she took care that he didn't notice the faint tremor in her hands.

"Everything's fine," she said.

"You look upset."

"I *look* like I haven't finished my morning coffee." Forcing a smile, she allowed her fingers to glide over the smooth silk that lay against his chest, her job completed. "There. All done."

"Will's coming to have lunch with you today?"

"He's bringing it in. We're eating in the employee break room, like you suggested. And by suggested, I mean *ordered*."

Eric sighed. "I know it's not the private meeting you had in mind, but it's safer. And I'm already tying up enough resources watching you. We've got every available man across the local Bureau and JSO hunting this bastard down."

She nodded her understanding. Bending his head, he brushed his lips over hers. Mia felt a wave of guilt, knowing how strongly he'd be against it. But her emotions had pushed her to a decision.

No matter the consequences, it was something she had to do.

35

He couldn't believe what he saw.

Allan jammed the van's gear into Park and cut the engine. The door to the cinder-block building hung open like a broken jaw. Forgetting the Venti-size latte he'd picked up on his way home, he launched himself from the driver's side and hurried across the gravel in the early-morning light.

Someone had trespassed while he'd been out during the evening.

Entering, his heart pounding, he saw the overhead light had been left on. He'd been violated, but by whom? Lupita? Those low-life, teenage thugs who lived nearby? They had been caught breaking into property before. He looked around hastily, checking for some sign of disturbance. Missing tools. Overturned furniture. But nothing appeared out of place. His throat tightened with anxiety as his gaze moved to the previously padlocked cabinet. Open. Breathing hard, Allan swung its doors wide. The vials containing his treasures remained inside. All still lined up perfectly, an exact half inch between each of them. None was missing, but someone had seen them.

Someone had been here.

A red haze clouded his vision. The monster he'd barely been managing to keep tamped down emerged. Bellowing his outrage, he picked up a metal stool, beating it against the table before finally flinging it against the wall. It smacked the plastic sheeting and crashed to the floor.

Panting with exertion, he worked to rein in the anger that had been bubbling within him ever since Macfarlane had ridiculed him on television, painted him as a pathetic loser in front of the whole city. And now this. It was too much. *Too much.* His eyes swung around the unoccupied room. He yearned for someone to take his fury out on, but there was no one now. Not anymore.

Calm down. Allan drew in several deep breaths and tried to think rationally about the problem at hand.

If the intruder had seen something of concern, wouldn't they have called the police? Wouldn't flashing blue lights have met him as he turned onto the gravel road? He looked objectively around the room again, trying to see it through another person's eyes. He was neat and thorough with his cleanups. The jugs of bleach lined up on the shelf were a common household item. And the hooks in the walls and ceiling could be purely functional, couldn't they? Perhaps whoever had been snooping in the cabinet had been looking for something else, the vials' labels and contents falling beneath his or her notice.

He'd gotten lucky before.

Probably kids, he told himself. Looking for weed or alcohol.

Allan remained long enough to take a complete inventory and make sure nothing was gone. His copies of the digital recordings were still there, too, burned on CDs and hidden in a drawer of the workbench. Then turning off the light and locking the door, he took the path through the woods to the house, irritated by the birds chirping overhead in morning song.

He couldn't leave this place even for a few hours without everything going to hell.

The stench of cigarettes was noticeable as soon as he reached the screened door that led into the kitchen. Gladys sat at the table in her frayed housecoat, an ashtray in front of her littered with butts. She didn't even try to hide it. Her oxygen canister was parked at her side, as was her damned Chihuahua, who growled and bared his teeth at Allan's entrance.

He wanted to punt-kick the mangy mutt into next week. Instead, he snatched the lit cigarette she held and extinguished it in the ashtray, then dumped the lot of it into the sink and ran water over it. "We've talked about this. Repeatedly. No smoking."

She merely stared at him with her faded blue eyes and drooping mouth, her lopsided expression somehow more defiant than usual. Her skin appeared chalky-white and dry as parchment. Behind her, the television on the counter was on and turned for once to a morning news program.

"Have you seen anyone lurking around here, Mother? Lupita or those horrible Larkin boys?"

Her eyes narrowed. "I woke up at five and you weren't here. Where've you been?"

Where he'd been was Jacksonville Beach, watching the bungalow the idiotic deputies had practically led him to from the covert of an unrented property across the street. He had spent hours there—had seen Macfarlane himself go inside the house where she'd been hidden. He had been trying to plot out some kind of fail-proof plan to take her. As daylight had begun to seep into the sky, he'd come home to get some sleep and attend to Gladys's needs. He would set up camp again tonight and wait for his opportunity to prove just how far from a loser he was.

"I had a morning pickup. A television set—"

"You're a liar," Gladys spat, surprising him. "Just like your miserable father."

He saw it then. The extra set of keys to the building he kept in a drawer in his bedroom. They lay on the table next to her teacup. The keys to the cabinet's padlock were on the same ring. Allan went cold.

"Your wickedness comes from *his* side, not mine." She shook a gnarled finger, her thin voice rising. "You've been on the television! I tried to tell myself that drawing wasn't you. But now I know what you've been doing out in those woods. All these years…I've prayed for that sickness to be out of you!"

Blood pounded in his ears. Gladys? How had she gotten all the way down to his workshop? She couldn't have walked, could she? He remembered her car, an old Plymouth she let Lupita use to run errands. With the housekeeper's departure, it had been returned and now sat in the carport. It infuriated him that after all this time, she chose *now* to watch something besides televangelists.

"You promised me after that little girl." A betrayed sob escaped her. She shook her head and pressed her fingers over her wrinkled mouth. "What you did to her... I kept your filthy secret because you were my son! We prayed and you swore you'd never do it again! Shame!"

Allan wished Gladys had a mute button like the television set. She was starting to screech.

"You've got the devil inside you, just like your father! Lucifer!"

"You don't know what you're talking about," he attempted, face hot. "Your medication has you confused—"

"Those vials." She took a phlegmy, anguished breath, wheezing. "I saw them. They've got women's names on them! Their fingernails, their teeth—it makes me sick! I won't hide your sin this time!"

Closing his eyes, Allan rubbed a hand over his face. He could feel Puddles under the table, cautiously sniffing his pants leg. This couldn't be happening. He tried to shut out her accusing shrieks.

"Be quiet, Mother," he warned under his breath. He needed silence to think. Gladys was a shut-in, an invalid. He could cancel the phone service and sell her car. She wouldn't be able to tell anyone...

"You're a perversion! Bound for hell!"

She began praying aloud, beseeching God to cast the devil out of him. To make him a real man instead of a weak, pitiful child of the dark. Her entreaty went on and on until it evolved into a self-pitying monologue. The burden *He* had placed on her by giving her such a wretched, miserable son. Allan's face grew hot and he began to shake.

I won't lose control. I won't lose control.

"I should've never had you! Should've turned you in for what you did to that orphan girl! But you were *my* child! My yoke to bear!" She pumped her fist against her bony chest. "I was glad when you were gone! No one asked you back here!"

As she continued her caterwauling, Allan drove his fingernails into his palms until his skin began to bleed. A tsunami of rage washed over him. *How dare she.* If she didn't shut up he wouldn't be able to contain it. He could feel it moving inside him.

The monster clawed to get out.

It was midafternoon by the time Eric returned to the FBI building in Baymeadows. He'd been out with another agent, following up on the leads still trickling in through the hotline—including a suspicious, dark-haired male who'd been reported loitering around a girls' softball team practice at the University of North Florida. The man had been peculiar and Eric figured he might end up being someone else's problem eventually, but he wasn't their unsub. They did run him off the campus, however.

"We heard back from the Maryland and Virginia DMVs," Cameron told him, sitting at his desk as Eric entered the third-floor office. They'd split up earlier, with Cam leading a recanvassing of the area where Karen Diambro's body had been found the day before. "None of the temp agency's workers are showing licenses in those states."

It was a disappointment. The absence didn't completely rule out the names on the list—the unsub could've been unregistered there or had a license under an alias—but it greatly lessened the probability. Eric draped his suit coat over the back of a chair, taking some relief from the heat in the building's air-conditioning. "Let's still run the full background checks."

"I've already got someone on it, but it might take a few days to get through all thirty-six names." Cameron added cynically, "Oh, yeah, some guy turned himself in to the JSO a little while ago, claiming to be The Collector. He vaguely matches the physical profile, but Boyet and Scofield are dubious since he doesn't seem to know any confidential details of the case. They're contacting hospitals to see if he's been under psychological care."

While it wasn't unusual for someone unstable to admit to high-profile murders as a way of getting attention, it did add to the static that made it harder to isolate the real contenders. Eric felt a growing frustration. It seemed as though they'd been through a maze of dead ends. And despite the press conference he had hoped would incite the unsub, there hadn't been so much as a blip on the radar. Sitting down at the desk adjacent to Cameron's to check his email on the computer, his cell phone rang. The name that appeared on its screen worried him. He answered.

"Agent Macfarlane, it's Will Dvorak."

Will was supposed to see Mia at the newspaper before flying back to Chicago. Eric asked, "Is everything all right?"

"I don't want to alarm you," he said carefully. "But

Mia isn't here at the *Courier*. She left of her own voli-
tion, apparently. She's gone."

"Gone?"

"She took my car."

Eric rubbed his forehead. "You need to explain yourself."

"We'd just finished lunch and I stepped out to return
a call to my agent. When I got back, she'd disappeared
along with my car keys. She left a note apologizing and
telling me there was somewhere important she had to
go—"

"Did she say where?"

"No. She promised she isn't in any kind of trouble and
that there's no need to send a posse out after her. I went
to the parking garage to try to stop her but she'd already
taken off. She isn't answering her cell, either."

Already, Eric was moving toward the door, irritated
and worried at the same time. Cameron gave him a look,
his interest piqued.

"How long ago?"

"I'm guessing about forty minutes."

He didn't try to control the censure in his voice. "You
waited that long to call me?"

Will sounded nervous. "The call with my agent went
long, and then after I realized she was gone I spent a
while trying to reach her by phone. She's my *friend*,
Agent Macfarlane. She asked that I not alert you at all,
but I couldn't do that. I thought it best to call."

"You should've called me right away," he said flatly,
walking down the corridor. "If you hear from her, you
let me know immediately."

Eric ended the call. Cameron caught up to him as he waited for the elevator.

"What's going on?"

"Mia took off from the newspaper."

He raised his eyebrows, surprised. "Why?"

"She said there was something she had to do." He had a growing certainty about where she'd gone, and he didn't like the idea of it. In fact, he'd specifically refused her request on more than one occasion. But Mia had been adamant about wanting to help in any way she could. Eric thought back to that morning. She'd seemed pensive, but he'd chalked it up to the early hour and the stress of being taken out of her routine. He hadn't read more into it than that.

"Find out about this guy the JSO is holding, all right?" he said as the elevator doors slid open and he stepped on. They'd be negligent not to look into it, but he knew in his gut The Collector wasn't going to just turn himself in.

Cameron nodded. "Do you know where she is?"

"Yeah, I think so."

His concern grew as the elevator plummeted to the lobby. Surely Wilhelm wouldn't conduct another therapy session with Mia, especially when he himself had warned against it for her own safety. Walking briskly across the heated parking lot to his car, he tried to reach Mia by cell phone. Like Will, he got her voice mail. He called Dr. Wilhelm's office next as he pulled from the complex, but there was no answer there, either.

The Naval Air Station wasn't too far from Baymeadows. Traveling above the posted speed limit, he took the bridge over the water, heading west. He arrived at the base twenty minutes later and used his DOJ shield to gain access from the guards at the front. Upon reaching the single-story building that housed Dr. Wilhelm's office, he felt a flood of relief. Will Dvorak's Porsche convertible was parked outside.

At least he'd found her. At least she was here and not somewhere in the city, roaming around alone. *Damn it, Mia.* Shaking his head, he emerged from the sedan. He appreciated her bravery, if not her disobedience.

Eric jogged up to the building. Inside, however, he found Dr. Wilhelm's office door locked. The interior lights also appeared to be off. He knocked loudly but there was no response.

She went into a fight-or-flight reaction she couldn't come down from, causing the hyperventilation and prolonged spike in her BP. If it went on any longer she could've had a heart attack.

He raked a hand through his hair. What if Mia had somehow managed to persuade the doctor into putting her under again and she'd suffered another reaction? He recalled carrying her across the parking lot to the naval hospital's E.R. as she struggled to breathe.

Eric dashed back outside and to the hospital entrance, feeling an uneasy déjà vu. The E.R. was busy, filled with naval servicemen and families, as well as medical staff moving about in scrubs. Upon flashing his shield and explaining who he was looking for, a nurse working the front desk paged Dr. Wilhelm. Unsure if he was even there, Eric paced the area, waiting to see if the psychiatrist emerged. Five minutes later, he caught sight of him coming down the corridor.

"Don't tell me you let her talk you into doing it again," Eric ground out, advancing.

"A private word, Agent?"

The two men stepped into a quieter alcove off the main hallway.

"I didn't have much choice," Dr. Wilhelm said, stone-faced. "Ms. Hale called me and threatened to run a feature article on my work and her involvement with it unless I cooperated. Even with her signed waiver, I would come under considerable scrutiny for practicing on a civilian, something even your father's clout wouldn't be able to defuse. As you know, the drug hasn't been cleared for—"

"She's bluffing," Eric interjected. "She wouldn't do that."

"I couldn't take that chance. I'm sorry. I took every precaution, including moving her to the E.R. before-hand."

"She's already been under?" Eric's jaw hardened. "How is she?"

"I'll take you to her." Wilhelm touched his shoulder, guiding him from the alcove and down the hallway. "She experienced another blood pressure surge, but we were able to manage it better this time with the proper re-sources in place."

Eric felt his own pulse rise as he followed Dr. Wilhelm into a private, windowless exam room. Mia lay on a gurney, hands folded over her stomach and her eyes closed. She was receiving oxygen, and he could see the shallow rise and fall of her chest. A heart monitor was also hooked up beside the bed, its leads traveling underneath her blouse. He swallowed tightly. She appeared to be asleep, but the dark veil of her lashes fluttered open as he came to stand next to her. Looking up at him, her soft brown eyes filled with tears. With a tense sigh, he smoothed her hair back from her face, his upset dissipating. Now wasn't the time for a scolding. Instead, he murmured her name.

"Did you tell him?" she asked Dr. Wilhelm, her head rising faintly from the pillow.

"I thought I'd let you."

Eric touched her cheek, wiping away a tear with the pad of his thumb. She seemed jittery. "Just relax, all right? Tell me what?"

"I went back to the cinder-block room…I saw something this time, Eric." Her voice trembled. "Syringes in a white bag."

He felt the hair on the back of his neck rise.

"The print on the bag said Walker's Pharmacy."

36

"There's a Walker's Pharmacy in Green Cove Springs southwest of Jacksonville," Eric said, closing his cell phone. He glanced at Mia from the driver's side of the car. "Agent Vartran's headed there now. If the pharmacist recognizes the man in the sketch, we may have him. Syringes don't require a prescription in Florida, but if he bought them there, there's a chance he's also had prescriptions filled. They'll have his personal information."

"You didn't have to bring me back." Mia understood he was anxious to get to the location. "I could've taken Will's car—"

"You're still shaky and in no condition to drive. And I don't want you out alone. A JSO deputy is taking Will to pick up the Porsche, and I'm delivering you to the safe house. Agent Vartran will handle things until I get there."

He reached across the seat and briefly intertwined his fingers with hers.

"I thought you'd be angry with me."

His profile was somber. "You put your own safety at

stake. I couldn't ask you to do that again. I wouldn't put you at risk like that."

"That's why I took the decision out of your hands," Mia replied softly. She thought of the grim photos of Karen Diambro's remains. "He's a malignancy. I couldn't let another woman suffer and die, not if I could do something to help stop him."

Eric frowned. "You're brave, Mia. But the session could've gone very differently."

She knew what he was thinking—her previous attempt that had sent her to the E.R. in cardiac and respiratory distress. It still surprised her that Dr. Wilhelm had caved in to her threat, and that she'd managed to get through the therapy without another serious complication. Lying on the gurney as she waited for the drug to take effect, she had missed the comfort of Eric's presence. She hadn't realized how much strength she'd drawn from him until he wasn't there.

They headed into Jacksonville Beach, the late-afternoon sun a little lower in the sky. Mia gazed at the expanse of white-capped ocean as the car turned left onto the A1A.

"Was it bad?"

"I got lucky," she murmured. She'd been there with The Collector—gagged, woozy, her wrists bound to the table. But somehow she'd managed to stay calm enough to look around for something useful. She recalled the pliers he'd placed on the table in front of her. If she had stayed in the memory even another minute, she might have had to relive his torture. The thought of it sickened her.

They drove onto the dead-end street and past the row of sun-worn beach houses. Mia saw the deputy squad car already parked in front of the bungalow. Eric pulled into the driveway and escorted her inside, closing the door behind them. As she waited at the entryway, he checked through the interior, making sure it was secure. When he returned, he walked to her and touched her face.

"If we get this bastard, it's because of what you did. This could be the break we've been looking for."

"Be careful," she urged.

"I'd like the deputies to come inside with you. There may be some aftereffects from the drug—"

"I'm fine by myself," she insisted. Mia felt the dull throb of a headache, something not uncommon following the therapy. But the dizziness she'd experienced earlier was gone. "I'd really like to have some privacy. I promise, I'm going to lie on the couch and watch television."

He sighed in resignation. "Set the alarm behind me. Don't turn it off for anyone except the deputies."

Eric kissed her, a lingering touch of his lips to hers. Mia's hand lay against his shirtfront. When she looked at him, she could see both tension and excitement on his face. Mia locked the door behind him, then set the security system using the keypad. Moving to the gap between the curtains, she watched through the window as he walked across the sand and grass lawn to the squad car. He talked to the deputies inside it—probably giving instructions—before getting into his own vehicle. She remained there, fading sunlight slanting through the pane, until he had driven away.

Alone now, arms crossed over her chest, Mia glanced

around the room. She had no doubt it would be a long evening as she waited to hear for some word. There *were* things she could do, including a call to Will to apologize for pulling him into the fray, and another call to Grayson to explain her disappearance from the paper. Mentally, however, she just wasn't up to it yet. Restless, she wandered to the sheet-draped couch. Dropping onto its cushions, she picked up the television remote.

As she listened to the six o'clock news, her gaze fell on the papers Eric had left on the coffee table. He'd done some work here, apparently, after the deputies had escorted her to the newspaper that morning. Mia picked up the top several sheets, which were on the letterhead of a temporary staffing agency in downtown Jacksonville. Eric had mentioned his theory that the killer might have been an outsource repairman who had worked on security cameras at the Bargain-Mart where Anna Lynn Gomez was abducted. Her eyes scanned the list, stopping at one particular last name. She'd seen it before.

She went into the bedroom and returned with the retired detective's notepad, which she had brought with her from home. Mia flipped through the now-familiar pages until she found it.

It was probably a coincidence, even though the surname wasn't all that common. Locating her cell phone inside her purse, she used it to call Eric.

"Everything okay?" he asked, answering.

"I'm fine. But I was looking at the list of workers from the temp agency. You left it here." She pushed her hair behind one ear as she spoke, uncertain. "There's a man on the list named Allan Levi. Detective Dugger's notes mentioned that one of Joy Rourke's caseworkers was a woman named Gladys Levi. I'm wondering if there could be a connection."

"I'm still on my way to Green Cove Springs. I'll call Agent Vartran and mention it."

"It might not mean anything—"

"You never know," Eric said seriously.

Once they'd ended their call, she looked again at the television screen. A female reporter stood in front of the tire store where Karen Diambro's body had been found, doing a follow-up report. Mia half listened to the broadcast, her mind still on Gladys Levi. She was one of the people she had tried to make contact with, but she hadn't been able to find a current address or phone number in Jacksonville.

Another realization took shape inside her head— undoubtedly a coincidence, although it was a chilling one.

Levi was an anagram for *evil*.

Cameron approached Eric as he exited his car across the street from Walker's Pharmacy. The business was located on a downtown waterside square, in a one-story, stucco building with striped window awnings. Verdant shade trees lined the brick sidewalks.

"According to the assistant pharmacist on duty, the male in the sketch bears a resemblance to one of his customers." Cam's expression was triumphant. "And Mia was right—the son of a bitch's name is Allan Levi. He picks up prescriptions for his mother."

Eric felt nearly light-headed. They were so close. "Did he provide an address?"

"He looked it up in the customer database—although he wants to keep that off the record due to privacy laws." He handed over a piece of paper with the pharmacy's name and logo, the address written below it. "It's in a rural area about thirty minutes from here. This is it, Eric."

Cameron briefly clasped his shoulder.

A short distance away, the St. Johns River held glints of gold as the sun set over the water. People were fishing from a concrete pier rimmed by a park. Green Cove Springs lived up to its name—the place was like Mayberry, not at all a location where he expected to be closing in on The Collector. Eric pulled out his cell phone, his nerves taut.

"I'm calling for a warrant. Let's go ahead and get backup out here."

A violet dusk had fallen over the heavily wooded property. Law enforcement officers including a dozen federal agents were assembled at its border, preparing for a two-pronged attack. Cameron would lead the group entering the ranch house, while Eric's team traveled through the woods in back of the property. Clad in a Kevlar vest like the others, he gave a signal and the dual squadrons swarmed.

"Allan Levi! Open up! FBI—we've got a warrant!"

Eric heard Cam's barking order at the front door as he ran around the side of the house and toward the trees with his men. Flashlights marked their path as they traveled through the dense thicket behind the residence before emerging into a clearing. Eric felt his heart pumping. Everything here was as Mia had described—the concrete structure with a slab roof and single door, a makeshift gravel path that led up to the rural road. The steel skeletons of stripped cars stood at the forest's edge.

Repeating Cameron's command, he pounded on the building's locked entrance. A thin shaft of light was visible along the bottom of the door. When there was no response, Eric kicked it twice before it crashed open. The team fanned cautiously inside with guns raised.

The room was unoccupied.

"Clear!" Holstering his weapon, Eric looked around, his throat dry. At first glance, it was a standard workshop with all the basic accoutrements—a long Peg-Board holding tools, a wooden workbench and metal-top table bearing a deep dent. The place appeared obsessively clean. But it was the other trappings that told the real story, like the sheeting protecting the walls and metal hooks that along with a chain or rope could be used as restraints. Again, things Mia had relayed in detail. The antiseptic odor of bleach was overpowering. A box air conditioner hummed in the far wall, its condensation dripping onto the concrete floor. He had an image of her inside this prison—injured, drugged and somehow managing to push the unit from the single window in order to escape.

"Agent?" a deputy asked.

Eric turned to see the cabinet that stood with doors open. There were plastic medicine vials—ten of them—

lined up on the lower shelf. The realization of what they contained hit him like a punch.

Stepping closer, his eyes scanned the names printed neatly on the labels in red marker. The fifth one was marked with the name *Rebecca*. Despite the muggy heat and the weight of his vest, Eric felt a numbing coldness, the surrounding noise created by the other men fading from his ears. He had the presence of mind to ask for a pair of investigational gloves. He put them on and picked up the vial. Twisting off its cap, he spilled its contents carefully into his palm. Fingernails and two molars. Eric briefly closed his eyes. Tamping down the surge of raw emotion he felt, he placed the remains in the vial and returned it to the shelf. It was evidence now.

"Get a forensics team in here," he said hoarsely, walking out. "I want the place sprayed down with Luminol."

There was a reason for the half-dozen gallons of bleach in the room.

A field agent with a communications radio approached him. "Vartran's requesting you at the house ASAP."

"Is Levi up there?"

"No sign of him."

Cursing under his breath, Eric sprinted back through the dark woods. He wondered where Levi was. As he came into the backyard a few moments later, lights glowed from inside the house. Winding through the crowd of law enforcement standing outside, he reached the rear porch and screened door that led into a kitchen. Eric paused in the threshold. Cameron was down on his haunches beside the body of an elderly woman. She lay in a congealing pool of blood, her housecoat soaked and her eyes beginning to cloud. A butcher knife protruded from her chest.

"Gladys Levi, I presume."

Cameron looked up at him. "The body's already in rigor mortis. I'm estimating she's been dead about ten to twelve hours. And there's two vics, actually."

He indicated the other side of the table. Eric moved carefully around the blood pool, aware of the sickening, coppery scent that hung in the air. A small dog lay on its side next to a mobile oxygen canister, its tongue lolling out. Wall spatter and the condition of the body indicated it had been beaten to death.

"And you were worried you hadn't set this guy off." Cameron scratched his forehead with a gloved hand. "Agent Warren is in back. I sent the others into the yard to avoid scene contamination."

Eric noticed the small counter television with a shattered glass screen. "I'm going to have a look at the rest of the house."

Backing out of the kitchen, Eric entered the living room, which contained a chintz couch and damask curtains, doilies on end tables and Tiffany lamps. It was old-ladyish, if anything. Nothing to imply a monster lived here, other than the bodies in the kitchen.

At the end of the hallway, he found two bedrooms. The agent Cam had mentioned was in the more masculine one, already filing through items in the closet.

"Find anything?" Eric asked.

"Just your usual stuff so far."

He went into the adjacent bedroom, the one that obviously belonged to Gladys Levi, with its feminine, floral bedspread and eyelet dust ruffle. Antique baby dolls sat against the pillows, chubby infants in ruffled sleeping gowns with delicate porcelain faces and full heads of hair. There were ten of them. Still wearing gloves, Eric picked one up. Its vivid blue eyes closed as he held the doll horizontally.

"I've got the M.E. on the way." Cameron stood in the doorway, one hand on its frame. He nodded to the doll Eric held. "I guess the old lady collected them."

"They were gifts from her son."

"How do you know?"

He walked over to show Cameron. A portion of blond, human hair had been carefully braided in with the doll's synthetic tresses. The shade and quality were different, although it was a close enough match. It was what he did with the victims' hair he lopped off. An elderly woman's degenerating vision might not even have noticed.

"Do you think the mother knew?" Cameron asked.

"That her son is a serial murderer? Maybe. I don't know." He thought of Gladys Levi lying in the kitchen. "Giving her the dolls might've been a passive-aggressive way to flaunt who he was in front of her. They obviously had issues."

Rebecca's hair had been blond, the same color as the doll he held.

They knew who The Collector was now. In the hunt, they were light-years ahead of where they'd been even that morning. But a hard wave of disappointment passed through him. They didn't have the bastard, not yet.

He was still out there somewhere.

37

Eric watched from the doorway as forensics techs sprayed the workshop with Luminol, a chemical agent used to illuminate latent bloodstains. As they dimmed the lights, he felt his jaw clench at the telltale, glowing blue. The vinyl sheeting had protected only the walls. The amount of blood on the floor was shocking.

"Goddamned slaughterhouse," one of the techs muttered.

The area around the drain in the room's center was especially revealing. Levi had used a hose and bleach on the concrete after each kill, pushing the blood and water into the grate. A fluorescent cobalt hue practically pulsated around it.

"Get it on video," Eric instructed somberly. He went back out into the clearing and took a deep breath of humid night air. A sedan with two FBI agents had been covertly stationed on the rural road, in case Levi returned. His vehicle was a black van with Clay County, Florida tags. It was currently missing from the property.

Eric didn't know yet how Levi had escaped the DMV

checks in Maryland and Virginia, but they had his license plate number and the make of his vehicle here. An APB had been issued. It was only a matter of time, unless he was driving around in another stolen car, his van ditched somewhere.

"Macfarlane, we need your sign-off," another agent called to him.

He went over to an SUV with a raised back door. As lead over the investigation, chain of custody procedure required Eric to sign off on evidence seized and removed from the site. The vehicle held a number of items, already bagged and labeled. His eyes scanned the vials that contained fingernails and teeth, CDs with the audio recordings, the ten dolls taken from Gladys's bedroom, as well as the knife that had been plunged into her heart. Inside the cinder-block building, it was likely the Luminol would reveal other objects used for torture and murder.

Eric thought of the mess inside the ranch house. For someone compulsively neat, Levi hadn't attempted to conceal the bodies or clean up. That wasn't his practice. It was another sign he was losing control.

He signed the evidence forms and then stepped to the edge of the clearing, away from the others where it wasn't as noisy. In the rural area far removed from city lights, the night sky had darkened to an inky, starless black. Taking his cell phone from his pocket, he requested a patch-through to the deputies watching the beach house.

"What's the status?" he asked the one who answered the call.

"All's quiet here, Agent."

He recognized the deep voice as belonging to the heavier of the two men who'd been assigned the evening duty. "When's the last time you checked on her?"

"I knocked on the door about a half hour ago. Ms. Hale said she had a headache and was going to lie down for a while. We saw the lights go off in the bedroom a little after that."

He checked his wristwatch. It was nearly 9:00 p.m. "Let her sleep another twenty minutes. Then go up and tell her I ordered you to stay inside with her. She's going to argue, but do it anyway."

"You got it, Agent."

He closed the phone. Mia wouldn't be happy about the intrusion, but the scene out here had spooked him and he wanted her in the deputies' direct line of sight.

Cameron approached, carrying a padded envelope.

"Where was it?"

"Inside one of the drawers in the workbench." He handed him the unsealed package. Like the others, it was addressed to Eric at the Jacksonville Bureau offices. Something Levi hadn't yet had a chance to mail, apparently. He wondered if it contained the audio of Anna Lynn Gomez or Karen Diambro's murder, or both.

"There's something in it besides the recorder." Cameron appeared tense. "Like I said, you really pissed him off with the psychological profile."

Eric opened the envelope and took out the sheet of paper with its familiar, neat script.

You're a dead man, Macfarlane. I'm going to enjoy making you suffer as much as I did your wife.

At the threat, he simply pressed his lips together. He placed the note back inside the envelope.

"More evidence," he said tersely.

The bungalow sat like a moonlit seashell, the last in its row of run-down beach houses. From where Allan stood, hidden deep in the shadows of the unrented property, he could hear the tinkle of wind chimes on its porch.

A while ago, one of the deputies had gotten out of the squad car and knocked at the bungalow door. He had briefly glimpsed her sleek, dark hair as she spoke to the man, the sight of her whetting his appetite. Then she'd closed the door again and the deputy had returned to the unit. Jittery, Allan scrubbed a hand over his burning eyes.

The gun equipped with a silencer felt both heavy and thrilling in his hand.

He itched to sneak up on the squad car and take out both men, like the bad guy on a television show. But common sense told him his chances with such an approach were limited. He might get one before the other shot *him*. And Allan had no intention of dying tonight.

So he continued watching.

Tall pampas grass grew along the edge of the driveway, their white-fringed fronds waving at him in the night air. Nearby, the squad car's powerful engine was running to keep the air-conditioning going in its interior. Allan leaned against the house's siding, eyes narrowed, biding his time. He let his dark fantasies entertain him. And they were very dark. He could wait forever—Gladys was no longer his problem. A brief spark of grief ignited, then died out.

Another long stretch of time passed before the unit's engine died. The driver's side of the squad car opened again and one of the deputies emerged. Allan stood alert.

"Look, I'm starving," the deputy said to the one still inside the car. Allan strained his ears to hear. "You go on in. I'm going to make a run to the convenience store around the corner first. You want anything?"

He couldn't make out the response from the vehicle's interior, but the one who had exited jogged off down the road. *They were going inside.* Allan felt his pulse speed up. With the two officers separated, this could be his best—and only—chance.

Although the cruiser's interior light remained on, the other man hadn't yet exited. The deputy's head was bent, as if he were completing paperwork. Another sign this was meant to be.

Now or never.

Leaving the protection of the shadow of the house, Allan crept carefully across the dead-end street, gun poised and avoiding the reach of the streetlight. His blood coursed. He prayed the deputy remained engrossed in whatever he was doing. Reaching the hardy pampas grass, he ducked down behind it and waited.

Finally, the deputy got out and stretched. He was tall and beefy, with a blond crew cut. He lumbered over the sand and grass lawn, passing the metal sign that indicated the bungalow had a security system. Perspiring, his nerves thrumming, Allan stood from his hiding place and fell silently into step behind him. When the man went onto the porch, he quickly advanced. Sensing his presence, the deputy began to whirl, but the tip of the gun barrel pressing against the back of his head made him halt.

"If you want to live, you knock on the door and get her to open up," Allan ordered in his ear, voice low. "Do it now."

He jabbed the barrel hard for emphasis. He could feel the deputy quiver in his uniform. Thinking he had gone stupid with fear, he repeated, *"Do. It. Now."*

The deputy hesitated, then knocked. Head buzzing with excitement, Allan shrank down behind his larger form. It took a minute, but he saw the curtain move at the front of the house. There were four muted beeps as the alarm was turned off inside.

And then the door opened. He heard her voice.

"Everything's still fine in here, Deputy. I—"

Mia stumbled backward as Allan shoved the man inside, keeping the barrel of the gun at the base of his skull. He felt a rush of power as he saw her eyes go wide and the blood drain from her face.

"You scream and he's dead." Allan kicked the door closed behind him.

He grinned at her.

Then he shot the deputy in the back of the head, anyway.

38

The silencer muted the noise, making a satisfying *thwap* as the man toppled. Blood poured from the wound in his skull, soaking the bristle-blond hair. Allan swung the barrel toward Mia. She looked exquisite—hair disheveled around her face, her mouth open in shock and horror.

With a choked cry, she sprinted down the hallway, her only free path. Allan launched after her, wedging his shoulder into the door she tried to slam closed. He rammed it open with such force she fell backward onto the carpet. His excitement spiked at the terror he saw in her eyes.

Crawling, she reached the rumpled bed and pulled herself up. What was she searching for? Her purse. It lay on the comforter. She was going for her cell phone. Allan lunged and tore the bag from her hands. Cornered, she picked up a brass lamp from the nightstand and threw it at him. He deflected it with his forearm but felt the bruising contact. *She'll pay for that.* She dove across the bed, still trying to escape. He caught her by the waistband of her shorts before she made it off the mattress. Screaming, she turned and kicked, her bare heel catching him painfully in the thigh and missing his groin by inches.

He grabbed her by the ankles and dragged her back across the bed, jerking her up. If he didn't quiet her, the other deputy would hear from outside. Warding off her small fists, he slapped her hard across the face with the back of his hand, a bone-jarring blow. She fell back onto the mattress.

Allan leaped on top of her and wrapped his hands around her slender throat. He began to squeeze, thrilling at the bob of her small Adam's apple under his thumbs. Mia kicked and scratched, gasping for air. He continued choking her, kept his fingers clamped around her throat until her movements grew clumsier and her eyes finally fluttered closed, her hands dropping limply onto the bed.

Breathing hard, he loosened his grip. He wanted her out, not dead. At least not yet. He ran his hands over her soft skin.

His eyes latched on to the bedroom closet. There was a collection of men's silk ties—tasteful, expensive— hanging inside. Allan went over and removed two. He used the first to bind her wrists together. Already, she was starting to come around. She resisted weakly, cough- ing as he knotted the second one and forced it between her teeth, tying it at the back of her head.

Then Allan scooped her up and carried her to the closet. Dumping her onto its floor, he slammed the door closed and put a chair under its knob. That should keep her quiet long enough to dispose of deputy number two.

He couldn't help but smile. Things were going so much better than he'd ever imagined. Before, his only hint of a plan had been to somehow kill the guardsmen and burst through the bungalow's door, spiriting Mia away as the alarm screeched like a banshee. It would have been a haphazard approach. So much could have gone wrong. Here, hidden snugly inside the house, he had the element of surprise and so much more to gain.

Reentering the living room, he pulled the gun from his waistband and stepped around the deputy's body that lay facedown in a spreading pool of blood. He was just in time, he thought, as a knock came at the door. Allan peeped out from behind the curtain, liking what he saw. The other deputy stood with hands full, bearing two plastic soda bottles, chips and hot dogs.

He swung the door open, his gun pointed. The man startled.

Thwap.

He fell backward onto the porch. Bright crimson bloomed on the tan uniform. He'd shot him in the chest. Allan looked around for witnesses as the deputy writhed and gasped for air. He saw no one.

"Who sent you inside the house?" Leaning over him, Allan nudged him hard with his shoe and wielded the gun. "On whose orders?"

"Macfarlane," he managed to croak out. Pink froth formed on his lips. Pleased, Allan shot him a second time, putting him out of his misery.

He picked up the man's booted feet and dragged him over the threshold and inside, lining him up next to his partner. Then Allan went back out to the porch, noticing the bloodstain on the thick, woven doormat. He flipped it over to hide the mess, then picked up the drinks and food and went back inside.

Looking around the quaint but comfortable interior, Allan removed one of the hot dogs from its paper packaging and took a bite, smiling to himself as he thoughtfully chewed. He had some time to play with her before Macfarlane returned.

And then he would have them both.

Monsters lived in the dark closet. Her mother had told her they liked to eat bad little girls.

Mia banged on the inside of the door, her face wet with tears. "Please, Mommy. I'm afraid! Let me out!"

But all she heard in return was silence.

Mia awoke with a start, disoriented and in blackness, her right cheekbone throbbing as it pressed into the carpeting's scratchy pile. It took a few seconds for her mind to flash back to what had just occurred.

He was here, inside the house. He'd killed the deputy in front of her.

She couldn't stop her rising panic. Hot tears leaked from her eyes. All of it came flooding back to her. Her windpipe felt raw and bruised. She'd expected to die right there with him straddling her and his big hands squeezing her throat, but she now realized he was saving her for something far worse. The thought caused a cold sweat to break out on her body. Desperate, she twisted her wrists, trying to loosen the binding as her tongue pushed against the hard knot of fabric in her mouth. She was panting and not getting enough air through her nose, the lack of oxygen feeding her terror. It took all of her willpower to concentrate on her breathing, to force it to slow down or else lose consciousness again.

Good, Mia. In and out.

Managing to get to her knees in the cramped, unlit space, she pushed at the door but it wouldn't budge. What had happened to the other deputy? Was he dead, too? Or maybe he was looking for her. She had to make some noise. Whimpering through her gag, she pounded on the wooden panel with her bound fists. She prayed for someone to find her before the real-life monster returned.

The low voice that came through the door sent ice water trickling down her spine.

"I can hear you crying, Mia."

Her heart stopped. *Oh, God. No.*

"You've been a very bad girl. Running away from me. Twice." He chuckled. "That's not going to happen again."

The closet door swung open. His bland face studied her, his pale blue eyes curious and cold. Then he grabbed her by her bound wrists, hauling her to her feet. Mia's head swam at his closeness. There were spots of blood on his shirt from where he'd shot the deputy at point-blank range. The gun was tucked into the waistband of his chinos.

"You and I have some catching up to do."

He walked her into the hall, keeping a hand braced firmly on the back of her neck. Her skin was damp with perspiration, and her knees felt like gelatin as he pushed her forward into the living room where the nightmare had begun. Mia cried out, the sound muffled by the cloth in her mouth. The two deputies lay on the floor side by side, a large circle of blood beneath them. More of it flecked the white wall.

"Sit," he ordered, pointing to a spindle-back, wooden armchair he'd moved from the dining area. The chair now faced the sofa. When Mia hesitated, he dragged her over and shoved her down hard.

She trembled as he strolled around behind her, unsure of what he was about to do.

"If you start screaming, it goes back in. Do I make myself clear?" When she gave a small nod, he untied the gag. She took a quavering breath, filling her lungs with air. He then dropped down on the couch facing her, appearing smug. He pulled her chair closer so their knees touched.

"Do you know who I am?"

She blinked back tears, struggling to find her voice. Mia knew the answer in her gut.

"Your name…is Allan Levi." The words were rusty in her damaged throat. When he seemed to be waiting for something else, she added, "You abducted Joy Rourke in front of me twenty-five years ago."

A chilling smile spread over his face. "You *do* remember. I was at the group home that day to drop off papers for Mother. I never made it inside. I was too entranced by the little girls sitting on the sidewalk holding hands. So sweet and innocent."

She wanted to add "helpless." It was why he'd started out on a child. He reached out and ran possessive hands over her forearms. "You still remind me of a little girl. So small and delicate."

Biting her lip, she closed her eyes, her skin crawling at his touch.

"Joy was an easy mark. Trusting. But you ran from me. Imagine my surprise when I recognized you in the newspaper all these years later, covering my…work. It was as if it was meant to be. Well, I *had* to take you, didn't I?"

She thought of the dead women. Disgust filled her. "How…how did you find me?"

"You mean at this run-down beach shanty? I suspected you weren't at your apartment, since there were no lights on and you've been keeping the place lit like a church on Christmas Eve. But a call to your office receptionist confirmed you *were* still working, even though I haven't seen your name in the paper lately. What did they do—bump you down to obits because of me?"

He indicated the two dead men. "When I saw the squad car leaving the employee parking garage yesterday, I suspected you were inside it, being delivered to wherever the FBI had stashed you. I trailed it here, and I've been watching and waiting ever since for the right opportunity."

Her desire to keep working had gotten those men killed.

"You should have come to me that day outside the foster care home." His clammy hand squeezed her bare thigh. It was all she could do not to use her bound hands to shove him away, but his size and the gun at his side were a constant threat. He leered at her. "I'm not a fan of disobedience."

He leaned closer, his face inches from hers. "I can forgive a frightened child, but running away from me three weeks ago…that's going to cost you."

Allan looked into her eyes, searching for her fear. Mia did everything she could not to give it to him. She tried to sound brave.

"Did you steal another car to abduct me in?" she asked blithely.

The light huff of his laugh fanned her face. "Sorry. I won't be carrying you off into the night this time. I have a better plan. We're going to wait right here for Agent Macfarlane to arrive. He *is* staying here at night?"

The words chilled her to the bone as she suddenly understood. Eric.

"He radioed, apparently. He sent the two deputies in to sit with you. They were on their way when I *dispatched* them." He smirked. "Pardon the pun."

Then he would find nothing unusual about the squad car being unoccupied in front of the house. He would think the deputies were inside. Mia felt her pulse race. Eric would be walking into an ambush.

Allan stood and went around behind her again, forcing the gag back into her mouth despite her resistance. Then he returned to his seat in front of her. He took her bound hands in his, paying particular attention to the left one with its two scabbed nail beds. Mia felt nauseous. Fresh perspiration broke out on her skin. She wished for a drug to sedate her, but she was painfully alert.

His cold eyes pinned hers. "It might be a while before

he arrives. But I have an idea of how we can pass the time. Shall we continue where we left off?"

The cloth stifled her agonized scream as he used his thumbnail to dig into the first of the healing wounds.

39

They were starting to learn more about Allan Levi, including the fact that his real last name was Bolstrup—Levi was the mother's maiden name. Gladys had dropped the Bolstrup upon her divorce thirty-seven years ago, and changed her small son's surname. When they contacted the Maryland and Virginia DMVs again, Eric wondered if *Allan Bolstrup* would appear in one of their databases. It would explain how he hadn't come up in the previous check. Going by his alternate name there would have been another subtle act of defiance against his mother.

"I just got off the phone with Gladys Levi's primary physician," Cameron said as he walked across the pine needle-covered ground toward him. "She suffered a stroke three years ago."

"The time line matches. It could have been what brought him back to Florida."

They stood at the edge of the property outside the ranch house, its tidy facade lit by squad cars. A van belonging to the Clay County M.E.'s Office sat in the driveway.

"Forensics is nearly done and the M.E.'s about to remove the body. I say we clear out of here soon." Cameron peered at him. As if he could read his thoughts, he said, "We're going to find him, Eric. It's just a matter of time."

He traveled off again, yelling directions to keep the recently arrived media farther back. Their presence guaranteed Levi wouldn't return here. Left alone, Eric heard the low hoot of an owl coming from somewhere deep in the pinewoods. Disregarding the current chaos, the setting was bucolic—a disquieting contradiction to the grim torture chamber hidden out back. It was interesting that despite their evident dysfunction, Levi had still accepted responsibility for his ailing mother's care. Whether it was out of a sense of obligation or a possible future inheritance of the property, he wasn't sure.

He also wondered if he might have taken a perverse, extra pleasure in knowing his mother was only a short distance away, unaware, as he tortured and killed.

We're going to find him. Every fiber of his being hoped Cam was right. They knew who he was now but he'd dropped off the face of the earth once before.

Taking out his cell phone, he used it to request another patch-through to the deputies at the bungalow. A male voice emerged over the airwaves, shrouded in radio static. "Deputy Cutshaw."

It was the other one who answered this time.

"This is Agent Macfarlane. Are you inside the house?"

"Yes, sir. Have been for a while now. Ms. Hale's gone on to bed," he drawled. "She probably just didn't want to sit around here with us all night."

"Stay alert. Don't get caught up watching television—"

"We know how to do our job, Agent. We've got the place sewn up tighter than Fort Knox."

Eric blew out a breath, telling himself she couldn't be safer than with two armed guards in the next room. "I should be there within the hour. We're locking down the crime scene now."

He closed the cell phone. Cameron was right—it was getting late and there wasn't a lot more they could do here. Alerts were out for Levi and the black van throughout the state and into portions of Georgia and Alabama. He would leave a few men stationed on the property, go back to the bungalow to get a few hours' sleep and then start up again early the next morning. He felt exhausted and wired all at once. Eric had briefly considered having the deputies wake Mia. He'd wanted to hear her voice but decided to let her sleep.

The more oblivious she was to the drama the better.

Mia watched through watery eyes as Allan tossed the deputy's shoulder radio onto the coffee table and went to stand in front of the television again. Hearing Eric through the static had caused her throat to clog with tears. She'd cried out to him through the gag, but he hadn't been able to hear her.

She felt a spiraling hopelessness. There was nothing she could do to help him or herself.

White-hot pain radiated from the reopened wounds on her fingers, the gouged flesh pulsating and dripping blood onto the carpet like two slowly leaking faucets.

When he'd grown bored with using his thumb, he had opted for a ballpoint pen lying among Eric's papers, driving it into her exposed nail beds. Each time she'd started to pass out from the agonizing pain, he had slapped her back to alertness. Her wrists were now tied to the arms of the chair to further restrain her movement. He had been torturing her intermittently, allowing her short reprieves while he kept an eye on the evening news.

Drowning in dread and fear, she prayed it would continue to hold his attention.

The screen showed a ranch house from a distance, lit by the blue lights of police cars. Although he'd lowered the sound when the call came through, Mia could read the caption.

Break in Jacksonville Serial Killer Case.

She looked at the bodies of the two deputies on the floor.

The news broke for a commercial segment. She felt her panic rise as Allan waltzed toward her again. He had Deputy Cutshaw's name bar pinned to his shirt, his idea of a joke, apparently. *No, please. No more.* Frantic, she struggled, nearly rocking the chair off its legs as he neared. Her muffled scream burned inside her already ravaged throat. He raised an inquisitive eyebrow.

"What's this? I thought we were having fun together."

She tried to gulp air, barely able to breathe through the confining cloth wet with her saliva. Towering over her, he tucked a few strands of her sweat-damp hair back behind her ear. She wore only a bra and panties, her outer clothes cut off her with a kitchen knife he'd also pressed against her throat.

"You're acting like a frightened child."

Mia glared at him despite the fresh tears that slipped down her face. With a feigned sigh, he sat across from her, lounging back on the sofa cushions as if they were having a casual chat.

"What were we talking about before the call came through? Oh, yes, I remember now. My initial fascination with you. After the heat died down, I went back to the group home looking for that sweet, dark-haired child. But by then you'd been moved somewhere else. I learned your name from Mother's files, but I couldn't find out where you'd been placed. I had no choice but to forget you."

He leaned closer. The pale blue eyes danced. He traced the scabbed numeral on her stomach, the touch of his index finger sending chills of revulsion through her so intense Mia feared she would vomit. If she did, it was likely she would choke on it. She fought the urge.

"It's fate that after all these years you've come back into my life. I have to admit I've become a little obsessed with you. What's the old saying? The one who got away. Or at least you *were*."

His predatory smile made her go cold. Dropping his gaze to her two damaged fingers, he tsked softly.

"I've made a mess of these, haven't I? Tell you what…"

Allan dug into the pocket of his chinos. *No, God, please.* Mia whimpered, her throat convulsing at the small pair of pliers he withdrew.

"I found them in a drawer. You heard Agent Macfarlane—we've still got some time to kill. How about I leave those two alone and start with a fresh one?"

Headed back to Jacksonville Beach, Eric spent part of the drive making requisite phone calls, including one to SAC Johnston to update him on the break in the investigation. Afterward, he closed the device and returned it to his shirt pocket. He needed the solitude to process the emotions he'd been holding at bay until now.

It was impossible not to dwell on what the final hours of Rebecca's life had been like. Seeing her name on the vial, grim pieces of her inside it—all of it had taken him back to her murder three years ago. He released a pent-up breath and passed a hand over his eyes. *Forgive me for not being able to save you.*

Mia's name had been on one of the vials, as well. At least when they caught Levi, she would finally be safe. There was little doubt she had been scarred both physically and emotionally by what she'd gone through, but unlike Rebecca she would still be alive. Mia was strong. She'd be able to get on with her life.

If he put an end to Levi's reign, at least one woman he loved would survive.

And he *had* fallen in love with her, he realized. Lost in thought, he drove past the inlet marina and brightly lit shopping complexes that were only a short distance from the Atlantic. His cell phone rang. Eric glanced at the screen before answering.

"Boyet and Scofield located a cousin of Gladys Levi in South Carolina," Cameron told him over the airwaves. "They interviewed her by phone. She shared quite a bit of information on the family, including the fact that the father was a convicted felon. Arnold Bolstrup went to prison when Allan was six years old."

Eric turned onto the A1A, pale sand and the blackened plane of ocean to his right. "What for?"

"Rape and battery of a coworker at his factory job. Bolstrup was a violent drinker and an after-hours flirtation got out of control. He died behind bars twenty-five years ago—shanked by another inmate."

It occurred to Eric the father's death would have been around the same time Levi took Joy Rourke, his likely first victim.

"According to the cousin, Gladys was a bible-thumper who got even more religious after her husband's arrest," Cameron continued. "She hated Arnold for what he'd done and soured on men in general."

"Did Allan Levi have any contact with his father in prison?"

"The mother forbade it. She wouldn't even allow them to exchange letters. The cousin described Allan as aloof, odd and not very masculine. Not all that surprising considering the mother's domineering personality and the removal of any male figures from her son's life. Gladys sent Allan to college out of state—he got a degree with honors but never did anything with it. The cousin said he moved around a lot. She'd heard he was living in Maryland before returning home after the mother's stroke."

"What about his relationships with other women?" Driving past, Eric noticed the convenience store on the corner was particularly busy, with a pack of teenagers loitering in the parking lot. He turned onto the residential street a block off the beach and traveled down it. The white-and-blue squad car sat unoccupied in front of the bungalow.

"To the cousin's knowledge, Allan never had a girlfriend—not in high school or college. She suspected he was gay, but she'd never heard of a boyfriend, either. She also mentioned an incident when he was around twelve. He got caught torturing and killing neighborhood cats—he removed their claws. They were still living in metro Jacksonville at the time. Gladys didn't move out to the country until she retired from social work."

A psychological pathology was beginning to emerge. Cutting the sedan's engine in the driveway, Eric went up the sidewalk to the front porch, still talking to Cameron on the phone. Light seeping through the bungalow's closed curtains cast a hazy glow onto the stoop.

"Are there any other relatives?" he asked. "Someone Levi might trust enough to give him refuge?"

"It's doubtful. The cousin is the last living relative on the mother's side of the family. Contact's been broken with the father's side since he was a kid."

The strong breeze coming in from the ocean ruffled Eric's hair. He wanted to finish the call before he went inside, so he remained on the stoop, listening to Cameron relay what else the detectives had learned. As he stood there, he noticed a line of red pharaoh ants, common to the South, marching over the concrete and under the doormat. The mat had been flipped upside down, its rubber backing exposed. Curious, he kicked up a corner with the toe of his dress shoe to see what was attracting them. The insects swarmed over a dark, wet spot on the woven material. Some of it had dripped onto the concrete.

It looked like blood.

He recalled from a forensics entomology class that pharaoh ants would consume almost anything…including plasma. Alert, his eyes searched the perimeter as Cameron continued talking. An alley ran behind the look-alike bungalows across the street. He barely made out the black van sitting in shadow. Eric felt his heart turn over.

Levi was here.

Based on the blood, at least one of the deputies had gone down.

He'd already been standing outside the bungalow for a full two minutes engaged in phone discussion. Trying to appear calm, he strolled casually back onto the sidewalk, pacing a short distance out with one hand on his hip and the cell phone pressed to his ear as if nothing had changed. He suspected he was being watched from behind the curtains.

"Cam, listen to me," he interrupted, voice low as he stared onto the road, his back to the house. "I need a SWAT unit at the rental property. Sirens off. Get them here but keep them covert—"

"What's going on?"

"I think Levi's in the house with Mia. There's blood on the front stoop and a black van's parked in the alley across the street."

"Jesus. Where are the deputies?"

"I don't know." His gut told him both men were dead

or incapacitated. Things were too quiet. How had Levi known where to find her?

Maybe Mia was already dead, too. The possibility felt like a knife through his chest.

"Eric." Cameron's voice was insistent. "I know what you're thinking and you can't go in there. If he *is* inside, you're as good as dead! Levi *wants* you."

"He's already seen me outside. If I don't go in, he's going to know he's been made." And then he'd get desperate. If Mia was still alive, she wouldn't be for much longer if Levi thought they were on to him.

There wasn't another choice.

"He's lying in wait for you! You'll be giving him exactly what he wants—"

"I won't leave her alone with him. I'm counting on you, Cam. Don't let them rush the place—it could get her killed. Levi can't know he's cornered or it's over." He recalled the sliding glass doors in back. They were covered by cheap vertical blinds that gapped slightly even when closed. It was possible a shot could be fired through the glass. "Get a sharpshooter here, too. I'll try to get him into the kitchen."

"He may not give you that chance—"

"Sounds good," he said loudly, facing the bungalow again. "We'll talk again in the morning."

"Eric!"

He closed the cell phone. Eric's heart pounded. He thought of Mia and prayed there was still a reason to risk going inside. Wind chimes danced in the soughing wind as he stepped back onto the porch.

There was a possibility Levi would kill him on sight,

but Eric believed his sadistic nature would make him want to draw out his victory over him, especially if he thought he had taken him by surprise and had all the time in the world. Hopefully it would be long enough to get the SWAT unit and sniper there. He put his key into the lock, briefly closing his eyes, and attempted to prepare himself for whatever he was about to walk into.

40

Eric felt a vortex suck the air from his lungs. The deputies' bodies lay on the floor in front of him. In the same instant, he heard the metallic clink of a round dropping into a chamber. He froze; he hadn't drawn his own weapon. To do so would be giving away that he'd known of Levi's presence before entering.

"Good evening, Agent Macfarlane." He stood about ten feet away, his gun trained. "Careful now. Keep your hands where I can see them or this gets ugly fast."

"Take it easy, all right?" Slowly, Eric lifted his hands and looked around. Mia was in a chair on the other side of the room. Stripped to her underwear, her head sagged onto her chest, her curtain of dark hair obscuring her features. The sight of her hit him hard. She appeared unconscious but alive.

It had to be good enough for now.

"She's an exotic little thing, isn't she? Now, I want you to very slowly remove your gun. Then slide it on the floor to me and close the door."

He did as told. Once Levi had confiscated the weapon,

he motioned Eric farther inside, keeping carefully behind him with his own firearm raised. They stepped around the deputies. The larger of them—the one whose last name was Graham—lay facedown. The back of his skull was a gory mess. The other one, Cutshaw, had at least one gunshot wound to the chest. Eric's pulse thudded, his mouth dry. Both men's weapons were gone.

"I'm afraid you're going to lose your cleaning deposit," Levi commented drily.

Moving closer to Mia in the room's subdued lighting, he felt his insides twist. His neckties had been used to bind her forearms to the chair, another used as a gag. Her right cheekbone appeared swollen and her neck bruised. Her eyes were closed, her dark lashes in stark contrast to her deathly pale skin.

Eric winced. The wounds on her fingers had been reopened and were bleeding badly. Two more fingernails had been removed. He wondered how long Levi had been here—how long she'd had to endure his torture. He shoved down his anger, knowing it would get them both killed. One of the deputy's shoulder radios lay on the coffee table on top of his paperwork. He realized that when he'd called the second time, he had been speaking to Levi instead. It confirmed he'd used a voice disguiser in the audio recordings.

"As you can see, we've been having a little fun while we waited."

"Waited?" he asked.

"For you, of course. Are you carrying any other weapons?"

"No."

"Mind if I check? Hands on your head. Now." Levi kept behind him, shoving the gun into his spine. Eric raised his hands like a suspect being placed under arrest and interlocked his fingers behind his neck. He remained motionless as Levi patted him down, keeping the firearm's barrel snug against his body as he checked for another gun. He took his cell phone. When he was satisfied, he said, "Now turn around slowly."

They came face-to-face. Nearly as tall as Eric, Levi was an animated version of the artist's sketch—receding dark hairline, finely arched brows, a somewhat weak chin. A face that could easily blend in or be forgotten. But the pale eyes were bloodshot and cold. He smiled thinly, enjoying the fact that he had the upper hand. The gun was pointed at Eric's chest.

"You raided my home tonight. Did you find my girls?"

He gave a faint nod. "We found your mother, too."

For a split second, the cool veneer disappeared. Regret flashed in Levi's eyes before it flickered out again. "Then you saw the vial marked Rebecca. Very lovely woman, your wife. I recall how she screamed for you as I was cutting her up. But you know that already. I sent you the audio to remember her by."

Eric's jaw tightened but he held Levi's stare. He had to stay calm.

Mia moaned, her head moving weakly. She was beginning to come around.

"You attract the pretty ones, don't you?"

When Eric made no comment, Levi added, "Oh, come now. You're quite handsome, Agent Macfarlane. I saw the two of you outside her apartment building that night. You practically made love to her in the shadow of the squad car. You've been spending your nights here with her. A convenient setup, I think. The sheets on the couch are a nice touch, but I'm sure you've been slipping into her bed. A lonely widower like you must have needs."

Keeping the gun on Eric, he ambled around behind Mia. "Let's help her wake up."

Eric's hands clenched into fists as Levi roughly grabbed her hair with one hand, snapping her head back. Her soft brown eyes fluttered and she cried out through the gag. Tears trickled down her face when she saw him, her gaze locking with his. Eric's heart ached.

"There's your hero, Mia. But he won't be able to save *you,* either. You'll be the second of two loves he's failed." He reached into his pocket with his free hand, pulling out a pair of nickel-plated handcuffs. "I went through your things while we were waiting—I hope you don't mind. I thought these might come in handy."

He tossed them to Eric and nodded to a second spindle-back armchair that had been relocated from the dining area. "You know what to do. Your right wrist, please."

The chair faced Mia but was about a dozen feet away. Levi put the gun to her head to show he meant business. Eric had no alternative. He sat down in it and snapped one of the cuffs on his wrist, the other on the chair arm, giving it a tug to show they were secure.

Satisfied, Levi walked over. His lips twisted into a sneer. "I didn't appreciate what you said about me at your press conference."

Hauling his arm back, he struck Eric's temple hard

with the gun barrel. Pain exploded inside his head, his vision blurring and the room tilting. He heard Mia whimper.

"I'm in charge now, Agent. And I'm hardly the underachiever you think I am."

Don't black out. Warmth ran down the side of his face. Several heavy drops of blood splashed onto his shirtfront.

Levi returned to Mia. Her injured fingers were splayed on the chair arm, secured tightly in place. He applied pressure to the oozing wounds with the heel of his hand. She released a muffled, agonized scream and tried to lurch off the chair.

"Don't touch her!" Breathing heavily, dizzy from the hard blow, Eric attempted to draw Levi's focus back to him. "It's me you're pissed off with! *I'm here.*"

"I have to admit, I *have* been playing with her fragile fingers for a while now. All right, Agent. You don't want me to touch her—let's move on to a new game."

Levi took something from the table. A transparent dry cleaning bag. He snapped it in the air to open it. Every muscle, every nerve under Eric's skin jumped to attention. His clothes had been inside it, hanging in the bedroom closet.

"It's interesting how one can find lethal instruments in the most mundane things," Levi said with a smile.

Eric felt his throat close with dread. He understood what the placement of the chairs was about. Levi's compulsion to kill and torture in front of a witness—a witness destined to be his next victim—hadn't been satiated in some time. What he wanted was for Eric to watch.

"For better suction." Levi took the gag from Mia's mouth. She sobbed, her narrow shoulders shaking.

"Don't," Eric pleaded. He gave an involuntary shake of his head. Things were moving too fast. He needed more time for the SWAT team to assemble, to strategize the best way inside.

"Why so glum, Agent? You've got the finest seat in the house."

Eric's eyes held Mia's for a bare, emotional second before the plastic bag went over her head.

The SWAT team was assembling two doors down, out of visibility from the bungalow. Vacationers staying at the nearby properties were being warned to keep indoors. Men in body armor, equipped with assault guns and stun grenades, stood waiting for the command to strike. Overhead, iron-gray clouds had eclipsed the moon, further darkening the sky and promising to bring the rain the meteorologists had been talking about.

Cameron felt a rush of anxiety, though he kept it hidden from the others on standby in the sparsely grassed yard. He had been heading back to St. Augustine when he'd made a sharp U-turn on the road.

Eric had cut off their phone conversation to walk willingly into a death trap.

From here, watching through binoculars as he stood among the SWAT team and other federal agents, things appeared deceptively quiet. Thin, yellow light leaked from behind the bungalow's closed curtains. Cameron wondered what the hell was going on inside.

Either way, they had Levi—he would be theirs, dead

or alive. But what about the others who were in there? Cameron felt the heavy weight of responsibility. He had called Eric in on this; he was the one who had brought him down here.

I'm counting on you, Cam. Don't let them rush the place—it could get her killed.

Anytime law enforcement was forced to enter a hostage situation, the chance of casualties grew. But for all he knew at this moment, it was too late already. Eric, Mia, the two deputies—all of them could be dead.

"We can snake in a thermographic camera," the SWAT team captain said as he approached. He was buzz-haired and heavily muscled. A tattoo on one forearm indicated him as former military. "Body heat readings will tell us where they are."

"How long to set it up?"

"Hard to say. We'll have to find an entry point, like a vent. But we're going to need it to determine specific locations before we go inside. It's the best chance you've got. Otherwise, we can throw in the grenades, storm the place and hope we get to your suspect before he takes anyone out."

"Get the cameras in there," Cameron said, stomping sand off his shoes. He described the house's ventilation system. "What about the sniper?"

"He's on his way—he got caught in a traffic snarl on I-95." The captain held a command radio in his right hand. "Until he gets here I've got a man outside the fence in back with binoculars and a limited view into the kitchen. But he says no one's visible from that vantage point."

The wind had picked up and the first rain began to fall—hard, fat drops plunking onto the earth around them. Cameron heard one of the field agents curse. The downpour was expected to worsen throughout the night.

Damn it, Eric. He blew out a tense breath, perspiring in the muggy night air. If Levi didn't kill him, he just might do it himself when this was all over.

He only hoped he got the chance.

Levi was a cat toying with his prey. For the fourth time, Mia's body twisted against its restraints as he tightened the seal over her mouth and nose, pulling the thin, transparent plastic taut with one hand.

Thirty seconds. Forty seconds. Too long without oxygen. Cuffed to the chair, Levi's gun on him, Eric watched in agonized helplessness before the bag was once again loosened enough to keep her from slipping into unconsciousness. She wheezed, sobbing, the flaccid plastic making smacking sounds against her lips as she feebly drew in air.

Face hot and eyes red, he felt as though he were being slowly pulled apart.

"You son of a bitch," he whispered, voice ragged.

Levi's expression back to him was one of unadulterated glee. He waited for her lungs to fill a few more times and then he tugged the plastic tight again. Forearms tied down, Mia's back arched off the chair, her throat making a desperate choking sound as she fought in vain to breathe.

"That's a good girl," Levi muttered, enthralled. His titillation was repulsive.

Chest heaving, Eric yanked hard at the chair's arm, the cuff clanking against the wood. "Don't do this! Deal with me!"

Levi grinned, watching him. He *needed* his witness, Eric realized all over again. He needed to see the anguish and fear of his observer as much as he needed it from his victim. He craved someone to behold his power. And this time he had a male—a federal agent, his own nemesis—as his spectator. The feeling of supremacy had to go far beyond anything he'd enjoyed with the drugged women.

He felt his panic rising. Levi had cut off her air for a good forty-five seconds this time. She was getting weaker, the fight beginning to go out of her by degrees. Her bloodied fingers that had been clenched now uncurled. Eric's heart beat out a rapid staccato. He couldn't take this anymore. Muscles straining, he pulled so hard at the chair arm the metal cuff cut into his wrist, opening his skin. He felt the arm's dovetailed joints loosen. Another series of forceful, painful yanks and they pulled apart. Sliding the cuff from the wood, Eric rose.

The dry cleaning bag went instantly limp. Levi gripped the gun. "Remain seated!"

"No." It was a risk he had to take or watch her die a slow and excruciating death. Eric was betting his own life on Levi's need for an audience. He remained standing. Mia breathed in tight little rasps, her head wobbling under the plastic.

"I said, be seated or I'll shoot you now!"

"Then shoot me," Eric challenged between clenched teeth. "Because I'm not going to watch another fucking second of this."

Turning his back on Levi's outrage, he waited to feel the hot force of a bullet, see his world fade to nothingness as the metal slug passed through his skull. But instead all that came at him were more hurled threats. Pulse thrumming, Eric moved slowly toward the kitchen. If Levi killed *him,* there would be no one to watch.

"Say goodbye to her, then!"

He stopped but didn't turn around. His throat ached as he heard the bag snap tight over Mia's face again. Her chair rocked on its legs as the asphyxiation continued. Eric walked away on knees that threatened to buckle.

Leaving her was the hardest thing he'd ever done.

But it was the only way to lure Levi away from her.

He stepped over the dead men's bodies, his shoes leaving bloodstains on the kitchen floor. The phone line here had been cut. Aware of the tremor in his hands, he took a glass from the cabinet and filled it from the faucet. The handcuffs dangled from his bleeding wrist. Staring blindly at the backsplash, Eric took a small sip and waited. *Come after me, asshole, and leave her the hell alone.* But he heard nothing from the other room, only the sound of rainfall beating on the curtained window over the sink. The silence was as unbearable as her torture. Wiping at the blood trickling down his temple, Eric closed his eyes and prayed. If he'd failed her, if he was wrong and she was dying right now, he wanted his own release next. Levi could put a bullet through him for all he cared.

He wasn't wrong.

He palmed a small paring knife from the counter as

he heard heavy footsteps approaching. They stopped in the doorway. "You're going to get back in here now!"

Eric turned. Levi's face was a mask of fury. He remained several feet away in the shadow of the refrigerator, pointing the gun.

"You want to kill me, then do it."

"I get that you're not afraid to die. How brave. And I promise you, *you will.* But on my terms. You're going to *watch* her succumb to me first." He tilted his head in bemusement, his lips lifting in a cold smirk before he spoke again. "This must all seem like some kind of curse to you. First your wife and now her—both of them taken by *me.* You're the one who's *powerless,* Agent Macfarlane."

He indicated the sliding glass doors. "You obviously care for her or you would've escaped. You can't bear to leave her, can you? Now get back to your seat or I'll make her death especially painful. Would you prefer that I cut her up like Rebecca? We'll start with some superficial slashes before moving on to the mortal ones."

Eric felt the threat in his veins. Still, he remained controlled.

"It must suck to be you, Levi," he said quietly, baiting him. "Your mother emasculated you to the point that you're a weak, sexless excuse for a human. And yet you spent years caring for her, still hoping for her approval. You never got it, did you? She was embarrassed by you. No wonder."

"Shut up," he warned, eyes glittering with anger as he clenched the weapon harder. "You don't know anything about me!"

"I know everything about you I need to." Eric slipped his fingers around the handle of the concealed knife, prepared to fight. "My profile wasn't wrong. You're a dead loser."

With a snarl, he advanced from the shadows, his gun aimed at Eric's face. A sharp pop filled the air and the side of Levi's head exploded. Brain matter splattered the cabinets as he dropped to the floor in a red mist.

The sniper.

A small hole was visible in the glass door. Stunned, Eric remained frozen for a half second. Then he began to move.

"Mia!"

She remained tied to the chair, barely conscious, the plastic bag still over her face. Yanking it off and whispering her name, Eric knelt in front of her, hands shaking as he used the knife to saw through her binds. Her breathing was labored and uneven. He freed her just as the SWAT team burst through the door, shouting commands to get down. Holding his shield in the air, Eric wrapped his other arm around her protectively.

His eyes briefly met Cameron's as he carried her out to the waiting ambulance.

41

Subdued voices coming from the hallway woke her. Mia lay in a faintly lit hospital room, her body sore and the fingers of her left hand wrapped in heavy gauze. Eric sat in the chair beside her bed, dozing. His dress shirt was untucked and open at the throat, and there were splotches of dried blood on its collar and front. He had a heavy bandage on his temple. She gazed at him groggily, amazed.

It was hard to believe either of them had gotten out alive.

A wall clock indicated it was nearly four in the morning. She'd lost hours, she realized, sedated by the E.R. physicians. Vaguely, she recalled Eric lifting her into his arms and pushing through the crowd of law enforcement to get her to the ambulance. Then he'd climbed inside with her, his face tense and pale. He had told her Allan Levi was dead. That he could never hurt her again. Just after, her world had faded to black.

For a time Mia listened to the steady beep of the heart monitor. Even now, she could feel the terrifying burn of her lungs and the pounding of her blood as Levi pulled the plastic bag tight over her face. She turned her head to the side on the pillow and closed her eyes, her insides knotting.

I'm still here, she reminded herself. *I survived.*

Reaching out with her uninjured hand, her fingers caressed the sterile dressing wrapped around Eric's wrist. Her touch caused him to stir. Seeing that she was awake, he sat up and leaned forward in the chair. His moss-green eyes stared into hers. She watched them slowly fill with tears.

"Eric," she whispered, her heart constricting.

He bowed his head, bringing her fingers to his lips and kissing her knuckles, then rubbing his stubbled cheek against them.

"I'm so sorry," he said hoarsely.

"It's not your fault."

"I moved you to the bungalow." The words were thick in his throat. "I thought you'd be safe there."

Mia's voice in return was gentle. "He followed the deputies from the newspaper. You couldn't have known."

Those same two men were dead now, one of them murdered right in front of her. She wondered if they had families, children. It made her sad that she had failed to ever ask them.

"They ran some tests. The doctor doesn't think you suffered any brain or organ damage from the oxygen deprivation." He released a shaky breath. "But it's likely you have some nerve damage in your fingers, honey."

The local anesthetic that had been shot into her injured fingertips had worn off. Even with the pain medication she was receiving through an IV line, she could feel their dull throb as her bandaged hand rested on the bedsheets. "How bad is it?"

"They don't know yet."

Mia tried not to think about it. Instead, she looked at Eric as he rubbed a hand over his bleary eyes. She understood his intense emotion. Levi's death represented the close of three arduous years in his life. She couldn't imagine what it must have been like to come face-to-face with the man who had tortured and murdered his wife, the woman he'd loved. To be forced to sit helplessly by as he came close to killing *her,* as well. Mia's fingers grazed his forearm. She suspected from his bloodied clothing he had never been too far away from her. He obviously hadn't taken the time to change.

"Have you been here this whole time?"

"I was debriefed in one of the hospital conference rooms." He appeared tired, and she noticed the small lines etched around his eyes. "Agent Vartran is handling statements to the media."

"Eric, it's your case. If you need to go…"

"I'm staying here. I'm not leaving you." Pausing, he bent his head again, struggling with something he needed to say. "When I realized Levi was inside the house with you, I was so afraid you were already dead."

Then he'd known from the beginning. He hadn't been surprised upon entering. He'd come inside for her, knowing full well what awaited him and that he was as likely to die at Levi's hands as she was.

"I couldn't lose you like that…" Shaking his head, he

swallowed hard. "I couldn't lose another woman I loved the same way."

Mia felt her eyes mist.

"But I almost did…lose you," he said haltingly. "I couldn't stop him from hurting you."

"I'm here. I'm going to be okay."

He laid his head on her stomach, asking again for her forgiveness. Mia stroked his hair as he fell silently apart.

The night was warm, the dark waters of Matanzas Bay stretching out as far as Eric could see. He stood on the deck with Cameron at his house in St. Augustine.

"They seem to be hitting it off," Cameron remarked. It was after dinner, and Lanie and Mia were visible through the window, the two women talking in the kitchen. Mia had been released from the hospital four days earlier. She sipped from a coffee mug, her cheekbone marred by a bruise and her left hand still heavily bandaged.

"How's she doing, by the way?"

Eric continued watching her. "She puts up a good front, but we both know she's been through hell and back. I've asked her to see a counselor dealing with post-traumatic stress."

He'd brought up the topic on more than one occasion, actually. Both times, Mia had jokingly told him her sessions with Dr. Wilhelm had filled her psychiatry quota, thank you very much. But the nightmare she'd had the previous evening worried him. He'd been there to hold her, and he wasn't sure how well she would cope once he was gone.

"You're in love with her?" Cameron asked.

Eric leaned against the deck railing. He thought of Rebecca. Levi's death had allowed him to finally gain closure, some justice for her. He gave a small nod of acknowledgment. "We're taking it slow."

Cameron sipped his beer, seeming to process the information.

"For what it's worth, I would've done the same thing." He looked at his wife. "If Lanie had been inside with that psychopath, I'd have walked through fire to save her. When's your flight out tomorrow?"

"Seven o'clock." After closing down the case Eric had remained in town, taking vacation time to be with Mia. She'd been fragile after leaving the hospital and with Will and Justin still in Chicago, also alone. Eric had moved into her apartment. They'd slept late, lounged poolside and made love as if they would never see one another again. Danger had a way of heightening passions, but Eric had discovered his feelings for Mia remained the same even in the calm after the storm.

"Long-distance relationships are tough," Cameron pointed out.

"I'll come down for a weekend and she'll come up there. We're going to try it that way for a while." Eric turned and peered out over the water again. "She understands my job, Cam. Why I have to do what I do."

"I appreciate you coming down here, Eric. Lanie and I care about you. We want you to know that."

"Then check in on her for me?"

"You got it."

Just then, the women appeared at the door, their conversation capturing the men's attention. Lanie cupped her pregnant belly. She seemed to have gotten a bit larger in the time since Eric had last visited them.

"I'm going to slice some watermelon, Cam. Mind giving me a hand?"

He took Eric's empty beer bottle and his own and followed his wife into the house. Mia came onto the deck. She was stunningly beautiful to him. The wind blew her sleek, dark hair as she approached.

"I like Lanie." She added wryly, "And I think Agent Vartran is warming to me."

"Cameron," Eric corrected with a faint smile. Using his fingertips, he pushed back a few strands of hair the breeze had blown across her face.

For a time, they stared out over the languid bay together, Mia's head against his shoulder and his arm wrapped around her. The lighthouse on Anastasia Island cast a glow into the dark night, reflecting on the water where, at twilight, they had spotted a small group of frolicking manatees.

"What're you thinking?" he asked when she'd remained silent for a while.

Her voice was somber. "Just that they're still out there."

Eric knew what she was referring to. Cissy Cox's remains had yet to be recovered, although her death had been confirmed by the chilling audio recording. The Bureau's forensics team had used cadaver dogs to go over Levi's property but nothing had turned up. Eric suspected her remains were moored somewhere in the St. Johns.

And Joy Rourke, the little girl taken by Levi more

than two decades ago, now existed only in Mia's dreams. She'd been forgotten by the system, the only real proof of her life in Hank Dugger's notes and the newspaper archives.

"I've talked to Grayson. I'm going to do a cold case profile on Joy. He liked the idea."

"I don't want to leave you," Eric whispered.

She looked up at him in the darkness. "I know."

He bent his head and kissed her, even now feeling a hunger for her. It was their last night together for a while, and Eric vowed to share dessert with Lanie and Cameron and then take Mia home where he could have her all to himself. Already, he dreaded her absence in his life.

"I'll be fine, Eric." It was as if she could read his thoughts. "Will and Justin will be back in a few days. Justin's mother's improving and they've found a live-in caretaker for her until she's fully recovered."

"You could come with me to D.C. tomorrow. Miller told you to take off whatever time you need."

She shook her head. "The summer ballet classes I'm teaching start at the center next week. I don't want to disappoint those little girls. I also have a doctor's appointment I need to keep."

For now, all they knew was that the sensory nerves in her fingertips had been damaged, impacting her sense of touch. The doctors would have to allow the wounds to heal further before determining its permanency. Mia had taken the news like a soldier, blithely mentioning that it might make using a keyboard interesting. But the reality was that it could also impact even basic skills like chopping vegetables or buttoning a shirt. Eric felt a lingering sense of anger about what Levi had done to her.

Her voice distracted him from his thoughts.

"Besides, if I come back with you now, we aren't really giving this whole long-distance thing much of a try, are we?"

"I'll be back down again at least once before Lanie has the baby," Eric promised.

"And I'll come up to see you at least once before then."

Hurricane lanterns had been set out around the deck. It was a romantic setting, but one that was also bittersweet. Eric stared into Mia's eyes. He wanted to memorize this moment and call on it often during the times they were apart.

"Do we really need watermelon?" he asked in a low voice. "We could leave now."

"Lanie's carved baskets out of cantaloupes to hold the fruit. She went to a lot of trouble. I think we need to stay." She slid her arms around Eric's neck and placed her lips against his ear, adding, "When we get home, I'll make the wait worth your while."

Eric held her in his arms, reveling in the feel of her. She'd been through so much in her life. He thanked God he had gotten her back. If they were meant to be together, they would manage things, somehow.

I haven't left yet and I miss you already.

Gently capturing her face in his hands, he lowered his lips to hers.

<u>Epilogue</u>

Four Months Later
Chantilly, Virginia

Mia felt her heart lift upon seeing Eric among the throngs of people inside Washington Dulles International Airport. He was dressed casually in khakis and a button-down, his sunglasses clipped to his shirt pocket. Spotting her at nearly the same time, he began making his way through the crowd to her. She went into his arms.

Their kiss lingered despite the passengers bustling past them in the busy terminal.

Eric had been down to Jacksonville a month earlier to celebrate the birth of Rosalie Marie Vartran. But to Mia it seemed an eternity since she had last seen him. The way she felt made it even clearer they were doing the right thing.

"How was the flight?" Taking her carry-on bag and sliding its strap over his shoulder, they began walking toward the baggage carousel.

"Crowded." She looked up at him. "But worth it."

"It's the end of the summer vacation season. People are getting in last-minute trips."

Mia was there in part for an interview with a D.C. newspaper, the meeting arranged by Grayson. He hadn't seemed surprised when she'd told him that she and Eric were ready to take their relationship to the next level. The phone calls and occasional long weekends weren't enough. She had been touched by his offer to contact an old friend who was executive editor at one of the metro dailies.

"You look beautiful," Eric said as they waited for her luggage to wind its way from cargo to the carousel.

"I *look* like a wrinkled mess." Self-conscious, Mia smoothed her hands over the sundress she wore. She was meeting Eric's parents for the first time, at his insistence. They were going directly from the airport to dinner at their home in Falls Church. His sister, Hope, would also be there.

"Hey," he murmured, apparently sensing her nerves. "You're going to do fine. Besides, I'm not a kid. The only approval you need is mine."

"That sounds ominous."

"Actually, my father is looking forward to meeting you. He followed the investigation and he thinks you're a very brave woman."

She felt a little intimidated at the prospect of having dinner with the associate attorney general of the Department of Justice. "And your mother?"

"You're on your own with that one." His teasing smile softened, his eyes becoming serious. "They both just want me to be happy. Don't go in with preconceived notions. I'm pretty sure they're going to love you as much as I do."

Taking a step closer, he tilted her face up to his and kissed her again. Mia's hands rested against his chest. He felt so solid and strong.

"You keep doing that and we're going to miss my suitcase," she said a little breathlessly once his lips left hers.

Cradling the fingers of her left hand in his, he examined them, frowning. "How are they?"

Although her nails had mostly grown back, the scar tissue underneath was evident, the keratin ridged and bumpy when it should be smooth. It was strange. Most of the time, her fingertips were simply numb, something she was slowly adapting to. But occasionally she felt a sharp flare of pain, an undead nerve vocalizing its outrage.

"The same," she said mildly. "The doctors have done about all they can do."

Compared to all those other women, she knew that she was the lucky one. She thought of Rebecca, Penney, Joy. Eric touched her face, his gaze questioning. Mia was unembarrassed by the tears in her eyes.

"I'm just so glad to be here, Eric. I've missed you so much."

Only her suitcase broke the spell between them as it appeared on the carousel amid other passengers' luggage. He stepped forward and dug it out, then pulled it on wheels with her carry-on stacked on top of it. As they went past the two-story, glass wall that provided a view of planes taxiing on the runway beneath a lavender, early-evening sky, they talked about his most recent case—a string of murders that had taken him to Portland, Oregon. Eric had been gone for a week and a half, acting as a consult to the local police there.

In the parking garage, he put her luggage in the trunk of his car, then opened the passenger-side door for her and went around to the other side. Before starting the engine, however, he turned to her.

"Whether or not this job works out, I'd like you to go ahead and move up here, Mia. As soon as possible." His expression was earnest. "I don't want to wait any longer to be with you."

Over the past several months, they had talked about so much during their regular phone calls. His cases, her return to the daily grind of news reporting, and what they both wanted from life. Eric had a crucial job at the VCU, no one knew that better than her. She understood his hectic schedule and heavy travel requirement, but if they lived in the same city, they *would* see each other more. Mia also wanted a deeper connection to him. She wanted to wake up in his bed every morning and share a home with him. They'd made the decision that she would be the one to relocate.

"I also know you've been toying with the idea of doing something different," he mentioned carefully. "Maybe *not* being a reporter anymore."

Despite the interview she was in town for, it was something else they had discussed. Mia was back at work and functioning, and she'd been seeing a trauma counselor. Grayson had returned her to her former crime beat. But there was no denying that what she'd gone through had impacted her. She felt as though she was at a cross-roads in her life.

"A lot of journalists make the move into media relations," he continued. "Instead of reporting news, they start *disseminating* it."

"I get the feeling you're talking about something specific."

He looked at her in the car's darkened interior. "There's an inner-city arts program in D.C. It includes dance. It's gotten some pretty decent grants and donations but it needs publicity to keep the funds rolling in. They're looking for a media relations director."

Mia felt her heart bump at the unexpected opportunity.

"If you're interested, my father can get you an interview, maybe even while you're here. He sits on its board. Your background combined with your media skills—I think you'd be a good fit. It's just something else to consider."

"I'd like to talk to them," she said, grateful. "Thank you."

He leaned over and kissed her again. Then he started the engine.

As he pulled the car from the garage, his fingers intertwined with hers on the armrest. Mia felt her throat tighten a little at all the changes occurring. She had lived in Jacksonville her entire life. She would miss it in so many ways. Will and Justin, her San Marco apartment, the ocean and sandy beaches that were minutes away. All of it was part of her.

But there were also bad events in her past that she was

ready to leave behind. She had a chance to start a new life here with the man she loved, and D.C. was an exciting place.

They were moving in together. It was a step she had never taken before with anyone. But for the first time, she had truly given over her heart and her trust. Mia gazed at Eric's profile as he drove. She understood that she was *his* chance to start over, too. All she wanted was the best for him. *To be with him.*

It was a leap of faith, she knew, but nothing had ever felt more right.

* * * * *

Acknowledgments

Many thanks to my editor, Susan Swinwood, at MIRA Books, and to my agent, Stephany Evans, at FinePrint. It's a pleasure to work with both of you. Thanks also to the following who have helped in so many ways: Michelle Muto and Vicki Jacob, for being both beta readers and friends; Deborah Damerell for scouting territories; and Dana Cogan and Soon Mee Kim, for holding my hand now for too many years to count. Also, a special shout-out to my "DB girls" who always make me laugh and hold a place in my heart.

The chilling Krewe of Hunters trilogy from
New York Times and *USA TODAY* bestselling author

HEATHER GRAHAM

SOME SECRETS REFUSE TO STAY BURIED...

Available wherever books are sold.

Intoxicating romantic suspense from
New York Times **and** *USA TODAY*
bestselling author

BRENDA NOVAK

Available wherever books are sold!

REQUEST YOUR FREE BOOKS!

2 FREE NOVELS FROM THE PARANORMAL ROMANCE COLLECTION PLUS 2 FREE GIFTS!

leslie
TENTLER

32934 MIDNIGHT CALLER	__ $7.99 U.S.	__ $9.99 CAN.
31313 EDGE OF MIDNIGHT	__ $7.99 U.S.	__ $9.99 CAN.
31246 MIDNIGHT FEAR	__ $7.99 U.S.	__ $9.99 CAN.

(limited quantities available)

TOTAL AMOUNT	$_____
POSTAGE & HANDLING	$_____
($1.00 for 1 book, 50¢ for each additional)	
APPLICABLE TAXES*	$_____
TOTAL PAYABLE	$_____

(check or money order—please do not send cash)

To order, complete this form and send it, along with a check or money order for the total above, payable to MIRA Books, to: **In the U.S.:** 3010 Walden Avenue, P.O. Box 9077, Buffalo, NY 14269-9077; **In Canada:** P.O. Box 636, Fort Erie, Ontario, L2A 5X3.

Name: _____
Address: _____ City: _____
State/Prov.: _____ Zip/Postal Code: _____
Account Number (if applicable): _____
075 CSAS

*New York residents remit applicable sales taxes.
*Canadian residents remit applicable GST and provincial taxes.

MIRA | HARLEQUIN®
www.Harlequin.com

MLT0212BL